THE
KING'S
PEACE

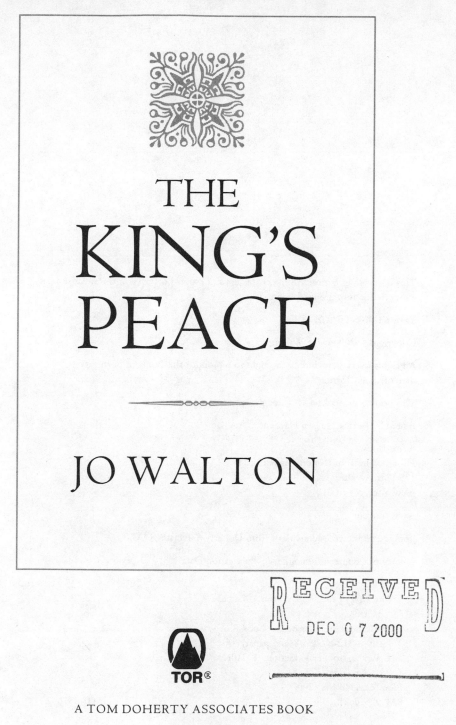

THE
KING'S
PEACE

JO WALTON

A TOM DOHERTY ASSOCIATES BOOK

NEW YORK

THE KING'S PEACE

Edited by Patrick Nielsen Hayden

A Tor Book
Published by Tom Doherty Associates, LLC
175 Fifth Avenue
New York, NY 10010

www.tor.com

Tor® is a registered trademark of Tom Doherty Associates, LLC.

Library of Congress Cataloging-in-Publication Data

Walton, Jo.
    The king's peace / Jo Walton.—1st ed.
      p. cm.
    "A Tom Doherty Associates book."
    ISBN 0-312-87229-1 (alk. paper)
    1. Women soldiers—Fiction. I. Title.

PR6073.A448 K56 2000
823'.92—dc21   00-031682

Printed in the United States of America

0 9 8 7 6 5 4 3 2

DEDICATION, THANKS, AND NOTES

Gracious as gift given   nine nights later
when words came back   changed for keeping.

Wool I wefted,   who warped it?
Relish this, Riddler,   thy own I give thee.

This book is for the four people who lived with the story as it was being written, who caught errors, made suggestions, and helped in their different ways to shape it as it grew. Sasha Walton, my son the Jarnish partisan, for taking it for granted and being insistent. Emmet O'Brien, for love, help, delight, and support all the time I was writing it. Hrolfr F. Gertsen-Briand, my military adviser, for the hard work on detail he put into it, for showing me how to do Caer Lind, and most especially for sharing the dream and showing me there's more than one way of not being able to have it. Graydon, my non-union muse, without whom there would not only not be this but there would not be anything; for always seeing clearly what was wrong and for being so awfully good at being himself.

This book also gained inestimably by being read in manuscript by Janet Kegg, my fairy godmother, my aunt, Mary Lace, and Michael Grant.

I'd also like to thank Pamela Dean for inspiration, wise advice, reassurance, and conversation about writing; Mary Lace for driving me to Oxford and Caerleon and other helpful places; Patrick and Teresa Nielsen Hayden, for taking notice of it; and Jez Green, Andrew Morris, Ken Walton, Helen Marsden, Steve Miller, Bil Bas, and Art Questor for the inspiration that came out of a game.

For those to whom pronunciation of names is important, they have been rendered as easy for an English speaker as possible. *C* and G are always hard (as in cat, gold), and all letters should be pronounced as read. Doubtful vowels are more likely to be long than otherwise. *Ch* is hard (as in Bach) except in Malmish names.

This is not our world, and this is not history. Anyone seeking information on the history of Britain in the early Sixth Century would probably do well to start with John Morris' *The Age of Arthur,* not an infallible book but a very readable one. From there I'd highly recommend the wonderfully illuminating recent work of K. M. Dark, especially *Civitas to Kingdom* and *External Contacts.* As far as primary sources go, many of them are collected together in Coe and Young's *The Celtic Sources for the Arthurian Legend,* the most useful of the many useful volumes Llanerch Press have made available in recent years. For technology I'd highly recommend Gies and Gies's *Cathedral, Forge and Waterfall;* and for religion Fletcher's wonderfully thorough *The Conversion of*

Europe. I'd like to express my gratitude to the staff of Sketty library for their unfailing cheerfulness in ordering me in great piles of strange volumes from the ends of the Earth. I couldn't have managed without them either.

"I will have it so that though King, son, and grandson were all slain in one day, still the King's Peace should hold over all England! What is a man that his mere death must upheave a people! We must have the Law."
 —Rudyard Kipling, *Rewards and Fairies* (1910)

"If I heed your words that is all
that I shall ever have.
If I have no sword
where then shall I seek peace?

"A sword might win
a Peace's time from tumult;
no peace have the hungry,
and so the Peace is made
from the work of gathered days
the many's many choices."
 —Graydon Saunders and Jo Walton, from *Theodwyn's Rede* (1996)

What it is to be old is to remember things that nobody else alive can remember. I always say that when people ask me about my remarkable long life. Now they can hear me when I say it. Now, when I am ninety-three and remember so many things that are to them nothing but bright legends long ago and far away. I do not tell them that I said that first when I was seventeen, and felt it too. Although only one person heard it then, of all the people I said it to. Nevertheless, it was as true then as it is today. So I have been old by my own terms since I was seventeen, although that seventeen-year-old who had my name seems very young to me now when I remember her.

Yet now that I am fit for little more than telling stories to the children it occurs to me that my memories will be lost if I do not see them passed on. All of them are things that nobody alive but I remembers. Some of them are things that are truly passing into legend. In the legend there is no room for me. I was not important to the story they tell. My story has no drama; a land defended, vows unbroken, faith upheld. That is not the stuff of legend. I am nothing but an old woman, even if I am still lord of these

few acres of land. Lord Sulien they call me still in courtesy, but I could not
defend my people now. It is my great-nephew's word that counts in the
king's council, and that is as it should be. My king is dead.

Dead, long ago.

So long ago. Too long ago. I wrote those words, "my king is dead," and
my pen stopped in my hand and I was lost again in dream. Fifty years and
five it is, since Urdo fell, and yet my memories of him are still very clear.
The years I rode as his armiger shine brightest of all the memories of my
long life. Yet to the children I tell stories in the autumn sunlight they seem
like legends of another age. I suppose they are. The world has changed, and
changed again. The king my great-nephew serves now is more Jarn than
Tanagan. He follows the White God. The ways of the Jarnsmen are mingling with our ways, and the customs and languages of the two people are
becoming one. This was our dream of course, but I do not think we imagined how the world would be when that dream came true.

Now I shall write down my memories, but I do not know who will
read them. Nobody can read these days but the priests of the White God
and those they teach. My mother was old-fashioned even in her own day in
insisting that all her children could read and write. She was born in the days
when the Vincans still ruled. When I was a child she was much given to
praising the virtues of Civilization and Peace, two things the Vincans
brought to our island and which my lord Urdo fought to restore. Which he
did restore. The Peace we built in Tir Tanagiri lasted, despite everything.
This is still our land, and I am still lord of these few families, these little
fields. My people come and go in peace. The flocks safely graze.

So I do not write for my great-nephew and his friends, or for the children of the estate. These days lords' children learn honor and farmers' children learn the land; none of them can read. I do not write for the priests. I
have been a worshiper of the Radiant Sun all my days, and although I
respect what my king did in accepting the White God into our land I have
small liking for the priests and their ways. I do not write for the living who
care too much and not enough, or for the dead who may care but who
cannot reach me. I shall write for any in the future who care about us, our
little kingdom, and our ways. I shall write small, in neither the harsh Jarnish
tongue nor the old language of the farmers which was my own first language. I have lived to see those languages change, and I do not think that
change is over yet. I shall write in the clear Vincan I learned from my parents. It is most likely to last without changing, and it is, after all, my mother
always told me, the language of literature.

When I have finished I shall seal my writing in clay and set on it the holy seals of the Sun in Splendor, Lord of Light, and of the Shield-Bearer, Lady of Wisdom. Then I shall cast it into their protection for those to find who may. If you are reading these words then I pray that these two gods have guided you to them. Further, I pray that the names of those you read about in these pages will not, even after all that span of time, be entirely forgotten. I know he would have freely given all his wordfame to make the Peace. All the same, there is a wistful hope in me that if there is any justice, my king's name will still be a trumpet blast in a thousand years.

1

THE KING'S PEACE

—1—

First came the Tanagans, hop along, hop along,
then came the Vincans, dance along, dance along
then came the Jarnsmen, run along, run along
the gold-headed Jarnsmen to chase you all home!
  —Children's step game

If I had been armed on horseback, I could have taken them all out. Even afoot I could have made a good showing with a sword. Hand to hand I think I could have given one of them a fair match, for all they were full-grown men and I, at seventeen, had not quite all my woman's growth. I was already veteran of ten years' training and one brief battle against raiders the year before. I was strong, not just strong for a woman but strong by any measure. These were but common Jarnish ship-raiders, all but untrained in land fighting like most of their kind. They had not spent their childhoods as I had, lifting weights and swinging staves to develop their strength and speed. But here I was alone and unarmed, and there were six of them. Worst of all, they had taken me unawares.

I was on my way home from one of the little farms that lay in those days inland about five miles, well within my father's lands. One of the farmers was ill, and my mother had sent me with a healing potion and a hymn to sing over her bed. I had stayed to teach the woman's son that hymn, which was needful to help keep up his mother's strength. He had a liking for tunes, so while I was there I taught him a few other lesser hymns to the Radiant Sun, two of them my own translations into the tongue of the people. The farmers in those days had their own names for the gods we all worshiped, few indeed had heard of the White God then in Derwen or elsewhere in our part of Tir Tanagiri.

I was walking back singing across the fields. I was thirsty in the hot sun and thinking longingly about the little stream of good clear water that ran in the shade of the trees. I was looking up at the smoke rising over the wood from the direction of the house. I wondered who had put what on a bonfire to make such a billow on the wind. The wind was coming out of the southwest and blew the smoke away from me, the smell might have warned me. As it was, the first I knew anything was amiss was the appearance out of the trees of half a dozen burly sea-raiders, yellow-haired, white-skinned, and ugly. I had seen a troop of them the summer before, but they still looked strange to me then. There were no Jarnsmen settled anywhere near this part of the realm in those days. They laughed to see me, showing their bad teeth, and shouted to each other in their own tongue.

I fell at once into a fighting stance. I shifted my grip on the bottle that had held the potion. It was baked clay, not a good weapon but all I had. They came on, bunched together. I held my ground and looked around for what there was to help as they closed in. It was a meadow, grassy, covered in buttercups and daisies, a pleasant place where the farmers grazed the cows. There was earth to throw in their eyes. I could see no stones. The trees were not too far away, if I could make their cover I should know the ground better than the men and be able to get home. There would be fallen wood I could use for a club. Somehow I assumed without thinking about it that the raiders had just come out of their boat, and that these six were all there were of them.

The first one reached me, only moments ahead of his companions. He carried a single-edged blade, typically Jarnish; it could be thought of as a short sword or a long knife, as suitable for cutting brush as slashing an enemy. It was loose in his hand. He did not think me much of a challenge. I kicked his arm hard, aiming for the elbow. My foot connected with an impact I could feel all through my leg. I spun, completing the movement. He dropped the blade and clutched his arm. The second man was on me then, and I was facing him. I brought the bottle up in his face and brought my arm down hard on his knife arm. I wasn't fast enough, and his knife caught me a gash across my sleeve. It would have been nothing if I'd been wearing leathers; as it was the cloth tore and it cut my skin. I felt nothing then, although I saw my own red blood flowing. It was a shallow cut but it stung badly later. I never feel wounds in battle. Some say this is a gift of the gods, others have said it is a curse. Urdo always said I would die fighting of wounds I never noticed I had. I never did, though I suppose I may yet.

The third man was there, his spear pointed towards me. The first was reaching down for his fallen knife with his good hand. I stooped for it, ducking under the second man. I was lucky in that they were not trying to kill me, for he could have had me then easily, my throat was exposed. He did not try though; the Jarnsmen in those days did not kill young women. They saw me as not only their own sport but as booty. Women had a resale value on the continent even then, when the market was glutted. They probably hoped to get as much for a strong girl like me as for a horse.

I had the sword, and as swift as thought I stabbed at the second man's knee. It was a good target from my position. These Jarnsmen wore leather tunics and leather sea boots, nothing like as hard or as well made as my boots. The knees are unprotected in the old Vincan style, nobody is supposed to be that low in the line of battle. The sword was heavier than the short knives I had practiced with. It had not the reach of even our short swords, let alone the long cavalry sword I was used to. He toppled, and I was drawing out the knife when one of the others grabbed my arms from behind. I brought my head up hard to jar his chin. I felt the force of the blow through my skull. He reeled a little, but held firm, and the others were there. I had wounded two of them, but four were whole and I was captured.

If they had taken me back to the ship then I should no doubt have spent the rest of a short unpleasant life as a slave on the continent in some Jarnish or other barbarian encampment. Maybe I would have escaped and found some other life in the parts of the continent that still clung to some shred of Vincan civilization. I have often wondered how I would have survived. I had skill at arms and languages, I knew a few useful devotional charms, but I had few womanly skills such as they might expect. But they were greedy and wanted to taste their prize themselves. One of the men quickly cut off my clothes using a short sharp knife he had at his belt, ruining the good green cloth and leaving me quite exposed. I stayed limp in their grasp, hoping for an opportunity to escape. I had no body-shame, of course, though I had been told the Jarnsmen suffered from this badly. My siblings and I had always trained for athletics naked, Vincan fashion.

They jabbered in their own language. I understood no word of what they were saying. They poked at me, and dragged me, unresisting, back towards the trees. I was ready to fight at any moment there seemed to be any possibility of advantage in it. I ignored the irrelevancies of my nakedness and vulnerability, stayed limp, and concentrated on tracking where they all were. This was Duncan's advice for being in a bad spot, and it came back to me now that I was in one. They were laughing at the ones who had been wounded, though one of them bound up his companion's knee. Looking at him then, I thought that if that was the level of their treatment he would surely lose the leg. He never walked without a limp again even as it was; that was a good blow with my strength behind it. I had clean severed the muscle.

The loud laughter was a bad sign. They had no worries about being overheard, or they thought only their own friends were near. I remembered that rising smoke and worried. I should not have called for help over that distance in any case, nobody would have heard me. But now I heard them laugh and shout out jests at each other I shouted too and screamed for help as loudly as I could. This was not only foolish but against Duncan's teaching, and I have found it hard to forgive myself for that. They gagged me with part of what had been my sleeve. I could taste the blood on it from the knife cut.

The trees' shadow was pleasantly cool. The sound of the stream trickling nearby was a torment. The leaves were green and fully out, all at their best, stretched wide gathering summer light to last through the winter. They tied me under a great oak, using cut strips from my clothes. They fastened my wrists and ankles to tree roots. They were careful never to let me have a chance to be free and hurt them. The bindings were very uncomfortable, especially on my wounded arm. The little roots and last year's leaves were hard and rough beneath me. I stared up at the three-fingered leaves, sending my mind up away among the pattern of twigs and branches, determined to ignore the pain. I tried to relax into it as Duncan had taught me, although it hurt like a vise. The leaves, the tree, I can see it now, the shapes the leaves made against the blue sky that did not care for me in my pain. People have told me they have taken pleasure in the act of begetting life, and some of them have even been women. That was the only time I ever did it, that thing which in most people's lives is so important, that thing for which, and for the lack of which, kingdoms fall and grown men turn into little boys. It hurt me worse than any wound I ever had. I believe there may be pleasure in it for some people, but I was not made so.

The fifth of them had just begun his thrusting and I was staring up into the leaves and wondering if I would die of the pain when the man fell forward suddenly upon me and I saw my brother Darien's face between me and the light. I had thought never to see sight of those I loved again, and it was almost too much for me. I wept.

"Sulien!" he said. He dragged the body off me and bent to cut me loose. So it was that he did not see the last man, the man with the wounded knee, come up behind him, though I did. I tried to warn him, but I was gagged of course and could make no sound. He was bending down, and the Jarnsman took him from behind in the thigh with the knife. Poor Darien had no chance, he fell forward almost at once, quite dead beside me. The wounded man limped forward, pulling up his tunic. I was quite sickened, and that time was the worst of all, both for pain and for violation. Darien's dead body lay only inches away from me, and I could send no part of my mind away, all that happened happened to me. Worst of all I knew for sure that he would kill me when he was done, and Darien and I would lie together, unburied in the wood. I believed all the rest of my family were dead already. Nobody would say prayers for us to the gods of earth and sky, our names would not be given back, and we would all walk the world as unavenged shades forever. He had to kill me. He was one injured man alone, and he had sense enough to know he could not get me back to his ship if he untied me.

When he was done he pulled out my gag. I stared at him, sure I was about to die. I did not scream. I wanted to keep some dignity in my last moments.

"You know spells?" he asked, in broken Vincan. It was the most unexpected question I had ever been asked. I almost laughed hysterically, but just managed to restrain myself. I raised my chin in cautious assent.

"You hurt my leg, you mend it," he said.

"Why?" I asked.

"You hurt, you mend," he repeated.

"Why should I if you're going to kill me after?" I asked.

"What?" he looked puzzled.

"Why mend if you kill me?" I said, slowly. His Vincan was not up to much subtlety.

"You mend, I no kill," he said. "Swear by One-Eye, Father of the Slain." This was one of their old gods. I had heard the name even then, enough to know it sacred.

"All right," I said. "If I can. Let me up." He shook his head.

"You up, you run," he said. I would have, too. I sighed.

"You give me water," I said. My mouth was unbearably dry. He took a water bottle from his waist and held it to my lips. Enough of it made its way into my mouth for me to choke, and some went down.

"Where sword?" I asked. He held up his own blade. "Where sword that did wound?" After some searching of bodies he limped back with it. "What your name?" I asked. His ugly pale eyes narrowed. I hated those pale Jarnsman eyes; they did not seem to me at all like human eyes that are dark and full of thoughts.

"Name secret."

"Need name to do spell," I said. He must have known that was true, however little his people knew about it.

"Ulf Gunnarsson," he muttered, reluctantly.

"Put knife against wound," I instructed. He did so, then knelt and touched me so that I could work the charm on him. With the most reluctance of my life I sang the charm of healing of weapon-wounds, an invocation both to the Lord of Light for healing and to the dark battle gods. Into

the charm I wove Ulf's name, and by the time I had finished I could see
that it had worked inasmuch as it could on such a wound—it was like a
wound he had suffered ten years ago and not like a fresh wound. His leg
would never be as it had been, and there was nothing anyone could do
about that.

"Now let me go," I said. He smiled, showing his dreadful teeth again.

"Never said so," he said. "You know name, know spells. You dangerous. I not kill you. I swore. But you stay here, sacrifice to Father of the
Slain, make corn go strong." I heard this with absolute horror. He took the
sword that had wounded him and cut the ball of his thumb, then squeezed
out a few drops of his blood to fall on my stomach. Ignoring my screams
and protests and threats to curse him, and being careful not to touch me to
give my curses a chance to work, he walked away, leaving me to die beside
my dead brother. Ulf Gunnarsson, I swore, if I get free and we meet again
you are a dead man. I knew no real curses, then.

—2—

To the land of the dead in the dusk returning
all deeds done, time gone, life ending,
no more amending, this is what you are,
this is your name, you know it all at last.
We, who are left on life's shore, mourning
as you walk on, into dark, not turning,
we cannot go with you, this journey all make alone.
However loved, and you were loved,
however strong, and you were strong,
however brave, and you were brave,
however skilled, and you were skilled,
you will come alone to Lord Death's halls
speak there your name and deeds,
for them to stand alone, for what you were.
You go on, shine bright, begin a new life,
taking from this all of the beauty,
learning from this all of the mistakes.
Do not grieve for us, though we are sundered,
you were what you were, you will be remembered,

learn to be what more you can be,

and we will mourn with the name you left us,

on life's shore, bound by old choices,

go free ahead, on new paths, returning.

—From "The Hymn of Returning"

When I was quite sure Ulf was gone I began to test the bonds. The one Darien had started to cut was frayed partway through. I craned my neck to look at my wrist, then saw what I had hoped to see. Darien's knife lay near it, in a large clump of fungus that sprouted beside the root my wrist was tied to. I could slowly force my wrist and the twisted linen down on the blade, which was lying sideways rather than point up. Because of the angle of my arm and the tree, I could either see what I was doing or do it. I alternated between doing and looking, with no thinking. It was a long time, and I did not know whether the cloth or my wrist would be sawn through first. If it had been my wrist it would have been a quicker death than Ulf would have wished on me. I cannot say how long it was before my wrist was free. After that it was a short time before the rest of me was free. The cramps when I stood and tried to walk were agonizing.

The first thing I did was to walk to the stream and drink until I could hold no more. Then I bent down and washed myself, over and over. The cold water was soothing, and it was good to wash away the blood. Hardest to scrub off was the dried blood on my stomach with which Ulf had dedicated me to the One-Eyed God. By the time I was clean I was chilled through. I walked back to the bodies. I had Darien's knife already; now I took his sword and his leather jacket. It had no bindings for my breasts such as my own leathers had, but it would do. It was unmarked, although the breeches were drenched with blood from the one slash, behind, where Ulf had struck so treacherously. I took them back to the stream and washed them as best I could, then pulled them on, still wet. They fit me well enough. Darien was close enough to my height—if he had lived he would have overtopped me soon. He was my closest friend, as well as my brother. We were equal in most ways, for though I was the elder he was the heir. Often enough we were rivals in prowess, but this only encouraged us both to strive the harder. I was better with the sword, having what Duncan, our arms master, considered an inborn skill for the weapon. Darien was a better horseman, and much better at aiming a lance at the target. He had had dreams of winning some great prize someday with his lancework.

All this I thought as I made his leathers mine. My thoughts turned to those of his hopes and dreams he had shared with me, of the times we had practiced together with wooden swords until our arms and shoulders were far past aching and then rubbed each other down with oil. I remembered the times we had lied for each other to Veniva, our lady mother, always so Vincan and proper, protecting each other's secrets. Well, Darien had come to protect me one last time. Without him I would be enslaved or dead. It was then that I realized for the first time what it meant to be old.

I knew it was foolish, but I stopped to build a pyre for Darien. I knew there might be other Jarnsmen around seeking their lost companions. But I could not leave my brother unburied in the wood. I built a pyre of fallen branches at the edge of the meadow. I put the weapons and gear of the men he had killed into the pyre. I set Darien upon the pyre in his linen underclothes and with his enemies' weapons beneath him; I left the Jarnsmen unburied for the dogs and birds to eat. All this took some time, and I was only just finished in time to be ready at dusk.

I lit the pyre with Darien's flint and steel and sang the great "Hymn of Returning," all alone beneath the twilight stars. I thought about Jarnsmen, but I had a sword now, and it would have pleased me to kill them and add their weapons to Darien's glory pyre if they came. I was lucky. No Jarnsmen came. Nobody came at all. If anyone saw the smoke they probably thought it just more destruction. Alone, and not half a mile from home, I mourned my brother. At last, when the pyre was burning brightly and all the hymns were sung, I took his sword and cut off my hair in the Vincan mourning custom. It made a thick black double handful. I cast it onto the pyre, where it flamed up with a singeing smell almost enough to mask the roasting smell of poor Darien. He should have had incense. He should have had sacrifices. He should have had his killer's arms beneath his feet. Swearing that one day I would bring them to add to his grave, I turned away and walked back through the woods towards the house.

I was not sure what to expect as I came out of the trees. I could smell smoke and knew there had been a great burning. There was no sound at all, and the wood was as quiet as if even the night predators had fled the Jarnsmen. Part of me, it seemed, expected to be home at any moment where I could fling myself down on my own bed and weep until I felt better. The rest of me knew the Jarnsmen had done their usual trick and fired the house, and the dead with it. The shape of the stone walls stood yet, but the silhouette looked strange in the starlight. The concrete and tiles of the roof had cracked with the heat and fallen in.

Cautiously I scouted around the walls. There was no sign of Jarnsmen. There were no bodies, although I had little doubt there would be bones in the ashes inside. I had left the house not long past noon and had been away what was, by both sensible count and by the stars, not much more than seven hours. Yet it seemed months since I set out, and the ruin of my home seemed something ancient and over with, as if it had been done by the Vincans when they first took Tir Tanagiri centuries ago. Certainly it was sad, but I could not feel it as I felt Darien's death.

When I had circled the walls I did not know what to do next. I thought of sleeping the night in a tree. There was a red pine I knew nearby that had one broad branch flat enough to lie on and well out of sight. I wanted to pursue Ulf and get my vengeance upon him and the other raiders. I had no idea where they had gone, or where their boat might be. In the morning I might scout the cliffs and inlets, but at night I would see nothing but shadows in the coves. I could go to one of the farms and sleep, but I felt a great weariness, and horror come over me at the thought of company and questions. I leaned my face against the rough stones of the wall, unsure. At length I murmured a prayer to the Lord Messenger, Guider of Choices, to help me choose rightly. He must have been waiting to guide me because as soon as the prayer was out I knew I must go to the Home Farm, only a mile or so away.

I walked in the shadow of the trees as far as I could. As I crossed the fields I saw no living thing except a great white owl, who gave me a fright gliding down close to me in complete silence to snatch up a vole almost at my feet. When I came to the farm I saw firelight within. I approached cautiously, and listened beneath the window. I heard the voices of the farmers and then, to my joy and amazement, my mother's voice. I rushed to the door and scratched for admittance.

There was immediately silence inside, through which I could hear awkward snoring breaths. Then a farmer asked boldly who was there.

"It is I, Sulien ap Gwien," I said, "and I know my lady mother Veniva is within." The man opened the door a crack so he could see my face. His own looked drawn and frightened. He looked about cautiously, then let me into the house, barring the stout oak door with iron as soon as we were within.

The half of the room near the fire seemed filled with my father, sprawled unconscious on a heather bed. His eyes were closed, and he had a bandage round his head. It was his breathing I had heard from outside. Even felled he was a great man. Darien would have had his height. It took me a moment to take in my mother kneeling at his side. My eyes were full of tears.

"Darien is dead." I said. Veniva looked straight up at me. Her face was as calm as ever, although her greying hair was disordered as I had never seen it, and her clothes were filthy and bloodstained. I would hardly have recognized her as my civilized mother. "Dead defending me from Jarnsmen. I set him on an honourable pyre."

"Are you all right?" she asked. I jerked my chin up affirmatively.

"Father?" I began.

"Your father is badly wounded. He took a blow to the scalp in the first fighting when the Jarnsmen came up from the boat. Duncan got him away here and then came to tell me—I was organizing the defense of the house. Morien and Aurien are here. The Jarnsmen have left, taking some, slaying others, taking all the horses and valuables. Gwien will live, I think, but we must have help."

"Help?" I asked, stupidly. One of the farmers put a wooden cup of warm milk into my hand, murmuring a blessing to Coventina. I took a gulp, and then drained the cup. There was honey in it. The strength it gave me was wonderful. It was almost as wonderful as knowing that all my family but Darien yet lived.

"Someone must go to the king. There is nothing stopping these Jarnsmen from landing where they will and slaying and stealing as they please. We must rebuild, and where are the money and the hands to come from? Most of our troops and the people of the house have fallen, and now you say Darien, too, is dead." It was as if she was just now taking in what I had said. "Darien. We will mourn him later. There is no time now. Morien is the heir, then, and he is but thirteen years old. I will keep the few hands I have here and make a beginning. I cannot be sure if Gwien will live."

I wanted to go to her, to touch her, to weep with her and tell her what had happened, but the distance between us was too great. She was holding on to her calm and control hard, and they were showing cracks around the edges. "Are you fit to ride, Sulien?" The thought of setting my thighs on a horse seemed agony. But I nodded. "Then as soon as it is light you must set off for Caer Tanaga. Gwien swore fealty to this young king, which was his free choice. Now we need help, and the king must send it to us."

She had never sounded more Vincan. Yet even as she spoke she was lifting her hands and unbinding her hair. Soon it was hanging loose about her face in the old Tanagan custom for one who is mourning close kin. Then she stared at me, daring me to speak.

For all my life, and hers, too, the country had been disintegrating. The Vincans had left us to govern ourselves. They had been overrun at home and could no longer look after Tir Tanagiri. We had sent to ask them for help time after time, before at last deciding to look after our own defense. Now she asked me to ride to Caer Tanaga for help from this latest in the series of kings who were trying to grab something for themselves from the wreck of the country. It sounded in my ears much the same as the way she had always told my father that we should send to Vinca for an army. His retort to her in such dinner-table conversations was on my lips, but I bit it back. I could not stand there and say to Veniva now "As well send to ask the moon for help." Instead I simply shook my head. The farmers were hesitating in the door that led to the storeroom, clearly unsure whether or not they should witness this.

"He will be very sorry, Mother, but what can he do?" I asked. I could not stop myself from saying the rest of what Gwien said to her so often. "He is so far away. We have to help ourselves, not ask others to help us." Veniva bit her lip and looked down. Then she drew a ragged breath.

"Your father went and swore to him. We sent troops, last year, to fight when the raiders landed near Magor. He owes it to us to help us rebuild. And we must have help, we must. If King Urdo will not, then go to Duke Galba. Galba's son is betrothed to you; he is practically family already he will surely come."

This was not the time to tell my mother I could never marry, though my stomach churned at the mention of young Galba, who had seemed polite and personable enough three years before when my father asked me if I could bear him. It was a very good alliance for us. The older Galba was a duke and a war-leader, and we held scarce enough land to be accounted noble were it not for our exalted bloodlines. Gwien could trace his family back to the kings who had held this coastline before the Vincans came, and Veniva's ancestors had been Vincan nobles from the City itself.

I stood still, clutching the empty cup and staring at Veniva like a dolt. She knelt beside my father, hair unbound, quite composed. I was caught between obeying her and telling her she was being a fool. I had already said all I could fairly say as an objection.

"Go to sleep, Sulien," she said, with some softness in her voice. "You need not leave until daybreak."

I bowed to her and followed the farmer to the hayloft, where I lay down beside my brother and sister and the children of the farm. I think I fell asleep at once, though I remember thinking, selfishly and half-asleep, that if I left at least I would be gone, I would be in other places seeing other things, not dealing with the day-to-day difficulties that were going to be overpowering at home.

—3—

Bear me swiftly over the land
long legs, nurtured with roots
turning ears tuned to my voice
gentle mouth here to my hand
warm flanks under my thigh
faster than eagles.

Bear me swiftly down on the foe
long legs, first in the charge
strong feet shod with iron
brave heart thundering down
driving home the lowered lance
stronger than lions.

Bear me swiftly home at last
long legs, ready for grain
at end of day when night falls
never complaining, carry me on,
smooth feet, shadow in shadows
best of companions.
　　　　—Aneirin ap Erbin "Greathorse"

I woke in the night to a desperate clatter of hooves, followed by silence. Morien was awake beside me, rigid in the straw. Aurien still slept. I eased my way out of the hay towards the wooden upper door. Two of the farm children followed me. I peered down between the slats. Down on the cobbles of the outer yard was a black horse, a shadow among the shadows, nosing at the closed gate. There was no sign of any rider. As was usual when a farm had more than one building the barn and house stood at right angles to each other, forming two sides of a square with walls enclosing the other two sides. From the hayloft we could not see all the way round.

"Apple!" breathed the farm girl beside me. I looked down at her. She was no more than a shape in the dimness, perhaps thirteen or fourteen years old.

"You know that horse?"

"He's Apple. He's Rudwen's horse. She used to ride him down here and exercise him up on the sward. They'd always stop for a drink of milk and an apple for Apple."

If he was Rudwen's horse then he had come from our stables. I peered at him in the gloom. He did have a familiar look. All our horses had been taken. Either Apple had carried a Jarnsman here, or he had escaped them somehow. There was no sign of any human movement below. It seemed most likely the horse had fled and come alone to a familiar place. I could not imagine raiders having need of such a ruse if they wanted to attack us.

"Do you think Apple would come to you?" I asked, pulling on Darien's leathers over the woollen smock one of the farmers had lent me to sleep in. The breeches were still unpleasantly slimy. The girl whispered a quick assent. I took up Darien's sword and led the way down the ladder. I put my hand on Morien's shoulder as I passed him. I felt him tense under my touch, but he did not speak. I moved on. He was only thirteen and had seen terrible things that day; it is no shame to the half-trained to want to avoid danger. The farm girl followed me, leaving the other children burrowed under the hay. At the foot of the ladder I paused among the warm bodies and fresh dung scent of the cows.

"I go out first. I am armed and armored. If there is fighting I want you to close the gates and come back inside here and make as much noise as you can to wake Duncan and your parents and mine in the house."

"Yes," she agreed, definitely.

"In case something happens—you know my name. What is yours?" I asked.

I could not see her expression as she answered, but her voice was steady. "My name is Garah."

"I will remember."

The shadows made the yard very dark. I made my way carefully in what light the stars gave. Garah followed me towards the gate. I opened it slowly, drawing up the bolts one by one. Then came the most dangerous moment as I pushed it open away from me. I stood ready, sword in hand. No attack came. I could hear the ring and creak of horse harness moving a little. At a single glance Garah was beside me. She stepped towards the horse, murmuring something soothing under her breath. It may have been a prayer to the Horse Mother or a charm, or just the way she always approached horses. Certainly it worked. Apple came towards her, harness chinking a little. He allowed Garah to take hold of his bridle and lead him past me into the yard. I closed the gate carefully and drew down the heavy bolts.

Starlight glinted on the iron of the harness. I could see Garah's teeth showing in a grin, and I grinned back. We had a horse, a proper war-trained horse. I tried to make out details about his condition, but it was too dark. He was six years old, fully trained. Rudwen ap Duncan had ridden him to the skirmish last year. Such a horse was worth more than gold. This was a loss to the raiders and a great gain to us. It would have almost made my journey to Caer Tanaga sensible, if only there had been help waiting there.

We took Apple into the barn. The cows shifted aside. Apple seemed glad to be among them. I went up to the loft and reassured the children in whispers that all was well, and we had caught a horse. Morien lay as still as stone, and Aurien was breathing clearly and serenely as a child does who is deeply asleep. The younger farm children settled themselves down as I went back down the ladder. Garah stood soothing Apple. She helped me to take off the harness. She had much skill with animals but no idea how the complicated gear fit together. It was not an easy task in the darkness, but at last we had all the tack and harness safely off. Apple shied and kicked out when I touched his mouth, but let Garah remove the bit.

"I think his mouth is cut," Garah whispered.

"Perhaps he managed to pull free of a Jarnsman holding his bridle," I suggested. This suited me better than the other likely possibility, that he had managed to shake him off somewhere. Jarnsmen in general were poor riders. I did not want to think that the woods might be full of Jarnsmen. But now I had a sword and a horse the odds were much more on my side in any fight, and I was not afraid. I leaned my head a moment against Apple's warm and comfortable flank and deliberately did not think of Banner, the bay Darien and I had helped to train, whom I had ridden all this last year. I fetched my blanket from the loft, rubbed Apple down, and stayed with him until he seemed comfortable with me. When I went back up to the loft dawn was beginning, and even Garah was deeply asleep.

Everyone had good advice to give me before I left. Duncan gave me good clear directions to Caer Tanaga. He could not go himself. Not only was he still weak from blood loss, but he was needed in case of any further attack.

"I think they will have fled to sell what booty they have collected," he said. "They were sea-raiders—in strength indeed, but no more than pirates for all that. In the east these men are coming to settle, driving the people off the land, but not here." The word he would not speak in front of my mother hung heavy in the air between us: not here *yet*. "All the same I think it would be safer for you to head north through the hills aiming for the road north from Magor, and crossing the river at the fords near Caer Gloran."

"There is a ferry across the wide mouth of the Havren at Aberhavren," put in Veniva, frowning a little. I did not think she had slept, or left my father's side all night. He had still shown no signs of waking. My mother's hair still hung unbound all around her face. "It cuts more than a day off the journey's length."

"The ferry may not be there, or may not be safe. And I do not think the coasts will be safe." Veniva set her lips, as if she would insist. I wondered for a moment if my mother was truly sending me for help or if she hoped I would die on the way. Then she shook her head.

"Very well, Duncan, you are war-leader, and you know the land."

It was midmorning before I got away. From the farmers I took a blanket and a bundle of food. I embraced Veniva formally and Duncan gratefully. Then in front of everyone I knelt to Morien and made him my formal homage as my father's heir. I agreed with Duncan that it was wise to have this done now and openly in front of as many witnesses as possible. If Gwien died there might be those who said they needed an adult to lead them. I had little desire for such a thing, but if it was necessary I would do it in Morien's name for a year or two. It was best to make that plain. I wished to be the cause of no dissension.

Morien had dark shadows around his eyes. His hair hung loose about his face. He said the formal words by rote. He looked a little stunned and did not at any time look me in the eye. Still, he was the heir, and would be a man grown soon enough. In any case, Gwien might yet recover. I prayed so. I embraced Aurien and then on impulse embraced Garah who stood beside her. Garah had spirit enough to hug me back. I rode out inland into a fine rain just beginning, not looking back.

Apart from the pain in my thighs the next two days passed much as any ride through broken country passes—I saw trees on the hills and farms in the valleys. I avoided people for I had no desire for conversation. The peace and the silence did me good. As I rode along my head was full of daydreams of revenge and glory and of a noble death in battle.

I did not go far that first day. I was still tired, and riding was painful. I was still getting used to Apple and he to me. He was still a little nervous of me. I had to argue with him a little before he was happy to consider me an appropriate person to ride him. His torn mouth did not help in this, but he grew calmer as the ride continued. We stopped for the night in some woodland. One cannot hide a warhorse, and horses must eat. I did as Duncan said, and I had practiced. I tethered him where he could graze, and slept in a tree, with Darien's sword near at hand. I slept just as well as one always does in such situations and was glad of the dawn and a good reason to move and stretch and set off.

The second day was much the same, though drier, and the pain in my thighs was somewhat better. The birds sang, and the trees were in leaf, I saw only occasional distant farmers. The land was strange to me now, but I had little difficulty. With starting so early I made good time and struck the highroad towards sunset on the second day as Duncan had said I should. What he had not said was that I should strike it just as a battle was about to begin.

I thought it was a battle then. I should not in honesty call it more than a skirmish. The road there runs north–south through a narrow valley. I came towards it over the hill from the west. The Jarnish forces were coming across country from the east. It seemed clear they had rowed up the Havren and landed nearby. They were not more than three full ships' companies, about two hundred men, armed with spears and shields. Where the other force in full array had come from was less clear. I thought they must have been heading south down the road from Caer Gloran. They were all cavalry, about sixty of them, armed and armored, bearing long lances and long swords. As I crested the hill they were just about to charge the massed ranks of the Jarnsmen.

I had hardly taken in what I was seeing when they charged straight at the massed Jarnish shield wall. They seemed to be holding their lances in a way I'd never seen before, and to move them with a strange degree of speed and coordination. What I did then has often afterwards been called heroic, and equally often foolish. I will only say that I did not think at all. Apple smelled the scent of the excited horses, coming towards us on the breeze. He threw back his head in a loud whinny. He did not seem at all frightened. He had been trained for war, and here were other horses and something he understood. I did not stop and consider any more than he did. It was his decision and not mine to charge, but I did not even try to stop him. Once he began to move it felt like a good idea.

The cavalry hit with a great cry, and the shield wall broke. Some ran, others were fighting. As Apple bore me down upon them I drew my sword. Darien's sword. I remember thinking that my wrists were strapped, as anyone's would be who was riding all day across rough country, not as tightly as one would do it for battle, and then that it would just have to do. Then I was on them, striking as I could. It is hard to remember the blur of battle or to distinguish one skirmish from so many others in those years. Sometimes the sweat of someone who has been riding hard will bring it all back to me now, excited horses and excited people, the chafing of the thighs, the force of impact, the delicate dance of the moving weight and edge that is the sword, round helms and pot helms and leather helms and the forest of spears and axes and the occasional sword coming up at an angle that must be avoided.

Apple responded to me as if we were one being, moving to put all his weight behind my thrusts. That was only my second real fight. I was still a little surprised at both how like and how unlike it was from practice, how I struck at the spot under and to the right of a man's collarbone and an instant later he slid off my sword no longer a man whose snarling face and weighted club were a threat but only another obstacle on the ground. I remember laughing at the expression on one Jarnsman's face as Apple bit and worried off the man's nose and he dropped his spear, clapping his hands over his face in surprise. I fought as well and as hard as I could, going from instincts bred from long training, remembering always what Duncan had told me, that cavalry must always keep moving and never hesitate.

Although their line had broken as the lances hit them there was some hard fighting before they fled. They rallied to their leaders and made solid stands in small clumps. I found myself in a bad corner at one point, parrying two axmen at once. A horseman rode up to help me, a broad-shouldered man with a white cloak, so light-skinned I would have taken him for a Jarn were he afoot. Our swords fell together, aiming and striking. Blood sprayed up. He grinned across the dead foes at me as Apple wheeled away, then frowned, realizing he did not know me. I laughed again, and just then Apple reared up and lashed out at a Jarnsman. He went down, but I was struggling for a moment to keep my seat and when I was steady again they were all fleeing and we were pursuing, keeping them running until they were flinging themselves down on the ground panting and puking in the mud. Most of them were dropping their weapons and pulling off their helmets in the Jarnish sign of surrender. I killed a few stragglers who were disinclined to stop running. The river was in sight by the time those of us following took out the last of these, a silver glimmer ahead in the twilight. I could see the dreaded dragon-prowed shapes of pirate ships, two large ones and three smaller ones looming among the willows on the bank. This was a raiding party, then; they were not coming to settle but for loot. The ships were a sign that they did mean to leave.

As I rode back a woman rode up to me. She had just sent a small group of a dozen or so riders off in the direction of the ships. I drew up Apple beside her. She was clearly a leader among the cavalry and was wearing a white cloak embroidered with gold oak leaves on the shoulders. I had seen her in the very forefront of the charge. She was broad-shouldered and long-nosed, and her skin was as pale as a Jarn's. Her eyes, however, were dark and human. Apart from the one man I had seen in the battle I had never before seen anyone who was not clearly of one race or the other, although I had of course heard of diplomatic marriages made with barbarians. She slid down from her horse, holding on to the reins, and politeness compelled me to do the same. My legs were rubbery as I hit the ground, but it felt very good to be standing and not astride.

"I am Marchel ap Thurrig," she said, bowing. As she straightened, I saw that she was not tall, perhaps a span shorter than me. "I am praefecto of the ala of Caer Gloran. And who in the White God's name are you? And how did you come here to fight so fortuitously?" Behind her the man in the white cloak walked away from the prisoners. They were being roped together. He came towards us.

"I am the eldest daughter of Gwien of Derwen." The polite incomprehension on Marchel's face was a revelation to me. Lords must give their names, and I had never thought my father's name would be unknown. "I am traveling to Caer Tanaga to see the High King." She snorted. There was a faint smile on the face of the pale-skinned man who was standing listening.

"Well there's no doubt at all that you fought with us and not against us—" Marchel began.

"Why do you seek the High King?" the man interrupted.

I looked at him. He had not identified himself. I did not even know who these people served, only that they had come from Caer Gloran. Nothing bound me to answer him. But for that moment we had shared in the fight I somehow trusted him.

"Raiders attacked my father's land at Derwen, and my mother insisted I go to Caer Tanaga to seek help."

"We may be able to help, depending on what sort of help you need." There was no smile on his face now. "How many raiders? From where?

Jarnsmen? Derwen—that is down on the south coast, yes?" He frowned as if trying to remember. "Derwen—yes, Gwien ap Nuden, and his heir is . . . Darien?"

"Darien is dead," I said, feeling a lump in my throat as I said it as I had not had when I gave the same news to my mother. "And my father Gwien is badly wounded and may not live. The heir now is my brother Morien. Derwen is two days' ride from here across country the way I have come. We need help rebuilding and also knowing what to do if the Jarnsmen come again. There are not very many of us." I tried to remember the rest of his questions as he stood there looking patient and worried in the fading light. "I think there was only one ship's worth of them, by numbers, but they took us by surprise. I did not see the battle myself, but I met some of them, and they were definitely Jarnsmen. They took all they could take in goods and people and horses and left."

"Raiding season," said Marchel, as if continuing a long debate.

The man raised his chin absently, then looked at me straight. "What is your name, daughter of Gwien?" He had no right to thus ask for proof of my words by asking me to put my name to them. His eyes were compelling, and we had spilled blood together, and if he wished me harm, he need not go to this trouble.

I raised my arms, palms open upwards, and then downwards. "I call all the gods of Earth and Sky to witness that my words are true and my name is Sulien ap Gwien."

He smiled again as I brought my hands back to my sides. "It is as well you found us. You would not have found any help in Caer Tanaga; there is nobody there but the townsmen and traders at this time of year. We do need to arrange for defenses in the south. We will ride to Derwen and see what can be done." He turned to Marchel decisively. "Will we need to go back to Caer Gloran first?"

She considered a moment, glancing at the prisoners and around at the rest of the cavalry. The people who had been holding spare horses out of the battle were mingling with those who had fought, some were binding up wounds and singing charms to keep away the weapon-rot.

"Unless the report from the ships is other than I expect, it would seem to me most sensible to go back for tonight, have the wounded seen to, and leave the prisoners there to be sent on to Thansethan. Then we can set off fresh in the morning with supplies and rested horses."

"Yes. We do that then. Arrange it." Marchel raised her chin definitely and swung back into the saddle. He turned to me.

"You fought well, Sulien ap Gwien. If they can spare you in Derwen, I would be very happy to offer you an armiger's place with me." He clapped me on the shoulder and turned away, leaving me standing there open-mouthed, staring after him.

And that was how I met my lord Urdo ap Avren ap Emrys, High King of Tir Tanagiri, Protector of the Island, War-leader of the Tanagans and the best man of this age of the world.

"By the Radiant Sun in whom I hold my greatest trust, I swear to take
_____ as my lord, to have no enemies save as they are his enemies, to harm
none of his friends, to strike and to go and to do as he shall command me in
his service, saving neither House nor Name nor God, until he die, I die, or
these words be given back to me.

"By the White God Ever Merciful, I swear to have _____ as mine to house
and horse and arm in my service as befits an armiger and to keep them in their
age; a blow struck them is a blow struck me, and their deeds are my deeds,
save as they break my peace."
                                        —Tanagan Armiger's Oath

I rode to Caer Gloran among the ala. There was an hour of the long twilight of midsummer left, and Marchel wanted to make the most of it. Most of the armigers were friendly at once. It was some time before I realized how lucky I was to have met these people first in battle. Although few of them were heirs to land, they were almost all of noble blood. They were already, after only two years together, very proud of their skills and position. I learned later that many of them had been sent to the king by their clans as hostages or pledges of support. Urdo had received them all alike in honor, seen to it that they were appropriately trained, and given them position as his armigers. Most of them were fierce when crossed and slow to accept any outsider until proven. I was lucky to have proved myself to them with no baiting necessary.

As soon as Urdo left me they came up and spoke to me with no need of introductions. They named themselves to me with their father's names or their land names without even a thought. Some of them even that first night gave their own names, as family do, or those who fight together and may die together. Many of them thought that I must belong to another of the king's alae. I rapidly learned from their talk that he had three already and soon the whole country would have them at every stronghold and the Jarns would be sent back across the Narrow Seas where they belonged. Their horses snorted at Apple, and he snorted back, making friends and finding his place among them.

In much the same way, the armigers asked me who I was and how I came to have a fine warhorse, and how I knew how to ride him. They thought me trained because I had fought, although at that time I knew nothing of true lancework beyond tilting at a target. I could not have taken my place in a charge. One of them, older than most, named himself to me the son of Cathvan and said he had known Apple before he was given to my father at the coronation. He was one of the king's horse trainers. The five-year-old he was riding that day was now battle-hardened and ready to be gifted to a lord. He showed some regret at this thought. I knew how hard it was to train a warhorse, having done some of the work myself of saddle-breaking a colt. I had never really thought where all the horses the king had given to those who swore to him had come from. I had given it no thought beyond the old songs of the Emperor Emrys winning a thousand horses for a song in the land of giants, and the even older stories my nurse had told me about the white horses born of the wave that came thundering up the beach to stand whole in the breaking surf draped in seaweed to be caught by heroes.

I told them all my errand, and they dealt with the news exactly as I might have best wished, looking grave and saying that what was done was done, but we would be avenged. They were for the most part very young, no more than a few years older than I was, though they were battle-seasoned and seemed to me men and women grown. Few of them were women. Besides Marchel, there were only four other women in that ala of sixty. Lancework needs great strength in the shoulders. I looked at Marchel in time to see her mount by straddling her horse's lowered neck and having him toss her back into the saddle. She did this with unself-conscious grace, but I saw many envious glances, and one or two attempts to copy her that left the riders lying in the mud or sprawled awkwardly across their horses' rumps behind the saddle.

Marchel gave us a riding order—most of us were to ride on the road, four abreast, which was usual; scouts and outriders were given their positions clearly. The prisoners walked in front with four riders single file on each side of them. I took up a position with some of my new companions towards the middle of the ranks. Ap Cathvan the trainer stayed near me. As we began to ride I asked one of my companions about Marchel.

"Is she a Jarn?"

He laughed. He was a broad-shouldered man who had given his clan name, Angas. Even I knew that this was one of the great clans of the north. "Marchel? Not a bit of it. Her father is Thurrig, a Malmish admiral from Narlahena. He serves King Urdo now. He came to Tir Tanagiri thirty years ago with three ships, though they were lost in battle long since. He has fought all that time for one king or another, and Marchel, too. They say she was born in the saddle."

"They say Thurrig got her on a mare, too, but they make sure to say it quietly," put in ap Cathvan. Angas laughed again.

"When we all know her mother? But she's a fine fighter and highly skilled as a rider. Her father's a good fighter, too, though he's always pining for ships."

"Urdo has promised him some, and I'll be glad to see him get them. That would give us the chance to catch the Jarnish bastards at sea before they do any damage." The two men raised their chins at the thought, and I smiled, thinking of ships. Without knowing it I had caught the infectious hope that ran through the ala, the belief they had all caught from Urdo that we could make a difference, we could change things, we could turn the tide.

"I know very little of the Malms. Are they like the Jarns?"

Angas looked at me, considering. "I can't say I know much about them either. But Marchel and her father are loyal, and she's good to have beside you in a fight, none better. If Thurrig had some reason for leaving Narlahena in a hurry, as some say, then for my part I suppose he was justified in it. If I remember my history right then the Malms were the first of the barbarians to win a battle against the Vincans, years and years ago, away somewhere off in the east." The direction he waved his arm was south rather than east, as we were riding northwest, but I said nothing. "They may well plague the civilized people in some parts of the Empire much as the Jarnish raiders plague us, I don't know. But in the alae we don't judge people by the color of their skins but by who they are and how they themselves behave. When Marchel was first put over us there was some dispute over that, but as the king himself says, we should judge people each by their deeds, by the color of their blood, by who they are willing to shed it for and by the strength of their arms." He was looking at me very seriously.

I raised my chin. What he said was sense. "I hate the Jarns though," I said.

"The raiders yes, and so do I. We all do. They will destroy everything we want to build. But there are Jarns living among us, in the east, who live in hamlets and have settled lives. Some of them took up arms beside us and fought their cousins who came raiding last spring, when I was at Caer Tanaga with the king. Not many of them it's true, but some, and there will be more, Urdo says."

Ap Cathvan spat aside. "Take them by the each, you say, Angas, and that's fair enough, that's the king's wisdom, and the teaching of the White God. But when you see them ready to kill you that speaks pretty plain. Nothing against Marchel to be sure, but the Jarnish farmers who've sworn to the King's Peace, well, say what you like, but I'd not sleep the night among them and be sure to wake up with my horse and my throat whole. They're mostly thieves when all's said and done. Sure there's good people among them, same as there are bad ones among us. But we're mostly to be trusted and they're mostly not." This, too, sounded like wisdom. I wanted to believe the Jarnsmen a different species from myself so I could hate them cleanly.

"Nonsense!" I was surprised how vehemently Angas spoke. "You must have extremely honest farmers at home, and I'm glad to hear it. But the Jarnsmen are no different from us in kind, once they leave off worshiping their blood-loving gods." I looked from one to the other of them, uncertain. The older man laughed a harsh bark and looked over at me.

"Angas is talking like this because his father is giving him one of them to wife."

"A Jarn?" I found the idea revolting.

"A Jarnish princess," said Angas, looking at me and ignoring ap Cathvan. "And it was not my father's idea but the king's, and the girl is kin to the dowager Rowanna, the king's own mother."

"I say an Isarnagan alliance now and push them back to the sea," said ap Cathvan.

"And what would you pay for that alliance?" asked Angas, suddenly leaning forward in his saddle. "What do you know about the Isarnagans? I fought against the Isarnagans at home in Demedia every year until I came down here. Believe me, a burned harvest smells the same whoever fired the corn. You should see what the Isarnagans have done in the north, and whether the people there welcome them as cousins."

"And what will you pay for your Jarnish princess?" ap Cathvan sneered back. "The same as King Avren did for Rowanna? Land for her relatives to settle, a truce for a term of years, and then more of the maggots eating away at the island from the inside? And what gods will your children pray to? The Isarnagans are wild people, I agree, like we were before the Vincans came, but they know our gods, and when they give their word before an altar we can trust them, not like the oathbreaking Jarns."

"If it were not for Rowanna and Avren's Jarnish alliance, we would have no High King now!" retorted Angas passionately. "What happened to his elder brothers when Avren died, Queen Branwen's sons, the heirs everyone acknowledged?"

Ap Cathvan shook his head, and I raised my eyebrows. If I had heard any tales of them I had not paid attention.

"Young Emrys died in battle, yes," Angas said, lowering his voice a little, "but some say it was a blow from behind. My mother told me it was not the Jarns nor a fever that killed Bran. Rather it was King Borthas at Caer Avroc, though he had given them all his protection. She herself was in fear for her own life if she tried to claim the crown, and very glad to be given to my father even though she was but thirteen years old. What sort of ally kills the king's sons and uses the daughters to make alliances?"

"Treachery, yes. A shame that such a man still lives and bears the name of king. Yet nobody who was alive in those days can claim—"

Before ap Cathvan could continue Angas cut him off. "There's been treachery enough on all sides in the last twenty years, true enough, but nobody can say there was treachery on Rowanna's part. She took Urdo and fled to Thansethan in disguise, and nothing else would have served to keep him safe to grow up. Of them all it was the Jarn who kept faith in what she swore. And 'what gods' you say, ap Cathvan, making my blood boil, as if they all serve those bloody-handed gods of war? But you know as well as I do that she and all her kin have trusted in the White God. To be sure there was oathbreaking enough when people swore by gods not their own, but there is an end of that."

"For those who will turn their backs on their own ways, but not all of us will, and I wager not all of them will either. Oathbreaking is in their blood, as honor is in ours."

"Rowanna broke no oath, she remained steadfast to her vows when nobody else did, not even my own father behaved as well as she did in the years after Avren's death." Angas looked angry enough now to leap at ap Cathvan with any more provocation.

"Some say," I ventured, "that she fled with a baby, three, four years old, and who is to say that the man who stood up in the monastery fifteen years later was that same baby."

The two angry faces rounded on me, united now in their fury. Suddenly we were in the middle of a spreading circle of silence.

"Nobody loyal to the king says that!" spit ap Cathvan.

"Urdo is the best king we've ever had, and when he was crowned he asked if anyone disputed who he was or what he did, and if nobody would dare speak up then they should not mutter it behind his back!" said Angas.

"I am only saying what I have heard said, not that I believe in it." I said, holding Apple steady. He was tense between my legs, sensing a fight. Sure enough Angas put his hand on his sword.

"If you hold to what you said, then I shall challenge you for the king's honor."

I did not want to fight this man I liked, and least of all for this cause, but I could see no way to back down now without appearing a coward. I drew breath, and before I could speak the king himself was between us on his greathorse. He had heard, and ridden back between the parting lines while we had been intent on each other. He drew to a halt now, and the rest of us halted around him; the whole ala was listening. He leapt from his horse and stood firm on the ground before her head. He was the broadest-chested and most solid man I ever saw—even Duncan or Angas was like a silver birch in comparison to an oak. I felt quite certain I should be put to death for treason. I drew another ragged breath, but he ignored me.

"Is this how you defend my honor?" he asked, looking from Angas to ap Cathvan. They hung their heads. "She spoke only out of ignorance, as many people speak. It is the natural way for people to think when a boy has grown up hidden not knowing who he is. I could hardly believe it myself when I first was told, that I was the trueborn High King of all Tir Tanagiri, like something from a story. Some of you know that the path from there to here was not as easy as the stories will have it." There was a ripple of cheerful laughter, breaking the tension. Then he raised his hand, and there was silence again.

"If it was hard for me to accept it was true, how much harder for those who have never met me? Hard indeed for those to whom the names of my father and grandfather are tales, whose whole lives have been taken up with Jarnish wars and fraternal bickering? We will not bring the King's Peace by killing them when they find it hard to believe! The way to drive out that story is not by spearing every farmer who repeats it, nor by slaying every armiger in mortal combat either." He smiled at me then, and my heart leapt. "It is true I was raised in Thansethan. The way to drive out the rumor that I am not my father's son is not with the sword, and not even with the word of the monks who were there when my lady mother brought me, and are there still. The way to drive out that rumor is by my own deeds. I shall be king, but no man can be king alone. Your deeds must keep my peace, or the people will say that there is not justice when you come to take them who break it, and that Urdo is a false king, whose armigers are false. It is no part of my peace to murder over rumors, so put down your swords and embrace, whether the daughter of Gwien finds me king enough or no."

Angas and I dismounted, and embraced, making peace as the king bade us. In all this time since the king rode up I had said not one word. I wanted to say that I had not doubted him since I had seen him, and that he seemed the truest and most honorable king that there could be, and besides he had promised to help me. But no words would come that did not seem too foolish to pass my lips. As Angas mounted again I slipped to my knees in the mud before Urdo.

It was growing dark, and the gathered horsemen were but shapes in the gloom, moonlight glinting on their lance tips. Yet I saw Urdo's solid shape clear as he stood against the western sky, his horse behind him.

"My lord, I would swear to you," I said. He looked into my eyes for a long time, very gravely, and then took my hand. I had to ask him the right form of words and he told me and I repeated back to him the armiger's oath, only where one would say the name of the lord I said, "My true king, Urdo ap Avren ap Emrys, High King of the Tanagans" and as he raised me up to give me back my sword he smiled.

—5—

The Three Most Generous People of Tir Tanagiri
Elin the Generous, daughter of Mardol the Crow
Gwien Open-Hand, son of Nuden ap Iarn
Cathvan Soup-Ladle, son of Senach Red-Eye
but Urdo himself was more generous than them all.
                        —"The Triads of Tir Tanagiri"

When I was a small child Darien and I shared a nurse, a local woman who had been nurse to my father Gwien long before. Under my mother's eye she would tell us the stories of Vincan heroes and battles, famous victories and fortitude in the face of adversity. Last thing at night she would tell us old Tanagan tales of daunting quests, desperate last stands, and unexpected reversals of fortune. In those tales, heroes traveling the roads often found strange and inexplicably marvelous things at every turn—burning trees, giant fighting cats striped in black and gold, floating castles. Always these wonders had the likeness of some familiar thing but made strange by size or transformation. At my first sight of Caer Gloran I believed for a moment that I had fallen into such a tale.

The wall around the fortress was stone-built, like the wall of any house or farm, yet it stood twice as high as my head and stretched far out of sight. Caer Gloran was in origin a Vincan fortified camp, one of those built five hundred years before during the conquest. When things were peaceful the camp seemed to them a good place to station a legion. It stands on the highroad at the place where the Havren is first narrow enough to ford. When the province was properly peaceful Caer Gloran became the local center for tax collecting. A market town grew up around it as the country-folk rode in to trade with the troops and the administrators. The town had grown and prospered then shrunk when the bad times came. The wall was built in the time of my great-grandfathers, when the first barbarian invasions began to reach up the Havren. To anyone who had seen Vinca, or even Caer Tanaga, it was a paltry place. I had never then seen any city, never anywhere bigger than Magor where perhaps eight hundred people lived. I knew none of this history as I stared at the bulk of the wall in the moonlight.

I was tired. I had been looking forward to the thought of stabling for Apple and a sheltered rest for myself. Now I felt chilled and uncertain. It was hard to imagine a welcome within those great walls. When we reached the gatehouse I gaped even more, for the wall's width was fully in propor-tion. As the gates swung open and we rode inside I looked back behind me, as if to check that the hills and the river were still glimmering there. I was not entirely sure that a hundred years might pass in a night or if I might not wake up quite transformed.

The man who came to meet us did nothing to reassure me. He wore long brown robes and had a brown hood drawn up over his head. He pulled down the hood when he saw Urdo, revealing a thin dark face. Around his neck hung a white pebble, which caught the light from the lantern he held and seemed to gleam slightly. Had I known what he was and how much it would have angered him to have been compared to the Folk of the Hollow Hills, I would have leapt from my horse and proclaimed my thought at the top of my voice. As it was I stayed on Apple's back and followed the others to the stables as Urdo got down and greeted the man.

The stables at Caer Gloran lie near the gates. In the original plan the fortress, like all Vincan fortresses, had housed foot soldiers, a Vincan legion marching in disciplined conquest carrying all they needed. They built the same fortress wherever they halted from the deserts to the snows. Much later when I went to Caer Avroc and Caer Lind I found much of them familiar from knowing the ways of Caer Gloran. Very little of the town had changed since it had been built, but the stables were new and spacious. Most of the horses were kept most of the time picketed in the fields inside the walls, but we rode now to the stable block where eager grooms started up as they heard the clatter of hooves.

These grooms were mostly young people around Garah's age or a little older. I eventually managed to make one of them understand that even though I was coming in with the ala I had no prearranged place to put Apple. I told her he was well behaved and well used to other horses, but she took us to the transient's stable where there was plenty of room. There was so much room in fact that she found him a stall with a space on either side. This showed me she was used to handling stallions. I knew Apple wouldn't have given any trouble, but I was glad of the courtesy.

The floor was dry, and walls only slightly chewed. Apple headed straight for the manger. A young groom brought Apple the same turnips and carrots and armloads of fodder the other horses were having. He began to eat enthusiastically. She showed me the room where I could store Apple's tack. Before I had quite settled Apple, Marchel appeared. She had taken off her helm and I could see that her hair was the color of damp straw. She leaned over the side of the stall.

"Magnificent, isn't he?" she said. "Good appetite. He doesn't even look terribly tired. And he's a real fighter too. How old is he? A six-year-old?"

"Six, yes, he was four when my father brought him back from Caer Tanaga."

"So you've only had him a couple of years? Any luck with foals yet?"

I straightened up, all my joints aching. "He was given to my father's war-leader, Duncan, not to me. Duncan already had a greathorse of his own, though he was a gelding, being an unlucky color. Duncan came riding up out of the east twelve years back, and his was the only greathorse we had before my father brought those three back. Duncan did not want to change, so he gave Apple to his daughter Rudwen. The king had given my father and my brother each a mare. So last year we had two full-bred colts, each as pretty as their father, and this year one filly, paler in color but with a noble head. I was beginning to help train one of last year's, by Apple out of my father's mare Dauntless." I looked away, I did not want to think where little Hero was now. Apple was eating happily. I leaned over and patted him, taking comfort from his warm presence. "He would have been mine when he was grown. Mostly I rode my brother's mare, training, or Banner, who was a half-breed four-year-old that Duke Galba gave us as a colt. Apple had the run of our other mares as much as he would, the other stallions wouldn't come near him, and my father was well pleased with the general improvement of the horses."

"Anyone would be. But I didn't mean to make you sad talking about your stock, which has been lost. Not that the Jarnsmen will get much good of them. Greathorses don't do much good in twos and threes, you need a whole ala to be effective. Oh but he's a lovely beast. I was just admiring him and wondering if my Spring would like him as much as I do. If ap Cathvan says it's a good match, that is. He'll know, and care. He spent an awful lot of time getting so many horses mannered and ready to be given away at the crowning, but he remembers them all. Some of the monks at Thansethan didn't like Urdo doing that with the herd, not that they didn't have enough left. They've been breeding horses there for a long time."

"Are the monks there devotees of the Horse Mother, then?" I asked, putting one of my blankets over Apple's back and making the Horse Mother's sign. Marchel raised an eyebrow.

"They worship the White God, all of them, very devotedly. He watches over them well, and horses thrive in the pastures there."

"I do not know the White God."

Marchel looked up at me, frowning. "Where were you educated?" she asked.

I looked at her. "My mother taught all of us to read and write, and Duncan taught me fighting."

She laughed. "Forgive me. You speak such excellent Vincan I had thought you must have been sent away somewhere to school and had it beaten into you. The way you fight too—your Duncan must have been a very good teacher. Well, some of the best armigers among us came straight from the country. That does make sense of you not knowing. Well, the priests of the White God teach reverence for all life. Many of us in the alae worship him. Thansethan is one of his greatest strongholds in Tir Tanagiri. Urdo was raised there, as you may know."

"Is that why they let him have the horses?"

"They couldn't very well say no after he'd used their horses to save the place from Goldpate and a group of Jarnish outlaws. Even the Jarnsmen usually have some respect for a place of worship, but not those wolfheads. Most of them were people who were bloodcursed already for kinslaying or other crimes. That was the first ever proper charge, Urdo leading a load of monks and pilgrims and loose horses downhill onto a group of the most bloodthirsty pirates who ever deserved to get trampled to pulp. My father told me there was nothing left of Goldpate but one of her yellow plaits." Marchel laughed.

"Did he see it?"

"He was there in the guard of King Custennin. Thurrig was the first to speak up for the plan when Urdo suggested it, and he rode beside the kings in the charge." She sounded rightly proud. "I wish I'd been there myself. I would have been except that I was still nursing my youngest." She grinned. "If you're finished here, do you want to come with me to the baths? It'll be a couple of hours before dinner, and it would be good to get clean. My mother will probably be there with the children, she usually is at this time. You need to meet her anyway."

"You have hot water enough for everyone?" I asked. At home we had a hot pool as part of the heating, but it could only hold four people at a time.

"It's one of the best things about being in a town. You'll see. Say what you like about lazy and decadent Vincans I have to grant that they got it absolutely right about plumbing."

We walked together out of the stables. Many of the ala seemed to be going in the same direction, along a cobbled path that led away from the stables towards the main buildings of the town. It was fully night now and I could see it only as strange dark shapes. The place stank worse than anywhere I had ever been.

"I don't suppose you would anyway," Marchel said, as we walked along, "but I'll mention it while we're alone. It's better to be careful what you say about the White God. A lot of people won't like it otherwise."

"I hope I have done nothing to suggest that I am ever impolite to the gods," I said, uncertainly. "I only said I didn't know about him. There are many gods in the world, I meant no discourtesy. How can anyone know them all?" Marchel bit back a laugh. I saw her shoulders shake.

"We followers of the White God know that there are no other gods, that he alone is the salvation of all mankind," she said with conviction. This was the first time I had heard anything like this. At first it seemed simple nonsense, and then I thought that she, as a barbarian, had misunderstood. The gods are all around us. Even there in the middle of the city I could feel their influences—the Grey-Eyed Lady of Wisdom cast her cloak of protection around us and the cunning hand of the Lord Maker was evident in every stone. I did not even have to think or reach out for the threads that bound the world to know that it was so. Giving one's allegiance to a god above all others was something many people did, but to do that was not to turn one's back on the others.

"How can they say that the gods are not?" I asked. "I mean to give no offense, but they are everywhere."

"They are not true gods. They are sometimes demons who have deluded the folk into worshiping them, but usually they are spirits of Earth, who can be brought to see the White God's mercy and worship him. It is written that when the White God walked among us as a man he converted many such spirits and fought with many demons."

"He walked among you as a man? I have heard of such things in old tales. Did you know him?" If I had heard this in daylight and outside I might have laughed, it was the strange looming buildings and shadows within those strange walls that made me lean towards her and speak eagerly.

"No, it was five hundred and fifty years ago in the East, in Sinea. He was God, you see, the Creator, he made the world and everything in it. But most of the world forgot to worship him, and worshiped his servants instead, the little spirits. So he was born into the body of a man to remind us, to remind all that lives. He grew up and taught and walked among us. He died by stoning and rose up again forgiving his killers to become the Greater God, the One True God. All the world must worship him, people, animals, spirits. There are books, written by those who knew him well that tell all about his life and teachings." She was quiet a moment, and I said nothing, for that seemed wisest. We walked along together for a while in silence until we came to a huge pillared arch with a guard on either side. The guards acknowledged Marchel, and we went in.

I had heard much about bathhouses, but never been in one before. I looked around me with interest. The hall was floored with marble. In the center, raised slightly and protected by a marble step, was set a circular mosaic of the Mother of the Waters. It was a splendid swirl of blue and white and gold, hardly cracked at all and with only a few missing tiles. I caught my breath. Marchel smiled at me.

"This is the Large Bathhouse of Caer Gloran. The Little Bathhouse isn't much smaller, but it is reserved for the townspeople, and this one for the alae. That saves trouble. This one was designed by Decius Manicius, a

Vincan architect of distinction. It is widely considered the best bathhouse on the island. Manicius also designed the walls of Caer Tanaga. It was built at the same time as that city, about three hundred years ago"—she looked at me sideways and winked, adding—"before any of my ancestors crossed the River Vonar. Come in here and leave your weapons, we keep Tanagan customs here."

She led me into a room to my left which was stacked with an amazing assortment of axes, knives, and swords, long and short. There were wooden racks to hold them all. Shields were arranged around all the walls as decorations. An old man with one leg sat next to the door. He nodded at Marchel as she unbuckled her long ax, then grunted at me as I set down my sword and knife. I had never done this before—at home we kept weapons as was most convenient. Sometimes I wore my sword at my side and other times I did not pick it up from one practice session to the next. The feeling that I had fallen into an old Tanagan wonder tale was stronger than ever.

We went back through into the entrance hall. "Don't be offended by Vigen," Marchel said. "It's not that he doesn't talk, it's that he can't talk. They cut his tongue out, years ago."

"The Jarns?" I asked. Marchel shook her head, grimacing. "One of the kings of the north. I think it may have been Angas's father."

We went into the room on the right, and there I began to feel that I had fallen into a Vincan tale instead. It was a changing room, floored with marble and lined with wooden benches. Some of the ala were there, taking off their clothes. Ap Cathvan waved at us. He had a scar on his side and ribs he must have got from a long knife rather than a sword or spear. Angas was just walking out through the far door, dropping a shirt on the floor as he went. A servant picked it up, calling something after him. His laugh echoed back to us. I copied Marchel and piled everything neatly out of the way on the bench. I was glad enough to take the leathers off.

"Is my lady mother here?" Marchel asked a servant, offhand, in Tanagan. The girl ducked her head as if fearing a blow and spoke without looking at Marchel's face.

"The wife of Thurrig is in the baths," the girl replied.

"With any luck at all she'll have brought clean clothes," Marchel called over her shoulder to me as we went through the next arch. I could hear sounds of splashing and talking. On the other side of the arch stretched a great pool, steam rising from it. It was full of people, swimming, playing, washing, and talking as the mood took them. On one side of it stretched a mosaic pavement, mended in so many places so that it was difficult to see what the picture had been, except that there were vines in it. On the other ran a thin strip of soil, out of which real vines grew, reaching up the walls towards the roof, which was not stone but thick panes of glass so that one could look up and see the stars. I had never seen vines before but I recognized them at once from designs on tapestries and in books. I stared at them, both strange and familiar.

"I have brought clean clothes, and it's more than you deserve!" shouted up a deep voice from the water.

"My love!" said Marchel, surprise and delight clear in her voice. "When did you get back?" She straightened up onto her toes and dived headfirst into the pool, sending up a great plume of spray and surfacing beside a muscular man with long shaggy hair. Beside him in the water were a fair-skinned woman and two small boys. The woman was clearly by her face Marchel's mother, and the two boys immediately began to try and drown Marchel, calling her *Mother* so frequently that there was no doubt who they were. She did not look back at me. I walked a little way along the pavement and lowered myself quietly into the water, which was there chest deep.

There is no pleasure like really large quantities of warm water. I immersed myself entirely, then lay there floating on the surface. It felt indescribably good on my bruised and aching body. For the first time since I had caught sight of the Jarns in the meadow I began to feel really warm inside. For some while I ignored everyone and everything and just lay there basking. It was warm and clean, and the water was gently flowing, moving along the pool, which curved away out of sight past a series of dolphin fountains. I gave sincere thanks to the Mother of the Waters and to the Lord Maker for the wonder this place was. I began to feel truly comfortable as I had not for days. If it had not been for the danger of falling asleep I would have stayed still for hours. As it was I joined some of the people of the ala who were swimming to and fro. Osvran gave me some harsh soap that left my hair and skin feeling scoured. We discussed the relative merits of oil and soap for cleanliness and comfort. After a while we went in a laughing crowd to the steam room and thence to the cold room, which had warm and cold waterfalls as well as the plunge. It was pure delight to come back again to the long warm stream in the glass-roofed room.

When we were all climbing out reluctantly to threats and promises of dinner, Marchel's mother came up to me and bowed. In her hands she held what I recognized as a bunch of red grapes. There were some pictured in a threadbare tapestry in my father's room at home, behind the head of a smilingly androgynous god. I bowed back. My companions went on towards the changing room. She was very short, hardly coming up to my armpit. She had delicate bones and looked extremely elegant even though she was draped in a drying cloth. She gestured to a servant, who gave another of the cloths to me. It was worn and rough and not quite dry.

"I am Amala, the wife of Thurrig," she began. Her Vincan was very precise, each word sharply bitten off at the end. Although this was all the accent she had, it was highly distinctive. "I am in charge of the domestic arrangements of Urdo's people here. My daughter should have brought you to me before. I hear from her that you are the daughter of Gwien of Derwen? And you will need something to wear to dinner because you have nothing but some armor you have fought in? She forgot about you, and has gone off now to get dry and cuddle with her husband—she expects to be forgiven for her lack of courtesy because she hasn't seen him for a month." Amala smiled, softening her words, and I smiled, too.

"There has been no failure of courtesy on your daughter's part. I have been enjoying my bath exceedingly."

"Good. But I should have spoken to you and told you that you have a place to sleep in barracks and your horse will be stabled with the others as long as you are here. No doubt Urdo will be sorting out what to do with you later." Amala bowed again and presented me with the grapes. "We do not manage to grow many grapes here, but we do grow some. I believe these are the only vines on this island. We keep the grapes that ripen for visitors. That is the only thing I miss about Narlahena—there we had grapes enough for wine." I took them and turned them awkwardly in my hand, bowing in reply. I felt big and clumsy compared with this woman. I picked one from the bunch and ate it. It was far sweeter than any plum or damson. It also made me aware how hungry I was, and my stomach rumbled loudly.

"It is almost time for dinner," said Amala, laughing a little. "Come, let us find you clothes, and then I shall take you myself to the barracks, where you can leave your things and where you can sleep later. Then I'll show you the way to dinner. Urdo will eat with the ala tonight, he always does after a battle. He will expect you to be there." Amala patted my arm. "You will feel much better after a real meal."

I followed her through the changing room. With a gesture from

Amala one of the servants came up with a wicker basket containing cloth-
ing. There were several plain shifts and patterned overdresses, all clean and
well woven of good linen. The overdresses were exquisitely embroidered.
I would have been proud to have worn any of them, but it was immediately clear that even those which were nearly long enough were much too
narrow across the shoulders. I think they must have belonged to Marchel
or Enid.

Amala cut off my embarrassment before it was even clearly articulated.
She had dressed while I was looking through the basket and now she
looked more elegant than ever. I felt like a milk cow beside a deer.

"I can see I'd disgrace everyone in these leathers," I said, looking at
them. "But maybe I could borrow a tunic from Osvran? He's about my
height. Or I could just have some bread and go to sleep, I'm very tired."

Amala shook her head. "None of this is a problem. Wait a moment." I
sat down on the bench. There were only a handful of people still in the
changing room. Glyn of Clidar winked across at me. He had splashed me
earlier in the steam room, and I had ducked him under the cold waterfall.

"You'll be walking in to dinner with a fine silk cloak over your bare
skin I don't doubt. Good thing it's not so drafty in the Hall at this time of
year as when the icicles are rattling on the roof tiles." He laughed.

"You're a brave man, Glyn!" said one of the others. "Don't you listen
to him. She'll fix you up something good. Amala always gets things sorted.
I remember when there was no leather left at all, and we needed more harness, she had them begin tanning goat's hides." I smiled, and rubbed at my
short hair with the cloth. It was almost dry already.

When Amala came back she was carrying a folded length of white-
and-gold cloth, three gold brooches, and a knife. She looked pleased with
herself.

"This will do for a drape in the Vincan style, which will suit your
height admirably. Hold still and I will wrap it for you."

My mother would have admired how Vincan I looked going in to dinner. I felt sure everyone would stare, but nobody commented at all, and I
soon relaxed. Indeed, after a while I felt quite comfortable in it. It was surprisingly convenient, far more so in many ways than a shift, overdress, and
cloak, for my legs could move much more freely underneath it. It was
pinned with two Vincan cloak pins, but the piece of cloth I wore around
my head had a round Malmish brooch to hold it in place. When I came
back to Caer Gloran afterward I begged Amala to show me how to make

the clever folds and tucks in the material and I generally wore a drape on formal occasions afterwards.

We sat at benches by tables arranged in a circle. They almost filled the hall. Urdo sat at the table with everyone else. He ate heartily, laughing and talking with those around him. There was little elbow room. The center of the tables was piled with food, and there was an earthenware plate and cup set at each place. We had plates at home, but not so many nor so near to each other in color. My plate was a fine even orange. I had often heard my mother lamenting the fine pots of her childhood, and although she despised his work she had often tried to tempt the potter at Magor to move to Derwen. These would have pleased her, hardly any of them were cracked and those that were were mended most skilfully with rivets.

The food was wonderful. I had never seen as many kinds of sweet and savory pastries. There was thick barley soup and great platters piled high with different breads. There were three whole roast sheep and a dozen chickens. Angas said it would have been boars in the north, where pigs were not so rare. Osvran threw a piece of bread at him for complaining. Marchel was there, although I was surprised to notice that her husband was not. A look from her was sufficient for Angas to apologize. So many people told me that I should not expect to eat like this every day that I almost believed Glyn when he said that the usual fare in barracks was thin porridge with cabbage. The servants kept coming round and filling our cups with ale, and people kept raising their cups to honor each other. Everyone I had not already spoken to wanted to know who I was, and many toasted me. There were so many of them it was hard for me to keep hold of all their faces and remember who they were.

When the meal ended we drained our cups to the King's Peace. I was longing to lie down, but Urdo came over to me and asked to speak with me a little while. I followed him out of the hall and up some stairs into a chamber hung with tapestries. There was a neatly made bed in one corner and a large marble table piled with scrolls and pens and writing tablets. There were two spindly elegant chairs. Urdo sat down on one, and offered me the other, smiling.

"I have a map here, I want you to show me where Derwen is and how you came from there. Do you think a large group of horse can go that way?" I looked at the map and began to show him the headland where Derwen lay, and pick out my route. There was a scratch at the door and without a pause the brown-robed man walked in.

"Do you have a moment?" he asked, looking at Urdo and making the barest acknowledgement of my existence. Urdo raised his chin absently.

"What is it, Raul?"

"If you are really going off south in the morning, we have to arrange what's to be done about the prisoners, and also the ships."

"Write to Thurrig to collect the ships. He's at Caer Thanbard. The prisoners go to Thansethan in the usual way—they'll work for their keep until they get ransomed or swear at the high altar to keep the Peace." Urdo smiled at me as he said this last. "Raul is my clerk. He's a monk of the White God. I couldn't manage the accounts without him." Raul glanced at me again, and away.

"Talking about accounts, have you thought of how you're going to feed the alae this winter? We can't go on managing on booty like this." Urdo looked grave.

"Excuse me a minute, Sulien, I want to show Raul some figures." I moved over and sat down on the floor by the end of the bed. There was a sheepskin rug laid on the boards there. It was beautifully soft. Raul sat where I had been sitting and began to talk to Urdo quietly, seeming to contradict a lot of what he said. They were discussing figures. Raul confidently and rapidly multiplied figures from the ones Urdo gave for one horse to cover twenty-four, and then sixty-four. I'd never heard anyone do that before. All the same, it was tedious to listen to as they went on. I looked at the map for a while, the hills and the rivers and the few scattered towns. So large a coastline, so many Jarnish ships, I could almost see them in the painted waves. I found my head nodding and looked up quickly. Nobody had noticed. The drone of their voices was wonderfully soothing. If I laid my head down for a moment until the king had time to talk to me he probably wouldn't mind.

I woke to morning light on my face. I was still wearing the drape, though parts of it had come untucked, and there was a blanket over me. The blankets on the bed were pushed aside and rumpled. Urdo was standing by the table, fully dressed. He had clearly just thrown back the curtain. He smiled at me as I sat up, blinking sleepily.

"You were so fast asleep it didn't seem fair to wake you to send you to bed. But we must be up and riding soon. Show me the route on the map and go back to barracks and get ready." I noticed I still had the map clutched in one hand. I rubbed my eyes and tried to straighten the corner of the map where I had crumpled it.

"Yes, my lord," I said.

"You ask for help, but we have no help to send. The legions and allied troops are all deployed fighting the barbarians that are upon us. You complain that you have been stripped of men and arms. We are beset, and would ask you for more help if we could. You must band together to organize your own defense as best you are able. We will offer up prayers for you at the great altar of Victory, and our thoughts are with you as yours are with us. We commend you into the keeping of the gods."

— Letter from Gazerag, War-leader to Marcian, Emperor of the Vincans, to Emrys, sometime of Caer Segant, War-leader of the Tanagans.

It was a little over a year after that when I had sorted out the last of the problems left by the Jarnish attack on Derwen and was free to ride to join Urdo at Caer Tanaga.

Or so I have always said, telling the story, even after everyone knew, or thought they knew, all there was to know. But unless I am honest there is little point in taking up parchment and ink and time writing this down. If I were going to leave things out and lie then I have already told far too much of the truth. Not even the gods see all ends.

So, then, I rode south with Urdo and the ala, to Derwen. I was very surprised that first time how many more people than just the fighting armigers had to ride out, the grooms, quartermasters, doctors, farriers, and cooks made up what seemed an army themselves. I was surprised, too, how many spare horses we took. I was assigned two fine riding beasts, not greathorses but crossbreeds like my poor lost Banner. They were mares, both twelve or thirteen years old by their teeth. Riding them cross-country would mean Apple would be fresh if we needed to fight. We rode south down the road and over the hills the way I had come. It was pleasant riding even though it rained. We saw few people. We had tents to sleep dry, and there were enough of us that we only occasionally had to spend a few hours at night guard. Some of the armigers teased me about my night with Urdo, especially after they saw their wrong conclusions made me blush. Some of them stopped when they saw my confusion, and those who kept it up, especially Glyn, soon began to make me laugh. I saw that they would believe what they wanted to believe and guessed that most of them did not believe it anyway. We reached Derwen on the third day.

The place looked much smaller than it had when I left. We went first to the Home Farm where I was delighted to find my father awake and in his wits. That he would never walk straight again seemed a very little thing. He formally gifted me Apple and my sword, and informally gave his blessing on my riding with Urdo as armiger. It was too late for me to ask his permission. I tried hard to avoid speaking to Veniva alone. This was not difficult, for my family were living in the farm, and I was assigned to the third pennon, and busy.

Angas was my decurio, and Osvran ap Usteg was sequifer. Angas treated him as the second-in-command. He was a tall man, from Demedia, his parents were farmers, though he had been fostered with Angas and grown up with him. We slept six to a tent in the top meadow. By day we scouted up and down the coastline, going farther west than I had ever been, as far as the ruins of Dun Morr and even farther, as far as Tapit Point. We found four places where the pirates had landed. Everything indicated that they had taken sufficient plunder and left. It was raiding season, and we surprised one group of pirates who ran off back to their ship, and those we saw out to sea were too afraid to land once they caught sight of us. The Jarnish ships had the sea to themselves. Their square sails were visible far off, and then we would see their dragon prows cutting through the sparkling water, their oars rising and falling, sometimes even the pale-skinned faces of the raiders above the shields. Only one ship came in to meet us; the fight was nothing much—we had little difficulty driving them off. Angas found places along the cliffs where he said we should build lookout towers, as had been done near Caer Thanbard.

"They are no good unless we have enough armigers near to deter them, or unless we can fight them at sea, though," he said, scowling at the dragon ship slipping away eastward. "If Urdo can get money enough, he will build ships. These ships have come so far west because it is raiding season, and the coast around Caer Thanbard is closed to them. We need to hold the whole coast."

I began to learn to use a lance properly. Darien would have loved that training. He would have enjoyed life in the ala. I thought of him often. Lancework did not come naturally to me. It was not an easy skill to master, for much of what Duncan had taught me must be relearned differently. I came straight off over Apple's head several times and lost the lance more times than I could count before I got the trick of picking up stakes from the ground. Garah spent much of her time looking after the horses for me, and after half a month I asked her if she would like to be a groom and come with me. She had a knack with animals, and Apple liked her. Most of the grooms were nervous of him, and he picked it up and gave them good reason. With Garah he was always good-tempered, though she did spoil him with treats.

We spent much time visiting outlying farms seeking supplies, especially roots for the horses. When Angas paid at one farm with coin the farmer shook her fist at him.

"What good is this to me? You're as bad as the Jarns, taking half my turnips. Where can I spend this? What can I buy with it?"

"Peace," said Angas, angrily, then turned and wheeled away. He sent me back with Osvran, to calm her down.

We rode back to the farm, where the farmer was not pleased to see us. Osvran reassured her that she could spend the coin at any of the king's markets by the king's law, or that my father would accept it as proof that her taxes were paid. I heard this with some uncertainty. I had only the vaguest idea about taxes, but I had heard my mother say they were a terrible thing, the ruin of the gentleman class and the cause of the decline of the towns. I assured her that my father would accept the coin as worth the value of the turnips, and that she should plant more next year, perhaps one of the fields now lying empty. She knew who I was and subsided, I sang a charm over her cow's mastitis before we went, and she gave us both a drink of good creamy milk.

When we rejoined the rest of the pennon on the headland Angas was still red in the face.

"If a farmer spoke to my father so he would have her whipped!" he stormed.

"She has a right to be heard before the law, the same as anyone," said Osvran calmly, wiping the last drops of milk from his moustache. "They are her turnips, however much we need them. Think what Urdo puts up with people saying in council. People must learn to understand what the King's Peace is before they can want it."

"I sent you back didn't I?" he muttered, half under his breath.

Half a month later Urdo announced we would be moving on to Magor, leaving behind the second pennon with some carpenters and stonemasons to help with the rebuilding. Urdo also gifted my father with some horses and talked to him alone in the back room of the farm. At the end of the conversation my father limped out with tears in his eyes and called for Morien to fetch a spade. Ignoring my mother's horrified protests he sent Morien off to dig up our hoard, buried treasure that I had heard spoken of all my life but never seen. I sat at the table of the farm kitchen with my parents, Aurien, and Urdo. There was an awkward silence. Urdo winked across at me. He was wearing plain white wool, as he often did, finely woven but with no decoration and nothing to mark him as king except the way he held his head.

After a difficult while, Morien came back with the hoard. It was in a stained and half-rotted leathern sack with a ring around the top. He handed it to Gwien, who lifted it with an effort, pulled back the ring, and opened it. Two smaller leather bags emerged, and a great pile of gold coins spilled out. Aurien made a little sound in her throat as they poured onto the scarred wood. They lay there in a great heap, bearing the heads and bold mottoes of half-forgotten emperors. There must have been one there from the minting of every emperor since first the Vincans took this land. It lay there in a great glinting heap. A few coins rolled onto the floor. Morien bent and picked them up and set them down on the edge of the table.

Gwien opened the larger of the inner bags and tipped out onto the corner at his side a pile of small silver coins, some of them half-stuck together and almost all of them tarnished green and black. He opened the smaller and drew out a comb and some jewelry, wrapped in stained sheep's wool. He handed the comb to my mother, and turned over the jewelry with his finger. There were a pair of large gold brooches, one set with pearls and the other with amber. He gave the first to Aurien and the second to me. There were also some chains, which he pushed aside with the silver, and a heavy gold ring. This he pushed onto his finger. Then he ran his hands through the heap of gold coins, which were dulled from the earth but still had the unmistakable gleam of gold through the tarnish of water and time. He picked up one of them and turned it around in his fingers, angling it towards the light. *Vinca Victrix* was written around the edge, and the picture was a warrior with his foot on the body of a fallen enemy. It was the coin struck to commemorate the conquest of some province long ago, maybe even Tir Tanagiri, five hundred years before. He set it down again, and it chinked against the others. All this time nobody had said anything. Gwien set both hands against the great pile of gold coins and pushed it a little way across the table towards Urdo. He paled a little with the effort.

"That would be your taxes for the next twenty years or more," the king said, looking evenly at my father, not touching the gold.

"And in twenty years' time who knows what!" said Veniva, looking at Gwien as if wondering if his wits were addled after all.

"Well before that I may be dead, and all I am building may die with me, yes," said Urdo, smiling at my mother.

She looked disconcerted. "Another government wouldn't honor your intentions, however good they are," she said, uncertainly. Urdo laughed.

"It is very true," he said.

"Who else will help us to rebuild now?" Gwien asked Veniva. "You sent to ask him for help and see, here he is. He came. I gave him my oath, forgive me, lord, for the horses, not thinking much of it. Another little king claiming the whole island, I thought, here today gone tomorrow. But here he is, right here, and he does not give us empty air but solid help, stonemasons, carpenters, organization. He will station a pennon here when he has people enough, twenty-eight mounted armigers and all those who look after them, and he promises he will send craftspeople whose homes in the east have been destroyed. Craft workers, potters, and leather workers, maybe even a blacksmith, coming to live here at Derwen. This is not help from the moon, or help from the people of the hills that melts away in the sunlight. This is not a demand for tax that may do some good far away but benefits us little. He will give us the right by the king's grant in law, to hold a regular market here that uses the king's coin. People will come, and we can take coin from each of them who trades here."

"And this in return for our hoard? Our fathers' treasure?" My mother turned the comb over in her hands. It was the sort used to fasten up coils of hair on top of the head, and the word *Maneo* was engraved on it, "I shall remain." It would look good in her iron grey hair. What good had it done in the ground all those years? I turned over the brooch in my own hand. It was much larger and more splendid than most Vincan work. What forgotten ancestor had used it to fasten a cloak?

"I knew nothing about the hoard," said Urdo. "I would give the market right in return for the pennon being stationed here. They will be a protection, not just for you but for the whole coast, but you will have their keep to find and each greathorse eats two stone of roots a day, and green stuff. And then there are the people. Without supplies I can do nothing. I have not asked for this gold." Urdo still had not reached out or touched it.

"It all sounds well enough. But what if the Jarns come?" Veniva looked from one to the other of them, and then at Morien, who was leaning on the wall looking very young and frail. He stood to attention under her gaze, straightening the hem of his brown tunic.

"There will be more troops up and down the coast. I do not have enough trained riders yet, and it is hard to find and support them. I told you when I gave you the horses to have your children trained to fight from horseback. You listened—if many did, then in a few years we will have alae enough to sweep the land. When there are enough armigers and horses I will station an entire ala down here. It will probably be at Magor." Urdo sighed. "Horses and armigers who will train together, and lords' households who have training enough to ride out with them and loyalty enough to go where they are needed to defend everyone's homes. If the Jarns come we can win against them as long as we are there. They cannot burn our homes if they are well enough defended. Before mounted troops I have seen their shield walls break, time and again. If we are mobile and have well-found stone walls to protect us we can beat them off. As soon as I can I will be building a sea guard, too." Veniva looked no less uncertain.

"That is why I am giving him the gold now," Gwien said, patting Veniva's hand. "There will be no wealth and no market if the Jarns come in force and the whole land is ruined. We cannot eat gold. If we had all been killed in the raid, then this hoard would have lain still in the earth until the end of time. It would have helped neither us nor those who count on us. If there is peace, then it will count for our taxes for many a long year, and by then wealth will have grown again. If there is no peace, then it is no good to us anyway. My father buried it. He told me where it lay and said that if the bad times came, then we could take it and flee. Where would we go, now, Veniva? Far off to the East across the sea, to the lands of sunshine and story? There are barbarians there, too. And there are near two thousand families living on our land and looking to us. Will it buy them all passage? And on what ship?" My father shook his head and pushed the pile closer to Urdo. "All my life and all my father's life there have been war and invasion and raiding. This is my land, and my people. It seems to me that the chance this money can help you, that it will be more help now than next year, is a chance worth taking."

Urdo gathered up the gold and counted it. "I will have my clerk send you a receipt," he said. "And I thank you, Gwien ap Nuden, Gwien Open-Hand, with the whole of my heart for this generosity. If the priests speak truly who say that we are rewarded as we act then your open hands will flow with gold. It is with such service as this that I shall build this kingdom."

Magor was a bigger place than Derwen, though only the home of a lord and not a town. Urdo spent much time cloistered with Duke Galba, discussing defenses, I suppose. I know he persuaded Galba to send timber and tiles to Derwen, for he asked me what would be most needed. This was a courtesy only; he had a much better idea than I did. I was glad not to have been left at home with the second pennon, and only wished that Glyn had been. I was growing tired of his teasing about sharing blankets after every time Urdo spoke with me. We rode out every day along the coast, but we saw few pirates and no action. After a month I was no longer the worst with the lance for the younger Galba began to learn with us. He told me that he would be training as an armiger so that in time he could lead the ala that would be based on his land. He sought me out to tell me this in such a way that I realized it was past time I spoke to his father.

I made an appointment to see Duke Galba alone a few days later. He was gracious and polite, showing me in to his upper chamber as if I were an important person. The room was lined with tapestries, and there was a threadbare woven rug on the wooden boards. He bowed. I bowed. He showed me to a red padded chair. I wondered if perhaps I had made a mistake and should have chosen to tell my mother instead. I sat straight and decided to be as polite as I could while explaining as little as I could about my reasons. He handed me a beaker of warm cider. I accepted it, thanking him. It would perhaps have been possible to explain to Veniva how sickened I was by the idea of being touched again by a man, but not to this old and gracious man. His grey hair was worn in a square tail at his back. He looked like a Vincan bust brought to life. However, he was a stranger and would be polite, whatever else. He would not force me to the marriage bed, which my mother perhaps might. I decided to come straight to the point.

"Duke Galba, while I know the honor you do me and my family, and while I esteem you and your family, I am afraid that I am no longer able to marry your son. I have taken oath as an armiger, and my heart has changed since my father arranged the match." He frowned a little, but did not look surprised.

"I had heard something that made me wonder if you would be saying this to me." I had no idea what he could have heard. Had someone told him how much more suited I was to being an armiger than to running a household? That I was better with a sword than a needle? "Are you sure you are not being too hasty? My son is my only child, heir to all of Magor, this house, the great lands, and nothing the king has offered you can be sure or lasting."

"I am quite sure I have no wish to cease being an armiger, my duke, the life suits me."

"You are wise," he said. "But perhaps you may one day look on my son with more favor. You may feel sure we would not hold your previous status against you."

I should hope not. I sipped my cider and tried to think of a way to explain diplomatically that I could never think of marriage. "There is a goddess, my lord of Magor, in whose hand I have been, and she moves me to know that although he is a worthy companion I can never feel for your son as I should." I bowed from the waist, pleased with how well I had put this. As I mentioned the Moon Maid it crossed my mind that I had not felt her sickle when I should. I began to count days in my head. I supposed it must be all the riding, or the change of water. My nurse had always said too much riding upset the cycles.

"Well, our loss is Urdo's gain," Galba said, bowing again. "I believe your father has another daughter?" I assented, and he went on to talk about the land disputes, border problems, and inheritances I had been hearing about half my life and which my betrothal had been intended to settle. I praised Aurien to him, being perfectly honest about her ability with figures and fine needlework. Indeed, she was far better suited to be Magor's lady than I. I agreed that I would do all I could to persuade both Aurien and my father to the match, and he agreed that he would speak to his son and then write to my father concerning Aurien. This was a considerable relief, for it meant that before I had to face my mother she would have got over the worst part of her anger at me. I left the chamber with my heart high. I was free of obligations save those I had freely chosen and would be glad to fulfill.

No sooner than I was out of doors than I felt a wave of nausea sweeping over me. I ran for the midden and stood bent double, puking and catching at my breath. I had not known I was that nervous, nor had I ever been sick from relief before. Perhaps some of the herbs in the cider disagreed with me. I drank water that night and went early to bed. I woke early with my stomach griping. I wondered if Galba had poisoned me, and why. I barely made it out of the tent that time. Yet afterwards I felt well again and rode out that day with no more trouble. Over the next month it became habit to wake sick and be recovered before breakfast. It seemed a small matter. It was another month and a half, when we were back at Caer Gloran, before my dulled mind made the right associations and I realized I must be with child.

It was early morning, and I was in the barracks kitchen heating up water on the fire. The breakfast cook was up already, measuring baked oats and chopping dried plums. He ignored me; we had given our greetings when I first came in. He was used to me being there early. Soon the girl would come round with the milk, and he would ring the bell that woke the pennon. I had just come in from outside, through the dewy garden where I had picked some mint leaves. I had a cup in my hand. When the water boiled I would pour it onto the mint in the cup and sip it until my stomach settled. I was still shuddering slightly from nausea. My breasts ached. Suddenly all these things stopped being something I took for granted. Something moved inside me, a fluttering of butterfly wings inside my belly. I saw all the symptoms together—the sickness, two, no three missed bleeding times, the ache, the rape. Something was dancing inside me. Something had clouded my mind, and now it was clear. The water boiled, I poured it onto the mint. Then I set the cup down on the end of the trestle and put both hands on my belly.

I concentrated. I reached out and called wordlessly to the Lord of Healing and the Giver of Fruits. I could feel the life within me, just quickened, just become truly alive. Even now it would be the easiest thing in the world to loosen the hold of that life and let it slip away, go back to Lethe and choose again. It is so much easier for a new child to slip away than for them to hold on. Many will go with only a thought, even the most tenacious will yield as a prayer lets them know they are not wanted. A woman must truly long to bear a child, or see it as her grim duty, to send no thought of being free of it. It is hard for many to come through those first months I had come through all unknowing. Most women lose many in the early days before they ever carry one to term. Men know little of such things. It is always a woman priest who will sing the charm to open a woman's womb at her wedding. It should not have been possible for me to have this life inside me, this little heart beating inside the rhythm of mine. I had done nothing to seek this conception.

For a moment I longed to bear it, to feel its mouth suck milk from my breast and hear it call me mother. But only for a moment. Where could I keep it? I could not ride as an armiger unless someone else looked after it for me. I had no husband, and such a thing was unheard of. I had just pushed away all chance of marriage with young Galba, even had such a thing been possible. I had no desire for marriage, the idea brought my nausea back. I swallowed hard. Beyond sentimental dreams I had no real desire for the child. A day before I would have let it go without remorse. Even now it would do neither me nor it much harm to part. It would be better done sooner than later. I stood up, leaving my cooling cup, and made for the stinking barracks privy. "I am sorry my dear," I addressed it in my mind as I walked "I will have to let you go. There is more to giving life than bearing a babe, and I have nowhere in the cold world to bring you into to grow up whole. Go back, try again, find another mother, good luck."

I wiped around the seat with leaves, and sat down over the hole. I reached out my will to loosen the hold in my womb, and found I was touching nothing. The gods would not help me. I tried again, blending my will with the place where the gods were, this time quietly using the words of a hymn to reach out. There was no response. It was as if I reached out to take up Apple's reins and found them missing. If I sought to look at the growing child I could, if I sought to unbind the thread that held it to me, I could not.

Everything I had been taught told me that if the gods refused to act, then they had good reason, or were prevented. It was their part to preserve the balance of the world, and wrong for anyone to act upon it through their own will alone. I thought back to the rape, Ulf's dedication of me to the Father of the Slain. Did that one-eyed gallows god want me to bear this child? Was the dedication strong enough for that? I tried again, calling even on the Lady of the Dead to take back the child to her realm whence it had so lately come, but nothing happened.

I stood up and left the privy, head high. That an unmarried woman should be pregnant was unlikely enough. There were bastards in the world, but they were those married women bore to men not their husbands. Such a thing was a disgrace. I would be disgraced. My mother would never forgive me. Tears came into my eyes as I realized I would have to leave the ala. I would have to go home with no prospect of leaving, no hope of glory, only an obligation to a baby. I walked on blindly out of the barracks along the street, past the tannery towards the stables. I wanted to be with Apple.

I almost knocked Amala over. She was coming out of one of the bakehouses. When I had finished apologizing she frowned at me.

"What's wrong?"

"Nothing," I said, choking on words. She led me to one side, into the overgrown courtyard of a fallen-down house. She sat down on a wall and patted the stone to the side of her. I sat. Slowly she coaxed the story out of me. Remembering Marchel's comments about gods, I left out mention of the dedication.

"Well," she said consideringly when I had finished, "it should not be possible, but certainly it has happened. But I do not think it is a disaster. The king must certainly know. Unless he disapproves I do not see that it is too terribly hard to solve. He will be leaving this ala soon to go with the rest of his household to Caer Thanbard. You can go then to Thansethan. Everyone here will think you are with the ala of Caer Thanbard. At Thansethan you can bear your child. The monks of the White God Ever Merciful teach reverence for all life. They take in orphans and unwanted children. You can leave it there to be brought up with the others. That's an upbringing as good as the king himself had. You can then rejoin Urdo wherever he is, and he will find a place for you in one of the new alae he is forming, where nobody will wonder where you have been for the lost months. You can take your groom with you, the little girl, and she will be familiar company for you. I don't think there is any need to tell anyone else at all." Amala made a little gesture with her fingers that she used to mean that another complicated logistics problem was sorted, and I burst into floods of noisy tears.

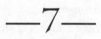

I wept, and He said to me "Why are you weeping? Soon you will all be
    free."
I replied "Lord, because you are going out to die beneath their stones."
He raised me up and kissed me, and said, "Kerigano, I am dying for all
    of us, that all our people will live. I will open up the way and be a
    door, that through me everyone may come to life everlasting."
Then Maram said "Lord, are you the Promised One?"
He was still a long moment, then He smiled at us all and set His hand on
    the door to go out. Then He turned, and said, "Is it not written that
    the Promised One is beyond death? My children, forgive these my
    blood. Remember me."
(That is why afterward we wear stones in His memory, and have
    forgiven the stones, even as He asked us.)
Then He went out and there in the sunlight the crowd was calling for His
    blood, and in their hands were stones, and behind them the soldiers,
    waiting.
        —*The Gospel of Kerigano*

The stone they put over Goldpate was so big it must have been dragged down the hill by horses. It would have been much too heavy for anyone to lift. If it was a pebble of the White God's mercy it was a mighty heavy one. It was the wrong color anyway; it was not marble but a great uneven chunk of dark granite. This was no part of their faith. Someone with rather different opinions had wanted to make sure she wasn't coming out again. There was no writing on it in any civilized tongue but angular Jarnish runes were carved on the rough top. Traces of dark red pigment could still be seen deep in the runes despite weathering. The Jarnish prisoners slid their eyes aside when they passed it, and made their odd version of the evil-eye sign. It was the most barbarous thing I had yet seen.

The stone lies about a mile from the east end of the monastery of Thansethan, on the monastery's boundary. It is there still, an odd memorial to stand so near, but nobody has ever dared suggest removing it. I walked out to it often in the months I stayed there. From it I could see far out to the east over the lands the Jarns had taken for their own. To the south rolling hills swelled and hid the view, but sometimes I could see a fog lying over the valley of the Tamer where distant Caer Tanaga lay. I would gaze out in that direction, then turn back reluctantly to the square golden-stone buildings that made up the monastery of Thansethan. I could imagine Urdo's first splendid charge with a following of two kings and their households and all the monks who knew how to sit astride a horse. It was such a peaceful place, it was hard to imagine it full of battle din.

Although I despised Goldpate as a barbarian and a bloodcursed kinslayer, there were days when I could quite understand her desire to destroy the monastery and all who dwelt in it. Thansethan was as big as a town. Within it, counting monks alone and not guests and children and prisoners, there were near two hundred people. These were severally wise and foolish, young and old, male and female, Tanagan and Jarnish, but they were all alike in their complete surety that they knew the One and Only Truth. They truly believed everyone else was misled, or mistaken, or deliberately deceiving. I found the smugness hard to bear, even among those monks I liked.

Once the king's party had left Garah and I were the only people sleeping in the guesthouse. We could hear the bells and bustle but were alone. The guesthouse stood within the outer walls along with the school and the infirmary and the prisoners' quarters. The stables were within the inner walls. Unlike visitors, horses had been part of their original plans of the founder Sethan. Most of the herds roamed out in the meadows and only rarely came within. The easiest way in and out of the monastery was through the stable gate. It was a mystery to me how anyone could design a large enclosure so that there was only one way in and out, and that at a great distance from anywhere anyone would be and on the opposite side of the place from anywhere anyone would want to go. The stable gate was a later addition, added apparently by some monk who found the clatter of horses on cobbles intolerable. They were good stables, dry and clean, with water butts standing near.

The best thing about the inside of the monastery was the water clock. I had read of such things but never seen one. It was an ingeniously designed thing, and carefully built. It measured the divisions of the day accurately so that the monks might give worship nine times a day at the prescribed hour. It stood in the center of the inner courtyard. When the time was near one of the younger monks would come out and wait, then when the water ran through they would ring a bell and everyone would go through into the great sacristy that took up the whole east side of the monastery. The first time I saw this I was amazed, for monks came rushing silently from every corner, from the cloister walk, down the stairs from the library, out from the kitchens and the storerooms, in from the school, the hospital, and the gardens. Only those who were actually preparing food and those whose duties had them watching the children or the prisoners did not move. It was strange to see so many brown robes swishing across towards the sacristy.

The word *monk* usually means a solitary worshiper, someone who dedicates themselves whole to a the worship of a god. There was a woman who lived in the hills near Derwen when I was a child who worshiped the Moon Maid. The farmers sent her food when they had spare, and my father sent her a cut whenever he took a roebuck, for such beasts are sacred to that goddess. Mostly she lived on radishes, which she grew, and trout, which she caught. My father would send me up with the meat, for she had taken a vow to speak to neither man nor married woman. She taught me some very good hymns to the Virgin Huntress, one of which I use to this day when I want to draw out a splinter. She never said anything to try and draw me to live with her, or live like her, and never said anything to me against the worship of other gods.

These monks were different. They came together to live in community, though each had a private cell where they slept and for their solitary worship. They did quite honestly devote themselves to worshiping their god, but the idea of converting everyone they met to similar worship was never far from their minds. Many of them seemed genuinely unhappy to know that anyone present did not follow their faith. Those who were themselves converts were quite sure in their own minds that once anyone had but heard about the faith in the way they themselves had learned of it they would immediately be converted. I found this really tedious. The faith had little appeal for me. Groveling before a god who desires everyone to praise and magnify him is no respectable thing. One must be polite to all the gods—after all, they are gods. But equally, one is a human being. There is beauty in the worship of the White God, but it has never seemed to me to be a polite or appropriate matter.

The chief among the monks of Thansethan was a man they called Father Gerthmol. He was an Isarnagan, though he had come early to Tir Tanagiri. He was thin and stooping, and had a habit of looking very deeply into the eyes of whoever he was talking to as if he thought to see into their soul. Many of the children and younger monks quaked in his presence. I had to bite my tongue to keep from laughing the first time he tried it on me. I think he was not much used to looking up at people's faces rather than down. He sent a young monk to fetch me to his office the second day I was there. She would hardly look at me but kept sneaking glances under her hood as she led me up the stairs and into his little office. I saw that she was a Jarn and probably little more than fifteen.

Father Gerthmol was polite, except for his searching glances.

"We put everyone to work here, everyone," he explained. "What we need to know is what you're good at. 'Turn any willing hand to the task at hand, and find the task most suited to the willing hand,' " he quoted. "What can you do to help while you are here, daughter of Gwien?" He smiled with more heartiness than the situation merited. His use of that form of my name seemed a little forced. The monks took new names when they were received into the church, abandoning their old one with their old lives. Most followers of the White God kept their new names in the same way they had their old, but the monks had theirs in the open for everyone to use.

"I have some small skills at most things, and what I do not know I will be pleased to learn."

This pleased him no end, for the White God sets great store by learning and knowledge for its own sake. He questioned me about my domestic and agricultural skills, and as I was about to go, he said, "If you truly like to learn, we will teach you to read." I smiled.

"I have this skill already; my mother taught me." He tested me with some prayers that were lying about his desk. When he found that I could read and write as well as he could he offered me free run of the library. He begged me to spend some time talking to the monk in charge of copying manuscripts to see what was most urgent and to lend a hand. He said this with so much more sincerity than he had talked about the value to the community of the skill at bottling apples that again I was hard-pressed not to giggle. If another of the ala had been there and winked at me I could hardly have kept a straight face.

I soon fell into a routine in my life at Thansethan almost as rigid as that of the monks. I would rise at dawn and drink minted water and eat thin gruel in the refectory. Later, as I grew larger, Thossa, the infirmarian monk, suggested to me that I should drink a preparation of elderflowers and raspberry leaves, so I took to drinking that instead. After this meal I would ride out on Apple for an hour while the monks prayed. Then I would go to the library, a delightful place, on the upper story. It was light and spacious and furnished with books. The monks had collected these from different places. I would copy manuscripts for a few hours in the best of the light. When the monks went to their noon worship I would stop copying, ease my cramped fingers, and read until their return.

I read *Memories of the White God*, partly to please the monks and partly from curiosity. Although it pleased me more than hearing it all secondhand, it did not please me very much. I found the fragmentary nature of the eyewitness accounts confusing, especially in the parts where they contradicted one another. I thought it would be much improved by some connecting narrative and explanation. I suppose many devout believers thought the same thing, for Raul's notes on such things have become popular with the priests recently. Despite the deficiencies, I did feel considerable sympathy with the White God as man; a man who believed himself the rightful king of the Vincan province of Sinea.

Yet in some ways I felt he deserved everything that happened—either he should have led the rebellion or discouraged it altogether. I think anyone in that situation who sacrificed himself to save his people and in doing this trusted the Vincan authorities to keep their word afterwards must have been crazy. Whether he was a god or not, I found him lacking in judgment. I felt no attraction for the idea of him as the One God, creator and savior of all mankind. I must admit some of his followers had miraculous luck in the destruction of the city, after. I did little more than skim the holy books of Sinea, for I found them and their insistence on their One God who made the world and the long lists of the doings of kings who were His servants and interpreters of the law most terribly hard going.

The shelves were full of fascinating volumes, so there was no need for me to restrict myself to theology. There were many of the Vincan classics my mother considered essential to any civilized education. There were also many books from all over the Empire on very diverse topics. I found some marvelous books on horse-breeding, and also on ancient cavalry. I read those with fascination. They had been recently recopied in a fair hand. When reading a chapter describing the use of light lance from ponies, I found a scrap of parchment in the same hand between two leaves. On one side of it was a sketch of a greathorse with a full-sized lance sketched beside it for the proportions. On the other was a design which appeared to be the organization of an ala—it was so labeled, ala, a wing, and the units pennon, feathers. There never had been an ala of a hundred and forty-four armigers, yet that was what was shown here. I realized that this must have been written by Urdo when he lived there, before he was the king.

I read other volumes on warfare, strategy, and tactics. There was no shortage of them. I even copied one old volume of thoughts on the Narla-henan campaign. The original was crumbling, and I was glad it should be preserved. I read one book written by a missionary who had been among the Jarns in Jarnholme that gave an account not only of their life but of their gods. His attitude seemed different from that of Marchel in that while he saw their gods as opponents of the truth he did not call them demons. He wanted to persuade them to the worship of the White God, too. He had been interested in everything, from the type of trees and birds to the Jarnish manner of worship. I learned a lot in that library, and had much practice in writing fair copies.

When the monks came back from worship I went to the afternoon meal. I grew heartily sick of porridge in my time in Thansethan, but at least there was plenty of it. There was plenty of honey to put on it. There was fruit, too, and some days fish. The monks ate no meat or cheese except at high festivals. Their high festivals were all connected with the life of the White God or the holy stories of Sinea. Many of them fell near the festivals I was used to, but others surprised me entirely.

In the afternoons I would walk out of doors, walking among the tilled fields or in the pastures where the horses, half-wild, ran from me, manes tossing, beautiful, glorious, and free. Then I would turn to the little spin-neys where fresh-fallen leaves crunched under my feet as they moldered down to join last years leaves, which were turning already to the earth of the woods. As autumn gave way to winter I walked more slowly, for the child weighed me down. After the first snows it was all I could do to walk out to Goldpate's stone and back.

When I came back I would help in the stables or with the beekeepers.

If there was nothing to do there, I would sometimes help in the kitchens for a little. Before I had been there long I grew tired too quickly to stand weaving, or grinding ink, or milking the cows, though I did all those tasks in the early days. I soon learned which monks were content to talk about the task in hand and which would take any opportunity to turn the talk to their God or reproaching me for my wrongdoing. As I had done nothing wrong I found this particularly hard to bear and tried hard to avoid those monks who made a particular point of this. Most of the women who came to Thansethan to bear children were indeed guilty of oathbreaking towards their husbands, so it was a natural thing for the monks to think. If they persisted I told them briefly that I was unmarried, or walked away.

I befriended the people who would talk about the tasks we were about, or horse-breeding, or the king. Whatever else I thought about them, I did not doubt their loyalty to Urdo. I heard many tales of him as a boy in Thansethan. Some of those who had ridden in the charge against Goldpate would talk about it. The young girl Arvlid had run ten miles to warn the monks. Goldpate, an outcast even among her own people, had made the mistake of revealing her purpose when trying to win more recruits. The monks were infuriatingly vague on the details of the battle, saying they just rode downhill, and the outlaws ran. Others said that King Custennin's men and King Talorgen of Angas's men did all the killing. It must have been something to see.

I would eat more of the endless gruel before I went to bed at dusk. The monks made good thick beeswax candles, the best I ever saw. I do not know what use they put them to, but they did not waste them on visitors. Sometimes Garah and I would sit and talk in the firelight planning dream stables and discussing which bloodlines of the horses we knew would give the most perfect cavalry horse. Sometimes Garah turned the talk to the baby I was carrying, but I did not like to speak of it.

I might have enjoyed my time at Thansethan more had it not seemed at the same time endless and bounded. I was not there of my own will. I was waiting, and forced to wait, to endure. Nothing I could do would make the time any shorter. Had it not been for the comfort of Apple and the support of Garah it would have been much harder.

As it was I could compare my lot very favorably to that of the Jarnish prisoners. There were a great number of them at Thansethan, all men who had been captured in battle and given a choice of life or death. Those who had chosen life were brought under guard to the high altar in the sacristy, where they swore not to escape. The White God would hold anyone's oaths. He would also punish oathbreakers severely. The White God's mercy did not extend to those who did not keep their word. The monks would send messages to their families at home and those who had kin to care about them could hope for eventual ransom. Some, however, who were not heirs to land, or who came from poor families or none, had been there for years. They could win their freedom at any time by converting to the faith of the White God and swearing never to raise a hand against the King's Peace. If they did this they could go freely into the Jarnish hamlets and settle there, or return home. Many of them so aware, and settled near Thansethan. If their families did not care enough to ransom them, then they would be unlikely to accept them home once alienated from the gods of their ancestors.

I watched the prisoners occasionally. They did most of the roughest work: hauling stones, shoveling manure, plowing the fields to plant roots, hoeing for weeds, digging the manure into the soil, dragging back wood cut in coppicing the spinneys. I wondered whether I would convert if I were in their situation. Arvlid told me that they checked the conversions very carefully and tested their sincerity; they would not allow someone to convert without meaning it. As my belly grew too great in the last half month for me to sit astride Apple's back, I comforted myself with the thought that, unlike them, I could leave. I tried not to look at the children in the school, keeping the same hours of worship as the monks. When I saw them playing in the fields, I smiled. When I saw them filing gravely into the sacristy I looked away.

My child was born the day after the spring equinox, on the very day that Sethan had founded the monastery sixty or so years before. It was thus a high holy day for the monks and even Thossa, who had been so kind to me through the months of waiting, was cross with me for having such bad timing. In the end the birth dragged on so long that they were all in the sacristy when he was born, and only Garah and Arvlid were with me.

Childbirth is a mystery; I put myself in the hand of the Mother. Garah made me walk up and down, up and down, squeezing my hand tightly. She had seen mares give birth, she said, and plenty of cows. She prayed to the Mother as Breda, and to the Horse Mother Riganna. Arvlid prayed to the Merciful One, but they seemed to understand each other. It was not a difficult birth, as these things go. The pain was endurable, though unlike in battle I felt every moment. The child was a fine big boy, perfectly formed though with lightish skin, of course. His first hair was very dark, and his eyes were at first the color of the sky before a sea storm. After a few days they faded and were the pale sea grey color of most Jarnish eyes. I could not like them. Nevertheless, his hands had a strong grip, and his feet kicked, and he tried to suck straight away, though there was no milk yet.

Thossa the infirmarian came back at dawn, extremely apologetic for having missed the birth. I was glad of him, for he got rid of most of the mess—the floor was spattered with blood and gory remains so that where I had been standing looked like the worst part of a battlefield. He opened the window shutter, letting in the cold spring air, and scattered clean rushes. I lay still, exhausted and still bleeding. The baby was asleep on my stomach. Garah brought warm water and began to wash my legs and feet, where the blood was beginning to dry brown. The infirmarian dropped some rosemary into the bowl, which gave the room a clean scent again. I almost fell asleep when Garah drew a blanket up to my waist.

Then all of a sudden Father Gerthmol was there, beaming. He picked up the child, who woke and howled a long shrill howl. He weighed him in his hands and patted his back in the practiced way of someone who has held many babies. I almost felt a pang of jealousy as he quieted.

"Well well, safe delivered, praise be to Merciful God," he said, handing back the baby and standing at the foot of the bed. I pulled the blanket up to my chin and wrapped the child in a corner of it. "A fine strong son, and born on holy Sethan's day, so. What a good sign." I smiled, warily. I wished he would go away so I could sleep. Battle never left me feeling so battered or exhausted. "So have you thought about what name to give him?"

I shook my head.

"So shall we be calling him Sethan, because he was born on Sethan's own day?" I think he must have been tired, too, to be so crass and direct about it. If he had asked me at a better time, or if he had acted as if it was his place to name the child he would, after all, be rearing, I would probably have said nothing. As it was, I shook my head again. Arvlid sat down on the edge of the bed and touched the child's cheek. It looked dark compared to her finger.

"Well, it is the custom in Thansethan. What could be better? Sethan ap . . ." He hesitated. "What is his father's name, now? Do you want to tell me?" I shook my head, this time fiercely, and drew breath. In all these months I had done my best not to think of the rape, the dedication, Ulf Gunnarsson, now that question brought the memories flooding back. If I must have a child I must, but he would be no tie to that cursed rapist.

"He is my son," I said. Garah sat down on the other side of the bed and took my hand, as she had done so often throughout the ordeal. It felt good to have the two of them there supporting me, even though I knew Arvlid would say nothing against Father Gerthmol.

"It is usual to give a child a holy name, and then his father's name," Father Gerthmol repeated. "What do you want to call him then?" My son would be clean of his begetting. He would start fresh. I would give him names he could be proud of.

"Darien," I said. "I will call him Darien." Darien would have no grandsons of his own to carry on his name. He had died too young to do great deeds to be remembered. He would have approved. Father Gerthmol frowned and looked disgruntled. Garah squeezed my fingers. Arvlid looked politely quizzical, the name meant nothing to her.

"Darien," he said, pausing again. "It is a pagan name."

"Which is well, for I am a pagan, as you know, Father." He bit his lip.

"And what else will you have him called? Shall we call him Darien ap Sethan as children are called who do not know their father's names?"

"Why are you so keen to have your holy founder's name as part of my son's name, Father?" Arvlid gasped at my impertinence.

He shifted from foot to foot and looked uneasy. "It is Sethan's day," he temporized.

"He will be known as my son, that is good enough. I know his father's name, but I will not speak it. His father is no saint, and nobody's business but mine."

Garah choked a wild bark of laughter. "He can hardly be called ap Sulien!" she said. I laughed, and even Arvlid smiled. Father Gerthmol looked at us as if we were crazy women. Little Darien stirred again, and I put him to my breast.

"He can certainly not be called that. It is an improper construction, certainly, and it would be very strange to put mother into the name." He was right in point of fact, for *ap* means *sired by* and could mean nothing else. I thought of Ulf again and felt even more resolute not to give his name. But the heathen form would do. The child was half a Jarn, and he would be growing up in Urdo's kingdom where there would be peace for those who would hold by the law. A Jarnish-shaped name would be little handicap.

"Let us call him Darien Suliensson." Father Gerthmol's mouth opened, then closed again as his eyes rested on Arvlid, who was smiling. Garah raised her chin in approval.

"So be it," he said, and turned and left me to fall deep down into blessed sleep.

So through the woods the old lord came,
to stand beside the ancient place
where he might hear his fathers speak
and cold and hard he set his face.
"Whose seed, oh ancient stones, oh trees,
grows in this boy I show to thee?
Whose child is this my wife has borne
who looks so wild and strange to me?"
There came no answer, then the wind
howled loud and shook the branches bare
and from behind his forebear's voice
came clear and cold upon the air.
"Know this, oh latest of my line,
and be content and ask no more:
to thee this boy shall be more true
than ever was a son before."
—"The Ballad of Cinon the Loyal"

I had just come in from riding, I was covered in my sweat and Apple's sweat. My breasts were tight and aching, and milk was beginning to leak through my shift at the front. Garah came rushing out of the stables towards me as I walked Apple towards the trough.

"Sulien! Quick, quick, the Queen of Angas is here and she wants to see you!"

"Me?" Sunlight and riding had made me slow. The routine of Thansethan had crept into me and did not want to be disturbed. It was time to feed Darien. I did not want people. "Why would she be interested in me?"

"She was interested enough in Darien." Garah looked a little uneasy. "He was crying. Brother Thossa sent for you, and I went up to tell him you wouldn't be long."

"I was late. Sorry. Apple needed a good run." I slid down from his back and patted the side of his neck. "We went like the wind. I'll go to Darien straightaway if you'll rub Apple down for me."

"No. Thossa's giving him cow's milk. It's time he started in on it anyway, whether he likes the cup or not. We'll be leaving in half a month when the king calls for us." I frowned. My breasts hurt. I was ready to feed him. Much as I longed to leave Thansethan, at that moment I only wanted to relieve the ache, the bursting feeling. "Anyway, the door flew open and this strange woman rushed in. She was wearing dark dark red with little pearls sewn on and a gold crown on her head like something in a story." Apple snorted at the water, finished. I led him toward his stall.

"If she's Angas's mother then she is the queen of the north, of Demedia," I said, remembering. "And the old High King's daughter; she's Urdo's half sister. She's entitled." My father had told me of the great crown Urdo had placed on his head at the coronation, the ring that symbolized his marriage to the country.

"She's nothing like Angas, nor Urdo either, who are both polite enough to notice that there's somebody there. 'Ah-ha!' she said, 'so this is the little summer hawk.' Then she laughed, and then when she stopped laughing she looked around as if she'd suddenly noticed there was someone else there, and asked what his name was. Brother Thossa said that he was Suliensson of Thansethan, and she asked who Sulien was and where, and said she wanted to see you right now. So Brother Thossa sent me to tell Arvlid to send some milk up for Darien and then to find you wherever you were and send you to the queen."

"You had better rub Apple down anyway, then."

Garah raised her chin. "I was going to!" she said.

"Are these her horses?" Six fine horses and a pony were standing in the stalls across the stable. I walked over to them. The pony was the color of fresh cream without a dark hair on him. He was in perfect condition. The horses were less striking, but all good beasts, shuffling a little in the unaccustomed place. One bay stallion shied away from my hand, and I looked closer. His mouth was torn. He wouldn't let me close, but it looked far worse than Apple's had been when he first escaped from the Jarns. I looked around, but the place was deserted; none of the brothers were there just then. I looked over at Garah. "If I'm not back before you've finished, see if you can get this fellow to take some salve on his mouth. The good stuff, there's plenty in the tack room."

Arvlid intercepted me as I walked quickly across the cloister towards the guesthouse. "I've just taken some milk up for Darien, and the Lady of Angas wants to speak to you."

"Is everyone going to tell me so?" I snapped, then, "Sorry, Sister, I was just on my way."

"She's in Father Gerthmol's room."

"Then she doesn't want to see me until later?" I was relieved. I could go to Darien.

Arvlid frowned. "They're *staying* in Father Gerthmol's room."

I was surprised. There had been visitors from time to time while I had been at Thansethan, although it was winter and not pilgrimage season. All of them had stayed in the guesthouse in the little narrow rooms all alike. Urdo had stayed in one when he stayed the night. I raised my eyebrows.

"The Lord of Angas keeps saying he will embrace the faith," Arvlid said, lowering her voice, "and Father Gerthmol says he has real hopes of it this time. His last pilgrimage here was to pray for a child, and a son was born nine months after, the fourth child. They are here now to have a ceremony of acceptance for that boy in the sacristy. I heard it's because it was the White God's intervention and something went wrong with the pagan ceremony. Which could mean that they may convert in truth this time."

"But how can he convert?" I was amazed. "He is a lord—Arvlid, no offense, I know the White God means a lot to you and you were brought up with the faith, but a lord must hold the land peace between the place and the folk. He cannot convert and be a lord. His ancestors and the holy ones would not allow it."

"King Custennin has," said Arvlid, looking at me as if I were a simpleton. "Holy Dewin scattered holy water on the land and converted all the Earth spirits in Munew. Dewin married King Custennin's sister, and they have built a great church at Caer Thanbard. He's one of the king's closest advisors."

I shook my head. "So who keeps the land peace in Munew?"

"God." Arvlid touched the stone hanging around her neck.

"On his own? A lord stands between the holy ones and the folk."

"The holy ones praise the White God, too." I drew breath again, but Arvlid patted my arm. "If you're interested, you can find plenty of people to talk to about it in great detail." We laughed. She knew how I went out of my way to avoid such conversation. "But now I have to help move a hive before the next bell, and you should get on to the queen."

I walked up the stairs still puzzling over this. I was about to scratch at Father Gerthmol's door when it opened and a child of four or five came running out, almost knocking into me. He was a beautiful boy, sturdy yet with a sure grace of movement. He had a little of the look of Urdo in the angles of his face, which must have come from his mother's side. He was dressed very finely in woven reds and greens. He ignored me and hurtled past me down the stairs. Immediately after him came a grey-haired man wearing riding leathers. He had a definite look of Angas, and I bowed my head politely. He smiled at me with an offhand charm that also reminded me of his older son.

"Excuse me, but I have to catch that rascal," he said. I stepped aside and he clattered down the stairs after the boy. Then I scratched, and went in.

The Lady of Angas was sitting on Father Gerthmol's best chair. She looked like an emperor on a throne. She smiled when she saw me. She was beautiful, and the tall gold crown suited her. She had the same grace as her younger son, and she reminded me of a great owl that can swoop so silently over the dark land.

"You are Sulien?" she asked. She knew my name of course, because she had been told my son's. I raised my chin in assent.

"I am Sulien ap Gwien, of Derwen." There, now she had a polite way to address me. "And you are the Lady of Angas, Queen of Demedia?"

"Oh yes." Her smile was perfect, but held perhaps a little too long. She looked at me. I felt very conscious of the horse sweat, of the milk stains, of her exquisite clothes and beautiful face. "Sit down, daughter of Gwien, don't tower over me like that."

I sat on the stool I used when I came to speak to Father Gerthmol. "So why did you wish to see me so urgently, my lady?" I asked.

"Why, to tell you I have seen your son in the water," she said. I gasped. She took my hand and stroked it gently. Looking into water to see the future was the work of an oracle. There were no oracles in Tir Tanagiri and had not been for many years. The last there had been had looked into tree rings and seen the end of the world, a hundred and fifty years ago. Yet, I believed her. Her voice was soft, low and gentle. While she spoke I was enthralled, listening to her. "I do not see the future, of course, such things are impossible. There are many futures, maybe many worlds, and I can see the different paths in them. I can see the roles people will play, if not how they will play them. I knew Urdo would be a great king when he was yet a small child. Your son will be a great hero, one of the best armigers in the world. He will succeed in a great quest. I see shadows in the water of what will be, or what has been elsewhere and may be here. I can act to bring such things to pass, or to prevent them. You though, you seem to have no shadows."

Dead of starvation in the wood. Or killed as a slave in Jarnholme. Dead of a spear thrust gone a different way. Maybe in those worlds Darien lived and took my place. I shook my head, and tried to speak, but it was very hard.

"In some worlds the gods walk tall and people cower before them. In others the gods are withdrawn altogether and it is hard for people to hear them. In this world have you given your trust to any gods especially, Sulien? You are not a follower of the White God are you?" I could not quite understand what she meant. I shook my head. I felt as if I was falling asleep, and knew I must not. "You are a thread in the pattern that is in this world alone, and I do not know what you will do. You will not tell anyone this, Sulien?" I blinked, and took a deep breath, forcing myself to think clearly.

"I—" I hesitated. "Why are you confiding in me like this, Lady of Angas?" My words came slowly and sounded very grating in my own ears. She was Urdo's sister, Angas's mother, we were in the heart of Thansethan, where she was a welcome guest, she was an oracle and wise and thus favored of the gods, and furthermore everything about the way she spoke seemed to encourage me to trust her, to give her my faith, to promise not to tell. Yet somehow I kept thinking about the bay horse's torn mouth. I wondered absurdly if that was her horse, she who was so gentle-spoken and regal.

"Do you trust me, Sulien?" she asked, explicitly. She was holding both my hands. I was not sure of the answer to the question. I was confused. If it was no, I could not say it without causing great offense. I would have to fight Angas after all. A tear ran down my face, for whether I killed him or he killed me it would be sad. If he challenged me, I should choose lances, and he would win, but he might in honor insist on swords, and then I should.

I knew I should say yes, or no, but could not. "Angas is going to marry Eirann Swan-Neck," I said. "And it is a terrible thing to die with no children."

"I don't know where my son Gwyn comes into this," she said, stroking my wrists. "Do you care for him, Sulien?"

"He is my friend," I said, thick-tongued. She should not have said his name, for Angas had never told it to me.

"And where does your loyalty lie?" she asked, almost purring, looking into my eyes.

Even in that strange state I was utterly sure of the answer to that one. "I am the loyal servant of Urdo, true king of Tir Tanagiri."

"A pity," said the queen, coldly, still holding on to my hands and still looking like an owl—beautiful, silent, and deadly—a creature of night. "But with a will that hard to overpower I do not think I could have let you live anyway." Then suddenly the room was dark, and I could neither move nor breathe. "Do any gods cast their protection on Sulien ap Gwien, that I may not slay her now?"

I had willed no protections, and had no will free now to seek any. In a flash of lightning the Lord of Light came towards me, his hand outstretched to protect me, an arrow pointing upwards towards the dark queen. In the shadows behind him stood others, ranks of them. They had come for me anyway. I felt breath beginning again deep in my lungs. She smiled, and spoke a word, and they faded a little, then grew more solid.

"By my name!" she said. "Your day is done, and this is not your place. Sulien spoke your names and was faithful to you, yes. You may give back her name and take her on to new life, there is no binding but that. Go, you are no stronger than my will." They wavered again, although I knew if I could have called to them they would have saved me. I tried to reach, to call, to exert my will, but it was out of reach, I was cut off from it. Then they were gone. I realized then in a detached and distant way that she was changing the world by her own will alone, without the sanction of any god. My breath was almost gone. I knew I was dying. I would never master the lance, never take part in a real charge, never see Urdo or Apple again, never see Darien grown. Then someone stood behind me. I could not see him, but I could feel a chill. The Lady of Angas looked up.

"You!" she said. "She can have sworn nothing to you!"

"She is my sacrifice," said a voice, dark and laughing, harsh as a raven's call. "She is dedicated to me, and my choice to take her or not to take her. I do not choose to give her to you, Morwen, Avren's daughter, whatever you may have given to me in the past." I was breathing again in the dark and could feel Morwen's hands tight on my wrists.

"She is not in the pattern," Morwen said.

"What are your patterns to me? She has borne me a son," said the voice, the one-eyed liar, the Father of the Slain. I had read about him in the monk's book, how he hung on the World Tree nine days to learn the secret of writing.

"Bah, begone!" said Morwen, tightening her grip. "Your day is done too, old fool, the White God will win and be worshiped everywhere, you will never have this land. I have seen it." The god laughed, with the sound of crows disturbed from their feasting on a two-day-old battlefield.

"Long is a night on the wind-wracked tree, queen with a fair face. Gapes, and grows hungry does hand-pledger's foundling; Terror's barley is still to be threshed. Embla's gift given to this weapon-tree as much as thee, and who shall say what is mine?"

Morwen blinked, and her brow creased. The god's voice was almost a chant. "Think you Necessity makes a hero's deeds?"

She drew in a sharp breath, as if this shot had gone home. "Oh no. I have found him," she spat "a different wife."

"Of course, of course," he said, and it was the cawing of dark birds, I felt their wings, and he was gone. Morwen lay back in her chair, eyes closed, her hands limp at her sides. Sunlight was streaming in through the window. I could move again.

I leapt to my feet and went down the steps and into the cloister, panting and gasping and drawing breath into my parched lungs. I must tell, I must tell, but as I ran I knew that there was nobody here who would believe my word against hers. She would smile and say I was gone mad. She would say I laid hands on her, she could kill me as easily with a knife or in the process of law. I needed to rescue Darien and be gone. Yet no. I stopped, two steps taken. Darien was safe here. She had seen him in her pattern; she would not hurt him. I must go to Urdo, who would listen to me, even though she was his sister. Urdo would be at Caer Tanaga, thirty miles.

I made for the stables. Nobody was chasing me, but monks looked up in surprise to see me run. Garah was there, crooning to the wounded horse as she spread on salve.

"This is terrible," she said, seeing me. "He's been wrenched and wrenched, poor fellow." I looked. It was worse than I thought.

"Could you ride him?" I asked. Garah sighed and smiled quizzically.

"No, really. Could you ride him if you had to? Is he too big for you?"

"He's not as big as Apple, and I rode him out when you were too near your time. But—"

"Saddle him up. I've got to go, now, Garah, no waiting for Urdo in half a month, and you'd better come. You don't have a horse, and this chap doesn't deserve to stay with someone who has done this to him and will again."

"Are you telling me to steal a horse?" Garah spoke to my back, I was fetching Apple's things from the tack room. "Do you know I could be hanged for it?" she inquired, as I began to saddle Apple.

"*Rescue* a horse," I said. "The woman is a sorceress." I half turned. Garah was getting a plain saddle. "She tried to kill me. Just do it."

Ten minutes later we rode out of Thansethan in the direction of Caer Tanaga as if the Wild Hunt was after us. The two stallions huffed at each other in rivalry, each trying to draw ahead of the other. "I don't know why

I'm doing this!" Garah called, when I finished explaining what had happened. "Nobody wants to kill me!"

"You're brave and you love horses!" I called back.

"The penalty is hanging if you steal a greathorse!" she said, as we galloped towards the river. "You can put on my monument 'Here lies Garah ap Gavan, she was brave, and she loved horses, and she listened to Sulien ap Gwien one time too many!' "

I did, too, but that was a long time after.

We laughed wildly then, and slowed down as we forded the river and turned south onto the road toward Caer Tanaga.

—9—

"Bare is back without brother behind it."
 —Jarnish proverb

She follows dark gods," Urdo said.

He let go of the window frame, turned towards me, and strode back across the room, frowning. He had not been still since I mentioned his sister's name. I found myself biting the skin between my thumb and fingers and pulled my hands together in my lap. I was here, and safe. Even if he did not believe me.

The journey had been uncomfortable. We had not known whether we were pursued and had spent the night in trees beside the high road. Every time we heard anyone coming we hid in the trees, or if there were no trees, in the ditch. My mother had often said I looked like a beggar's brat, but I never looked more like one than that day when I first came to Caer Tanaga, the great city. I was stained and muddy and the front of my clothes were stiff with sour seeping milk. If it had not been for the great luck of Glyn being the day's guard at the inner gates, we would never have got in. Now I was washed, Garah had dragged the twigs out of my hair, and I had borrowed Osvran's second-best spare tunic. Even so I had found it difficult to persuade the clerks and servants that I needed to see the king urgently on business I would not disclose. They took a message at last.

I waited in the marble-floored hall, trying not to bite my finger or rub my sore breasts. Both these things seemed to make the clerks uneasy. He had to believe me. They brought me to his little office. There was a large table in the corner in place of the bed that stood in his room in Caer Glo-ran, but it was otherwise very similar. The parchments and writing tablets and maps might have been brought two hundred miles undisturbed and set down again in the same piles and drifts. Sounds of armigers at practice in the yard below drifted up through the window. He was sitting writing at the table when I came in. He greeted me kindly and with concern. I wished I had come with good news to strengthen his arm and not to make his burdens greater. When I mentioned the Lady of Angas's name he sent the boy who was helping him out and told him to keep everyone away. Then he got up and paced while I told him my story.

"Very dark gods indeed," he said again.

"I think it is worse than that." I said. "I am almost sure no gods help her at all." Urdo paused, both hands gripping the back of his chair. He stared at me.

"But the cost to her soul, to have it gnawed away? No gods at all?" His knuckles were white on the wood, and I thought the chair might break. "Using her soul to power the enchantment?"

I looked up at him as evenly as I could. "I have heard stories of such things, my lord. She called on no name but her own. I have never felt any power like that. She sent the gods of my people away like a flock of pigeons." But they had come for me. She would not have eaten my soul and used it for her sorcery. If I had died they would have taken me down to the dark lands and given back my name. I would have lost this precious life, but I would have come back. Others might not be so lucky. I had to tell him, however much it distressed him.

"That is worse than I thought. But I cannot touch her!" He released the chair, and it tipped over with a sharp crash. He set it up again, patting it absently, then sat down, facing me. "She had done you a great wrong, Sulien, and would have done you a worse one if not for the shield of a god who never has only one purpose." I breathed a sigh of relief and closed my eyes for an instant. He believed me. "She wove such a spell on me once, that took my will away. She could not do it now, the powers of the land would not allow it. I thought that made me safe from her, but I was wrong. She has wronged you badly, and you are sworn to me, I owe you protection and vengeance and whatever recompense I can make. But I can do nothing openly against her!" He bounced to his feet again and paced up and down the length of the room, his hands bunched into fists.

"This is intolerable! Her husband Talorgen is the king of Demedia, the Lord of Angas, the greatest clan of the north. Demedia is a great land. It is the largest of them all if you measure by paces, though far from the largest by hides of cultivated land, for the most part of it is mountains. High mountains, where the folk still live in the forts in the hills they built before the Vincans came. I have not been there, the people do not know me, and they look to their lord, as well they might. He is a good king, in his way, harsh but within the bounds of the law, they respect him. He has supported me, he has paid taxes and sent me his heir as pledge. I am well pleased with his son, who is now one of my best and most loyal armigers."

He spun, rocking a fidchel board that sat on the edge of the big table ready to play, the white king in the center with his troops around him, the red pieces waiting at the edges to set up an ambush. "He has come south now to witness young Angas's wedding and also to see if I have an ala for him. He is beset by Isarnagans from the Western Seas. I doubt not that he also fears Borthas to his southeast. He does if he has any sense. But if I speak out against his wife, even were she not my own sister in blood, it would mean war. We would lose everything, and it would be a bloodfeud to shame the old songs. Only the Jarnsmen would be victors in such a war, for Talorgen has many allies among the other kings. We might win the battles, but the kingdom would fall."

He paused in his pacing and spun round to face me. "Do you think she means harm to the kingdom?"

I thought of her words in the darkness, and how I had been held still, incapable of even calling on the gods to aid me. I shuddered. The sounds of laughter and the clash of weapons sounded loud from below. The square of sunlight lay warm on the wooden boards, just touching the corner of my boot. Although the linen rubbed on my aching breasts and I was very weary, it felt good to be alive and breathing. "I have told you what she said to me as near as I can remember. I thought she wanted to know everything and control everything. She said it was a pity I was loyal to you, but she said she had always known you would be a great king."

Urdo's frustration was almost palpable. "I think she must be mad. What can one do with the mad who have power?" He frowned. "I could send her a priest, some priests strong in their own power who could stand against her. I wonder if I might get my mother's priest Teilo to go to her. She might be a match for Morwen. In any case, I will speak to her. But I cannot let the kingdom take fire from this spark, Sulien. I will do what I can for you short of that. There is not always a way forward which keeps both honor and a whole land." He looked tired. "I will go up to Thansethan as I planned, and speak to her. The Lord of Angas will have his

ala, but I will not give Morwen back her son. I will honor young Angas
with a command in the south, though he will need someone very steady as
tribuno to balance him." Angas. How would I ever be able to look him in
the face again? "I will send Marchel north and make sure all who go are
loyal to her and to me. I will have a blessing said over all of them that will
be a protection. I will tell the queen I will allow no move against any of
mine."

"I wanted to warn you about her. And I wanted to warn other people.
That spell works only on the unwary. It works because people trust her."

Urdo sighed. "I will tell her I will not tolerate it. And see that all the
armigers I send to Demedia are protected against such things."

"I hope that's enough. I do not ask for vengeance, and certainly not for
war, but I would not like her to make any more moves against me." Urdo
laughed shortly and sat down again.

"She is not entirely lost to fear. That should have been warning
enough for her. 'And who shall say what is mine.' " He paused, and
repeated the words of the gallows god again, more slowly, " 'And who shall
say what is mine.' " He shook his head and looked back at me. "I will make
sure that anything she may try openly against you is stopped. Tell me if
there is anything I should know, at any time. Even warned, it might be as
well to see that you and yours are protected in case she is fool enough to try
more sorcery, but I do not think she will." I raised my chin in agreement.

"I will do that."

"And your boy? Darien Suliensson. That form of name was brave
of you."

"I was angry with Father Gerthmol," I muttered, looking down. The
ache redoubled in my swollen breasts at the thought of Darien, who would
not understand, who would not know that I had not come. "I asked the
gods to look kindly on him as soon as he was born. He is safe enough with
the monks, I think. She said he would be a great hero." I smiled at this
thought. Urdo raised one eyebrow slightly.

"Good. Then what do you want to do? If you wish it I will give you
land and a lordship of your own. It won't be anywhere safe, for I have nothing to give that is anywhere safe. You'd still have to defend it and support
the troops you need, but it would be your own, your own land and name.
That's more than I have myself. That would be much less than you deserve
from me for this."

I was shaking my head before I'd even thought about it, whether it was
supposed to be everyone's dream or no. "No. Please no. I don't want that.

Really. I'd hate to be a lord. There's nothing I want more than what I have, to serve you as an armiger, in the alae. I've been looking forward to coming back all this year. I've been practicing with the lance, as much as I could."

Urdo gave me an unfathomable look. "Then I think you should stay here in Caer Tanaga for now. There are rumors of unrest in the Jarnish lands to the east of the Tamer, so there will be an ala here, and plenty of people training. I shall see that my sister does nothing against you."

"I'd like that. There's just one other thing. Her horse? I mentioned that I stole him? Garah was only doing what I told her. Will you take him into the ala? If I gave him back she would probably do the same again." I wondered if there was a Horse Mother curse I could put on Morwen so that no horse would bear her again.

"Well with that small matter at least I can help you." Urdo smiled a little. "It's a greathorse?"

"Yes, a stallion, bay, nine or ten by the teeth. You should see his poor torn mouth, but it will heal."

"Will he fight with your black?"

I laughed. "My Apple puts most horses to shame long before it ever comes to fighting, and this one is no exception."

"Then I gift him to you. You will need more than one real fighting horse." As I stammered out thanks, Urdo went on.

"My mare, Twilight, had a filly last year. She's dappled like her mother, her father was black and white, his name was Pole Star. He's dead now, I lost him under me fighting the Jarns this spring. We've called the filly Starlight. I'll give you her, too. You can work with ap Cathvan to train her. That will give you three good mounts in a few years when you need them." I opened my mouth again to thank him, but he continued, raising a hand but looking a little shy.

"I was wondering—I don't mean to breed Twilight this year, I want to ride her, but next year—" I had already heard this request one way or another from half the armigers I knew who had mares. I knew what was coming.

"I'm sure Apple will be as honored as I am, my lord," I said.

I went out past the clerks without looking at them though I did notice them staring after me and muttering. Raul was there, waiting, and he went straight into the king's room as I collected my sword and went down the stairs. Urdo had told me to see ap Rhun, the key-keeper, who would find me a place in the barracks. I wanted to see the stables properly and also to go out to the fields and find my new filly. For that I would need ap Cathvan.

I went out through the archway and blinked. In front of me, a broad-shouldered heavy-bearded pale-skinned man was swinging a long ax at Angas. They both wore heavy iron Jarnish helmets with cheek guards, and heavy shoulder pads. The ax whistled down, and at the last moment, Angas leapt aside and swung up his ax, bringing it down just as heavily. The Jarn skipped out of the way, then called a halt.

"Uncover your shoulder to protect your head and you're as dead as ever you were with a split skull. A long ax will reach under your collarbone to have your life. It can get to that point you young folk aim the lances for, if the armor doesn't stand it, and if the armor does, near enough a broken bone or three and no long time of living for you that way either."

I had found the practice yard. Angas saw me as he stood panting. "Hey! How did you get here?" he called. He grinned at me.

"You know how Uthbad One-Hand got his name?" I called. "I've never seen anyone playing chicken with their head before." Angas laughed.

"The blows sort of glance off the helmet, if you're not quick enough."

"If the helm holds," growled the other man, looking up at me. "In Narlahena we say if it doesn't, it's Wise Mother's way of correcting her mistake in letting someone who learns too slowly come into the world."

The older man's voice went lower, and very serious.

"It's the disadvantage of being a king's son, Angas, you've never had less than that good coat of yours." Angas's armor was exceptionally fine, steel plates enameled red and green riveted to thick leather and covering from his elbows to his knees. "You learned in one, and your arms master would have done less than his job to teach you not to rely on the coat for what you could, fighting with swords. "These"—the long ax in his hand lifted in emphasis—"there is no stopping with armor. One of those heavy shields Urdo's having made for you youngsters might take one blow, or it might not. No armor will withstand a long-ax stroke square on, not until you get stuff of Wayland's wreaking. That's why the hafts of these are strapped with iron halfway down from the head, you've got to reach past his stroke from the side for his neck or rap his knuckles well and solid sliding your haft down his to turn him; you can't block, and you can't bounce around so much fighting in a line, and you surely dare not wear the blow. You're blooded, more than once, and you've seen these used against you, but keep trying to parry with your head, and I'll put that helm over a post and show you why you oughtn't."

Angas raised his chin seriously. I longed to learn how best to use a sword against an ax. Angas turned to me. I had guessed who this warrior must be, but Angas confirmed my thought. "Have you met Marchel's father?" he asked.

"Marchel's father, is it?" said Thurrig, a deep furrow appearing between his mighty brows. "A renowned father of my own, two sons, one of them regrettably gone off to pray for his god, no small accomplishments earned in nearly fifty years of life, and I am introduced to a beautiful lady as the father of my daughter!" I laughed, and he laughed too, swinging the ax towards Angas, who skipped aside very nimbly indeed.

"Ah, but while you, your father, and your doubtless famed sons are strangers to me, Angas knows I have met your honorable and courageous daughter," I said, still laughing. "And also your wise and accomplished wife." I only meant to be friendly, and was surprised at the result.

Thurrig flung down his ax, but rather spoiled the effect by catching it by the haft before it had fallen as much as a handspan and then dropped it rather more gently onto the cobbles. Then he sat down hard beside it and put his head in his hands. "Alas!" he cried, quite loudly. "Why is it that whenever I meet a beautiful maiden, a beautiful armed maiden at that, a veritable Amazon, tall enough to spear swans out of the sky, why is it that when I meet such a creature even if my wife is two hundred miles away it turns out the woman has managed to meet her first!" I was laughing so much now I had to lean on the side of the gateway for support. Some of the other people practicing came over to find out what the noise was about. Angas slapped Thurrig on the back.

"It'd be a brave man who'd take on the daughter of Gwien, even if he were free to make her an offer," he said, looking at me sideways, half-smiling. "You haven't seen her in battle. Didn't I tell you she charged alone towards three ships' crews of Jarns?"

"So that's who you are?" Thurrig sprang to his feet again. "My wife did tell me about you, though how could she have left out so much, the hair, the breasts—" He gestured. As my hair was sticking out in frizzles all round my head as an effect of trying to pull the twigs out, my breasts were presently swollen like cow's udders, and as Amala was the epitome of civilized manners, this didn't altogether surprise me.

"Both have grown somewhat while she's been away," said Enid ap Uthbad, drily, coming up behind us. "Glyn will be enchanted."

"Poor Glyn's seen her, and he didn't say a word," said Osvran. "He just came begging me for my clothes so she didn't distract Urdo in the middle of the afternoon by going in to see him naked. He took my tunic to the bathhouse. I think he will live, but the matter was in some doubt." They laughed.

"Well it was kind of Glyn, and of you, too, and I'm looking after it," I said, tugging the hem of the tunic. "I'll give it back when my own clothes are dry."

"At last I meet the woman with even less subtlety than ap Rhun," roared Thurrig, picking up his ax.

"Watch out!" said Enid, as he swung it. "I don't want a matching set."

"I noticed the scratch," I said. I could hardly have missed it, the great red scar curved down her cheek almost to her jawline. "You got it from one of those?" I nodded towards Angas's weapon.

"Some Jarn with a great longing for death knifed the king's horse from underneath," she said. "And while I was turning around to see if Urdo was safely up behind me, his friend with the ax got a little too close on the left side. Nicked my cheek first, so I was leaning away and it came down through my shoulder blade from the back and not my lungs, which would have killed me for sure. It was that very ax Angas has there; Emlin picked it up for me. I'm fine now——"

"But when you come to the rally banner holding your friend's hand but your friend's cantering off in the opposite direction with the king on her horse behind her at the time, you think you might have a little problem," said Osvran, grinning at her. "Why you didn't faint with the lack of blood I'll never know."

"I would say it's because women don't make a fuss about losing a few drops of blood every now and again," said Enid, deadpan, and we all laughed. "But in plain truth it was Urdo, and it was Urdo that fixed it on again, with the help of the ax there."

"Whatever will your mother say?" growled Thurrig.

"She said 'I've been telling you that having a dog painted on it is no substitute for keeping your shield close in between you and the enemy's weapons for the last two years. Just be glad that Jarn didn't have the reach to try for your head.' And I had to allow she was right. It's just as well it's my shield arm though." She paused. "It was my father said 'Turth's tusks, girl! How will we ever find you a husband with a face like that?' "

"Speak to Amala. Not that she consults me, but I think she's looking for a wife for Larig," said Thurrig. Enid made loud retching sounds. "I mean it. We Malms aren't so particular, we don't look for a pretty face. Breasts, hips, brains, that's all that matters. Strong arms, too. As long as he fixed it back on the right way round that is?" As Thurrig leaned forward to pretend to check, Enid pushed him backwards while he was off-balance. Osvran and I leapt aside, and he rolled through where we had been and came back to his feet on her other side.

"So, husband of Amala, you can move quickly—" With a great bellow, brandishing the ax, Thurrig rushed towards Angas, who charged away across the yard, dodging and weaving. It did me more good than I can easily say to laugh like that, after so long at Thansethan.

—10—

Anyone accustomed to a civilized climate will find the island chilly and damp. This makes it also very green, and there is nowhere a shortage of sweet flowing water. I came up the River Tamer from the sea to the place where Castra Tanaga had been before the fire.

The place is on the north bank of the river, on a low hill, at the crossroads of all the main highways of the province. There were docks on the river and much coming and going of goods and people. It was clear to me in the first moment that to try and build the new capital anywhere else would be folly.

I spent many days there among the ruins, looking at the lie of the land. As I walked the ash-strewn streets an old woman came out of a shack and spoke to me, saying that her son was an oracle, who had seen in the flames while the city burned that it would burn twice more and be rebuilt each time. I asked her where her son was now, but she just smiled with toothless gums and fled. I learned from others that he had thrown himself into the flames. I decided that the new town I would build must be able to withstand another such conflagration.

I had at first imagined something in the style of mother Vinca, but I soon saw that this would be inappropriate. Pillars and columns do very well for sunlit lands, but in Tir Tanagiri they are best kept indoors. I realized I would have to visit the other cities and spend time deciding what would best suit this place graced by nature with all a city needs.

At long last when I returned I brought with me red stone from the west, white stone from the east, clear sand from the south and an idea that was old in the north. I built the walls of layered stone, with tall fluting towers rising from the curve of the hill. The city had no need to be defensible—what enemy could come here so far from Vinca's long frontier? Yet they are strong enough to stand forever. Three years it took to build it to the design I had sketched in one night. Each stone was set in place, the red-and-white patterns rising to echo the hill's shape. I covered the walls with the sand, doing the work myself when I saw that my assistants could not understand what I intended. Then we piled up wood beside and between the walls and fired it. The flames leapt up high, and the sand melted and glazed to the stone as color to a pot. When the marks of the fire were washed away with the rains I saw that I had completed the task I had come to the island to do—I had built for my emperor a city that shines.

—Decius Manicius, *From My Foundations*

I f I set down every bruise and skirmish of my training I will be here until I die, yes, and use up four whole sheeps' worth of parchment and still not have it all in. It was little different from any armiger's training, except that we were among the first to learn the way of it. It is enough to say that that summer I learned lancework enough that I was fit to ride at the charge. Many days I came in aching and fit only for an hour in the hot bath. "Relax enough to let the horse do its share!" Angas would bellow at me, until at last I learned the knack of holding shield and lance with a light arm until strength was needed. I put long hours into picking up stakes and tilting at the target until I no longer infuriated myself with my clumsiness.

At the turn of autumn, at Harvest Home, when the winds are too strong for the pirates to cross the sea, there is always a time of truce. That year at that time half the kings of the island crowded into Caer Tanaga to see Angas married. There were so many of them it seemed impossible to go anywhere in the streets of the citadel without running into little knots of them and their people, talking. One would have needed a good map to know where all their kingdoms were. They did not all style themselves king, but they were all rulers and they all acknowledged Urdo over them. There was no way to tell from looking at them if they ruled a domain of two thousand families like my father or ten times that number like the lord of Angas. There was much feasting and fussing and formality. Gwilen ap Rhun was in despair about finding space to put everyone and driven to distraction with questions of precedence.

Of the kings I did recognize, the High King's mother, Rowanna, was the most obvious. She seemed gracious and regal and was always at the side of some king or other. She ruled the Royal Domain of Segantia, which was in name Urdo's but which she had controlled since her husband's death. Sometimes I saw the bride, Eirann Swan-Neck. She dressed much like everyone else, but stayed always veiled, as highborn Jarnish women do before they are married. Her parents were also obvious, as there were so few other Jarnsmen in the city. They looked splendid but barbaric in their Jarnish regalia. Their names were Guthrum and Ninian, and they were king and queen of Cennet. Ninian was Rowanna's sister. To the rumored horror of some of the other kings, Urdo had accepted their homage as lesser kings, and with that their right to rule Cennet. I was far more surprised to see Ayl, who ruled the Jarnsmen on the east side of the Tamer. We had fought him in the spring, and had truce with him only until spring came again, but he dared to show his face here with the others.

Duke Galba came. He hailed me as I was on my way across one of the citadel courtyards to the practice yard.

"I have letters from your parents," he said. I took them and read them rapidly. It seemed the new town was thriving. My mother's letter said more about the problems they were having with retting flax and storing linen than anything else. My father was well. He said that Morien was doing better with his riding. He mentioned also that Aurien's betrothal to young Galba had been agreed in principle, as far as might be without them having yet been able to meet. This was good news, and I congratulated Duke Galba on it.

"I expect they'll marry in three years or so," he said, smiling. "I have seen your sister. Although she is young yet it seems you are right, and she will be a good lady for Magor. I hope you are well? I hear the king has been honoring you with horses?" I would have spoken to him longer, for I liked nothing better than to talk of my horses, particularly the way Starlight was developing. We were prevented, however, for just then Rowanna came out of the baths, two of her veiled Jarnish attendants with her, and called to him.

"No doubt she wants to talk to me again about her new method of harvesting hay," said Galba, sighing a little. He bowed to me as if I were of equal rank, surprising me not a little. I ran off towards the practice yard, where the others would be waiting. The wedding parade still needed practice if it was going to be perfect.

The day after that I received less welcome news in a reply from Arvlid at Thansethan. She wrote that she did not believe the accusations of demon summoning Morwen had made against me. She said she thought Father Gerthmol did. She advised me not to go back there soon. She said Darien was well and growing, he was eating mashed food and sitting up well. I felt hot tears burning behind my eyes, but I hid the letter among my clothes and tried to put the news out of my mind.

Three days before the wedding Urdo spent a long time talking with

Angas. Many people suggested that he would be given some high honor. I said nothing. When Osvran came walking down to the practice field in the afternoon I was glad enough to get my aching legs off Beauty's back and join my friends who were pressing round to find out what he knew. The rest of the pennon seemed very surprised to hear that Angas had been given command of the ala of Caer Gloran.

"He's very young to be praefecto, but he deserves it," said Osvran decisively.

"It doesn't hurt that he made a good choice of father," muttered Emlin into his beard.

"He might not have had this promotion so soon without that," said Enid, patting her horse's nose to quiet her. "But it wouldn't matter who his father was if he wasn't good enough."

"Marchel's a praefecto, and she's a Malm. She's not even a highborn barbarian. Thurrig was nothing special in Narlahena, he says so himself, and when he came here he was just an exiled pirate," said Glyn. There was a mutter of agreement.

"Urdo's officially given Thurrig the title of Admiral of the Fleet," said Emlin, smirking. Thurrig had been calling himself an admiral since before most of us were born. We all liked Thurrig.

"He's going back to Caer Thanbard with King Custennin after the wedding to get on with building some more ships," said Osvran. "So he can be an admiral in truth as well as in name, and catch the Jarns before they get to the coast. Marchel is being promoted, too—she's taking the new ala up to Dun Idyn. I pity everyone in the north, between Marchel's ala and Teilo's new monastery it won't be very peaceful up there even without the Isarnagans invading from the west and the Jarns raiding from the east."

"Will the new ala be under Angas's father's control?" I asked. Osvran raised his eyebrows.

"Oh no. All the alae are under the High King's control, always. Talorgen of Angas will feed them, of course, and they will fight beside him and his men as necessary, but Marchel is sworn to Urdo and not to any other king."

"Are we going with Angas or up north?" asked Emlin.

"We're staying here for the time being. Urdo told me. We'll be having more training and new people coming for training, and we'll all be trying new things. We'll be practicing a lot, as well as fighting when need be. I may as well tell you the rest of it. I'm going to have command of our pennon."

"Well that nicely settles the issue of whether people are promoted on merit or because of their family," I said. There was a sudden appalled hush, in which the jingling of harness seemed terribly loud, then Osvran threw back his head and laughed. A moment later, everyone else joined in. I could feel my cheeks heating. "I didn't mean—"

"Don't worry, I shall certainly take it as a compliment on my merit, and promise not to repeat it to my mother," Osvran said, almost choking with laughter at my confusion. Everyone came crowding around to congratulate him, and I tried to disappear into the background. What I'd said was even worse than it appeared, for there was a rumor, although I'd neither believed it nor paid attention to it, that Osvran had been fathered by Angas's father and not by Usteg, his mother's husband. The two men were too much unalike for me to give that credence. Osvran was as tall as I was, almost half a hand taller than Angas, and temperamentally they could not be more different. Although I had meant no harm I wished that the mud would swallow me up.

Amala and Marchel arrived at Caer Tanaga the next day. Marchel went in to see Urdo as soon as she had washed off the dust of the road. Amala caught me coming in from the stables. I had been picking up stakes with my lance all morning. I had promised to help young Galba with his sword strokes after lunch.

"How are you!" she cried. "And how is your little one? Did it all go well? You are looking healthy. I am sure you have grown two thumbs' height since I saw you last! I am looking for Thurrig."

"I am well, and my son is thriving in the latest news I have. But if you want your bold and noble husband you'll have to wait until this evening. He's taken a boat out on the river to show Duke Galba and the Dowager Rowanna how it is he gets it to turn to the wind when he goes out to catch Jarns."

Amala's face fell at this. I took her off to the barracks with me. I was ravenous, and she looked weary from her long journey.

I put my head into the kitchen as I went past. "One extra, ap Cadwas," I said. Ap Cadwas waved a hand without looking up from his pots, and then when we were almost into the eating room he did look up, started in surprise, and bowed deeply to Amala. Then he went back to his bustling, seeming to move twice as fast as before and calling to his assistants.

"I do hope Marchel manages to persuade the High King not to send her up to the wild north," she said, as we sat down at the end of one of the long benches beside the tables.

"Why?" I asked. "I think he's set on it, it suits everything very well for him to have someone he really trusts up there." Amala frowned. I ladled our mutton stew for her from the crock set in the middle of the table, then filled my own bowl.

"You cannot build a kingdom by tearing families apart. My Thurrig must be in Caer Thanbard, well. I could be there, except that Marchel and her little boys need me, and I am more use to Urdo as key-keeper in Caer Gloran. Now he will send Marchel up to the barbarians in Dun Idyn, and me with her." It seemed strange to hear this tiny Malmish woman talking of the northerners as barbarians. Yet she was right in a way—Vincan ways had hardly touched the lands of the north. "This would be all right, too, I suppose, though it is pleasant to see Thurrig now and again. But Marchel is young and has only two children, and her husband will not go."

"He won't? Why not?" I blew on the stew and swallowed rapidly.

"He is a swordsmith. A good swordsmith. A Tanagan, a good man. Ap Wyn the Smith they call him. His passion is making swords, and Marchel's passion is fighting, but they do well enough together." I nodded. I had thought they had looked fond of each other in the bathhouse. "Always he bought the raw iron for the swords from Narlahena. That was how they met the first time, at Caer Thanbard, which is the port where the Malmish ships come, when they can come. He was bargaining for the raw iron, and Marchel helped translate what the traders were saying. Every year he goes down to the port if the Malmish ships can come, to buy good iron. Sometimes he goes off to look for iron in the hills, but he never finds any."

"Now he has found iron in Tir Tanagiri, and it is all your doing, actually. He went down to that place you come from, Derwen, because there was a ship put in from Narlahena to buy linen. On the way between he found good iron, he says, nearly as good as the Narlahena iron. So now without buying any more iron from Narlahena than before he can make more swords, swords and spear blades and maybe make other things, too. Scythes the king said he needs when he wrote, scythes for cutting hay enough for all these horses. He needs very many people to work at his iron, he has been trying to steal my bathhouse workers." She smiled, and I thought that I would not like to try to steal her workers. Then she sighed. "But ap Wyn will not leave his iron of course. He wants to go and live right down there." I wondered which of the hills I had ridden over was made of iron. Apple's hoofs had not struck sparks, which was how one could distinguish iron mountains in the stories. I wondered how my parents had dealt with the news. "Caer Gloran he can bear—he can get to his iron in a day there and a day back—but Dun Idyn is too far. She doesn't want to go without him." One of the cooks came out of the kitchen bringing hot bread, fresh from the bakestone. A spontaneous cheer rose up from the armigers. We didn't often have bread when it wasn't a special day.

I sighed. "I don't know who else he'll send, but I expect he'll listen to that as an argument. There isn't likely to be another iron mountain up in Demedia."

"He could send my Larig, perhaps. Or he could send steady old ap Meneth from Caer Rangor? Or there is Gwair Aderyn at Caer Asgor. But that will leave him short somewhere. The trouble is that he has six alae now and only five commanders. Urdo needs more good commanders, I have been saying that for some time. Larig would rather be on a boat like his father. Angas is very young, really. King Custennin is not much good for leading a charge, even if he rides with the White God beside him. Worse, he is a very cautious man, even if he has my Thurrig and Bishop Devin with him to give good advice." I passed her the bread, and she took a piece and smiled. It was a larger piece than one would have expected such a small woman to take.

"I think he is training them as fast as he can," I said, indicating the people eating around us. Amala smiled, and lowered her voice.

"All my life I have been around fighters. My father fought for his hire, and so has Thurrig, all the time we have been married, which is more than thirty years. Taking the best of the sons of your lords you will find some who are very good, but if you want real leaders you must find professionals. If he wants year-round fighters he should send to Narlahena or Jarnholme. There are landless enough to come."

I looked around, but fortunately ap Cathvan wasn't there. I didn't know what to say. I could see the disastrous consequences of explaining to someone a Malm herself that if you hire a thief to catch a thief, the first thief will not leave you in peace afterwards.

"Why are there? I mean, why are there plenty of landless people there? They don't have more children than anyone else, do they?"

"No. Of course not." Amala rolled her eyes. "There are plenty of Malms in Narlahena who do not like the place though—it is a hundred and fifty years since their ancestors conquered it, and they are growing restless. There are always wars in Narlahena, Malm against Malm, and the losers looking for new homes. As for the Jarns, well, the sea is rising and their country is shrinking, they must leave, will they or no. They will come here across the Narrow Seas whether anyone likes it or not, and it seems to me it would be better if we were sensible about it."

Fortunately I was spared making a response for just then Marchel came in. She was greeted enthusiastically by many of the armigers, and it took her a moment to get free of them. She came over and sat beside Amala. She said something rapidly to her in Malmish. It was strange how much faster she spoke in that language than in Tanagan or her usual Vincan. I raised my eyebrows.

"I will go north, but only for a year," Marchel said. "Now food and no questions." Her mother filled her plate with stew. I silently passed her the last of the bread on our table.

—11—

> Grief in my heart for kinslaying,
> the red fire dies low
> brother killing brother
> bright swords together.
>
> Grief in my heart for warstrife,
> fire to grey ashes
> towns abandoned
> the din of weapons.
>
> Grief in my heart to see thee fall
> cold ashes scattered
> the kingdom broken
> black crows calling.
> —"Lament for Avren"

The next day ap Cathvan caught me on my way out of the baths. I had been in there a long time getting the soot out of my hair. Thurrig had been using smoke pots to show us how to fight in a burning building. But now, clean at last, I was wearing my drape and the great amber brooch my father had given me. I was on my way to a feast the pennon was giving for Angas. "Starlight's got a swelling on her rear off leg," he said. "I've

brought her in and put her in the king's stable. I've put the special ointment on it, hard to tell how serious it is. I'm keeping an eye on her, and that
groom of yours is down there, but I thought I'd tell you."

"Is there anything I can do to help?" I asked.

"Nothing right now," ap Cathvan said, looking at me. "Going to toast
Angas?"

"I was, and I really ought to, but if Starlight needs me, I'm sure he'll
understand."

Ap Cathvan paused, and rubbed his beard, thinking. "No need. There's
nothing to do at the moment. Not as if she's on her own. Better to give the
stuff time to work. Go down around midnight and put some more ointment on. See how she is. If she's feverish, wake me. Probably she's just
pulled a muscle training too hard, but better to be safe. She's in a stall on
her own down at the end, away from the rest."

Some of us had crossed the river the day before so we could surprise
Angas with a roast boar. There were many more in the Jarnish woods than
there were on our side. Fortunately nobody asked us where we had found
it. Such hunting could have been seen as technically breaking the truce
with Ayl. The boar sat, resplendent with crackling and roast apples, in the
center of the table. The meat was sweet and succulent and plentiful. There
were fresh and toothsome buttered turnips. Even Osvran, who most times
turned up his nose at turnips as horse food, was pleased with them. There
were also great plaits of oven-baked honey bread. When the servant carried
in this dish Enid drew out a single acorn-flour griddle cake such as we
sometimes ate on patrol and offered it gravely to Angas, bowing. He
snatched it from her, gave a great bellow, and threw it out of the window.
He had been feasting on his best behavior with the king and his family and
the great ones for the last ten days. He ate, drank, and belched like an
overexcited Jarn to make up for it, all to the laughter and echo of his
friends.

The cider went around, and around again. Everyone wanted to toast
Angas. Everyone had something scurrilous to say about him. I almost forgot Starlight, laughing and drinking with the others. Gormant brought out
a harp and played an old wedding song, full of old jokes about plowing
wheat fields and ripening fruit. Then he passed the harp along to any who
could play, and there was singing as good as ever we had when bards came
to play before Urdo. After laments for those dead in my grandfather's day
and a long song about how the hero Kilok stole the bristles from the giant
boar Truth, ap Erbin sang a song his brother had made about the beauty

and prowess of the greathorses. We were all silent a moment as the notes of that died away, then roared and stamped our feet in approval and toasted ap Erbin and his absent brother. Angas was very drunk by then, but he swore he would have that song sung at his wedding. It was near enough midnight when the feast started to break up, and I remembered I had to see Starlight. I made my way down the long curved streets to the stables. My head was spinning slightly from all the music and cider. The streets grew quieter, darker and smellier as I went downhill from the citadel. I had almost grown accustomed to the stench of cities, but it could still make me gag a little on a warm, still night.

There was a lantern hanging in the high-arched entrance to the king's stable, and another in a stall towards the back. Garah was in the stall with Starlight. She looked up and grinned as I came in. "I think ap Cathvan's making a fuss about nothing again," she said. "Look." I walked over, past the ropes marking off the backs of stalls of the other horses. Everything cast strange doubled shadows, black and grey, making the place seem larger than usual. Garah held the lantern so I could see. Starlight nickered softly and one of the other horses answered more loudly. The swelling did not look large and was not inflamed. I ran my hand over her leg, carefully. She tried to shy away. "It's gone down since I saw it earlier," Garah said. "I don't think it's anything to worry about."

"Good." I trusted Garah more than ap Cathvan if it came to it. She was my friend, and she understood animals and bodies. On the road on the way back from Thansethan she had made me drain my painfully engorged breasts into the ditch, showing me how and telling me stories of cows she had seen with mastitis. When I went to the doctor at Caer Tanaga for a charm to dry up the milk she told me how right Garah had been.

"You go to bed."

"Soon. I'm drunk, and I think I'll sit with Starlight a little and then go to bed. You go on—there's no need for us both to be here."

"She really is going to be all right." Garah stood up. "Oh, I forgot, you've got another missive from your admirer." She offered me a letter and I groaned. Glyn had recently taken to tormenting me by writing me extravagantly romantic poems claiming he was pining away for love of me. I glanced at it, to check that it was nothing more interesting.

"In Apple's stall again?" I asked. Garah raised her chin, grinning.

"He brought it round earlier. He's got it bad." I sighed again. "Can I have it?" she asked.

"Of course. But why?" I handed it back to her.

"I thought I might use it to try to learn to read. They started to teach me letters in Thansethan, but it was always their silly book. I thought this might be more interesting."

"I'll help you if you want to learn. But why do you? I mean my mother made me, and it's useful sometimes, but not all that much fun."

"You know how Glyn's the assistant quartermaster? Well he was talking to me when he brought this, and he said that Dalmer, the quartermaster, started off as a groom in Avren's service." She shrugged, making the shadows jump. "I'm never going to be big enough to be an armiger, but I'll be as big as Dalmer is."

I found it hard to imagine anyone wanting to do the dull and difficult work of quartermastering, working out the amounts of everything to take on the horses when an ala set off. It was hard and thankless and there was little glory in it. If it was what she wanted I would do what I could. "I'll help you," I said. "Keep that poem. But in good light, and not now. I'll just put some more ointment on this swelling like ap Cathvan said, then sit with her a little until my head clears properly. I'll look in again before breakfast, and I'll be surprised if she isn't ready to run." Garah came out of the stall, still holding the lantern.

"Will you be able to see if I take this?" she asked. "It's the one from Apple's stable; either I take it back now or you'd better later."

"Take it," I said, "there's enough light from the other to see well enough for this." I was pulling the wooden stopper from the jar of ointment as I spoke.

"See you in the morning then," she said, yawning, as she made her way out past the horses. I sat down on the little stool she'd been sitting on and made sure Starlight couldn't kick me as I put on the ointment. She was sleepy and I tried to be gentle and had no trouble. When I saw the light coming in I looked up. I thought it must be Garah coming back, or ap Cathvan. It was Urdo and another man, one of the kings I did not know, a broad-shouldered man with a black-and-white beard and grey hair. He was carrying a lantern, and Urdo was carrying a wine jar and a golden goblet. Where the light lit the strange king's cloak it showed red; where the folds fell in shadow they were dark, blacker than any black cloth could be. Urdo wore a white cloak as was his custom. I could see them very well though they could see me only as a shape among shapes and shadows. I was about to stand up and greet them as they walked towards me when the strange king mentioned my name.

"There are those who would have you wed ap Rhun or ap Gwien," he said. The strength went out of my legs, and I sank down again hard, bewildered. Gwilen ap Rhun was the key-keeper of Caer Tanaga. It was well-known that the king sometimes shared her bed. Urdo laughed, and I saw that he had already been drinking for some time.

"There are those who would have me wed anything that could walk and had a womb and wit enough not to disgrace the kingdom at table, yes," he said. "Do not tell me you have become one of them, Mardol? Do not be afraid to speak. You have never minced your words with me, and from you I look for forthrightness."

I knew now that this must be Duke Mardol of Wenlad, the man they called the Crow from his habit of profiting by battles others fought. He set down the lantern on the wall of one of the empty stalls and sat below it on a low bench the shorter grooms used to stand on when they were saddling up greathorses. "Forthrightness you will get, and always have," he said, looking up at Urdo. Urdo sat beside him. "Ap Rhun is a good key-keeper, though not noble-born. Ap Gwien is of passable enough blood and proven fertile. You would make no enemies by marrying either one. It is past time you were wed, man. You have done miracles in the last five years, but it is the next five years that count. I was a fool. If you had married then you might have had a son near as old as that young brother of the bridegroom who's been riding his fancy pony under our feet all week. You have no heir, and you are not immortal. You ride in the charge too often to think you are. All you have built rests on you, and you can't count on living thirty years more to see an heir grow up."

"I do not count on anything," Urdo said, loudly, with great passion. One of the horses kicked against the stall. I shrank against Starlight's side and hoped hard that they would not notice me. There was no way out except past them, and from the first word I had heard too much. Urdo set down the cup, filled it from the jar, took a deep drink, and spoke more quietly.

"What is it to be a king, Mardol? For you are one, too, for all that you call yourself a duke."

Mardol spluttered for a moment. "Duke is a higher title than king. Anyone can call themselves a king. Dukes can trace their title to Vincan grants of authority." Urdo raised his hand.

"The Vincans had no word for king. They had emperors, and they had war-leaders, for that is what *Dux* means in Vincan. That is the title they gave your ancestors. But to be a king is a word, a magical word. I know they call me the Duke of the Tanagans, because I ride in the charge. But that is only part of it. A king stands between the gods and the people. You know that. You do that. The land, the gods, and the people." Urdo stared off into the darkness, and I tried not to breathe. "What is Wenlad, Mardol? Some white-topped mountains that give it its name, some farms with hides of land my clerk could number for me, three towns, six fortified places, and a seacoast? Or is it the people who dwell in those places? Or is it only a word? And if the Jarns come in force again, only a word that will be spoken no more though the mountains still stand and the waves still crash on that shore?"

"I would say it is all three," said Mardol, sounding a little taken aback at how strongly Urdo was speaking. He picked up the cup and drank.

"But without the name there would still be a place, but it would not be Wenlad. There might be some people, fleeing, but they would not be Wenlad either. You've been fighting so long you've lost sight of what it is you're fighting for. That's easy to do. I could see it because I came to it fresh. It is not only our people and the Jarnsmen who are fighting over Tir Tanagiri, it is our gods and theirs battling over the land. If I lose, if this chance I am making loses, then I have lost, Mardol. Lost. The Jarnsmen will win. It won't matter if there is a child with my name as part of his name, there won't be another chance. The land will belong to the Jarns-men, and to their gods, or perhaps by the greatest mercy to the White God who will hear everyone. Tir Tanagiri will be gone, fallen. Maybe you will hold them at the border of Wenlad, maybe Angas would hold them at the border of Demedia, but Tir Tanagiri will be no more. The name will mean nothing. There will be no use for a High King." He reclaimed the cup and drained it, then turned it in his fingers a moment so that the light glinted off the gold. A dark cat slunk across in front of his feet, intent on its hunt.

"So what good is an heir if I die? There is nobody who will be regent who could hold the land. There will be no hiding the babe away in Thansethan and hoping for another miracle in a generation. It will be too late. If we are in time, we are only just in time. Besides, there is nothing magical in the blood of kings—who among all of you does not have as good a claim as my grandfather Emrys to make himself High King and Emperor over all of the island? If there is such magic then Gwyn of Angas has as strong a claim on the kingship as any son of mine might. You make me feel like a horse of good breeding who will be ridden to battle—make sure he has got foals enough first, when in fact it is not one battle but a long race that must be run full strength. I know full well that I might die any day, but I will not allow that to change the way I shall live while I live, or I might as well be dead already. I will live long enough to leave behind an heir or I will not—I am but twenty-four years old. Either there is time enough or there is not." He refilled the cup and passed it to Mardol, who took it, looking only at Urdo's face.

"You will not tell me you are living in chastity and saving your strength for the fight?"

Urdo laughed. "If I tell you different, will you promise not to mention it to Rowanna or Father Gerthmol?" Mardol laughed, shortly.

"Then why not take a wife?"

"Who should I take? You know I am not set against marriage. But I will not rush to marry just to beget an heir. There is no purpose in that. I will not marry a woman who pleases half the kings while setting the other half against me. I will not marry a woman I cannot want, or one unworthy to take her place at my side. So who should I consider?"

"Five years ago you asked me for my daughter's hand." It may have been the flicker of shadows, but it seemed that the same expression of sorrow passed over both man's faces.

"Five years ago you refused me your daughter's hand."

"I would not do so today, if she were alive to give you."

"She did well to feed the whole of Wenlad through a plague like that."

"I nearly died myself. We would all have died without what you sent from Thansethan. I thank you for that. I should thank the monks for it. Even though I despise their God, I was more glad of their surplus food than you could easily believe. We were all ill throughout Wenlad, scarce anyone could stagger to the fields. The food rotted in the ground. It was like a curse in an old story. Many thought it was the end of the world, and some called for me to be plowed under. Yet I did not feel the gods were angry with us, and since that one season we have prospered as before. Poor Elin. The worms ate her alive from inside. There never was a key-keeper like her. She knew what was in every storehouse, and her last words were about how best to share out what you sent us." They sat in silence a moment, then Mardol shook himself. "I was wrong, five years ago. I have said so. I was not prepared to bet so much on you. I gave you one son to train as an armiger, I did not want to risk my daughter, too."

"Elin would have made a fine queen. I wanted peace with you and your backing, and I wanted a woman like that to wife. But gone is gone." Urdo took a long pull from the wineskin and passed it to the older man. "So now. No sooner had I found an honorable solution to my mother's plan to marry me off to Eirann Swan-Neck she forms a conspiracy to marry me to Lined of Munew."

"She is heir to the land, and will remain so unless Custennin has a son." Mardol's voice was carefully neutral.

"Oh yes, heir to Munew, sixteen years old, and as pale a princess as Eirann in her way, a pious follower of the White God. You don't like that, and the land doesn't like that, and I can just picture the faces of the other kings." Urdo sighed. "I might wish Custennin had not converted, for all that his people were mostly pleased and for all that Dewin runs his country for him. I would send Dewin and Linwen up to Demedia to found a monastery if I thought Munew would survive without them."

"I thought you were sending your mother's priest, Teilo?"

"You heard that? It's true. Teilo is very holy and very sure of her own righteousness, and my lady mother can manage without her. The north could do with her. But I was saying, Mardol, that my own priest, the monks of Thansethan, Dewin, Custennin, and Rowanna would all have me marry Lined ap Custennin. Talorgen of Angas wavers and will not decide. I think he is waiting for his daughter to be old enough. I cannot marry her even when she is, she is impossibly close kin, her mother is my sister. Borthas of Tinala would have me marry his sister, though she is twice my age, and in any case I want no close alliance with that snake. Penda and his allies want me to marry the Isarnagan king Atha ap Gren, and bring in an Isarnagan army and sweep the land clear of the Jarnsmen. Everyone who has a daughter or a sister wants me to choose her, and if I do, then everyone else will resent it. Everyone has their own candidate, and their own scheme—it seems to me best to stay uncommitted and decide when there is some advantage to the decision."

"Why not Atha ap Gren?" Mardol wiped his lips and set down the wineskin. "I've heard she's beautiful, and she fights from a moving chariot with throwing spears and has many followers."

"The Isarnagans have never had a High King that lasts, and their little kingdoms are always at war with each other or with someone—they've been attacking into the west of Demedia recently. I would want to be very careful if I got embroiled there. Such a match would bring its own complications. In any case Eirann is marrying Gwyn of Angas, and I do not want to set Demedia and Cennet against me, to say nothing of upsetting Rowanna and Custennin and the monks of Thansethan." Both men took another drink and this time Mardol finished the cup.

"Do you think we can win?" Mardol asked, setting the cup down gently.

"Is there any alternative?" Urdo smiled grimly, but his voice was light. "I will say again what I said to you six years ago at Thansethan, and three years ago here to all those who came to the crowning. It will not be easy, and you won't like everything I have to do to do it, but if we believe we can do it, then we can. The gods of the land are on our side, and the Church of the White God supports me. I even have reason to believe that the gods of my enemies are not quite so implacably opposed as I had imagined. If we fight among ourselves, if we do not tax and struggle to support the alae, then we will lose, and lose forever. If we win it will be a victory for a moment only, maybe a few lifetimes. It is not possible to win forever. But it is possible to lose forever." Urdo stood up and put out a hand to help the older man up from the bench. "Now if you've said what it was you wanted privacy to say, I think it's time we found our beds."

I waited until they had gone, then stood up. My foot had gone numb and agonized me with pins and needles. Starlight was asleep. I wondered if poor Urdo had gone through all that with each of the kings. The moon was up when I got outside, and all the walls of the high city were gleaming slightly in the silver light. Caer Tanaga was the most beautiful city in the world. It looked delicate, like an exotic bird or butterfly perched on the hilltop. By moonlight it seemed promising, magical. It was always a sight to lift the heart, to make one believe that peace and civilization were possible things.

Standing there in the deep night I did not doubt even for an instant that Urdo would win.

—12—

Cold hooves on the highroad	who came by night
bearing bad tidings	leaves on a stormwind
swirling together	gathered against us.
There Guth fell	and Gunulf,
Randwine and Rankin	fresh come from Jarnholme
Edfrith and Egbold	in the far kingdom.
The battlehorsemen	invoking death.

Steady on sea-strand   strong sons of Sigmund
landlonging took them   far from their hearthhome
longspears found them   red blood in grey morning
shoulder companions   won graves not gain.
      —"The Winning of Tevin"

Those three years at Caer Tanaga were the happiest my life had yet known. I was young and well and among friends, learning the craft I was born to. We rode, we trained, we fought, we grew, scarcely noticing, a little older, and if things seemed not to be better they seemed also not to grow worse, for the first time in long years. We called it peace, who had never known peace in our lives, or our parents' lives before us. We drank to peace and spent all our time learning war. Sometimes, when we had a truce with Ayl and winter closed the seas to the raiders, we would go two months together without having to fight. We stayed at Caer Tanaga, for we were Urdo's Ala. Many of us were promoted away, and with our congratulations there was always a note of commiseration. When Urdo had three pennons and everything else an ala required he would send them where they were needed to build up another three pennons there. He now had eight alae of six full pennons each. We were always taking in new recruits and training, but we knew we were special. Urdo trained with us and fought beside us often, and away from the troops he sat in council, gave judgments, and made laws. He did not call it peace, for he alone of us knew what peace was and why it was worth fighting for.

Training was exhausting. There were times when we were glad enough to hear of a raid, for glorious war seemed almost like a rest in comparison. I had thought I was fit and strong before I came to Caer Tanaga but it was only now that I came into my full strength and stamina. I could practice riding formations to signals all morning and teach swordplay until the light left and fall asleep exhausted to wake and do it all again the next day. On rare days off we drank ourselves silly and got into fights with the other pennons. We played endless games of fidchel or dice. We complained constantly. It was always too hot, too cold, too wet, or too dry, the floppy practice lances too floppy, the real lances too hard, the weighted swords too heavy, and we were always tired and muddy. Yet if anyone stopped me to ask, I knew that I was happy.

After two years Osvran was made praefecto of our ala. At that time I was made decurio and given command of the fourth pennon. I was twenty-one then. I felt proud and confident, even though I had shaken in

my boots when I'd been picked out to lead a real charge as signifer only a
few months before. I swore I would go easier on my armigers than Angas
or Osvran had been to me, but after only half a month Masarn was complaining that he knew my face better than he knew his wife's. I worked us
all hard until the Fourth Pennon was the best, and then we worked to make
sure we stayed the best.

A year later, Urdo sent us north to Tinala in the autumn.

"It's not the dead but the fled I'm worried about." Osvran was tugging his
moustache and staring down over the edge of the bank. Down in the reeds
at the edge of the river the shells of two Jarnish ships were burning. "We
know how many we killed, or we will when Glyn comes up with Borthas
and his foot soldiers," he went on. "I didn't count them on the field. There
wasn't really time—anyone?" He glanced up at us. I shook my head along
with the other decurios.

"Four hundred?" I suggested. Osvran frowned, still looking down at
the two smoldering ships. In three years the raiders had learned enough not
to let us capture them. Their own boats in Thurrig's hand were our best
weapon against them, and they were coming to know it. Last spring, bold
Larig ap Thurrig had even taken the war to them and raided Jarnholme.
Everyone envied the troops who had gone with him, even though only
two of his eight ships made it back.

"It's a shame we couldn't have been after them faster," ap Erbin said. I
agreed that King Borthas had been slow in signaling that we could pursue,
but held my tongue.

"They came this far, or some of them. Whether the king and his sworn
men were here, who knows," Osvran said, wisely ignoring this remark.
"Maybe they had more ships and went off in them. Maybe they went to
ground. I just wish I knew where they were now."

"If Urdo were here," said Galba, voicing what we were all thinking. To
a king, the rivers and trees will sometimes speak of the passing of strangers,
and the abode of men. They had little enough to say to us. If the wind had
news, it was only that the grey clouds would send rain again soon.

"Unless the land twists terribly, then this is the Don, and over the river
is Jarnish land," Enid said. "We must be looking at what the map calls the
province of Valentia. Tevin, as they call it now." I looked over at it. It
seemed the same rolling grassland with broken woodland we had been riding over since we left the highroad. On a hillcrest stood a crumbling stone
tower. There was no sign of life, except for one incurious sheep grazing on

the riverbank. They could have been in the nearest clump of trees; laughing at us, or many miles away. It was just before noon, as far as I could tell through the clouds. It was always hard to tell how long a battle had lasted.

"There's another river four or five miles off away east," said Rhodren, gesturing. "According to the map. The"—he squinted at it—"the Derwent? Then it all becomes fenland, low-lying and marshy, lots of little channels, until you get to the sea. I don't know if the channels are freshwater or salt. Can't think why anyone wants this soggy land anyway. It's unfarmable by civilized methods. Can't we just let the Jarnsmen have it?"

"Jarnholme was a lot like that." Enid stared across at the moorland on the far side of the river. "But shut up, Rhodren!"

Rhodren made a face at her and looked back at the map. "Anyway, Caer Lind's not far downstream on the Don, southeast. Fifteen miles or so. If they're still living in Caer Lind, which we don't know. Fifteen years since anyone's been to see."

"I don't envy Raul," said Galba, looking at the ala where they waited, still mounted, for us to decide what to do next. "I wouldn't go on an embassy to a new Jarnish king in a country nobody's been into for a generation for a dozen mares. Has old Borthas found out about that yet?"

"Not as far as I know," said Osvran. "The High King specifically told us not to mention it. Urdo doesn't want the Jarnsmen to take Tinala. But we don't want to help Borthas to Tevin either. Borthas isn't our friend, in case that's slipped anyone's mind." We laughed. "What we want is peace, not conquests. Nobody much lives in Tevin now except Jarnsmen—it's wet and boggy, and it gets invaded a lot, and almost everyone from there is dead, living somewhere else, or enslaved somewhere and out of our reach."

"My old arms master came from Caer Lind," I said. "But he didn't talk about it much. He left when it fell to the Jarns."

"Rhodren's right in a way," said Enid. "We did just abandon it to them."

"That was a long time ago, and that's not the point," said Osvran. "Urdo would recognize a Jarnish kingdom of Tevin, the same way he's recognized Aylsfa and Cennet. He sent us up here because Borthas asked for help. Borthas isn't warring with either the Jarns up in Bereich or King Penda in Bregheda this year, and Borthas had heard that a Jarnish king has landed in Tevin, and he doesn't want trouble. He told Urdo he was frightened about an attack. If they've a new king, then maybe they're going to get organized, he said. So we're here, just for this season, Urdo's most loyal ala. It has to be admitted that the Jarns were attacking into Tinala today though. We got there in time to fight them in a place of our choosing. We're going to stop the Jarns, but when Borthas comes up he's going to want to cross this river and burn hamlets, and it's my decision whether we do. Now, helpful arguments about where they've gone, please."

"If they've gone north there's at least a shipload of them heading upriver straight towards Caer Avroc," said Galba. "Let me see the map?"

"That map would be a sight more useful if it wasn't two hundred years old," muttered Rhodren. We had already learned that it told the hills and rivers and Vincan towns well enough but gave no indication of Jarnish hamlets. The Jarnsmen seemed to site their settlements with what seemed deliberate willfulness as far out of sight of the highroads as they could. Those we had found on this side of the Don were nominally part of Tinala, but they were little pleased to see representatives of any king.

"North towards Caer Avroc, southeast towards Caer Lind, or overland towards the Derwent into Tevin," said Galba, looking at the map.

The rising smoke drifted away into the dark clouds. "If they had enough hands to crew even one of these ships, they'd have taken it, even towing," I said.

"We've beaten them on the field. They've taken casualties. No question of that. The problem is what to do next," said Osvran. "There are still enough of them to do damage, we ought to either press them to a more decisive battle or make a truce. If they have crossed the water, they may melt away into the Jarns who live there. They will have kindred and guest-friends enough among the Jarns who are living quietly and doing no harm, no doubt, up here the same as among Ayl's people. If they have time for that, we will never catch them, and maybe stir up the major war Borthas fears. If every Jarn settled in the east takes up arms it will be a disaster."

"I think that's what Borthas hopes for," said Rhodren, staring out over the sluggish water. "I hate it up here. He wants the Jarns to fight, to fight us."

"Can I say something?" asked ap Erbin. "It isn't a suggestion about where they are, but I think it's relevant."

"If you think it's relevant, always say it," said Osvran. "I know you've only been decurio a little while, but haven't you been to any of Urdo's strategy feasts yet?" Urdo believed that everyone who was in a position to give orders needed a minimum training in history, strategy, tactics, and knowing when to speak up. His strategy feasts could be both an ordeal and tremendous fun. Everyone above the rank of signifer would be invited, and the conversation could become very testing. He was inclined to assign reading to be done by next time. Enid was given to complaining that I had cheated by reading about the Lossian Wars as a child. I couldn't see the distinction between being forced to read Fedra's interminable prose by my mother and being told to read it by Urdo, except that Urdo's reasons were better. It wasn't my fault she had a bad memory.

"Just one of them," said ap Erbin. "Well, this may be silly. But why have they got ships at all?" We all looked at him like an idiot cousin. Jarnish raiders always had ships. He blushed. "I mean, when Ayl crosses the Tamer he doesn't. These aren't local raiders. They can't have got here without coming all the way from the sea, past Caer Lind. Those are big ships. Their king was there. They were fighting quite well, not like pirates. They were disciplined. They were doing ever so well against Borthas's infantry, and they were really solid against the charge, they stood it as well as I've ever seen anyone stand it. They retreated in good order, too. They were a nasty piece of work."

"They were," agreed Galba. "Ap Erbin's right. They're well-disciplined Jarns, a king and his house lords. They're not raiders, but they came from somewhere in ships for some reason. Probably they're going back there, if they have any sense."

"Or they burned their ships to show they're here to stay?" suggested Enid. "That they'll take the land and not retreat, even if they're retreating right now?"

"This isn't Aylsfa," I put in. "We don't have any truce with these people, or even any habit of having a truce with them. Maybe they don't know how to ask for one? If we go south along the river, to see if we could cut them off, then Borthas could take his army back to Caer Avroc in case they did go north. If we found them, we could send people back to him; we needn't engage them straightaway. The same if he found them; he could send a rider and we could come back. If they're going back and we find them, well, maybe they'd listen to sense if they heard it first. My signaler and a couple of people in my pennon speak Jarnish."

"That's not bad thinking," said Osvran, making my cheeks heat with the unexpected praise. "We have our own supply system, and that way we don't have to spend more time with Borthas than we have to." He grinned decisively. "Mount up, get ready, we may as well start moving. Enid, send a messenger to the main force explaining what we're doing."

"What if Borthas doesn't want to?" asked Rhodren.

"That's why I'm not waiting about to argue with him," Osvran said. "Send a messenger to Glyn, to Glyn himself, also explaining. Get all our supplies and spares to come after us as soon as they can. Tell Glyn we'll wait for them within three miles downstream, and we'll have something to eat and a rest when they reach us."

I walked back to where my pennon was waiting, smartly drawn up. They'd drilled so much that at last it was more natural for them to be right than wrong. They were all looking to me. We were one man down, poor Senach had taken a thrown spear through his eye. Indeg, my signaler, had a hand to his trumpet already, ready to pass on the orders. I grinned up at them all as I swung myself up on Apple's back. "We're going to head downriver, probably camp tonight, find out what's going on, no fighting." There was a satisfying chorus of groans. They'd fought once today already, and we'd come out of it very well, despite the unexpected high quality of the Jarnish troops. Their blood was up. They wanted to go on and do it again.

"At least we're not going back. I'd much rather fight than face another one of those terrible banquets at Caer Avroc!" said Geiran, pulling a face. Everyone laughed, and there were mutters of agreement.

"Fight?" I said, pretending to be surprised. "I should think we'd all rather fight. Personally I'd rather go on an all-night foot patrol with a forty-turnip pack in deep winter." They laughed again, good-naturedly.

"Who hasn't been offered double pay and a promotion to transfer to old snake-face's personal horse-band?" Bran ap Penda asked.

"Horse dancers," sneered Masarn ap Sifax. "Did you see them holding back in the battle behind the foot soldiers?"

"He doesn't have the first idea how to use horses in battle," said Bran, smiling a little.

"You'd think after the first hundred and fifty times they'd heard no they wouldn't bother to ask us again," said Geiran. "What did you say?" They were taking up their right places in the forming ala without my having to say a word. We were used to each other and comfortable together. The column was in fours without anyone giving an order. Geiran and Bran took up position alongside me. Bran was signifer, and he held the pennon banner and the golden charge banner strapped to his saddle. Geiran was sequifer and had the white rally banner safely strapped to hers. I had let them carry them in the charge, though I could have decided to take one of them myself. Indeg rode behind me, ready to catch my signals and relay them. I didn't even need to glance back to see where he was.

"Oh, I told him who my father was, and he backed off at a very fast gallop." Bran giggled, not pausing in his conversation as we rode off. "He'd be at war with my father now if the High King would let him. See those hills way off to the west? There's been almost as many battles between Borthas and my father among them as there have been between us and the raiders. What did you tell him?"

"I said I was suited well enough as I was, thank you kindly, sir," said Geiran. "I heard that Borthas's sister, old cow-eyes, promised Osvran her favors if he'd join them."

"What did the captain say?" They were both giggling, and I should have told them to pay attention, but I wanted to know, too.

"He said to try asking Glyn, as such an offer might be more to his tastes."

"Ah but Glyn—" Bran dropped his voice and muttered something.

"Have they asked you, Sulien?" Masarn asked from my other side.

"Flavien ap Borthas offered me the dubious honor of commanding his little band of half-trained horse." I grinned. "It was easy enough to refuse, if less easy to remain entirely polite." He had approached me when I was sitting with Galba, and he had leaned heavily on the supposed indignity of those of our high birth-rank serving under Osvran. Galba told me later that Urdo had told him before he left that when we went back he would be ready for the command he's long been promised over the ala at Magor and Derwen. We'd spent the rest of the evening designing a suitable motif for them. He'd asked me if there was anything Aurien liked that would work. He had been writing to her, and knew more about her present likes and dislikes than I did. They were due to marry at midwinter.

Masarn laughed. "I'll be glad when we've beaten these wretched Jarns and we can leave this horrible place and go home."

"I must say I'm not the least bit worried about losing anyone to the seductions of Caer Avroc."

Glyn met us as arranged. We ate and moved on. There was no sign of the Jarns that afternoon. At evening we made up a camp on a hilltop with a good view all around. When we led the horses up to it we found a large stone on the very top, of the sort that the people say belong to the Folk of the Hollow Hills. "That explains why it's marked as Foreth on the map," said Rhodren. "That means Table Hill." Some of the armigers were making an interesting assortment of aversion signs. Osvran called for silence.

"See this table?" he called. Everyone was either looking at it or carefully not looking at it. It was grey rock that came up to just above Osvran's waist as he stood by it, and stretched perhaps twice his length. "It was put here by our ancestors, maybe when they were fighting the Vincans.

It means this is a good hill to defend if we have to, and we chose right."
The mutters died out after that, and we settled down to spend the night. "If
we don't find anyone by noon tomorrow we'll head back," Enid relayed to
me, and me to my armigers. The rain had stopped. We were glad of the
chance to rest, and most of us barely complained at all.

—13—

> Take up your sword and go,
> take up these fair-won horse,
> go afloat in your cockle-boat
> that drew us from our course.
>
> Heed, heed these words I speak
> heed them and depart
> for I swear if we stay for breaking day
> this land will break your heart.
>
> You've won five games on the shining strand
> won them with your song
> and the stallion wave falls loud and brave
> to say we've stayed too long.
>
> Home, home, my lord, I say,
> that green familiar shore
> we must now leave or, lord, I grieve
> we'll see it nevermore.
>   —"The Ballad of Emrys"

It is always chilly in the deep night, even in the heart of summer. The
next full moon would mark the Autumn Feast and the start of the apple
harvest, so I was glad of my wool cloak. I would have been even more glad
of the full moon. The half-moon that showed now and then through the
scudding clouds cast odd shadows on the ground. All the trees seemed to
have eyes and arms. When the clouds covered the moon it was very dark.

I walked about a little, to keep myself warm and wakeful and to check
on the others. Too many cold camps Osvran or Angas had come checking

and found me almost asleep. Fourth Pennon would do sentry as well as we could. If the Jarnsmen came we were all ready to mount and be off the hilltop almost before they knew for sure we were there. It is foolish to fight good infantry at night when they know the ground and you have the advantage of mobility. None of my sentries were asleep. Nothing was moving except a few wakeful horses, who shifted and snuffled now and then. Another hour by the moon, and I could wake Bran ap Penda to take my place and set out the other half of the pennon on sentry duty. First and Fifth Pennons had armigers out there, too, in the outer ring. There would be enough time for sleep. The Jarns wouldn't either surprise us or wear us out.

I walked the circle of the camp, the whole hilltop. There were ruins of earth and stone that showed where people had lived, once. I stood and leaned on the old stone that gave the place its name—Foreth, the Table Hill. However reassured the others may have been by what Osvran said, I knew different. My mother had told me that such stones meant that people had worshiped here once. I reached out to feel for the old connection. There was hardly a trace to take comfort in. I could not even tell if it had been the Mother or the Smith whose forgotten names had once been called on this hill. It was very long ago, and there were none of those people left. The gods barely took account of this hilltop any longer. It would take some terrible act to wake them here. Those people were all dead, and forgotten, with no heritage. My Tanagan ancestors had killed them or married them, but there were none left to come up to the Foreth and make sacrifices. The hill took little notice of people anymore. I shivered. I don't think I had really understood, before that, what Urdo had meant about the name and the country. The stone still sat in the darkness, only itself, while the Tanagans had been driven out of Tevin, too.

I heard movement and spun round, my sword half-drawn, but it was only Osvran. The golden oak leaves on his white praefecto's cloak glimmered silver in the moonlight.

"I was awake," he said, in the low tones people use when people are sleeping close by. "Anything?"

"Nothing. Rabbits, twitchy horses, clouds across the moon. I don't think anyone knows we're here," I said. Osvran leaned on the stone beside me.

"They could. I don't see how they can't. You can't take two hundred horses across country without leaving clear signs for anyone to spot." The half-moon came out between the rags of cloud, silvering the winding river. I could see half of Osvran's face, level with mine as he stared out at the empty fields. "I wish I knew what they were doing. I had a message from Borthas—he's back in Caer Avroc and no sign of them there either."

"This is going to make a very odd report," I agreed. "And then they vanished . . ." Osvran snorted.

"Went inside a hollow hill. Maybe even this one." He was still staring out. I felt a cold unease pass through me.

"There's a lot of this country. They could be anywhere," I said. "Maybe we won't find them."

"I hoped if we camped here we might tempt them to attack. Then we could break out and catch them in the open early tomorrow."

"No sign so far." I straightened and walked all the way round the rock, looking out. My job might have been to keep the sentries alert, but I couldn't feel comfortable facing one direction for long. I settled back beside Osvran as the clouds covered the moon again.

"I just want to get this over with and go home," he said.

"It may be chilly, but everyone's happier on this hilltop than in Caer Avroc."

He laughed a little. "Me most certainly included."

"Did Borthas's sister really try to seduce you?" I felt a kind of horrified curiosity.

"Well . . ." Osvran was smiling, but without much amusement. He spoke very precisely. "Her name is Rheneth ap Borthas, Borthas's father having the same name, and his elder son, too, it's a tradition in their family. Stupidity and lack of imagination running in the blood if you ask me, along with their Tinala arrogance. She's been married twice already, both times to useful men who died rather too conveniently for Borthas. She has a half-Jarnish son about twelve years old who has some claim on Bereich that his uncle may push for him at a good time. Gah. She's been offered or offered herself to every king in Tir Tanagiri. She has the manners of a young girl who is pretty enough to be excused. She's getting a bit long in the tooth for it. You may have noticed."

"I have met her," I admitted.

"She also has the intuition of a sow. No, that's unfair to sows. They can be quite intuitive. It's the shape of her nose that made me say that, not her intuition." I giggled, and hastily muffled it. "But she's *really* not used to hearing no."

"She's just spoilt. Did you tell her to send a kinsman?"

Osvran snorted quietly. "No. No mortal insults to their House. Besides, young Flavien ap Borthas might have tried it. Is that what people are saying?"

"No. Don't worry. The gossip says you told her to ask poor Glyn." My eyes went back to the horizon. "I just thought it might have done her manners good if you had said that. Are there no men in the north who prefer each other?"

"*I'm* from the north," said Osvran, drily, then laughed. "But then why do you think I left?"

"You're not from Tinala, though, are you?" I asked.

"No, thank the White God, from Demedia. In fact where I was born is part of what's now Bereich. My parents fled the Jarns and now farm land that belongs to the Clan Angas, near Dun Idyn. I was brought up with our Angas as a companion, being much of his age, and got a noble war training out of it," Osvran hesitated, then continued, "There are some who say that the Lord of Angas paid my mother some attentions in the year before my birth. I have to fight everyone who says so, of course." His tone was cool and even.

"Why are you telling me this?" I'd heard this whispered, of course. But that he should repeat the slander himself seemed beyond belief.

"I always thought I'd never marry. I prefer men to lie with, always have. And I am not heir to land. But Urdo has promised me an estate, a name, something to leave to heirs. Not now, but when the Jarnish wars are over and we have peace. If the gods are kind and all this comes to pass and we both live to see it, I was wondering if you might like to consider a marriage. I know you turned down honorable marriage from Galba and Glyn, and you've turned down half the ala for something or other. But we wouldn't need to bother each other too much to what we don't have a taste to, though I think I could bring myself to conceive a child, or if not you might want to bear another to someone else, or at the least we could bring your boy back from Thansethan. We could do that anyway, I know you miss—"

"Osvran." He clearly had a whole life planned out as he might a foray. I had let him say so much because he had startled me. It was so strange to hear his calm tones setting out this logical series of suggestions in the darkness where I couldn't see his face. He went quiet at once at my tone of voice. I drew a breath, stood, and walked around the rock again to get calm enough to speak. I doubt I'd have noticed if a whole army of Jarns had been heading uphill along with an infantry legion painted for war, but it did me good. He was standing absolutely still. "No. I'm sorry. I have no taste whatsoever for that sort of love with anyone, man, woman, or beast." I shuddered a little remembering it. "We'd both be forcing ourselves, and I don't want a child that much. I like being an armiger. I don't want to be a key-keeper and run an estate."

"You could carry on riding, it needn't change anything."

"Yes it would, and you know it. Look at Enid and Larig."

Osvran shrugged. "She got him to take her on the Jarnholme expedition. She's here with the ala. What's changed?"

"That she has to beg him for permission to do what was her right? The awkwardness of all the men who used to share blankets with her after a fight and don't know quite how to talk to her anymore?" I suggested.

"Well, true, but she's dealt with that well enough, and being made decurio helped. That wouldn't apply to you anyway."

"What about the fact that when she can't keep hiding the fact she's going to have a baby you'll send her off away somewhere and she'll waste a year? Or more if she's fair to it. Fine for people who want to, but not for me. I lost one year already, I don't want to lose more. No. I like riding. This life suits me. And when it comes to it if I have ambition, I'd like to be a praefecto one day, and I'd hate to be a lord."

"I suppose it's because your parents would have a fit at my birth."

"What?" I blinked at his face, suddenly silvered as the moon came out again. I'd seen the expression once before, the time he vaulted over his horse's head unexpectedly while striking at a Jarn with an unusually soft skull. "Don't be ridiculous. You know I don't think like that. I truly don't want to marry anyone, ever. Not you, not Galba, not Urdo himself if he were mad enough to think it, not Elhanen the Conqueror if he were still alive. You're my friend, and I value you. If I wanted to marry anyone you'd do better than most."

"Oh well." He sighed. "Never mind."

"Thanks for the offer all the same. You'll think of something," I said, comfortingly.

" 'The good commander always thinks of something,' " he quoted Urdo quoting Dalitus. "Is Enid really having a baby?"

"I didn't tell you! She'll kill me. She didn't tell me, I noticed the signs, but she knows I know." I had been afraid she hadn't recognized the signs, but she had laughed at me. "She's not far on enough for it to stop her being able to fight yet, or she'd not have come however much she wants to. She has sense. She'll tell you at the right time, and you can send her off to Caer Tanaga or wherever Larig is now."

"I think he's at Caer Segant with the dowager Rowanna," said Osvran, abstractedly. Then he went on briskly: "I haven't noticed anything different about Enid. I won't take notice until I need to. I'll do a round of all the sentries and then get some more sleep. Let me know if you change your mind."

I paced to and fro. His was far from the first proposal I'd had in the ala, but it was one of the strangest. I wondered how long he'd been working it out as a sensible strategy. I pulled my cloak closer round me. It was almost time to wake Bran. I needed to catch any sleep I could if we were going to fight in the morning.

The morning was overcast, and brought us no sight of the Jarnsmen. Between Foreth and Caer Lind we found two Jarnish hamlets, both empty. Both showed signs of recent but orderly evacuation.

Just outside the second, a cow startled us by running across the track in front of us.

"She wants milking," said Glyn.

"They turned the herd loose," said Osvran. "What do they think they're doing?"

"Shall I have her milked?" asked Glyn. "A couple of gallons of fresh milk wouldn't hurt, and ap Gavan can milk anything."

Osvran looked around. There were scouts out ahead, of course. Where we were happened to be fairly clear ground.

"We'll stop here and eat. Make a fire. Make porridge. Milk the cow if you can manage it. If they care, then they know where we are already. Eat by numbers." This meant that no more than half the pennon would be dismounted and eating at any time. "Get water from the river, not from the well in the hamlet."

"Why?" asked ap Erbin, and then, "You mean they might have poisoned the wells?"

"It would be a logical thing for them to do," said Osvran.

"What color was the cow?" Bran asked Garah, as she came up to eat with us.

"Brown," said Garah, in the firm tone of one who has already answered the question too many times. "And if you don't like the idea of drinking the milk, then don't eat the porridge, that's where it went, two whole buckets, near enough forty cups. She wasn't milked last night either."

"I'll have yours," said Masarn, hopefully, as Bran stopped eating.

"Milk in porridge is good for you, that's the way they make it at Thansethan. It's good for people who're going to fight, gives you strength," I said authoritatively. Bran started eating again.

"If the People of the Hills had taken the farmers, they'd have taken the cow too," said Garah, holding out her bowl to Talog for her share. "She wasn't a happy cow, either. She won't have to put up with it long because of Cadwas is going to make her into dinner." Masarn cheered up at that.

"Will there be enough for everyone?" he asked. Just then Osvran blew the trumpet for the decurios to assemble. I gulped down my porridge and went off to join him.

"The first scouts are back from Caer Lind," he said, as soon as we were all there. "The report is that the place is deserted. It may have been deserted for years. My plan is that we ride on it as quickly as we can, secure it, send messages back to Caer Avroc for Borthas to bring up troops and supplies. We can use it as a base and send pennons out from Caer Lind to look for the Jarns."

Ap Erbin looked uneasy. "People are worrying about sorcery," he said. "Nothing seems to make sense."

"When we find them it'll be clear," said Osvran. "We can't just do nothing, and we have to be somewhere defensible or keep moving. Any other problems?" He glanced at us all. His expression was perfectly natural when he looked at me, which was a relief. Nobody mentioned any other problems. As soon as we could ride we made for Caer Lind.

I did not have long to see that strange deserted town that day. Osvran had an urgent need for information. The broken gates hung open, parts of the walls were crumbling. Inside the streets of the fort were laid out on the pattern the Vincans built from the Desert to the Ice. But they were cluttered with Jarnish buildings of wood and mud thatched with straw built into the old house walls. Grass grew among the cobbles of the streets.

"I think they left because they couldn't stand the smell," murmured Geiran. The smell was notably bad, worse than a midsummer midden.

Osvran called us together in the gatehouse. He had hoisted the golden-tree banner of the ala, and the green-and-red flag of the High Kingdom of Tir Tanagiri. He was just sending out messengers back to Borthas, a day and a half's ride away at Caer Avroc, and also to Urdo at Caer Tanaga, six or seven days away at best. He marked out clear routes on the maps for the pennons he was sending out. We had orders to send back a messenger every two hours, and to be back by sunset, and to return without engaging any Jarns we found in force. If we found any farmers we were to find out as much from them as we could. "I don't know what they're up to, but they're up to something," Osvran said. "Be back by sunset, but take overnight supplies in case. And drink from the river. The wells in this fortress are poisoned, so it makes sense to think they all are. You know how to patrol, you've done enough of it. But don't engage. Find out where they are, and get back to tell me so we can fight them. If we can find them and make them fight, we'll beat them."

—14—

TABLE OF ALA ORGANIZATION
(with supplies to move five days and 250 miles and fight on arrival)

Praefecto
(in command, field tactics and leadership)

Tribuno
(second in command, also in charge of logistics issues, with
    Quartermaster)

Six pennons.

Each pennon consists of:

COMBATANTS:

    one commander (decurio, tribuno, or praefecto)
    twenty-four armigers
    one sequifer (carries the rally banner)
    one signifer (carries the charge banner)
    one signaler/trumpeter

PEOPLE 28   GREATHORSES 60   RIDING HORSES 30

NON-COMBATANTS:

    one cook
    two assistant cooks

ten grooms
thirteen quartermaster auxiliaries
(to see to packhorses and supplies)

PEOPLE 26   RIDING HORSES 26   PACKHORSES 138

Quartermaster's Command

Quartermaster
  (in charge of supply and coordination)
10 messengers
20 scouts
1 trumpeter
1 signaler
1 doctor
2 doctor's assistants
1 horse doctor
2 horse doctor assistants
1 farrier
2 farrier assistants
2 clerks

PEOPLE 44   RIDING HORSES 74   PACKHORSES 216

TOTAL

COMBATANTS: 168
NON-COMBATANTS: 200
GREATHORSES: 360
RIDING HORSES: 590
PACKHORSES: 1,044

That day we found nothing. More empty villages with no sign of human life anywhere. We slept uneasily at Caer Lind. The next day we stayed in the fortress while the other three pennons took their turn patrolling. Osvran was getting worried. A message came from Borthas at sunset, saying he was in Caer Avroc, he still had no sight of the Jarns, and he would advance to join us with his army. "He leaves out more than he says," said Osvran, unsatisfied. "But that is always his way."

The third day I patrolled again, endlessly frustrated. In the afternoon a scout brought news there were Jarns in a nearby hamlet. She had seen movement from a distance. I sent the news back to Osvran. Almost as soon as I'd done so a messenger reached me from Rhodren, who was patrolling to my south. He'd heard the same news and wanted to investigate it. He'd also sent a message to Enid, patrolling to the west. If we all three converged we'd have enough force to confirm the sighting for Osvran and deal with it if necessary.

I was as ready to fight as he was. I led the pennon towards him, and together the half ala made for the settlement. The place was empty.

"If we started burning these places to the ground whenever we found one, that might persuade them to come out," said Rhodren. I just shook my head.

"Remember what we're fighting for, eh?" I said.

"Both your scouts saw something," Enid said.

"Something's wrong," said Rhodren, suddenly. "I can feel it. Let's get back to Caer Lind, fast. I think we've been stupid coming here. I think we're being watched." I gave the signals to Indeg, who was passing them on to the pennon. Rhodren and Enid did the same with their signalers.

"I feel it too," said Enid. "Let's get away from here."

"I'll lead," Rhodren said, and turned to do so. Enid followed close behind. Fourth Pennon followed them down the muddy track that led away from the hamlet towards Caer Lind. I was trying to work out why they felt the sudden panic. I hadn't felt anything.

Up ahead the trees were closer to the road. As we rounded a curve we saw a small force of Jarns standing blocking the way. These weren't villagers. There couldn't have been more than twenty of them. They had long shields and long axes and looked strong and determined. Now I had a bad feeling. Why were they here? Where had they come from? Blithely ignoring orders, Rhodren raised his charge banner and bore down on them. He didn't even change horses, and I saw his sequifer moving off to the side, with the spare horses and the supplies, at a speed we had practiced but never needed in the field. We always picked our own ground. Sixth Pennon was copying him, and raising the charge banner, moving slightly to the side to have room to charge. They were mad. We'd never attacked with as little thought as this, or in a crowded space. It must have been the frustration coming out in a rush as they finally saw a target before them. I felt something of the same urge. In any case, I couldn't possibly abandon them. Besides, I didn't have time to stop and consider.

I gave the same signal, and charged in support. Bran raised the charge banner and led the charge. It was something we'd practiced many times. Geiran dashed off to the left, I charged at Bran's shoulder and was there to snatch up the pennon banner from him almost as soon as the arrow struck his back and he fell.

They were all through the trees, and it was uncomfortable fighting. I gave the general rally signal at once, and Indeg trumpeted it out to all three pennons, but even so we were hard-pressed to fight our way out. The ranks of Jarns had stepped aside to reveal ropes strung between the trees. In the woods, abbatis of cut trees and crossed branches protected the archers. Rhodren and his front rank had gone down almost at once. The heart-rending screams of the broken-legged horses went on and on.

If their archers had held their fire slightly longer they would have had us all in that first moment. It is surprising how much of a battle is decided right at once. As it was it we couldn't charge into the trees, but we could rally and fight our way back. Once we knew about the bowmen we kept our shields ready. All I could think was to keep moving, to use what we had, to get away. At last we cut our way out. We rallied again with the baggage train on a little hill a mile or so off.

Rhodren and Enid had fallen in the first seconds. Bran was dead. Of the three pennons that had been ambushed I had only slightly more than two pennons' strength left. Very few of those left were primos, those who charge in the front rank. Most were dead, but some had been captured. Many of those with me were wounded. Garah was cutting an arrow out of Masarn's arm as I watched.

"Back to Caer Lind?" asked Geiran. "By a different route?" She managed a wan grin.

I was tempted to agree. But even though the fight had seemed only to take moments, it was growing dark. I turned to Garah. "Did they take any horses?"

"None of ours, not alive," she said. "I didn't see if they could have got any of the others. I don't think so."

"Then they're not mobile, and we are. But they're between us and the town. They didn't come after us, but they know the land. We can move faster, but they can do that again anywhere they know of a place. I think we'd better wait for daylight."

"Osvran will be frantic," said Masarn, wincing as the arrow came out. It had gone all the way through.

"Would you like me to heal that?" I asked. He looked at me and raised his eyebrows.

"It depends how long we're going to be out here fighting," explained Garah. "It'll heal better with time and exercise than with prayers, but much quicker with prayers."

"I think I'll go for quick," he said. I laid the arrow on the wound and sang the charm with all my heart. When he was well I put him in charge of the other pennon—I kept what was left of Fourth Pennon, with other people filling the gaps. I organized the demoralized armigers so that they felt like a fighting force again. I did what I could for the other wounded, which was little enough. Few of them had the weapons that had inflicted the wounds. We settled down on the hilltop for a truly horrible night.

We had lost friends before, but we'd always been able to recover their bodies. We'd never let the Jarns take prisoners. What I remember clearest of that night is the screams. I didn't know who made them, but I impotently cursed the whole race of Jarns until they stopped. I still knew no real curses. We stayed alert, and I at least slept very badly. I kept blaming myself and trying to see how I could have done it better.

We ate before dawn and mounted to set off as soon as there was light in the sky. Everywhere was eerily quiet. There was no sign of the Jarnsmen at all anywhere. They could have vanished back into the hollow hills. We kept outrunning our scouts out of a deep reluctance to stay in one place too long. We found our way back to Caer Lind with some difficulty and arrived there around noon, so far as one could judge in the rain. Then we saw what we had been looking for for days. A huge Jarnish army, four or five times the force we had beaten with Borthas, was gathered around the fortress of Caer Lind. Our banners were still flying. Osvran was still in there. But we had no way of getting to him.

The Jarns were drawn up in front of the fort in a way clearly designed to make it difficult for us to charge. They were on the higher ground, and there were very many of them. Also they had wagons set up as barriers all along one side, with troops in and among them, and along the other stood their best fighters, heavily armored. In the center stood their king, his arms wreathed with gold and a short red cloak falling from his shoulders and holding a long ax with murderous familiarity and intent. I had seen him use it in the first fight. His house lords were close around him. There there was no way to flank them. The flanks were in the forest, and we had learned our bitter lesson there. There was no way to Caer Lind except straight through them.

"Borthas's troops should be here really soon," muttered Geiran.

"Why am I not reassured?" answered another voice. It was Edlim,

Rhodren's sequifer. I'd given him my charge banner, with the full intention of taking it back if we had to charge. It seemed we would have to.

Suddenly, everything was very simple. Whether Borthas was coming or not was scarcely the point. I scanned the troops for a messenger. There was only Indeg, and I needed Indeg to give my signals.

"Garah, no arguments, ride for Caer Avroc and make sure the information about the situation gets to Urdo as well. If you have to go to Caer Tanaga yourself do it." She opened her mouth to protest, but she didn't argue, she just turned and did it. I saw her disappearing northwards as I talked it over with my surviving officers. The Jarns were laughing at us and banging on their shields.

"Well," I said, as loudly as I could. I stood up in the stirrups so they could see me. It wasn't a good beginning for a great rallying speech, and a great rallying speech was what they needed, for the faces on my troops were uncertain. We'd lost badly yesterday and had a miserable night. Losing wasn't something we were used to. The Jarns were howling in rhythm to the banging now. At least it had stopped raining. "Well. You know what we're here for, you know what we're fighting for as well as I do. If we're going to die, we're going to die together, and there are much worse things. They're barbarians, and they killed our friends. They don't deserve Tir Tanagiri. They don't even deserve Tevin, horrible place though it is. They deserve death, so let's go and give it to them. We charge at the king. If we don't take him out right away, we rally back here, be ready to signal, Geiran, and charge at him again really fast, and that will surprise them. Let's avenge the fallen."

I took the charge banner and made sure everyone was ready. The Jarns were ready, too, of course. I raised the banner, Indeg blew the trumpet, and we were off, at top speed. Apple led the way, going flat out as much as he could uphill. I was shouting something as my lance hit, great nonsense no doubt if one could hear it after, but it helped me then. We hit them with great force, but they were expecting it and stood like a wall of ice. I crossed swords with the king himself for a few brief blows. Then we turned smoothly, rallied, and made a second charge at the same place before they had time to prepare themselves again.

This time they broke, and we were almost through except that they brought up horsemen in the gap. Pony men I should say. They had been behind the wagons, Jarns on little hill ponies, laughable compared to our great horses but enough to cause confusion and plug the hole before we were through. Geiran raised the rally banner and we re-formed. I looked up at the city. I could not understand why Osvran didn't sally out to help us, but presumably he had his own problems. The pony men followed us, and found out it is not easy to fight on horseback in the open when the other side knows what they're about. Not one of the ones who came past their lines survived. I took down two myself, and Apple bowled over one pony and pulped the rider beneath his iron-shod hooves. He had blood right up to his fetlocks.

We re-formed back where we had begun. "Another charge?" panted Masarn. The horses were winded, too.

"Pull back a little and let's think while the horses get their breath," I said.

"They're sending an embassy," said Geiran. I looked. They were. Two of the sturdiest footmen who had been standing near the king were advancing towards us. They held green branches, the signal for a parley.

"Pick up a branch, and go forward and ask them what they want," I told Indeg. "I won't talk to them unless they're serious."

He came back quickly. "They say they come from Sweyn, King of Tevin and Emperor of Tir Tanagiri, and want to discuss surrender terms."

"Ha. Tell them we accept their surrender if they give up their claims and leave the island now and forever." I said. My blood was pounding in my ears, and I wanted to kill them all.

"I don't think that's what they mean, Sulien," he said, very serious. Indeg rarely picked up on irony; Geiran and Bran were always teasing him.

"I know. Go and say it anyway. You're a herald; they'll know it's me saying it really."

Indeg returned again. "They say if we surrender now, they will grant us our lives as slaves; otherwise, they will kill us all."

"How terribly tedious that would be," said Geiran. "Sulien, I know I shouldn't ask, but would you mind awfully if I charged this time? Edlim can take the rally banner, he's a very good sequifer, and I haven't even got my lance wet today."

"We'll all charge this time," I said. "Tell them if that's really the only choice, then we'll take death, thank you very much, and they can be our honor guard to speak for the worth of our sword arms in Death's dark hall."

Indeg went to deliver the message, not questioning it this time, nor even quibbling over theology. They returned to their lines. "Change horses, those who can. Masarn, take Beauty, he's used to you, Apple has another charge left in him but Whitefoot is bleeding. Everyone here knows how to charge, even if you're not all primos, this time everyone's going to charge. Sequifers, quartermasters, grooms, cooks, everyone. This is what we practice for. Get on the best horses there are and dump all the gear. Be ready to follow my signal. What we're going to do is charge straight at the king again, just like last time, and at the last minute wheel and make for the wagons. The troops there are nothing like as good, they're the second-raters, they may well break. Then half of us—everyone on a tired horse and everyone who is not usually an armiger—is to get down and fight on foot. Armigers to protect, the others to move two wagons. The rest are to pull back and rally. Geiran, you be ready to lead that rally. Everybody make sure you know which half you are in right now. What those of us on feet must do is clear the wagons—fight and clear the wagons, so that when Geiran's lot charge again they can get right through and hold them off while we make for the fort. I don't need to explain how important it is. We have to make a gap. Geiran, as soon as there's enough gap you lead the charge through. Then we mount up again and get through up to the fort. Now or never. Everyone ready? Anyone unsure?"

Nobody was unsure. We'd never practiced moving wagons, though we'd practiced turning at the charge and changing weapons. I tightened the straps on my wrists and made sure my sword was ready. I grinned at them, and they grinned back, bless them, and then we charged.

We surprised them. I laughed out loud to see their faces when we changed direction at full speed. I was still laughing when I leapt down and began to engage on the ground. I killed someone there, laughing, I don't remember it at all. I only found out about him when his sons named the circumstances three years later when they came to take vengeance on me. The fight was very bloody, but our swords were better than the Jarnish spears in such a close and confused melee.

I stopped laughing when one of them killed Apple over my shoulder, a spear in the neck. He kept on going forward steadily beside me, though the blood was pouring out. He trampled the spearman and kicked the man next to him hard in the head with one high-stepping kick. Then he fell without a cry, like the brave warrior that he was. He was the bravest horse I ever knew. After that I fought in silence. I just killed them as fast as I could, protecting the people who were clearing the wagons. It wasn't long before there was a gap, and those who had rallied were tearing through it. Geiran was in the lead, tears on her face, shouting "Bran!" in a voice loud enough to rock the sky and shake the crows up from the branches where they were waiting.

I got up on a horse again then, I don't know whose horse, it belonged to someone who had been in Fifth Pennon. We charged together behind

Geiran's armigers just as she hit the pony men. They were coming up to help their comrades like before. One of them was Ulf Gunnarsson, and in the frenzy of the battle I was not even surprised. I could not come near him, whenever I tried people swept between us. I learned later I yelled loudly that I would kill him and set his arms on my brother's tomb, because several people later asked me who this Ulf was. In any case, we showed the pony men what it meant to be cavalry. All went very well indeed, and soon we were making at a gallop for the gates of Caer Lind.

I could not understand why the gates were closed when Osvran must have seen us coming. They opened when Masarn shoved them.

The Jarns who met us in the street inside died too fast to lose their smiles. In that first moment I was too busy fighting to be surprised, or to realize what this meant. The little ambush they had set up had no chance of holding us, and soon they were scattering like sheep. We were all inside, and the Jarnish king and nobles were running up the slope towards us. I slammed shut the gates. "Masarn, hold this gate!" I yelled, and galloped off into a strange town with my mixed troops at my heels, killing and cutting down all the Jarns I found like a wolf falling on sheep. I knew the shape of the city. It was exactly like Caer Gloran. I sent people to the ends of quarters, where we could trap them. They were confused, and not expecting us. We moved too quickly for them to be able to get organized. I had privately thought the practice in street fighting was a waste of time, now I blessed Thurrig in my heart for insisting on it. Masarn held the gate. They were not trying very hard to take it, for reasons I did not discover until later. The rest of us retook the city. I gave orders almost faster than I could speak, and was amazed for years to hear them praised as cogent and clear. It seemed at the time as if I was giving them faster than I could think. All those dues paid in training came to fruition. My sketchy orders were correctly implemented by those around me as if we had practiced just this emergency.

The fortress had been taken by treachery. There was a secret way in. I found it, open, and had it stopped later by the simple expedient of throwing down the stones until it was blocked. For now I left Geiran and some troops there. By this time the mere sight of a heavy horse and a lance was enough to send the Jarnsmen in the city running. They were not the best, nor even the second-best troops. In fact they were not King Sweyn's men at all but people who had been settled in Tevin for some time under their own king, Cella, who Sweyn had coerced into helping him. I learned this later. Edlim herded the prisoners into the barracks, where he found what was left of the ala. The first I learned of this was when ap Erbin and Sixth

Pennon came charging out to help me. They were armed with everything imaginable—Jarnish short swords, eating daggers, clubs, and even cobblestones. My heart lifted. I had thought they were all dead, even though I had not had time to think at all.

Time seemed to jump rather than to flow as we fought in the streets. When things were somewhat settled, I asked ap Erbin what had happened and where Osvran was.

"Dead," he said. "The Lady of Angas and King Sweyn tortured him in the tower last night."

It made no sense for Morwen to be here. And why would she torture him? If she had been here, where was she now? Had she killed him to steal his soul for power? I had seen no women in the field. "Are you sure it was her, ap Erbin? It's a serious thing to say."

"I remember her from Angas's wedding. She didn't remember me. I think she must have meant to kill us all, though the Jarnish guards were saying we would be maimed and enslaved." He touched his ankle where some slaves had a ring set between the bones to prevent them from running and escaping. "Thank the Lady of Wisdom you made it here."

"Oh, we'll probably all die yet. Our survival is entirely dependent on Borthas being on the one hand not a traitor and on the other well organized. Not much to bet our lives on. But do you know where that foul witch Morwen ap Avren is now?"

"How do you know her name?" he asked, his eyes widening.

"She's one of the great queens of this island, how do you not know it? Whoever heard of someone in such a position keeping their name secret? Lords' names must be known, it is part of the covenant with the land." Ap Erbin raised his chin but looked startled.

"I've never heard her name spoken before," he said. "I don't think I knew it. I didn't know it, even though her husband is kin to my mother."

"She has kept it secret because she is a witch," I said. "A god told it to me. Now where in the name of seven silver fishes is she?"

"I don't know. She may have gone out with Sweyn. But a lot of Jarnish women and children are still here. They're being guarded in the praetorium."

She was not among them. When I got to the praetorium Masarn informed me with great glee that King Sweyn's wife and baby daughter were there. "Don't harm them!" I said. "In fact send out an embassy, send Indeg up on the wall, to make sure that Sweyn knows they're safe. That explains why he didn't try a frontal attack. Get the other gate blocked right now."

"Galba and some of Third Pennon are working on the other gate," he said. "But I can't send Indeg on the embassy. Indeg's dead. I thought you knew. You were there. In the fighting around the wains."

It was just one more death. The pain would come later. I shook my head. "All right. You go. Or send someone. Gormant speaks some Jarnish. Just let them know their people are safe and won't be harmed if they don't attack. We need time. Or maybe I ought to go?"

"I'll send Glyn. You're absolutely covered in blood. You'd terrify them, and they'd shoot you." He grinned, and went. I set off to search the fortress for Morwen. It was Apple's blood, and maybe Indeg's. He had been right by me at the beginning of the fight, ready to echo my orders. Some of it was mine too, I had been wounded and bruised in several places but still had too much energy to notice.

—15—

Never betray an ally. If you wish to make an end to an alliance inform your ally that the alliance is over from this time. If you once betray an ally, it will never be possible for you to make another alliance, either with them or with anyone else, for nobody will trust you.

To make an alliance, it is not enough that you and the person desirous of being an ally share an enemy. When making an alliance you should consider what you will gain from it, and what your ally will gain from it. If you will gain much and they will gain little, you should make the alliance. If they will gain much and you will gain little, you should consider if that little is worth the trouble. It may be; sometimes a little is much. If by the terms they offer they seem to gain nothing, you should look carefully at their reasons for making the alliance. Either it is a trick, or you have overlooked something. At all times while the alliance continues you must consider who is benefiting in what ways, and if things change, you should consider ending the alliance.

If it seems that you will both gain different things and in equal amounts, then this is the best kind of alliance; you should make the alliance and keep it.

—Caius Dalitus, *The Relations of Rulers*

When I had seen the gatehouse tower room before, it was bare. Now the stone walls were badly draped with heavy, wrinkled tapestries depicting stick-figure Jarns, fighting. There was one carved chair, placed precisely in the center of the room. By turning her head she had a view from one of the high windows. She was facing the stairway when I came up.

She was sitting very calmly. She looked, if anything, more regal than ever. Her hands were folded in her lap. She was wearing a gold torc. Her robe was dark red, embroidered with Demedian thorns and the running horse of the House of Emrys in gold thread. It would have given me great pleasure to kill her.

"Sulien ap Gwien," she greeted me, smiling a little.

"Morwen ap Avren, Lady of Angas, Queen of Demedia," I replied, looking straight at her. "And by the gods of my people you will pay for this day's work. I would kill you now with this bloody sword—" (it happened to still be in my hand) "—except that it would be better for the realm to bring you to justice in Caer Tanaga. There are too many to swear to this treachery for you to escape this time."

"It would tear the realm to pieces if Urdo were to try me," said Morwen. "Even if—especially if—young Galba ap Galba survives to speak against me." She smiled, thin-lipped. "But don't waste your breath on what will never happen. The realm is over. Sweyn will kill Urdo, and soon."

"Then why don't I kill you now?" I suggested. I raised my sword, irrelevantly noticing the new nicks in the blade. She leaned back a little in the carved chair, looking up at me.

"No, dear. You don't dare kill me because I'm a bargaining piece with Sweyn, much more so than his wife and girl are, as it happens. For people with such strong gods they're surprisingly ignorant about power. You might even be able to persuade Sweyn to let you out of Caer Lind, not that it will make any difference. You're a fool, but you're not such a fool as to kill me and risk killing everyone in this fortress." She smoothed her hand over the stuff of her skirt.

"Borthas will be here later today, or tomorrow," I said. "He's no hero, but between us in here and him out there we can break Sweyn's army." I wasn't as sure of that as I tried to sound. We'd lost a lot of horses.

She laughed. It was a particularly unpleasant laugh. "Putting your trust in Borthas is even more misplaced this time than it usually is. The snake is dead. We attacked his army almost as soon as you were out of sight. He never made it back to Caer Avroc. Your messages from him were forged. I killed him myself." It had to be true. It explained where they had been.

"Then nobody knows we're here, and we're going to die anyway," I said. In that case I might as well kill her now. The point of my sword came up and was steady. I stepped forward.

"My brother knows," she said, quietly. She didn't even pretend to be frightened. "That message got through. I want him to come up here. He can't possibly bring enough with him to dent the army Sweyn has. And he has no idea how many men Sweyn has. The reports were sent before anyone saw the extent of it. Sweyn has come from Jarnholme to rule this island. And Sweyn has alliances with Bereich and Aylsfa. They will be kings under him. Bereich are even now attacking into Tinala, and as soon as Urdo leaves Caer Tanaga Ayl will cross the Tamer."

It all had a nightmare plausibility. If she'd been lying she'd have said he had an alliance with Cennet as well. Urdo wasn't a fool, and it wouldn't happen the way she thought, but she could well have set up the Jarnish side of it. "What do you get out of it?" I asked. "Last time you talked about Urdo as a great king."

She laughed. "There are many paths, and I have found a better one. My husband is dead. Did you think I would stay powerless in Dun Idyn where that prating priest won't leave me alone?" It was news to me that the Lord of Angas was dead. No word of it had come to Caer Tanaga before I left it. "I get the western half of Tir Tanagiri to rule through my son. He is ready for it. The people will follow him. What else I get you wouldn't understand. Now go out and strike a bargain with Sweyn—he will let you hold out here until Urdo comes if you let me go."

"Oh no." Even in my state I could see how long she would keep that bargain once she was free. "If you are a bargaining piece I shall wait and think what I want to trade you for." The only reason I didn't kill her at that moment was that I wanted to do it too much. I called down the stairs. Geiran and ap Erbin came up from where I had left them waiting. "Tie her up. Don't listen to anything she says. But she may be useful to us, so we don't kill her yet." I walked over to the window and looked out. The Jarnish army covered the fields outside. It was already reorganized to face the Caer.

"She tortured Osvran to death," said ap Erbin. "The whole fortress heard."

"So if we don't need her as a bargaining piece we try her in Caer Tanaga in front of everyone," I said, miserably. My left leg and my right side and my left wrist were starting to hurt. I was going to have to tell everyone the bad news.

Geiran brought the rope and advanced towards Morwen, who did not move and continued smiling faintly. "We can probably prove that she killed Osvran for sorcerous reasons, and ate his soul," I said. She had tried to do it to me. Geiran stopped and looked at me, eyes wide. Ap Erbin drew in a sharp breath. "She would have needed it to get enough power for her black sorcery."

Morwen looked at me with a momentary hatred, and I knew I was right, I had caught her in a weakness. But when she spoke her voice was calm and almost amused. "Oh no. I killed Osvran because he was my dead husband's bastard. It was an insult to me to let him live."

It was too much. I clenched my hand on my sword. She was completely mad in her self-centered pettiness. How dared she kill a man, my friend, a good man, one of Urdo's best men, not for himself but for an accident of birth? I gritted my teeth. How dared she even lie and so insult his memory. Geiran, beside her, drew back her hand and slapped Morwen across the face. As her hand touched Morwen I felt a wave of heat. Suddenly, Geiran was burning like a torch, all the fat in her body burning at once. I could see her bones through her flesh in that first instant. This was nothing like the spark almost anyone knows how to bring, to start a fire, it was an evil unearthly flame. I took a step towards Morwen, raising my sword. I think I could have killed her. I don't think her sorcery could have hurt me.

Geiran carried on moving forward to touch Morwen, her arms open now. She enfolded her in her arms even as the flesh ran off them, even as she was consumed. Morwen laughed, and I saw her reach out for power. I took another step. The tapestries behind her suddenly billowed forward. Morwen was burning. Ap Erbin was screaming and rushing forward, his sword drawn. Morwen wasn't laughing anymore, and I saw in her eyes that no power was coming, and she knew it. She had burned up her own soul at long last, and now her flesh was burning. She tried to rise, and poor Geiran's bones scattered to the ground as my sword and ap Erbin's met in Morwen's throat. If she wasn't dead already then we were more merciful to her than she deserved.

We stood and stared at each other a moment, as our swords clashed together. Then the tapestry fell and a child hurtled out, running straight towards the burning thing that had been Morwen.

"Mother!" he screamed. I snatched him up only instants before he would have touched what was left of her. He would have caught fire in that unnatural flame and died there with her. He was only nine years old. There were so many times later when I wished I had let him burn.

He struggled and fought me, trying to draw the short sword at his side, trying to bite me. He was hard to hold. Then ap Erbin screamed again, and pointed, and I saw that the wooden floor was burning around her body in a quickly expanding circle of white fire. We turned and ran down the stairs, ap Erbin first and I behind, still struggling with the boy. We came out into the cobbled courtyard. The tower fire rose up from the top of the tower, sending up a high plume of greasy black smoke. The stone would not burn. I handed the child to ap Erbin, who sheathed his sword and held him with both arms, making comforting noises. The boy bit him. People were coming out to see why the tower was burning. Ap Erbin called over Celemon ap Caius, his sequifer, and gave the struggling boy to her.

"Put him with the prisoners," he said. "Have him watched. He is the son of a traitor, but only a child, and he is an orphan." He was screaming curses and the names of gods as loudly as he could as Celemon took him away.

"Shall we try to put it out?" asked ap Erbin, staring up at the black smoke twisting unnaturally in the dusk.

"No. It's Geiran's pyre. And Osvran's, too." I stood and sang the Hymn of Returning then, pulling off my helmet and cutting my hair with my sword, as I had for Darien my brother. Ap Erbin sang with me, and the others who were there were quiet, listening. I prayed with all my heart that Osvran had passed into the quiet halls of Death to speak for his life and go on to make new choices. I feared very much that he had not, that she had stolen his soul and he was gone forever. At least she was gone, too. Morwen had unraveled her own soul for power until she came, unexpectedly, to the end of it.

When we had finished ap Erbin turned to me. "What in Coventina's name are we going to tell Angas?" he asked softly.

"If I ever see Angas again I will be so pleased I don't care if he kills me," I said, putting my helmet back on. It had acquired some new dents and a nasty crease, no wonder my head hurt so. She had said she was going to rule through Angas, but I knew he would never betray Urdo. "The first thing is what we're going to tell Sweyn. How defensible do you think this place is?"

"We can hold it for a few days. Do you know a well blessing? If we had a clean well we could hold it longer." Garah knew a well blessing. But I'd sent her off into who knew what danger. I'd heard her give it. She would be furious with me for letting Apple die.

"I can try one."

"We need to talk to Glyn about supply. But I think we can hold out until Borthas gets here."

"Borthas is dead." Ap Erbin gaped at me. "Get Galba. Get Glyn. Get Masarn, I put him in charge of the other pennon I brought in. Get someone else fit to be a decurio who can lead First." Osvran's pennon. "We need to have a council and decide what to do. Get—" I remembered with a start and a warm glow of strong relief that Galba would be in charge. I gave sincere thanks to all the gods of war. He was highest-ranking survivor, and Urdo had promised him command of an ala. He was just getting it sooner than he expected. He could make the decisions, which was good, as my head felt as if it had been stuffed with wool. It wouldn't be up to me to decide what to do next. I didn't want to be a praefecto after all. I wanted to get very drunk and sleep for a week and after that do something simple and boring like days and days of lance-drilling exercises where the worst of my worries was getting Apple to change feet at the right time. Except that Apple was dead. I rubbed my eyes with my raw hands. My gauntlets had vanished somewhere.

"What shall I get, and where shall I get them to?" ap Erbin asked. He had been waiting while I stood with my mouth open.

"The praetorium, I think. I can't remember what else I was going to say. Galba can decide what we're going to say to Sweyn. Oh, and tell Galba he's in charge, will you? Don't get someone for First Pennon. Galba can do that."

Galba blinked at me when he saw me in the praetorium. "Are you hurt, Sulien?"

"A few scratches I think. I haven't looked yet. It's mostly Apple's blood, and Jarnish blood. Yes, one of these years I'll have time to wash all off it off. There are things you need to know."

I waited until everyone was there, then told them everything Morwen had said and done. Ap Erbin confirmed the way she had died. I told them the titles Sweyn claimed and the surrender terms he'd offered before the battle.

"Let us assume," said Galba, "firstly, that Urdo will not fall into the trap. If he comes, he will come with sufficient force. He may not come. He may assume we're all dead."

"If ap Gavan reaches him he will know more than they think," Masarn pointed out. "Sulien sent her via Caer Avroc. It'll take her six or seven days to get to Urdo."

"The immediate problem is what to say to Sweyn now. We have his family, he has us trapped," said Galba.

"Is he an honorable man?" asked ap Erbin.

"He made an alliance with Morwen, and according to her, he needed her," I said. "On the other hand the people of his household I fought today did nothing dishonorable. I think he might not openly break a public agreement before his people."

"So do we ask him to let us go in return for his family?" asked Glyn. "We've supplies for about ten days."

"Six days to Caer Tanaga, six days back here," muttered ap Erbin.

"We can hold out twenty days if we must, but it will be hard going," said Glyn.

"He won't let us go, that will spoil his trap if we get to Urdo and tell him," said Galba. "I think we ask him for supplies in return for keeping his family safe. They need to eat, too, after all. And we tell him that the witch is dead, and so we serve all traitors." We all raised our chins. "Do we have a herald?"

Glyn started to put forward suitable names of people who were alive, on their feet, and spoke the Jarnish language. It wasn't a long list at all. I stopped listening. It was still a question of when we were going to die. I couldn't even see a way of avoiding taking the kingdom down with us. The discussion swirled about me like a fog as they thought out loud. I tried to concentrate, but I could feel my eyes closing.

"We need a miracle," said Galba, summing up. "We'll keep going until one happens." He then assigned us a sector of the city each, and work that needed doing. "But get your wounds seen to and sleep first, Sulien," he said.

I agreed, but as soon as he left the room Glyn dragged me off to bless the poisoned well.

"I know it's raining, but the sooner we have a good water source the better," he said.

I remembered the words. I opened my heart to the Mother and addressed her as Garah did, as Coventina, the leaf that floats on the forest pool, Lady of Good Waters. There was a loud gurgling sound and the well shot up high, soaking the courtyard, then settled back. Glyn sent down a bucket.

"It's sweet," he said, tasting it cautiously. I felt curiously more cheerful myself.

"Good that someone's on our side," I said.

"And good that some people are still teaching their children the old ways," he said. "That's a woman's blessing. I never learned it."

"I had it from Garah. She uses it to bless muddy ditches when we need water, and it always works. She's a marvel. I do hope she makes it through."

Glyn raised his chin soberly. Though we didn't say anything, we were counting days and food in our head. We had heard the good news that Sweyn had agreed not to attack that day if he could see his wife alive, which was done.

I sat down in the praetorium and went to sleep, knowing Galba would not relax the guard just because we had a truce. Visions of the battle spun in my head, but I kept on counting days and food. To get that twenty days, Glyn must have been counting on eating the horses. We needed a miracle.

The way people tell it now, they say that the miracle was there when we woke the next morning, men sprung from the ground as corn from seed. The timing was not quite as good as that. It was three more difficult days before we saw that incredible army. They passed uncomfortably. Sweyn attacked, feinted, made brief truces, tried to take the city by the secret way, pushed hard at the gate and once almost succeeded in scaling the walls. On the fourth day of the siege Galba came and woke me at dawn.

"Come and see," he said. I came, rubbing the sleep from my eyes. I had slept in my leather armor. I wanted hot water and hot food. On the plain before Sweyn's army stood a host of a size I had never imagined. In the center flew the banners of the ala of Caer Gloran, along with Angas's own banner, the thorn of Demedia, the single great purple silk royal banner of the High King of Tir Tanagiri, the red-and-green kingdom banner and, just catching the light, Urdo's own personal banner, the gold running horse on white and green. So many times I had charged beneath that banner. I felt tears prick in my eyes to see it again. He had come. This sight would have gladdened my heart, but far stranger was what stood to left and right of the ala.

It seemed to all the world an army raised from the warriors of Tir Tanagiri who had been here before the Vincans came. I had no idea how Urdo had raised the dead to come and rescue us, but there they were in great numbers, long beards, blue-painted faces, and arms with swirling black-and-white battle designs. They had little round shields with more such designs on. They had only one banner, though many of them flew it, a blue background with a black naked man. I had never seen it before. They were armed with short stabbing spears, and some of them even had swords. The wonderful thing about them was that there were so many of them they covered the whole area where we had rallied and fought three days before. In the bare space between the two armies Raul was meeting the envoys of King Sweyn.

Nobody fought at all that day. It was noon before they had an agreement anyone bothered to tell us about. I would have stayed on the wall all that time if Glyn hadn't dragged me off to eat. We had no idea what anyone was saying. Galba brought Sweyn's wife and daughter onto the walls so that they could both witness and be seen to be alive. He also had them bring the boy. I did not know his name then, but I will give it here— Morthu ap Talorgen, of Angas. Sweyn's wife was a cheerful brave woman called Gerda, who did much to keep the prisoners content and felt great faith in Sweyn. I liked her, even though I suspected her of indicating more to Sweyn than the fact of her health and presence. She looked exactly like a Jarnish woman should with long, plaited, straw-colored hair and a broad bosom. This was because she was nursing the baby, though she never did it where anyone could see, being very body-shy.

When the agreement was made, two heralds rode up to us. One was Angas, and the other was one of the same men Sweyn had used for his embassy to us before. They explained that we were to open the gates and ride out, then all of us were to leave Tevin to Sweyn. The prisoners were to be left inside, unharmed. The herald was to enter the fortress and see that everything was done according to form.

"Where is my mother?" asked Angas.

"Dead by the sword, the day we retook the fortress," said Galba, smoothly. It is hard to tell from above when a man is wearing a helmet, but it seemed to me that Angas looked relieved.

"Then bring my brother out to me when you come," he said.

We made a brave show as we rode out, but the effect was spoiled by the shortage of horses. Morthu had to be tied to a horse behind Glyn, as he refused to go willingly. Most of us were wounded, and none of us were very clean.

Galba led the way with half a pennon in as good shape as he could muster. Then followed the wounded and those without horses. We had burned those of our dead who fell in the fortress. The rest of us brought up the rear in marching pennon order. We could have fought if we needed to, and it was good to let the Jarns know it. They drew aside for us as we passed in deep uneasy silence. We could hear every rustle and every footfall of our passing. It made me edgy. I looked straight ahead of me and ignored them as much as I could as I led my pennon through them.

As we came up to the ala of Caer Gloran they parted for us and raised a great cheer, which was echoed by the blue foot warriors on either side. I wept to hear it, and Beauty began to pick up his feet high, as he always did when he heard cheering. I suppose Morwen must have taught him.

Urdo came forward and embraced Galba, bringing up spare horses for us all. Then he embraced me, before the other decurios. "Sweyn tells me you are a female demon out of his legends," he said to me. "Well done, Sulien ap Gwien, it was all very well done."

"How did you get here so fast?" I asked. "And how did you raise the ghosts?" Urdo smiled.

"Morwen wrote to her son Gwyn of Angas to tell him his father was dead and what her plans were, at least as far as telling him to be ready to attack me. The moment he had the letter he raised the ala of Caer Gloran and rode to Caer Tanaga to let know me. Such loyalty delights me, and has saved us all." We were standing in a crowd, and Angas was near enough to hear. He blushed. "It happened that I had an Isarnagan ambassador there that day, urging an alliance on me as some wars of theirs had recently ended." Urdo smiled. "We had to move very fast, but I got them to bring troops up the coast by ship, while we rode up. I sent to Gwair to bring the ala of Caer Thanbard to Caer Tanaga in case of trouble there. We did it all in eight days from when Angas reached me." The cheering broke out again.

"It's wonderful," I said.

"Now we ride to Tinala," he said. "The great war is beginning, and there is a great chance for peace on the other side of it."

"And the Isarnagans?" ap Erbin asked, as Urdo embraced him in his turn.

"It was an emergency," said Urdo, smiling. "I got married."

—16—

Those who went to Caer Lind were battle-ready
a power of horses, blue armor, shields,
lances held high, shining spear blades,
of mail there was no shortage, nor any weapon.
So long to grieve, those left behind them,
the great deeds done to be remembered
Those who went to Caer Lind, shouting for battle,
green mead was their drink, bitter the aftertaste,

a hundred warriors, fell-armed, fallen
and after exultation, there was silence.
        —Aneirin ap Erbin, "Caer Lind"

W hen I woke, Garah was there, cleaning my face with a warm cloth,
      and muttering under her breath.

"You could have some consideration for other people. Honestly, Sulien!
You let it dry on like this and how am I ever going to get it off again?"

"Hello," I croaked. For a moment I didn't know where I was. I was
lying on straw in a tent, not my tent. By the light it was afternoon. The tent
was empty except for my armor, piled on a stool, and a heavy ironbound
chest. Then I remembered. Apple dead. Osvran dead. Geiran, and Morwen, and Indeg, and Bran . . . —I felt sick briefly, so many gone. But Garah
and I were alive, and here. I took a steadying breath. "When did you get
back? Where are we?"

"We're outside Caer Avroc, and I came up with King Cinon and ap
Meneth and the ala of Caer Rangor this morning." She dipped the rag and
scrubbed at my face. It stung a little.

"Did you get all the way to Caer Rangor?"

"Oh yes. I found the remains of Borthas's army before I got back here.
It was easy to spot by the crows. I could see he wasn't going to be coming
to help you. I went forward slowly and almost ran into the other Jarnish
army, the one from Bereich besieging Caer Avroc. So I started making for
Caer Tanaga like you said, except that I thought any help I could get would
be too late, so I went by way of Caer Rangor." She paused to rub hard at
my cheek. It hurt. "I think you really do have a scrape here, it's not just
dried-on blood."

"I don't remember hurting it."

Garah laughed. "You never do. You're not really hurt. Some spectacular bruises, though." One of them was under her hand. I winced. "Raul
and a doctor had a look at you when you didn't want to wake up and they
said it was nothing serious. There were so many wounded who were serious that you haven't really been cleaned up. I think some of them were too
afraid of you. You do look a sight. What have you done to your hair? And
I hope you're going to help me sand that armor because nothing else will
ever get it clean. Glyn wouldn't let me touch it, he said you seemed to want
it like that, but that's ridiculous."

"Cut my hair off with my sword," I muttered, then I realized how
good it was to be alive and have her scolding me. I lay there a moment

without speaking while a tear of relief ran down my face. "Of course I'll help you clean the armor," I said, my voice catching in my throat. "As soon as I get up. Have I slept all through the day? I suppose I was awfully tired."

"I'm not surprised. And you've slept for nearly two days. You've woken up enough to stagger to the latrine a few times, so they knew you weren't really dazed. They moved you on the wagons with the wounded because you wouldn't wake up enough to talk coherently, Glyn said." I didn't remember at all.

I sat up. I felt stiff and awkward, as if I had had a fever that was just leaving me. My bruises and scrapes screamed in protest as I moved, and my knees ached. "Where are the latrines anyway?"

"We're in camp. You've already proved you can find them in your sleep." I giggled, and proved her right. I came back in after a few minutes, yawning.

"I'm hungry. Do you think there'll be anything to eat? What's happening? Everyone was rushing about. Where's Fourth Pennon?" I had only vaguely recognized faces.

"Let me finish cleaning your face first. Nearly done, and you shouldn't really eat with it like that. Sit down again." I sat down gingerly on the edge of the straw. "There's only the one scrape on it, I think. All the rest of this blood is just dried on and then forgotten about. That's the last time I ever go off and leave you to fight a battle." She picked up the cloth again.

"No it isn't," I said. "You're not my servant, Garah, you're a member of the ala. A valuable member of the ala. You did exactly what you should have done, you followed orders and went for help. You might have saved all our lives. Thank you."

"I don't quite see why everyone's making so much fuss about it." She shifted her shoulders uncomfortably. "I didn't do anything. By the time I persuaded King Cinon and ap Meneth to move the messenger from Urdo had almost reached Caer Rangor. He met us less than a day up the road. Just as well, really, or we'd have gone to Caer Lind."

She said this so calmly it took me a moment to really take it in. "You managed to persuade them to bring the whole ala? That's who we're camped with now?"

"It was an emergency."

"It was indeed. I never thought of that. It would have worked, too." I was counting days in my head. If she had got here this morning and I had slept a night and a day she would have brought them to Caer Lind by last night. They would have been in time. That would have been before we had to start eating the horses. Caer Rangor had never crossed my mind once as a source of help. I'd forgotten it existed. "Why Garah! Garah—if you were in my line of command, I'd promote you."

"Too late. I have done it already." The doorway darkened as Urdo came in. He was wearing full riding armor, and his helmet was on his arm. "She belongs to Derwen and to your family no more. Garah ap Gavan is sworn to me as armiger in her own right. She may not have the weight to wield a lance in the line, but she has already given me such service as I will never forget." Garah blushed, and I stood up and hugged her.

"It was just lucky that ap Cathvan was there and knew me," she muttered. Urdo was beaming. He looked at her as if she were a new trained horse who had just done an exercise perfectly.

"At last I have people around me who will do what is necessary," he said, stressing the last four words. "Between Angas and you two what could have been the defeat of all my hopes has become the beginning of the long road to victory." I had never seen him look so happy.

"So what next?" I asked.

"I heard word you were awake, so I came to ask if you are well enough to ride? The army of Bereich is drawn up outside Caer Avroc. Flavien ap Borthas is holding out inside. Angas's ala is getting ready, and ap Meneth's ala is getting ready, and the allied Isarnagan foot soldiers are getting ready, and I have come to ask you if you are well enough to ride as signifer for my ala."

"She wouldn't say no to that if she were at death's own gate, and you know it," said Garah, before I had even opened my mouth to say that I would do it if I had to ride through all the hosts of Jarnholme to do it. I laughed at the two of them.

"I am fit to ride, and I would be honored to ride as signifer." I said. "Raul has looked at me and seen that my injuries weren't serious, you told me so yourself, Garah. I was just tired. It would be better if I could eat something first."

"There might be time for some gruel if you are quick," Urdo said.

"I'll get it," said Garah, sighing. I looked down at myself. I was wearing someone's brown-wool shift. It was too short for me. My sword leaned on the side of the stool, on top of it my armor lay, in a pile. I had not really looked at it while I had been wearing it. My shield looked as if some great monster had been chewing on it. As for the rest, Garah was right about the sand. I shrugged off the shift and reached out for it reluctantly.

"See if this fits," said Urdo, looking shyly proud as he did when he made someone a gift. He opened the chest and lifted out some armor. I blinked. It was leather set with metal plates, far finer than in my armor, or even Angas's enameled armor. These plates were polished so that they might almost have been silver like the scales of a great fish. There were strange hair-fine curling designs inscribed on them, dragons and serpents and strange beasts. It looked as if it had been made for a woman my height. "When my grandfather Emrys returned from the land of the giants, he brought one of the giants with him, as well as the giant horses whose descendants we ride today. The giant was a woman called Larr. The armor was hers. It has been in a chest in Caer Segant for the last fifty years or so. My mother Rowanna found it there and sent it to me, thinking it might fit you. The leather has been well cared for, and this is close to the pattern of all the armor we use today to fight on horseback, as you can see."

I took it from him. "My thanks, lord. I am honored. And I think it will fit." I was awed. It was armor that might have been forged on the anvil of Govannen the Smith in the morning of the world.

"I don't think she can have been such a giant as all that, then," Urdo said. I began to put it on, carefully joining the beautiful tooled leather and brass connections, smelling the leather and fresh oil.

"Perhaps that's why she left with your grandfather. Perhaps she was as a dwarf in the land of giants. If they were all so big that our great horses were like ponies to them?" Urdo made an adjustment to the back and I pulled what was left of my hair out of the way. It fitted as if it had been made for me.

"Well, records are terrible for that time when the Vincans were leaving," he said. "Fascinating as it is. All I know about her is that her name was Larr and she came back with the horses after his famous voyage, and she died in one of the battles my grandfather fought when he made himself High King. She must have been wearing her second-best armor at the time." Garah came back in with the gruel, and gasped at the sight of the armor. Her eyes widened as Urdo stepped out from behind me to look at the effect.

"Yes, a very good fit," he said. I couldn't speak.

"Well it's clean anyway," Garah said. I took the hot gruel and swallowed greedily from the bowl. It was marvelous.

"We're very lucky all the horses didn't get killed in those battles," Urdo went on, pensively, turning my new helmet over in his hands. "There weren't all that many of them then, you know, not really enough for a proper charge. They could all have been lost if not for the monks deciding to breed them. I give thanks to Horse Mother and to the Lord of Moderation for Thansethan."

"You do what!" I turned to him laughing and took the helmet. "Do they know? Father Gerthmol would turn blue and die." Urdo laughed his deep laugh.

"I haven't mentioned it to him," he said. "He did his best to bring me up to be a good worshiper of the White God, and I am, in my way. But the land will speak to the lord, as they say. Anyway, you look magnificent, the very thing to put fear into the Jarns. Are we ready?" I tightened the buckles and set my helmet on my head. I bent for Garah to straighten the crest, then she handed me the pennon banner and the golden charge banner with a proud smile. Urdo set his helmet on his head and we strode out to lead one more charge.

It was a hard-won fight, especially where the king and his house lords held the field. We beat them, but by the truce terms the people of Bereich kept control of all the northern hills of Tinala.

After the battle Angas came up to me in the bathhouse. He had cut off his hair, the way I had, though his was cut all in one line. The heating system for the baths of Caer Avroc was long since broken, but the clean cold water felt very good to me that day.

Angas came right up beside me as I stood under the falling water and spoke very low, so that I could hardly hear him and there was no chance of our being overheard. "I have to know what happened with my mother." I would have spoken but he held up his hand. "I've spoken to Galba, and I've spoken to my brother Morthu, and they tell me completely different things. I won't pursue a bloodfeud. Whatever you and ap Erbin did there's no question she deserved to die. She was mad. She was an oracle, you know, and they are often driven mad by seeing the future and then not seeing it. I think she didn't expect my father's death, and it drove her mad and then to this treachery."

"How did he die?" I asked, really not wanting to say anything about how long she had been mad and treacherous. She was dead. It was for Urdo to say if it needed to be said.

"A boar who was stronger than he was made it up his spear." Angas smiled grimly. "Not an unfitting death. He always enjoyed the hunt. But my mother—even apart from her outright treachery in raising arms with the enemies of Urdo, she killed Osvran, who was my foster brother and her guest-friend. I am grateful to you for making it easier for me in that she is dead already. The law in Demedia would have had her whipped around a birch tree for that. Even by Vincan law she had earned death. But I am Lord of Angas now, and King of Demedia when I go home, which I must do as soon as I can. I will always be your friend, no matter. But I have to know if it would be wrong for me in the eyes of the Mother to break bread with you."

"I don't know," I said, and shrugged, stepping out of the water and wrapping myself in a towel. I sat down on the step beside it, and Angas sat down next to me, the cold water lapped our feet. I spoke quietly in the water's sound shadow.

"She admitted treachery, and she admitted murdering Osvran." Angas's face twisted a moment in pain. "Geiran struck her, with her hand, for an insult to Osvran's memory. You don't want to know. I'd have done the same if I'd been closer. She then released a sorcerous fire which burned Geiran, killing her. Geiran touched her, and she began to burn herself. It looked to me as if she had not the power to control the fire. She was burning up in the fire and dying. She may have been dead by the time my sword touched her, I think so. My sword and ap Erbin's are marked by the blaze and have had a strange blue shine to them since. But if intention counts then I would have killed her, if she had still been alive. I wanted to bring her back for trial, but I was angry. Geiran was my sequifer."

"I hate all this," Angas said. "If you had killed her it would have been just. That is what I told Morthu. He's very young and he adored her. It's hard for him. It will be hard to tell my sisters. But if that's the way of it, then by my thinking she died by her own hand, and you and ap Erbin are guiltless even of the action. So I will ask you both to sit with me and Eirann at the feast tonight, as a sign that there is nothing to forgive."

"Of course I will. I'm just relieved that's how you want to look at it."

"So am I," said Angas, wryly. "But if she went mad before she died better to forget as much of it as possible, I think. That was Eirann's advice."

"Eirann's here then?" Angas stood and pulled me to my feet.

"Yes, and our baby son. We're on our way to Dun Idyn." We walked through the baths and back to the changing room, which was warmed by a cheerful iron stove. "Stopping here and at Caer Lind to fight can be seen as just pauses on the journey. I have to take oath as king, and marry the land in the old way. Eirann doesn't like that, but there's no chance of turning the whole of Demedia to the White God in my reign; these things take time. Even Custennin didn't have it altogether easy in his conversion, and he was king already and most of the land gods and almost all the people were in favor. Which reminds me, have you heard that Custennin has an heir at last? His wife has had another baby, at the age of forty-five. They're saying it's a miracle and calling it Gorai, after the apostle of the White God."

"I'm glad you're going with tradition and the proper way of doing things," I said. Angas snorted. He reached into a sack that was underneath his pile of clothes and brought out a leather flask that sloshed.

"Did you know they call your mother the last of the Vincans?" he asked. I did. There was a great deal of truth in it. He drank from the flask and passed it to me. "They don't mean any harm by it. They like her. I like her. She was splendid when our baby was born. She's really doing well organizing the town at Derwen, too. The place is thriving."

"I'm glad to hear it. Did Galba tell you he's going to have a whole ala down there?" I drank, and blinked. It was good strong mead from the west.

"Now? I doubt it. Urdo's going to need to keep us very mobile. This is a real war we have coming, not just some cattle raid. We won't have the Isarnagans forever, and they'll need paying." He looked somber, and I passed him back the mead.

"You don't think it was a good idea?" I asked. I finished drying myself and began to dress.

"What else could Urdo have done? He really needed them just then. I'm afraid he may regret it later. It was lucky in some ways. Their ambassador was there, offering an alliance. A great big war in Tir Isarnagiri has just finished, and the princess's betrothed was killed in it by Black Darag, one of their maniac berserkers, leaving her conveniently free."

I pulled my cloak on, and took another pull of mead. "Will I see her at the feast? I expected to see her on the field."

"She's in Caer Tanaga. And I don't think you'll see her on any battlefields." Angas reclaimed the leather flask and took a hefty swig. "She's strictly the decorative type of woman from what I've seen of her. She came with a bard's song saying she's one of the Three Most Beautiful Women in the Island of Tir Isarnagiri. An extremely pretty face, and good hips as well, as Thurrig would say." He settled his white praefecto's cloak on his shoulders, twitching it so the oak leaves were straight.

"I thought she was a warrior?" I stood up, confused, as we made our way out of the bathhouse.

"I don't know where you heard that. She's only sixteen or seventeen. Very odd for her if you think about it. Her betrothed killed in battle and apparently at one point her mother was offering her to anyone who could kill Black Darag. Only nobody could. Then suddenly she's whisked over here, married to Urdo, he spends the ritual night with her, and at dawn he's away off up here to fight. All of it absolutely necessary and the least much that would do, and I expect she's been brought up to expect it. All the same I'm ever so glad I had longer to make friends with Eirann than that."

"Who is she then? You've just saved me from another famous howler. I sort of assumed he'd married Atha ap Gren. That's who everyone's always mentioned in terms of an Isarnagan alliance. But I know she's a warrior. There are songs about her."

Angas laughed. "Well that's saved you very narrowly from making one of the Three Most Tactless Blunders of Sulien ap Gwien—so sorry, I mean of the Island of Tir Tanagiri." I poked him. "That would not have gone down well if you'd said that in front of any of our painted friends. Atha ap Gren is married to Black Darag, since last year. We've allied with the other side. The new High Queen of Tir Tanagiri is Elenn ap Allel and don't forget it."

We came out onto the street laughing together and almost immediately saw Rheneth ap Borthas. She was wearing a dark overdress and had her hair loose around her head in the Tanagan mourning custom. It made her look older, but also more dignified. She was, after all, a woman over forty, twice a widow, not a young girl. Her eyes were red and swollen and there were tracks of tears on her face. I felt real pity for her. Although I had not liked her brother I knew she had been close to him. I hated to think that he had been killed by Morwen and almost certainly lay unburied. Not even Borthas deserved to have his soul eaten. If I had been alone, I think I would have stopped and given her my sympathy. As it was Angas slackened his pace when he saw her, but she almost ran up to us as if she feared we would flee her.

"Laughing, are you?" she said. "Traitor. When your own mother opened the gates to them. You Angarides have always hated us. My brother shouldn't let you inside the city walls in case you do the same." I was completely taken aback by her outburst. Angas stood still, rocking back a little on his heels as if struck.

"The High King knows well that Gwyn of Angas has been loyal to him above loyalty to his own family," I said.

"What do I care about that half-breed coward Urdo," she hissed at me. "Oh you think yourself so wonderful with your horses, but whose land have you been giving away to the barbarians today? A pox on the whole house of Emrys. My brother held Tinala whole for more than twenty years, three reigns. No matter what anyone did, he held the land that's always been in our family. Always, since before the Vincans came. Nobody cares about land anymore, except us in Tinala. I hate you all. Thank Riganna Flavien survived. I'll see you all eaten by serpents before you get any help from me." She spat suddenly, on Angas's beard, then ran off quickly down the street.

Angas wiped his face and stared after her.

"She's been drinking," I said.

"Oh yes. That doesn't mean she doesn't mean it. Borthas never was a friend to Urdo. Well, he's paid for it. But that did seem rather excessive. All the same it's impossible to answer. Borthas did hold the land, and we have given some of it away. And my mother was a traitor. I do hope everyone isn't thinking that about me underneath." Angas leaned back on the wall and began to laugh. "We have to go to a banquet and appear like reasonable people on good terms with each other when all that's seething below the surface. It was just like that when my mother's letter arrived, I felt as if I'd been handed a nest of snakes. Please don't go mad and start shouting abuse at me, Sulien."

"Of course not. Come on, get up, we really do have to go. Nobody will be thinking that about you, if they have half a brain. If you were a traitor, you'd have joined with her and the crows would be eating all our eyes this fine night."

"It's a horrible thing not to be trusted," he said. "I've never had a problem with it before, I always thought it was like Dalitus says, be trustworthy and you will be trusted, seek out associates that are trustworthy and you will not be betrayed. I always tried to do that, as much as I could, especially once I was an armiger. My father sent me as a hostage in a way, and Urdo treated me with such honor."

"Come on, Angas." I wanted to say that everyone trusted him, but it wasn't a time for comforting lies. "Anyone who doesn't trust you is an idiot. Urdo understands and trusts you, and all of us in the alae will stand with you. Anyone else will realize what that means."

"I am going to miss Osvran," he said quietly, standing up again.

"I am, too," I said. "Come on now." We walked off together down the street. "Oh and another thing. About the Three Most Tactless Blunders on the Island of Tir Tanagiri? I'd put what Rheneth ap Borthas said just then pretty high up among them."

It was a surprised laugh, but it was a real one. The feast was long. I caught some strange looks from Flavien ap Borthas and from King Cinon of Nene, and from some others. I hoped it was because of the colors the

bruises were turning my face. Afterwards Angas and I went off to Urdo's
big tent with Urdo and ap Erbin and Garah and Glyn and Galba and ap
Cathvan and drank up all the mead we could find in the camp. We talked
about Osvran and our other lost friends and drank until we had all laughed,
and all wept, and several of us had lost our dinners. I got to bed when the
sky was starting to pale and slept the day through again. When I woke I had
a headache, and I knew that Angas would already have left for Dun Idyn. I
remembered that Galba was going to lead his ala. Then I remembered that
I had promised Urdo that I would do my best to lead what was left of ours.

—17—

I trust you, don't you know,
(throw ball to next person in circle)
and I trust you, even so,
(bounce ball to next person in circle)
and I trust you, have a go,
(throw ball to next person in circle)
don't you trust me, no, no, no!
(throw or bounce ball to an unsuspecting player and run away.)
—Tanagan children's ball game

I couldn't make out all the words through the thick wooden door, but
Raul was shouting something about "Next year" and Urdo was roaring
something about the truce and the thaw. I backed slightly. Being a praefecto might give me the right to approach the High King without permission; it didn't necessarily give me the right to walk in on him when he and
his chief clerk were yelling at each other. Everyone knew Urdo and Raul
yelled at each other sometimes. They'd grown up together after all. Walking into the middle of it was another matter. After two months spent
mostly in the field pursuing Jarns who never stood to fight, I was still
uncomfortable with my new rights and status. Galba and I looked at each
other and took another two steps back up the hall.

"I think we should come back later," Galba whispered, and I assented
gratefully.

"If you do that you'll find you're feeding them on grass, and then see
how they fight!" shouted Raul, storming out through the door. He almost

tripped over us. He looked absolutely furious, and his glance at me would have curdled fresh milk. "Excuse me," he said, with clearly strained politeness. We leapt aside and he brushed past us. We looked at each other again, uneasily. I felt twelve years old.

"You may as well come in, whoever you are," Urdo said. We went in. Urdo's hair was sticking up all over as if he had just been running his hands through it. The heaped-up pile of writing tablets and parchments on his table seemed higher than ever. On the top was a map of the north with new lines drawn on it in black ink. He looked at us with an expression which looked as if he was trying to pull together the tattered edges of patience. "Yes?"

"It's not a good time," Galba said. "It isn't urgent. We'll come back." Urdo sighed, and ran his hands through his hair again, smoothing it down.

"It's not going to be a good time for quite a long time, so you may as well tell me now."

Galba shifted his feet and took a deep breath. "I'm supposed to go to Derwen and get married. You said—"

"What, now?" Urdo's voice rose, then he suddenly laughed. "Well, yes, now. You've been planning it for years, haven't you, and I'm in no position to complain about getting married in the middle of a war. Derwen. Yes." He glanced at the map, saw it was the wrong one, and started to reach for another from underneath. I leapt forward to catch the pile as it slithered inexorably towards the floor.

"It'll take about half a month to get there, and then about the same to get back," I said, straightening most of the pile and sliding it back onto the table. Urdo's eyes were shut. I picked up the map and a scraper and put them on the top. I bent down again to pick up the rest. I picked up a slate covered in the drearily familiar calculations of the arcane art of logistics, chalked and erased and redone so that the slate was ghostly white. I put it down very carefully.

"Somebody needs to be down there anyway," he said, opening his eyes one at a time and looking at Galba. "Take the recruit pennon. Take both recruit pennons. Go by way of Caer Gloran. Make sure there's a pennon there. Tell Amala and—and—whoever Angas left in charge of whatever troops are there that you're in charge there now. Then head down to Magor and Derwen, get married, and send me back three good war-ready pennons. Send them to Caer Tanaga, I'll be there by the time they get there. You'll have a whole ala, counting the recruits, and you'll have a chance to train them up."

"I'm to stay down there, then?" asked Galba, looking worried. I put the green-and-brown stylus Urdo had said was made of the shell of a Lossian creature on the table and stepped away from it. The pile looked as if it was about to slip again at a breath. I held mine and backed away.

"Yes. For this year at least. Marchel won't like it, but you've a family claim, too. She's going to be coming up here in any case. If you're going to marry, you ought to have a little time at least somewhere near your wife. I'm not completely stripping the south and west, but the troops are going to be needed along the Jarnish line whether Raul likes it or not. You'll have one ala there, there'll be another at Caer Thanbard, and that'll be it. We have to stay mobile. The Jarns have to think we're everywhere. If I really need everyone who can ride I'll summon you back." Galba's face cleared a little at this. Poor Galba. I was glad I wasn't going to be stuck down in Magor while the war was all happening miles away. That was for those too old to fight full-time. "You should be able to hold that whole area against anything that's likely to come up against you. If you really need help— which means if you're invaded, which could happen—hold on, send to me, and I'll get it to you from somewhere. Cooperate with your father, with Gwien ap Nuden, and with old Uthbad One-Hand at Talgarth. They'll supply you as much as they can. Have you written to Uthbad, Sulien?" His glance swung round to me.

"Why?" I asked, and then I remembered. Uthbad, the Lord of Tathal, was Enid's father. "No, I haven't. I didn't think. I wrote to Larig."

"Well copy it out and send it to Uthbad, too, and give the letter to Galba to deliver. Give him my regrets, too. Tell him I liked Enid, she saved my life once. She'll be much missed."

"Of course. Would you mind telling my mother I can't go, though?" Urdo looked at me as if I'd started to whinny instead of speaking Tanagan. I changed feet, uncomfortable. "My mother's very insistent I go to Galba's wedding. He's marrying my sister. I thought if you explained that 'in the circumstances' doesn't just mean that Galba and I used to be betrothed and I changed my mind but the fact that the land's at war and I'm needed, she might understand. You have met my mother," I added. Urdo raised an eyebrow.

"You can go," he said. "Half a month there, and then six or seven days to Caer Tanaga, you'll be there nearly as soon as I will. I'll take the ala down, don't worry. It'll make it easier in a way because you can bring the pennons back with you."

"I don't mind not going," I said, hastily. Urdo laughed.

"I can tell. But if you're not afraid to charge the might of Jarnholme uphill and almost single-handed, it's about time you stopped being afraid of your mother. It'll probably do both of you good to see you've grown up. Which you have, Sulien, and don't forget it. We have a truce for the time being. There won't be any fighting until the thaw. I don't think the White God himself knows when next this will be the case. I can spare you, briefly. Oh, and call at Caer Rangor and tell ap Cathvan that I don't care whether he's been kicked by a mare he should make his way to Caer Tanaga to be there when I get there. I need him. Tell him I don't expect him to be up to training horses, I do expect his mouth to be working. He knows the horses better than anyone. Make sure he's sitting down before you talk about the Isarnagans, though. I'd hate to hear he'd expired of joy." We laughed, and laughing he accepted Galba's thanks and gave him his blessing. We left him to his work.

It was bitterly cold and frosty when we set off south. We rode out of Caer Avroc in a mist of our own breath and the horses' breath. The ground was hard as stone. We stopped one night in Caer Rangor and one night in Caer Gloran. The other nights along the way we camped to give the pennons practice at making and breaking camps, cold camps, camps with fire, and night camps. Galba and I took a pennon each and raced each other, practiced tracking each other and pacing each other. We took turns going cross-country. The recruits were more than half-trained already and merely needed a lot more work, especially at charges and close-order discipline. They learned quite a lot before we reached Talgarth, though we didn't have to fight at all. I quite enjoyed the journey. I think the recruits did, too, for all that they raised the usual loud groans and complaints whenever they thought we were out of earshot.

We reached Derwen the day before the full moon, the day before the wedding. We made the best procession we could, coming up. Galba led with one pennon, and I brought up the rear with the other.

I hardly recognized my home. It had developed wharves on the river and a town wall all around. There was a forge, and a mill upstream, merrily turning. The house had been restored and looked larger than it had been, with a much larger stable, two blocks, big enough for three pennons. Outside the house a gaily striped yellow-and-white awning had been spread and pegged like half a tent. The winter sun shone on it and through it. The place looked almost like a Vincan town, though half of it was built of wood instead of stone. People came running up to us as the trumpeter blew a blast when we approached. I didn't recognize any of them.

We dismounted at the house and grooms came up to take our horses. I did recognize some of the grooms, but only some of them. I'd have liked to take Beauty myself, but it didn't seem courteous. Emlin came up and greeted me, then took charge of the pennons.

I went forward behind Galba to greet my family as they came out. We embraced, formally. Veniva looked thinner than ever, and there was no black left in her hair. It was twisted up tightly and held by the gold comb from the hoard. Her embrace was stiff. Gwien was still using a stick to walk but apart from that he looked well. He smiled as if he were truly glad to see me. Morien had all the growth he would ever have, though he was still shorter than I. He had not yet filled out to fit his bones and looked stretched and gangling. I hoped Galba would soon give him a good training as an armiger and help him build up his strength.

Aurien, however, looked beautiful. She was wearing the traditional orange overdress of a bride, fastened with her pearl brooch, over a long white shift, and her thick black hair was piled up on the top of her head. She was not yet at her full height, but it was clear that she would be tall and slim like Veniva. Also like Veniva, she looked regal. I have never understood Aurien. She gave up learning to fight as soon as she could defend herself at minimum competence. She never liked horses, and as soon as she could stay on one she gave up bothering with them. Even as a little girl she loved to do accounts and household management, and she could sew a seam that stayed straight for a mile or embroider a flower in four colors. She could draw, too, and read Veniva's improving books with an appearance of enthusiasm I'd never been able to summon. Now she was being married at the youngest possible age to a man ten years older. She had only met him twice, but she appeared to be thrilled at the prospect. It was fortunate for me that she was.

We embraced briefly and formally. Then I stepped aside and presented Galba to her. I realized a moment later that I should have left it for his father to do, but nobody noticed. Galba clasped both her hands and said a few formal phrases, then he embraced her decorously and whispered something in her ear that made her giggle. He looked very pleased indeed, and so did the old duke as he came up to greet me. Then I greeted Duke Galba and old Uthbad and his wife Idrien. They all three looked much older than when I had last seen them. Enid's death had been hard on them. They presented their two remaining children to me, Cinvar, the heir, and their other daughter, Kerys. We bowed politely. When this flurry was over Veniva announced that the wedding would take place at sunrise the next day and all were welcome to witness, and we all went inside.

The stone walls of the hall were hung with bright-colored tapestries. I regretted the old familiar ones, but was impressed how much had been done in so short a time. The carpenter Urdo sent must have been good, for there were wooden window boxes and strong shutters on all the windows. I went over and looked out. I could see the wharf below. People were unloading bales of linen and strong hemp-cloth from a cart into a warehouse just uphill. The place was bustling even though it was midwinter.

A servant came up to me with a steaming pottery beaker, which I accepted gratefully. He then offered me salted bread, and I realized he must have taken me for a stranger. I stared at him for a moment, taking in his green tunic, his plaited hair, the pebble around his neck. He must have thought me some soldier companion of Galba's, needing to be given the hospitality token. We had kept no such custom when I lived at home, any breaking bread with the family would be real and immediate. But then strangers were few at Derwen when I was growing up. I hesitated. I was in my father's house. In days gone by, I could have killed him for this insult. Even now if I did not keep the King's Peace I could offer challenge and take him outside to fight, though it would be as good as murder to do so. He did not know me. I tugged on my white praefecto's cloak, straightening it to make sure he saw the gold oak leaves, and his face did not change, though his smile was growing more forced. I did not believe my parents were casting me out. If they had wished to greet me as a stranger they would not have embraced me as kin outside. Where had this smugly smiling servant been then? In here heating the drink very probably.

I took the bread in my hand. If he had the right to offer it then I must take it or leave, no excuses, no other choices. Once he had offered it I could not speak, except the ritual words, anything else would be a rejection. All this rushed through my mind very fast. I truly meant no harm to any within and would keep the laws, and that was all this welcoming ritual meant. If I didn't know him then why should he know me? Any attention I drew would only make matters worse, and all my instinct was to have things go smoothly.

I bit into the bread. "Peace in this hall," I murmured.

"And a welcome to you who keep the peace within it," replied the servant. His expression now was one of intense relief. He cannot often have seen someone hesitate over accepting hospitality of the house, I thought. I wanted to laugh out loud.

"I am the eldest daughter of Gwien of Derwen," I said, and paused, politely, for him to tell me how he should be addressed. The blood left his face and he looked grey. The look on his face was as good as a picture. I took a sip of my drink to hide my smile. It was good spiced cider, ideal for a cold day. Just then, to my relief, my father came up to me.

"What are you doing, Dal?" he asked, sounding horrified. "This is no stranger; this is Sulien, my eldest child."

"Lord," he stammered. He tried to touch his hand to his head, but could not, because of the tray. He looked at me again, stricken. He either had really not known or he was a very good actor. "I beg pardon."

"He meant no harm, Father," I said. "It is a long time since I have been here." And in my heart it was not my home, my home was in the alae, looking forward between a horse's ears. I knew that then, but did not say it.

"Veniva will have your ears," Gwien said to him. "This is Daldaf ap Wyn, Sulien, your mother's steward. You will know each other again, no doubt." Daldaf blushed now. "Go on, take that cider round. Don't chatter about this mistake to the others." Daldaf bobbed his head and moved off with the tray. Gwien turned to me. "You're truly not angry, Sulien?"

"No," I said, and I was not.

"Let me tell Veniva about it then," he said. "It will have to be put the right way, or she might feel she had to send Dal off, and she has just got him trained to her ways. He is come out of the east and he is a great help to her now that the household has grown so."

"I was admiring how it has grown," I said, gesturing to take in the hall.

"I wanted to rebuild as a fortress," he said, "but Veniva wouldn't have it, it had to be Vincan style or nothing, 'our strength is not in stones but hearts,' you know her way. The walls are thick, though, and you will have noticed how the windows would give a good field to an archer?"

"I did indeed," I said. "But the next line of that is 'stone-strength shows how heart-strength holds,' and we need strong walls and strong hearts both, Urdo says."

Gwien beamed, straightened himself, and hugged me again. "I see by your cloak you're now a praefecto of the High King? When did this happen? You shouldn't have been away so long, Sulien, I've missed you. And you've grown taller than I am, I wouldn't have thought it." He seemed proud of it. The truth was that his back was a little bowed because of his injuries. We would have been eye to eye otherwise. But I didn't tell him so. I was very pleased to see him and to have him approve of me.

"I've missed you, too," I said. "But I have been so busy in the ala, Father, and I have enjoyed it so much. After Caer Lind Urdo has made me praefecto of his own ala."

"That's a great honor, wonderful thing," Gwien said, and clapped me on the back. "I always knew you'd do great things; Duncan and I used to say so when we saw you going at it with a sword when you were quite small, you and Darien." His face clouded, then he smiled again deliberately. "Sit down a minute and let me look at you, so tall and fine you are." We sat down together on the window seat. The shoulder piece of my armor caught the sunlight and blazed out. Gwien looked at it and said in quite a different tone. "Where ever did you find this, Sulien?"

"Urdo gave it to me. Isn't it splendid?"

"Is there a dragon on the other arm?" He looked, and there was. "You know, I think this is the very armor my mother used to wear. She was killed when I was just a little boy, but I remember her wearing this and showing me the pictures in it. I thought it had been lost with her."

"Urdo said it was in a chest in Caer Segant. He said the dowager Rowanna found it and thought it might fit me, and so he gave it to me after Caer Lind when I needed some new armor. He said they thought it belonged to a giant, but it could just as easily have belonged to my grandmother I suppose. How strange though."

"Not really, if it was size they were going by. There aren't many women big enough to wear this. It's beautifully made stuff, and I'm sure it's the same armor. Galba may remember it too. Galba! Come and have a look at this!" Duke Galba excused himself from a group that contained his son, Aurien, Veniva, and Idrien, and came over to us.

"You remember my mother, don't you Galba?" said Gwien. Duke Galba inclined his head.

"I was only ten or eleven when she died, but I do remember her," he said.

"Then look at this armor and see if it looks familiar." I stood and let the two old men look at it. I preferred the story about the giant in some ways. I tried to remember what I'd heard about my grandmother, other than that she'd been killed fighting in the civil wars. I couldn't even remember her name. I knew my male line ancestry, Gwien ap Nuden ap Iarn all the way back to Edwy who escaped the Flood with his eleven companions and was shipwrecked on our shore and married a woman made out of alder. They'd all had to make do with trees for wives and the trees were the only women's names I'd been made to learn. Duke Galba shook his head slowly.

"I think I do remember her wearing it. Well, well. Though it was all a long time ago. Getting on for fifty years. I wonder where Urdo got it from."

"From a chest in Caer Segant." I repeated the story. "The odd thing is that they didn't send it back here with her things, if it was hers."

"Things were very confused then," said Duke Galba, frowning at the memory. "In any case, if it was a royal gift, if it had belonged to someone from the land of giants before, perhaps Emrys took it back. I never knew her well, but wasn't she from Caer Segant? Maybe they gave it back to her family instead of to Nuden."

"I think she was a Vincan, but she'd certainly lived in Caer Segant, it's marked as her place of residence in the register when she married my father," said Gwien. "I don't know her father's name, she's just written down as Laris."

"Laris?" I said. I must have heard the name at some time because it was familiar, but it hadn't stayed in my mind. "Urdo said the giant was called Larr. She wasn't a giant, was she?"

Duke Galba laughed and looked deliberately upwards at me. "Your height on a woman would be enough to get called one, by sailors and farmers. Not a giant like in those Tanagan legends, big enough to wade the sea between here and Tir Isarnagiri, but maybe a giant like the ones Sextus Aquila mentions who live at the back of the North Wind. I can see why they said that in Caer Segant if the Emperor Emrys did indeed bring her back with the horses. Nuden married her when I was a child, and I don't remember any stories about who she was then, but then it wasn't the sort of story I listened to very closely in those days." The old man smiled.

"Well I never knew it if she was," said Gwien, smoothing a crease from the leather sleeve of my armor. "I thought you looked like my mother when I saw you riding up, and it's good to see her armor again."

"Giant's blood in my line, well," said Duke Galba, looking at Galba and Aurien, who were looking into each other's eyes. "I thought it was a magnificent gift when I first saw it, but this makes it even more special."

"Oh no," said Gwien, in a different tone. I looked at him. "Veniva's bringing out the musicians already." He sighed. "There will be dancing, I'm afraid, before we eat, and I shall have to stand with her." He limped off across the hall. I felt for him. He had loved dancing when I was a child.

"And now Sulien," said Duke Galba, "tell me what Urdo is going to do in Tinala?"

"You'll have to ask your son, I'm afraid," I said. "I'll have to change my clothes right away if there's going to be dancing."

It was an hour before I managed to get young Galba on his own, and then only in the middle of the dance floor. He had the dazed look of the newly in love, and he had hardly been three feet away from Aurien since we came inside. I had made my way through several dances already. I was pleased to see that people were more polite in how they issued invitations than they used to be when last I danced in my father's house.

"What's so important," Galba hissed as the line brought us together. "If there was an attack they'd have called."

"What's Urdo going to do about Tinala?" I asked him. He laughed, swinging me and catching me again.

"Who's asked you?"

"Your father and my mother and Duncan. I told them to ask you."

"Oh," He looked surprised and almost stopped backing. "It was your father and my aunt and Emlin who asked me."

"Well, what's the answer?" I called, catching Kerys ap Uthbad's hands, and spinning with her. She was wearing a very splendid overdress of red and gold.

"I told them to ask you," he said, and laughed again as we danced towards each other. "I told your father that Urdo isn't an idiot, and he said in that case he'd throw Flavien ap Borthas out and replace him with someone loyal. If it wasn't for that I thought they were worried about the Jarns." I had thought that myself.

"I didn't see any sign he was going to throw him out when we were there," I said, dancing away again. "And he hasn't done anything wrong."

"I don't know." He laughed again.

"Are you drunk, Galba?"

"Two beakers of hot cider, you can't call that drunk!" he said defensively. But I'd seen it before. He was drunk on the thought of Aurien. He was intoxicated over an arranged marriage that was just right for the families that he'd told me seriously only a month before that he was intending to make the best job he could of. I looked questioningly at him as we danced up to each other for the last time and touched hands. "If Urdo wants someone to reassure people politically down here, he should have sent Raul," he said, frowning. Then he bowed to me. The dance was over, and Aurien was waiting for him.

Duke Galba and Veniva both made for me as soon as I was alone. My mother reached me first, bearing down on me like a raider ship in full sail.

"Will the food be soon, Mother?" I asked. I was starting to feel really hungry. I also felt the need of a diversion. I looked for my father, but he was talking intently with Idrien of Talgarth. The light fell on her face from the side, and she looked much like Enid, except she had no scar.

"It won't be long, but never mind now," she said. "And I haven't come to ask you what you're doing dressing up as a Vincan senator—I suppose you have a right to those folds through my great-great-uncle, but I don't think you know it." She smiled a little grimly at my drape, which was folded the way I had been wearing it ever since Amala had shown me how. "I don't suppose anyone else recognizes it or cares. Quickly. Gwien tells me Galba said Urdo will depose Flavien ap Borthas, is it true?" We were standing near the musicians, and the sound of the lyres and horns shielded us from eavesdroppers.

Duke Galba reached us before I could speak, coming up very like a Vincan senator himself though he was wearing a usual tunic and leggings. "Tinala, child," he said, "my sister Idrien says my son doesn't know the High King's intentions, and it's important."

Looking from one face to the other, both so aristocratic in the Vincan model, I had no idea what to say. "Urdo's no fool, sir, Mother," I said, hoping it would work.

"Then he won't offend all the kings by throwing Flavien ap Borthas out?" said Duke Galba.

"Why would he?" I asked. Then I took a deep breath. If Urdo had wanted diplomacy, he'd have sent Raul. Very well, but I didn't think Urdo knew diplomacy was needed. "Look, to tell you both the plain truth, I have no idea what Urdo plans to do either. He told Galba to cooperate with both of you and with Uthbad One-Hand." Uthbad was dancing with Kerys now. His hair was still cut short for mourning. Seeing them together I saw the great resemblance between them; she was much more like him than either Cinvar or Enid. "He expects all-out complete war in the east with a chance to really win, to beat the Jarns, to make the peace."

"We all want peace for trade to flourish," said Veniva. "But more war first?" Behind her the servants were beginning to light the lamps. They were real Vincan oil lamps, not candles. I wondered in the back of my mind where they were getting the oil from. We were rarely so grand in Caer Tanaga.

"What news have you had of what happened in the north?" I asked.

"Very little," said Duke Galba. "That a great Jarnish army had invaded and Urdo has made a marriage and an Isarnagan alliance to beat them, and that he has beaten them indeed but allowed Borthas to be killed. That he has troops all over Caer Avroc."

"Beaten them would be a great exaggeration," I said ruefully. "We had a victory, but their army is still for the most part whole. As for Borthas, he was killed, yes, but it was not really our fault and most certainly not our design." I could see how it could be made to seem so. "We made a wrong guess, but we thought he was heading back to safety. We were almost killed, too. Our captain, Osvran, was killed. It's a long story. When I get back I will see to it that messengers send news regularly to all the kingdoms about how the war is going."

"That is a very good idea indeed," said Duke Galba. "Veniva raised her chin."

"There will be worse war than there has been, but mostly in the east, I think is what Urdo expects. The Jarns are a long way from beaten yet," I said.

"And what about Flavien ap Borthas?" asked Duke Galba.

"I don't know for sure, but I think if Urdo had been thinking about doing anything about Flavien ap Borthas or about Tinala other than defending it against the Jarns as well as he might, he'd have told us so we could reassure you. Why are you worried about it?" I was looking at Duke Galba, but it was Veniva who answered.

"He sent asking for help against Urdo," she said. "He sent to all the kings and all the lords, everywhere. He asked us to be ready to help him." The implication of this hit me rather thoroughly at once in the pit of my stomach.

"They'll think it's war." I realized I was reaching for my sword only when my hand jarred at my empty belt. Had Urdo possibly planned to remove Flavien? His father had been a traitor, but Borthas was dead. I thought of Urdo's table piled up with urgent things that needed doing. I thought of what he and Raul had been shouting at each other. "I am sure that is not what's in Urdo's mind," I said, as firmly as I could. "I spoke to Urdo just before we left, and everything he said was to do with moving troops to be ready when the truce ends with the Jarns. They are allied now, Sweyn and Ayl and Ohtar Bearsson of Bereich. Urdo's planning to go back down to Caer Tanaga soon, to be there by the time I get there. I don't think Tinala's in any danger from Urdo at all. But gods help us, Mother, he asked me to bring three pennons from here, and he is gathering in pennons from elsewhere to swell his alae. If Flavien has written to all the kings and then they see Urdo gathering in troops, what will they think? Will they take up arms against us?"

"Some will," said Veniva. "And whether Urdo fights them or not, then the Jarns will have us. It will all be the same as when Avren died."

"Only worse," said Duke Galba, looking grim. "I will send to all who trust me to tell them Urdo is no fool and will not do it, on your word Sulien. I would have sent Flavien no help in any event, but there are many who would."

"What gods do they want to rule in this land!" I said, forgetting to be quiet. People turned and looked, and then looked away. Galba and Emlin took a step towards me, then stopped as I waved them away. "Yes, what gods?" I asked again, quieter, a thought coming to me. "Who benefits most from this? Maybe it was not Flavien who sent the message. He may be a fool and afraid, and surely his sister is angry with Urdo, but would he be such a fool as to do that unprovoked? Maybe. But maybe it was Sweyn who sent. Did you know the messenger?" Duke Galba shook his head.

"She was a woman of the north," he said. "She had the accent and the look of Tinala."

"Or Tevin?" I asked. He drew in a sudden breath.

"When we have eaten, let us all sit down and talk and see exactly what we know," said Veniva, decisively. "After that there will be time for sending messengers when we know exactly what we want to say and who to say it to. It must be half a month since you left Caer Avroc. Who knows what might have happened."

"I have got to get back to Urdo. I have to take the ala to him. You can do better than I can to calm fears of allied kings."

"As you say," said Duke Galba. Then he put his hand on mine. Behind him I could see Galba and Aurien, their heads bent together in the lamplight. "We are allies, Sulien, we are one family already. We will stand together, and we will stand by your word as the High King's." This was the first real trust that had been given me as praefecto, and I drew myself up to be worthy of it. I realized suddenly how much Urdo's trust in me meant— not just that the near three hundred people of an ala were within my command, but that I could sway the great events of the island. My position made me an equal to Galba, and to my mother, and between us we could stop this new civil war before it was begun.

"You can leave immediately after the wedding," Veniva said. "Some of the messengers can set out tonight. Whether or not it was Sweyn who sent, we can say that it was. Everyone fears the Jarns. Most people will be uncertain what to do, and decisive action now will catch them if we are in time."

She caught a signal from a servant and raised her hand to signal dinner. Duke Galba took my arm to lead me in. Gwien and Veniva led the way, then Galba and Aurien, Duke Galba and I, Uthbad and Idrien, then Morien and Kerys ap Uthbad. Cinvar ap Uthbad came last, alone, looking a little

sourly at me. We went into the family alcove, the others followed, and
Daldaf fussed around seating them in other alcoves. I saw Duncan and
Emlin and others I knew, mixed with strangers. The dining hall looked
splendid, hung about with pennon banners like the one at Caer Tanaga.
Veniva smiled at me as she sat beside Gwien. I realized that she was dealing
with a crisis without suggesting sending to ask anyone for help. Show your
mother that you've grown up, Urdo had said. It seemed to me that she had
grown up a great deal, too.

—18—

I have been a prize in a game
I have been a queen on a hill
From far and far they flocked to see me.

White am I, among the shadows,
My shoulder is noted for its fairness
The two best men in all the world have loved me.

My crown is of apple, bough and blossom.
They wear my favor but my arms are empty.
The boat drifts heedless down the dark stream.
— "The Three Great Queens of the Island of Tir Tanagiri"

As I came up to the shining citadel of Caer Tanaga my heart rose. It
always did at the sight of those gleaming walls and rising towers.
They seemed graceful and airy even in the last of the light in a day made
darker by icy rain. We had made very good time. The banner of the ala of
Caer Gloran was flying under the flag of the kingdom, but no other ala
banners. We were here before Urdo. Emlin looked at me inquiringly as I
drew Beauty to a halt and called the decurios up.

"Find everyone barracks. Sort it out with ap Rhun. The place is going
to be crowded, and I don't doubt lots of us will be sleeping in tents, but not
tonight. Let them get to the baths, they've earned it." They smiled at me.
They looked tired. We had come half the breadth of Tir Tanagiri in six
days. We had taken the ferry crossing at Aberhavren and ridden as fast as we
could without hurting the horses. We were here. We had done what we

could. Galba and Uthbad and my father had sent out messengers to all those who trusted them, or might trust them, to keep the country calm. I had written to the commanders, though I did not know them well and did not know what weight my words might have with such as ap Mardol and Luth of the Breastplate. I did not know yet if this had done any good.

The decurios led the troops off to see to the horses. I took Beauty myself into his familiar stable. Sorrow for Apple swept over me in a great wave and almost bore me down as I went inside. Tears came into my eyes. This had been his home for so long. It still seemed to smell of him. I chased off the grooms and cleaned and settled Beauty myself. Then I went to say hello to Starlight, who was outside in the near field. She was grown now, and trained. She came to me at once, protesting that she had missed me, she was desolate, though it was clear she had been very well looked after and regularly exercised. I had to make my mind up soon whether to ride her or breed her this year. I had been intending to breed her. Now she was grown she was one of the most beautiful greathorses I had ever seen, with perfect coloring and clear markings. She looked like her mother, the High King's Twilight, except for the star she had on her head. But now, without Apple, I would need another mount if there was war, and there would be war. I could not decide. I was telling her Garah would be home soon and promising her a ride as soon as day came, when Marchel came out into the field towards me.

"Ap Gwien?" she called.

"Here!" I said.

"I might have thought to look here first," she said. "I mean, greetings and welcome to Caer Tanaga, and can you please come in right now because you're needed urgently."

I left Starlight and walked towards her. I looked at her in surprise. "Urgently? But Urdo isn't here yet—"

"Just come on." I followed her out and into the streets. The night was closing in already. "Urdo isn't here, no. The Queen is here, and I am here, and we have a Jarnish visitor who came with half a company of infantry and assorted followers, including a couple of wellborn Jarnish women, one of them young and veiled, which means unmarried among their people. And he won't talk to foreigners, as he so politely puts it." She snorted.

"A Jarnish visitor?" I followed her up the street. "What are you talking about? From Guthrum of Cennet?"

"Nobody I know. A stranger. He has a herald's branch, but he has not given his name nor accepted the peace of the hall. Why would Guthrum send like that? With women? You know how much that is against their custom."

"I thought he might send word if he has heard of civil war brewing among the Tanagan kings. Flavien ap Borthas, or possibly Sweyn, is trying to stir up trouble among them. That's why I rushed back. Or he might want to tell us if Sweyn is offering him an alliance."

"This man came from the east, not the southeast, but he might have come from Cennet through Aylsfa. I hadn't thought of that. He came from across the river. He is clearly a person of some consequence, and he has the troops with him. He has given up his weapons in accordance with the herald-peace. He said he wanted to see the king. He was disappointed that he wasn't here yet, and demanded to see the war-leader." Marchel was almost running, and I lengthened my stride to keep up. "When I got there he took one look at at me and refused to talk. He has spoken inconsequentialities about the weather with the Queen and asked politely if she is increasing, but he demands to speak with the king or a high-ranking Tanagan officer. He is here under a herald's peace, and he cannot eat or drink and make himself our guest-friend until he explains himself."

"That's ridiculous," I said. "Anyway, he might break bread with the Queen and give his business, he's unlikely to find himself across a spear from her. Or surely there are some strict priests here?" Priests of the White God swore to do no more harm to creatures of the world than they must. There were different schools of thought as to what was meant by *must*, some even going to the ridiculous length of saying that they should forego killing animals to eat. There were a number who considered that it precluded them from taking up arms except in immediate and personal self-defense. Such people were often used as heralds.

"He will have no priest near him." Marchel sighed.

"He can't be from Guthrum then. Guthrum is as devout a follower of the White God as even Father Gerthmol would wish."

"He is," said Marchel, very shortly. I sighed. We were never going to agree about matters of the gods, for as a follower of the White God she was never content to allow others to go about their worship in their own way.

"He ought to talk to you anyway. It's discourtesy not to."

"Oh and I know as much, but if he fears treachery from the Jarns and thinks I am one, then who knows? His brains may be completely addled, but he is dressed like a Jarnish noble and claims to be a herald. If we can't find out what he wants it's very difficult to know what to do with him."

We came up into the citadel and waved at the guard, who passed us in after a very perfunctory ritual challenge. Ap Rhun came out and called after us, asking me how many pennons I had brought and needed feeding. "Four," I called, as Marchel rushed me along. "The decurios will see you about them." Ap Rhun had shadows under her eyes and looked unhappy.

"What's wrong with her?" I asked.

"Too much work, as usual. And I expect she wants to kill the queen for being prettier than she is." Marchel laughed.

"Ap Rhun's a good key-keeper, not just Urdo's leman," I protested.

"She'll be looking after another of his fortresses soon if he has any tact," said Marchel. "The Queen's running her ragged trying to find everything out. Come on, he's in here."

They had put them in one of the smaller halls, but it looked huge and unfriendly and full of shadows. It was lit by a few wax candles around the walls. He was sitting on one of the carved chairs, and indeed, he looked just like a Jarnish nobleman, golden hair and beard and barbarian clothes in good dyed wool and leathers. He was about forty years old and looked well used to fighting. I had never seen him before, which made it very unlikely he was one of Ayl's people. We had been fighting them fairly regularly for years, and most of their great men were familiar to me. He might be from Sweyn. He straightened in his chair as Marchel walked in. He looked anxious and uncomfortable.

Marchel advanced into the room. "I bring to you the Praefecto of Urdo's Own Ala," she began. The Jarn rose, looking relieved. I followed her in and bowed to the Jarn. He bowed to me, but the look on his face changed from relief to dismay. He muttered a word under his breath in his own language.

"I thought the Praefecto of Urdo's Own Ala was Osvran ap Usteg?" he said, in even and polite tones, but looking at me suspiciously.

"He was, but he was most regrettably killed at Caer Lind, and I now have that responsibility. I hope you have been made welcome in Caer Tanaga?" I asked.

"He has spoken to me but not broken bread with me," said a very low sweet voice in the doorway. She spoke in Tanagan although we had been speaking Vincan, as I always did with Marchel. I turned and saw a woman who could only be Elenn ap Allel, Queen of Tir Tanagiri. She was even more beautiful than Angas had said, as beautiful for a woman as Starlight was for a mare. I had never seen anyone like her. She wore a very simple overdress in slate blue. She had a heart-shaped face and deep dark eyes. Her hair was as black as a raven's wing, and bound around it was a silver circlet set with pearls. It must have been an heirloom of her house, but it suited her as it would suit almost nobody else. In stories flowers grow up in the footsteps of exceptionally beautiful women, and I almost looked to see if this was the case with Elenn. She was holding a taper in one hand. I bowed to her as she came forward and began to light more tapers around the walls.

"I mean no harm to any here," said the Jarn, slightly plaintively. "But I want to speak to the King, or someone who has his trust."

"I am the Praefecto of Urdo's Ala," I said. "Will you tell me what brings you here to us?"

He bit his lip. "I know you lead the charge for the High King. But women do not conclude alliances."

Marchel drew an angry breath and choked it back. I did not know whether to burst out laughing or yell abuse at him. Alliances? I choked back both and whispered to Marchel, "Is ap Cathvan here yet?" Elenn spoke before she could reply.

"I am myself a girl, and newly come here," she said. She had her head tipped slightly to one side. She looked very imperious. She reminded me in a way of the dowager Rowanna. "But these two women are high in my husband's confidence and captains of his troops. If you cannot speak to them, then you cannot speak to anyone until the king my husband returns, which might be soon, or it might not. We have been exchanging politenesses since noon, and I am tired of it. I have heard that in Jarnholme they keep women veiled and locked up with the cooking pots, but it is not so here. You have come into our country now. Shall I fetch in some stableboy or scullion for you to explain yourself to what is inside his breeches? Or will you fast until my husband returns? Or perhaps you could bring yourself to speak to those the High King has found worthy of his trust?" She folded her arms and waited.

He stood there staring down at her for a moment, his mouth open and a most comical expression on his face. Then he turned and bowed to me and to Marchel.

"My name is Alfwin, son of Cella, son of Edgar Houndsbane, son of Alfwin, son of Otha, son of Tew," he said. "I have come to offer the High King Urdo my sword. The traitor Sweyn has killed my father, who was king in Tevin. I can offer him fifty armsmen of my house besides myself. I ask only that he uphold my claim."

Marchel and I exchanged glances. Her eyebrows were almost up to her hair.

"Greetings to you, Alfwin Cellasson, and welcome to Caer Tanaga. I am Sulien ap Gwien ap Nuden ap Iarn ap Idris ap Cadwalen." I stopped after six names because he had done so, and that seemed polite. "I am Praefecto of the King's Own Ala under Urdo ap Avren ap Emrys, High King of Tir Tanagiri, Protector of Caer Tanaga, War-leader of the Tanagans." I gave all Urdo's titles not just because it was a formal occasion but because I was trying to find time to think how to say what must be said. "Only the High King himself can fully accept this offer. I do not know if he is free to accept your claim by the terms of the truce he has made with Sweyn. I can promise, though, that he will not harm you or allow harm to come to you under his roof, or by his will, and that we can offer you and your armsmen and companions rest and comfort under his roof until he returns."

Alfwin bowed again, to my relief. Elenn gestured to a servant, who brought forward food and drink. We all sat around the low table. The servant brought plates and cups, a plate of bread, another of cold meat, and a pitcher of ale.

Elenn waited until Alfwin had taken his first bite, then gave instructions to the servant that food was to be taken to his companions. The servant left, closing the door.

"We are saddened to learn Sweyn has killed King Cella," said Marchel. If she had known more than the bare name of King Cella an hour before, it was more than I had. "Can you tell us how this came to happen? We had no news of a falling-out among your people."

Alfwin grimaced. From the way he was eating the bread and cold meat it seemed he had been hungry. "That doesn't surprise me, Thurrigsdottar," he said. "For there has been no such falling-out." He took another great mouthful and chewed loudly. "When we have eaten I will tell you," he said, speaking around the food. His table manners certainly owed little to Vincan propriety. My mother would have had severe words for him. I tried not to look at his mouth.

Elenn poured the warm ale, pouring for Alfwin first, then for Marchel and then for me. She had taken only bread and was clearly eating only out of courtesy. Marchel was eating bread and meat slowly and looking very intently at Alfwin. She hardly said a word. I ate quietly. I like cold lamb, the lean meat and the fat together. It was good bread, too. I was hungry. Elenn inquired about my journey, and I asked about hers from Tir Isarnagiri. It had been of no more interest than mine. She then set herself to charming Alfwin, at which she had much success. When we had quite finished she turned to him seriously.

"Will you please tell us about your father's murder?" she asked. "And could you tell me also who Sweyn is, for as you know I am newly come to Tir Tanagiri and these names and places confuse me." She smiled very sweetly into his eyes and leaned slightly towards him. I wondered at the time if she had taken a great liking to him, but I learned afterwards that this was her manner with all men of rank, and she meant nothing by it.

"Sweyn," said Alfwin, and then he swallowed hard, caught his breath and choked. I banged him on the back. He picked up his cup carefully as if it were something strange to him. Then he took a drink and began again, using the formal storytelling style of his people though speaking still in the Tanagan tongue. I had heard their skalds telling tales in this manner before, and he did it quite as well as any of them, giving our words an air of his own language and now and then using a word of it where no word of ours would do.

"Sweyn was the rightful king of Jarnholme. Now Jarnholme is sinking, every year the waters are rising. This has been so for three generations. Every year there is less land to farm, and less food for our people to eat. So many of us have left, when the seas came calling, and considered what we found in the south or across the Narrow Seas ours to keep, and none of Sweyn's to yield lordship to any of our kin we left behind us." He took a long drink and set down his cup. "Some of my people set off to the south into the rich Vincan lands there, and some went east inland. There they found the ravaging marauders, the brotherhood of the Skath, who have recently fallen on the Malms in Vinca and destroyed them."

"I have heard very bad things of the Skath," said Marchel. It was the first thing she had said since we started to eat, and Alfwin turned to her in courtesy.

"They are a dangerous people. The Jarns who went east had no profit in it and returned to their sinking homes, and those who went south in my grandfather's time and made themselves kingdoms are sorry for it now as the Skath attack them. I have heard that they pray to a god of rats, and also that when their leader married a Vincan princess he stole the luck of Vinca. The Vincans keep trying to steal it back again, but they are not having any success." He turned back to Elenn.

"In any case, my father Cella, my two brothers Harald and Edfrith and I came with all our people over the seas to Tevin twenty years ago. As the waters were drawing nearer Lord Tew came to Hild, my mother, in a dream. He gave her the news that we must leave by sea and take up the land he should give us. The wind he sent brought us to the shores of what was then called Valentia. We won the land fairly, taking even the city after five years of war. The night before the battle in which we took Caer Lind, Lord Gangrader came to my mother while she slept. He said to her that if we spared the Lord as he fled with his child set before him on his piebald horse, then the land would be entirely ours with all the Vincans driven out."

I started, spilling my ale and causing them all to look at me for a moment. I had not known Duncan was the Lord of Caer Lind, though who else would have had a greathorse? I wondered if my father knew. Marchel drew nearer to Elenn, away from both me and Alfwin. I had read the monk's book in Thansethan. I knew Gangrader was the Lord of the Slain, Old One-Eye. I wondered what he had wanted with Duncan and Rudwen.

"Do go on," I said, into the silence. Alfwin touched an amulet at his throat, and continued.

"Lord Gangrader said if we did this one thing then we would be prosper in the land and a king with the royal blood of Jarnholme would become High King of Tir Tanagiri. And this has come to pass, for Urdo has that blood through his mother Rowanna, though when we Jarns speak of kings we usually consider blood to pass from the father. The rest of what Lord Gangrader said came about immediately. The lord did flee on a piebald horse, with a child set before him, and we did not pursue. Once they had gone the land was ours, and we prospered in it. We named the land Tevin, for Lord Tew who had given it to us. Very many of our kin came there from Jarnholme, as the waters rose, and they built hamlets and farmed. Even though the water is rising in Tevin, too, there is much of it raised higher and inland. We lived there for the most part in peace among ourselves and with plenty of room for those of our kin who came from Jarnholme in later times. It is such land as we greatly love, with rivers and marshes for fowling and fishing as well as land for farming. We fought now and then with Ayl, and with Cinon of Caer Rangor, and most often with Borthas, but there we prevailed, for even if he won in the field, he could not stop us taking the land and farming it, and thus more of Tinala became Tevin as time went on." Alfwin took a deep breath.

"When Ohtar Bearsson and his men took Bereich, to the north of Tinala, at first they warred with us by sea, for they had an alliance with Borthas. His sister was married to their king Ohtar's son. At that time my mother Hild Haraldsdottar, called Hild the Red for her red hair, and my younger brother Edfrith Cellasson died of a camp fever. A little while after, Borthas killed his son-in-law by treachery and tried to take Bereich in his nephew's name. Then Ohtar made a truce with us, and I married a daughter of Ohtar and we warred upon Borthas. This was nine years ago, and it is the reason I am alive now." He smiled very grimly, looking at Elenn, who looked back with perfect composure.

"Sweyn Rognvaldsson, as king in Jarnholme, heir to his uncle Gunnar Arlingsson, believes he is king of all the Jarnsmen, wherever they may be in the world. He made an alliance with the witch-queen of Angas and wrote to all the Jarnish kings in Tir Tanagiri, calling them his underkings. Guthrum of Cennet returned him a rough answer. Ohtar and Ayl made an alliance with him. When he heard this my father said that we needs must do the same. I urged him rather to make alliance with Urdo ap Avren, who has the name of an honorable and powerful man. My father would not give up our gods, who have been good to us. We missed my mother's wise advice, for the gods do not speak to my wife or to my brother Harald's wife. My brother's daughter had confusing dreams and woke many times in the night calling out Sweyn's name but could say nothing clearly. So we also made alliance with Sweyn, and he gathered up the might of Jarnholme in ships and crossed the Narrow Seas and landed in Tevin. When his foot touched the shore of Tir Tanagiri he made the great blood sacrifice to the gods. He himself took the knife to his daughter, a girl of eight summers. As her blood soaked the soil he said that the land would be his and that the island would be known hereafter as Jarnland." I gasped, Marchel made a noise in her throat and sat wide-eyed, her hand clasping the pebble around her neck. Elenn sat still, silent, unmoving, calmly beautiful, her hands folded in her lap. I suppose as an Isarnagan she did not feel it the same way.

"He then commanded our farmers to abandon their dwellings, at the word of the witch-queen, and we fought and fled and fought again with Urdo's troops in Tevin and in Tinala. I think you know of this already, how there were was much fighting around and within our city of Linder, that you call Caer Lind. I was with my father-in-law Ohtar, fighting in Tinala, for my wife was with child and wished to be with her mother. Ohtar favored me and gave me a command. I fought against you on the field there, I think before Yavroc?" He said this last to me, and I raised my chin in agreement.

"I did not see you, but I was there. Your side fought well." It was true, as well as being a politeness; they had stood well.

"Sweyn thinks you are a walkurja, one of Gangrader's chosen. He fears you, daughter of Gwien." He laughed a little uneasily, and I grinned at him. I had not realized I had gained this reputation among the Jarns, but it did not displease me to have my enemy fear me. It would make their stand against the charge that much less stalwart.

"Well, Ohtar and I fought a little with your troops after that, until winter closed down on us all, and Sweyn made a truce with Urdo until spring. My new son was a month old. I left my wife and children with her parents and went to Caer Lind for a few days, meaning to speak to my father and my brothers. As I traveled through Tevin a man of my brother's household approached me, and told me that Sweyn had treacherously slain my father, Cella Edgarsson, and my brother Harald Cellasson, for arguing with his right to make disposition of lands in Tevin, calling this treason, but without holding any trial before the people such as the meanest peasant might deserve. He had done this almost as soon as he was secure on shore, before any of the battles and not long after I had left for Ohtar's camp. No doubt if I had stayed he would have slain me, too, for I would not see the land of Tevin given wantonly away any more than my father would. That land is ours. None of my father's thanes dared raise a voice, for Sweyn had so many huscarls at hand. As soon as my niece, Harald's daughter, learned of this she did not waste time making appeals for justice to Sweyn or his wife, she gathered up all the people of my brother and my father's households who she knew were loyal and fled, seeking me." He took another deep draught of his drink. I drank, too.

"Worst of all, I had seen Sweyn in that time, when he came to Ohtar's camp, and he talked to me and called me Cellasson, and he even drank ale and ate with me and with Ohtar and with our household there, but he said no word to me that my father was dead by his hand. I owe my life to the fact that Sweyn needs my father-in-law. Yet, when I went back to Ohtar with my brother's people Ohtar was in fear of Sweyn, and he said that my father must have been a traitor if Sweyn said so. He even spoke against my father, saying he was no great lord in Jarnholme and not even his father's eldest son. This is truth, but so much the better for him that he had won great lands in Tevin by his own might and main. Ohtar would not listen to me. He said he knew I was no traitor, and he would always give me a place at his court for my wife's sake and the sake of our children. Yet in my heart I could not stay with him unless he would help me take vengeance. I left him in peace, and my wife and children are with him still. She was not well enough for a long journey." He coughed, and took another drink.

"Ohtar gave me a ship to come south, and south I came to Aylsfa. I spoke to Ayl and he gave me soft words and said he would help me and with me make alliance with Urdo. Yet we fled from him last night, for my niece had a dream warning her that he meant to hand us over to Sweyn when he could and win Sweyn's favor."

"Last night?" I said, looking at Marchel. I could see that she was also calculating the places where Ayl might have been last night that were close enough.

"You know this land better," she said to me. At the same time she gave me the hand sign we use in the ala to say that I should take charge of the affair and do what I thought right.

"I reached here at noon," said Alfwin, courteously ignoring our exchange and saying the most he could without breaking guest-friendship with Ayl. Ayl had made no move against him, whatever his intentions may have been. "The rest you know. I think there are many in Tevin and indeed in Aylsfa and Bereich who will rally to my banner if I raise it beside the High King Urdo. Many do not love Sweyn."

"I think Urdo will be very pleased with this news," I said, and it was in many ways extremely good news for us. "And I have little doubt he will welcome you. For my part I will be proud to fight beside you."

"And I," said Marchel, after a moment's hesitation. "But will you swear by the White God when you swear to Urdo, Alfwin?"

"I will let him hold my oath, as he will hold any man's," said Alfwin, pleasantly.

"It is not necessary to do more, or even to do that, for I swore by the gods of my people when I swore, and so do many of the nobly born in the ala," I said. Marchel glowered at me.

"None have sworn by the heathen gods of Jarnholme," she said, with the fervor of a convert, when I knew perfectly well that although her brother was an exceedingly holy monk, her father's favorite expletive was "Thunderer box your ears." I laughed.

"It is in the sincerity of the oath and the oathtaker that matters," I said. "There have been Jarnish pirates who swore by gods not their own and broke their word, which is why the custom is to let the White God hold the oath. Alfwin is willing to do that. That is enough." Marchel was still looking furiously at me, and a spirit of mischief took my tongue, following on all Alfwin's Jarnish talk. "If he wanted to swear by his Lord Tew, I do not see that there would be any harm in it."

"Like my father, I do not wish to desert my gods," said Alfwin sensibly.

"Nor need you," said Elenn, who all this time had sat still, smiling just a little. "But Marchel, you must tell me about this White God of yours. I have heard very little about him for his priests have scarce gone to Tir Isarnagiri."

Some while later I escaped, leaving them engrossed in stories of the White God's doings. I took Alfwin with me, and told ap Rhun to find somewhere to house Alfwin and his people. Then I went to the barracks and gave orders to three of the pennons of Marchel's ala to patrol along the river because Ayl might be near and intending to cross. Then I went to my own bed and slept deep and sound until morning.

—19—

New folds in the knotwork, turning, returning,
What news from the west?
Is the land aflame, is the kingdom burning?
Should we stir from our rest?

In the cold gray dusk, the red-cloaks riding,
What news from the south?
Are they safe, do you know, do you bring us tiding?
What word in your mouth?

The sky hangs heavy, dark in the morning,
What news from the north?
Have you come to summon and bring us warning?
Should we venture forth?

The beacon flares, and the riders calling
There is news from the east!
To horse! To arms! The hoofbeats falling
and the crows will feast.
                —Aneirin ap Erbin, "The Messengers"

Emlin came to wake me just after dawn to tell me Urdo was there. Oh, that was just like the War, rarely a full night's sleep, never knowing who or where we were going to fight, always good news and bad news and orders and plans and trouble. We had six wild full years of it, and all those early mornings run together in my mind. I breakfasted with Urdo in his room and explained everything to him. His eyebrow rose a few times, but he said he was pleased with what I had done. He accepted Alfwin Cellasson into his service, as I had known he would. Alfwin swore to Urdo, with the White God holding his oath, which made no ripples. Then he raised his banner. Many Jarns rallied to him as he had said, and we had for the next five years both Jarnish and Isarnagan allied infantry. We learned how to make best use of them. I often wished they were better organized and more able to maneuver. There's nothing quite so frustrating as waiting for the infantry to come up before you fight.

We narrowly avoided a civil war that first spring. Duke Mardol wrote to Urdo that he would not have risen against him. He added that it made him easier in his mind to hear from Duke Galba. Some of the other kings were also reassured by that timely letter. Penda of Bregheda, for all that he was Borthas's ancient enemy, took his troops as far as the mountains between Bregheda and Tinala. Urdo sent me up there as soon as he heard of it. Raul and I met him with the ala, ready to fight if it came to it. He passed it all off as a misunderstanding once Raul had convinced him that Flavien was secure in Caer Avroc and the message was a forgery. On that trip I learned to value Raul for more than his skill with numbers and saw why Urdo used him so often in difficult matters of diplomacy. He was wonderful at hearing a remark without offense and replying to it politely with information to make the other person think again. He rarely lost his temper with anyone but Urdo.

I had to speak to Penda myself, for Bran had been his son and my signifer. He was short with me to begin with, but I persisted with him for Bran's sake until he became gracious and let me tell him how bravely his son had died. I liked the hawk-faced old man, though he was not much like Bran, who was always laughing. I made him smile saying that Bran had pointed out these very hills and said he was always fighting in them. He was kind enough to say that Bran had spoken well of me in his letters home. Later I told him some of the jokes Bran and Geiran had made, and we laughed and wept. We broke bread together that night, which was better than I had expected. Raul even got some supplies out of him before we rode off, and the promise of more. Supplies were the problem all through the long War.

As long as the alae stayed where the lords could feed both armigers and horses, Urdo's order worked well enough. But when the Jarns pressed us and forced us to be very mobile, food became a perpetual problem. Even if the lords were willing to give it to us when we were not settled on them for their own immediate defense, which was by no means always the case, it was difficult to transport great quantities of food around the country. The seas were highly dangerous because of raiders, the roads were bad anywhere away from the high roads, and there was always the danger of a Jarnish ambush. The danger on the roads and sea made all trading riskier, and many of our patrols seemed to involve running down raiding parties trying to intercept supplies. Near the borders goods and supplies had to have an armed escort or move where they were going at great speed. I remember getting a letter from my mother sometime the next winter, full of the problems they had by land and sea, and on the second page telling me of the birth of Aurien's first son, another Galba. They called this one Galbian, little Galba, to distinguish him from his father and grandfather.

We fought up and down the border. We had no great defeats, but no great victories either. It was hard to get them to stand and fight if we had enough force to beat them, and if they could get past us they could ravage our farmland and retreat. We fought continuously, with only the occasional truce to gather the harvest or in the dead of winter. We ourselves farmed whenever we could, planting a turnip crop around the stockaded forts we built. Some of the armigers resented doing this work, and not only those who were noble-born. To hear them talk I wondered if some of them had taken oath precisely to avoid farming. I wouldn't have blamed them if they had, but the horses had to eat or they could not have the strength to fight or be ridden long. We used captured Jarnish prisoners to do the work whenever we could, and some complained about that as well, saying we shouldn't let the Jarns at the land.

Urdo moved the alae where they could do most good, and moved himself with them. The King's Own moved with him, always in the thick of the struggle. We raided and patrolled and fought beside Angas up on the borders of Bereich, we fought often and always in Tinala, we fought up and down the long border of Aylsfa. We stopped in Caer Rangor for the night now and then, though Marchel and ap Meneth were both based there all the time and there was scarcely room for us to crowd in. We even fought right down in the southeast, in Cennet, when Sweyn brought many men around the coast in ships and tried to take the coast by storm. I thought it a holiday to fight from Caer Tanaga with hot running water and a chance to see Garah. It was the only place where I felt safe when I took my boots off. There were always two alae in Caer Tanaga, all through the War.

Garah was stationed there full-time: she and Glyn were working hard organizing the distribution of food and alae across the country. She also worked with Dalmer coordinating the alae messengers and collecting rumor and information to piece together a whole picture of what was happening in the country. This news she sent to Urdo, who valued it greatly. Official news of victories and defeats and how the War was going she sent out regularly to all the alae and to the allied kings. They did well. We had thin times, but neither people nor horses ever quite starved, and news and intelligence mostly arrived where it was needed. We built depots and forts in enemy land to store supplies, and garrisoned them with infantry and swift messengers.

Commanding an ala was different from commanding a pennon. It was lonelier. There were more people to care about and so it was more difficult to know them all as people. I tried my best. Ap Erbin was my tribuno, my second-in-command. Elidir ap Nodol was my signaler and banner bearer, taking poor Indeg's place. She was always close beside me, and though I trusted her and relied on her, she was always a little in awe of me and I could never quite relax with her. Two years after the War began she married Grugin ap Drust, my trumpeter, and they shared a tent. There were always messengers near me, too, though they came and went too quickly for me to grow very attached to them. Losing my armigers in battle always came very hard. We still trained whenever we had the chance, but everything was more in earnest now. I fretted that I would never be a good praefecto, until I talked to Angas about it, and he said that he felt the same and he knew that Osvran had. He added that I should try being a king if I wanted to know what it meant to be lonely in a crowd.

There was little enough time for it, and there were always good times. A good charge could always lighten my spirits. Then there would be times with old friends, drinking with Masarn and ap Erbin or with Galba or Angas or Thurrig as the chances of the War brought us together. And sometimes I would sit and talk with Urdo around a campfire, discussing the land, or the law code he would write in the Peace. Even as he directed the War and put all his strength into it, Urdo never lost sight of the Peace he would build. I eventually made friends with Alfwin Cellasson, once he stopped thinking I was half a demon. After a year or so he asked me outright if I worshiped the Lord of the Slain. I think he was relieved to hear I kept to the faith of my fathers. Yet if the Lord of the Slain rejoices to see brave warriors killed in battle I did him good service in those years. But then so did we all, including Alfwin, for all that his prayers were foremost to Tew.

There are so many things to remember of that time. Garah, in Caer Tanaga, delighted because Guthrum and Ninian had sent the whole amount of their taxes unexpectedly and there would be food. Elenn, hearing this, saying she must send them a present and finding from the treasure rooms a swan of blown glass and wrought silver, work from distant Lossia in time long gone by. Thurrig telling me how he had beaten six ships at sea, slapping his thigh and laughing "Son of the Shore! I had no idea where they were until we ran into them! Then our axes bit." Alfwin almost exploding at the idea that his niece Alswith wanted to train as an armiger, and Elenn very gently persuading him. Riding like the Wild Hunt all night to sing the Midwinter Chant outside Ayl's hall at dawn and riding away again, still singing, holding up torches and blowing war horns. The bards sing of how brave that was. They never mention how silly we were, nor how cold. Urdo quarreling with King Cinon at Caer Rangor, after the battle where the Jarns had nearly taken the city. Cinon was complaining about Urdo taxing the Jarnish hamlets instead of burning them. "You're treating them as if they have a right to be there. They're stealing my land!" Urdo slammed his hand down on the table and said loudly in a ringing voice "The problem is not that we do not have enough land!" Indeed, riding over it day after day it sometimes seemed that we had too much of it. Always we went to bed weary and woke too early.

The War went on, sometimes well, sometimes badly, and the joys and sorrows of the War filled my horizon until I almost forgot that there had been any before or could be any after. We were too well matched and could not find a way through the endless fighting to any lasting victory.

In the fifth year of the War Urdo was stupidly wounded in a skirmish when we fell on a raiding party that was larger than we expected. A thrown ax got through to the king when we were riding steadily down on them. There's nothing to do when that happens but keep on riding towards them and hope it will miss. This one hit and went through the armor on his thigh. We were not far from Thansethan. We fell back to the monastery by night to rest. It was the first time I had been there since I fled with Beauty and Garah. The muddy rutted track from the highroad to the stable gate was worn deeper. Otherwise, it seemed little changed, and my heart sank as I heard the bell ringing for a prayer as we rode up. Urdo begged admittance, for nobody could command the monks here in their stronghold. The gates opened to us, and we went inside.

We had an awkward reception. Father Gerthmol said nothing to me but touched his pebble every time he looked at me. Urdo was not badly hurt, but he had lost blood. He looked horribly pale; it worried me to see him like that. He needed rest and water and food—I knew it would only be gruel, but hot food would be better than any charms. The place also had good water in quantity, which he needed. The thing he needed least was the priests fussing, but I knew that was inevitable. He sent me away once he was settled in a guest room. He said that he could deal with Father Gerthmol best alone, and he knew I had people to see here.

I went off, feeling shy, to look for my son Darien. It was summer. I had to count it up on my fingers. He would be nine years old. I thought I ought to find Arvlid first. Then I thought I ought to check on the horses. I knew this for cowardice, but I thought that if I saw Starlight safe and sound. I would have courage to seek him after. I did not at all know what I could say to him. The stables were full and quiet, the horses had been cleaned and watered and fed. There was plenty of food. Thansethan was one of the places where food was stored for us, to be collected or sent out where it was needed. There were a few monks moving about, and here and there armigers seeing to their horses. Grugin raised a hand to me as I passed him grooming his horse. Starlight was down at the end, where it was quiet. Darien was in her stall with her.

I wondered how he had known she was my horse, and that I would be coming to see her. I did not have a moment's doubt as to who he was, even though he had only been two months old when I had last seen him. He had a look of my brother Darien, though his coloring was closer to Jarnish. He was tall, for a nine-year-old. He did not look much like his father, except for his winter-sea eyes. He was wearing brown homespun wool, like all the children of the monastery, and he had a pebble around his neck. He was talking softly to Starlight, who had put her head down to his hand. He was giving her an apple. She liked him. She was good-tempered and liked most people. I was glad he knew how to treat horses.

I came up behind him and stood there for a moment. "You found my horse," I said, and cleared my throat.

"Yes, sir," he said, turning. He looked up at me calmly, meeting my eyes. I wondered for a moment if giving him Darien's name, I had given him Darien's soul, he looked so like him. Such things have happened. "Is she your horse then? I thought she must be the High King's horse, because she is the most beautiful." When he said this I felt strange inside. He had come to Starlight because Starlight was beautiful. He did not know me after all, and I would have to tell him.

"She is the daughter of one of the High King's horses," I said, and my voice came out evenly though my heart was thumping so loudly I was afraid he might hear it. "Her name is Starlight, and her mother's name is Twilight. Twilight isn't here, she's at Caer Tanaga, she's in foal this year. Urdo's riding Prancer, who is in the stall just across there." I pointed, and he squirmed out of Starlight's stall to look.

"She's a good horse, too, but she's not as beautiful as your Starlight." Prancer was Urdo's favorite greathorse that year. She was Twilight's daughter by Apple, a seven-year-old then. She was almost as dark as Apple had been but not so broad-chested, and a sweet-tempered horse like her sister. Although Urdo always disagreed, I thought she did not quite have Starlight's grace.

"I think so, too," I said. "So you're a good judge of horses?" He flushed. With his pale skin it was extremely obvious.

"I like horses," he said, a little defensively. "They're the best thing here."

"I like horses, too," I said. "Do you want to work with horses when you grow up?"

He shook his head slowly, looking at me consideringly. Now his expression was nothing like my brother at all. "Oh no. I want to be an armiger and ride for the High King. Why did you never come before?"

My tongue stuck in my throat. "You know who I am?" I asked, idiotically.

"You are wearing a praefecto's cloak, gold oak leaves. The only women who are praefectos are Marchel ap Thurrig and Sulien ap Gwien, and I know Marchel. She comes here. So you must be Sulien ap Gwien. I am called Suliensson, and so you are my mother." He bowed. I knew I ought to embrace him, but somehow the way he held himself didn't at all invite it. He was very self-possessed, not at all the way I had been when I was a child, nor my brother either. I suppose it was growing up with the monks.

"Yes," I said, and remained still, though I wanted to move towards him. Starlight nickered softly and another horse answered her. "And I didn't come because I wasn't sure Father Gerthmol would let me in. We only came now because Urdo was wounded. I—"

"Is he going to be all right?" The concern was immediate, real and personal. He looked just as my brother Darien had looked when we fished Morien out of the river the time we tried to teach him to swim.

"Yes. He's lost blood, but he'll be well again soon."

"Oh, thanks be to the White God ever merciful," he said, entirely sincerely, with a real relief in his voice. It seemed odd to hear him pray to the White God, but if I had not wanted him to grow up in that worship I shouldn't have left him here.

"You know the High King then?" I asked, curious.

"Oh yes." Darien rocked on his feet. "He always comes to see me when he comes here. He brings me things. He brought me a toy sword, but I have outgrown it. He brought me some weights for practicing, and I have practiced and practiced, shall I show you?" He looked ready to run off and find them. I shook my head.

"I haven't brought you anything," I said. "I didn't know I was coming."

"That's all right," he said. "There's nothing I want." I knew I should have brought something. I should have come before, no matter how much Father Gerthmol disapproved. This boy was a stranger to me. "Did you really summon a demon?" he asked, leaning forward and looking interested.

"No," I said. "It was Morwen of Angas who did any summoning that was done. She tried to kill me, and then told lies."

"That's what Sister Arvlid told me," he said. "I knew she was right." By the set of his shoulders as he said it I knew that he was used to fighting the other children about this. I wanted to cry.

"It's all lies," I said. "Arvlid was right."

"Then—" he hesitated. "Then why don't you like me?" he asked, and stuck his bottom lip out. I wanted to reach out to him, but something in the way he was standing said that he would run away if I moved closer. It was hard to know what to say. I squatted down on my heels so my head would be closer to his level.

"I do like you. I don't know you, but I think I would like you if I did. It wasn't anything you did wrong!" He looked at me, very unsure now. "There isn't—I can't—" He raised an eyebrow. He must have learned that from Urdo. "I'm a praefecto, I don't really have a home I can take you to. If you don't like it here, I could send you to my parents in Derwen, or my sister's house at Magor, though the Mother alone knows what they'd say."

"I don't mind it here." He leaned back on the ropes that were the back of Starlight's stall. "I've never been anywhere else. The High King says it's one of the best places to grow up in Tir Tanagiri."

I was surprised into a laugh. "He never grew up anywhere else either," I said. "It's something people only get one try at doing."

"Will you come and see me again?" he asked.

I wanted to promise I would, but if I broke a promise now, it would ruin everything. "I don't know if I'll be able to come back soon. I don't know where I'm going to be or what's going to be happening. I'll come when I can. You're nine. You can't be an armiger until you're sixteen at the youngest. That's seven years. Come to me in Caer Tanaga then. If I'm not there, go to ap Gavan and tell her who you are and wait for me, I get there now and then. I will give you a place in my ala." He bowed again.

"Thank you, sir."

"Darien—" I said. He started and drew in his breath. He had not given me his name. He seemed surprised I knew it. "There's no excuse for why I didn't come. I was afraid of Father Gerthmol's disapproval, and I was busy, and time went on and you were getting to be a person and I didn't know. It wasn't that I didn't care about you. I wish I had brought you something. Is there anything you'd like me to send you?"

"There's nothing I want," he said, but I caught the flash of his eyes towards Starlight. I couldn't give her to him, she was Urdo's gift. There was Glimmer, the filly she bore in the first year of the War. Since then I had ridden her, despite ap Cathvan's advice to ride lesser horses and have her bred.

"If I left Starlight here," I said, "and you had her bred to a good stallion, one ap Cathvan chooses when he comes here in season, then she would give you a foal you could train to be ready to ride when you were ready to be an armiger." For an instant he looked thrilled, and as if he might unbend towards me. "And," I added, "then I'd have to come back next year to collect Starlight." His face closed up again, and I realized what I had said, that I would promise to come for the horse but not for him.

"Thank you, sir," he said, cold and formal. "That would be extremely kind of you. I would take good care of her." He looked at Starlight, and his face changed again. He loved my horse. I had made a bad beginning. I should have come before. I drew breath to speak, to try to set it right, and there was a great hammering on the stable door. We froze. One of the monks came down and opened it. There was a rider outside, a red-cloak, one of the Garah's messengers.

"Urgent news from Caer Tanaga for the High King," he said. "Do you know where he is?" I recognized his voice, it was Senach Red-Eye, who had been in my pennon once.

"I am here," I said, straightening up, raising a hand to Darien to signal him to wait. "The High King is wounded. Is the news worth disturbing him?" Darien shrank back against Starlight, who huffed at him gently. The monk stepped aside and let Senach in. He dismounted and stood dripping on the floor. He handed me a dry scroll from his leather bag. It was sealed with Elenn's seal and addressed to Urdo.

"From the Queen?" I asked. I wondered if she was with child at last. "Do you know the news? Is it personal?" All but the most personal and dangerous news would be entrusted to the messenger as well as to the scroll, in case some mischance happened. Messengers were especially chosen from loyal and discreet people. Most of them were armigers who had been wounded, like Senach, whose single eye no longer sufficed for him to ride to war.

"It is no good news," Senach said, taking off his wet cloak and nodding to the monk who led away his horse.

"Tell me." The monk was out of earshot if he spoke quietly. Senach looked at Darien inquiringly.

"I will see you tomorrow, sir," Darien said, bowed, and ran out past me through the stables into the courtyard. I bit my lip and turned back to Senach.

"What?" I snapped.

"Some assassin of Black Darag's has killed Maga, the Queen's mother, the king of Connat in Tir Isarnagiri. It is war there. Allel has sent asking our help."

"They want their troops back?" I stepped back, horrified. They ate a lot and wouldn't do any work but fighting and we had to wait around for them, but the Isarnagan infantry was a great asset in any big battle.

"They want more than that. They want our help in their war." I felt my teeth grind together.

"I think this is important enough to take to Urdo, even if he's asleep," I said, and sighed. There was no sign of Darien as I took Senach and the unopened scroll up to Urdo's room in the guesthouse.

—20—

It is very meet, right, and our bounden duty, that we should at all times and in all places, give thanks into thee, O Lord, Holy Father Almighty, who walked among us as a man in Sinea, died for us, and ascended into Heaven in renewed and restored strength.

Lo, children and the fruit of the womb are a heritage and gift that cometh of the Lord. Like as the arrows in the hand of the giant even so are young children. Happy is the man that hath his quiver full of them, they shall not be ashamed when they speak with their enemies in the gate.

O God, the strength of all of them that put their trust in thee, mercifully accept our prayers. Through the weakness of our mortal nature we can do no good thing without thee, grant us the help of thy grace, that we may please thee both in will and deed and bring forth children to praise and please thee.

Therefore, with Angels and Archangels and with all creatures living and dead, visible and invisible, yea with all the glorious company of Heaven, we

laud and magnify thy glorious name, evermore praising thee and saying, Holy,
holy, holy, Lord God of Hosts, Heaven and Earth are full of thy glory, Glory
be I to thee, O Lord most High.

      —Prayer for Fruitfulness as offered at Thansethan,
      early translation

I went to the dawn service in the chapel. I caught the edges of some puzzled looks from Elidir and from many of my armigers. Masarn was there
giving thanks that his wife had been safely delivered of another son. At least
Senach had brought good news for someone. I sat quietly unmoved
through the chanting and readings and praise. I had not come for the
White God, but to see Darien. I could not distinguish him among the
group of robed children, but I thought I could catch him as they came out.
I wanted to talk to him. The service was calm and peaceful, even if it still
made me think that this was no way for respectable people to address the
gods. There was a prayer for Urdo's health which named him as "our
Earthly protector." When the children filed out Darien was not among
them. My heart sank. Was he avoiding me? I caught up with Masarn as we
came into the courtyard.

"I'm going to see Urdo. I think we'll stay here today, but we'll likely
need to send out messages. Tell the other pennon commanders rest and
gentle practice, be aware orders might be sudden." Masarn grinned.

"For a change? Is there any chance we might head down to Caer
Tanaga, do you think? It would mean a lot to my wife if I got there to see
the baby before he has teeth."

I shrugged. "That'll be the High King's decision." I suddenly felt terribly envious of Masarn's uncomplicated family life. Yet the War took us all
away from our families. It had been at least partly my choice not to come
here before. I sighed, patted Masarn's shoulder. "It might not be today, but
I don't doubt we'll get there soon. If I send anyone there, it'll be you. I'm
going up to see Urdo. I'll let you know." After I'd spoken to Urdo I would
seek out Arvlid and ask her how best to approach Darien.

I went up the steps of the guesthouse. Urdo had one of the little narrow cells to himself. Haleth stood on guard at the end of the corridor. She
passed me through with the hand wave that meant all was well. As I walked
towards his room I heard Urdo speaking.

"I'll have my work cut out to get all the kings to go along with it." I
thought he must be talking to Raul, but to my amazement I heard Darien's
voice answer.

"But you're the High King. Can't you just say you'll chop their heads off if they don't do what you want?" Urdo chuckled, and I froze where I was for a moment.

"If I chopped off Father Gerthmol's head, do you think the rest of the monks would do what I wanted after? Being High King doesn't mean threatening people to get them to do what you want all the time, or else I'd soon have an empty country and a large pile of heads." Darien laughed, too.

"Then maybe you could take them out hunting and ask them to let you have all the alae while they're in a good mood?"

"Now that's a much better idea." I couldn't believe how happy and relaxed they both sounded. I wanted to be there. I moved forward and drew back the curtain. Darien was sitting on the corner of Urdo's bed. Just for a moment I saw them looking naturally at each other, then they both looked up at me. Urdo raised an eyebrow, and Darien slid to the floor and stood ramrod-straight.

"Good morning, sir," he said.

This time I was determind to do it right. I bent and embraced him as family. He stood still and stiff and endured it until I stopped. I stepped back.

"I didn't mean to interrupt," I said, awkwardly, shifting on my feet.

"Darien tells me you're leaving Starlight here to foal?" Urdo said, looking up at me shrewdly.

"Yes," I said. "It's time she had another foal, and he will need a horse." I found it very difficult to look at Darien in the morning light. He looked too like and too unlike my brother, and himself.

"A good thought," said Urdo, gently. "Ten is a good age to begin to train a foal, and you'll be ten by the time you start, won't you, Darien?"

"Yes, my lord," said Darien. He looked as if he thought he'd be put on triple duties if he moved out of line. "May I go, my lord? It's almost time for language practice." He looked like a colt ready to bolt. Urdo raised his chin, and he took a step towards the door. To get out he would have to pass me. He looked somewhere over my shoulder. "Good morning, sir," he said, again. I moved to let him go. I felt a burning in my eyes.

"Well," said Urdo, when he had gone.

"Well he likes *you*," I blurted. Urdo half laughed.

"He likes me, and he likes Starlight, and if you don't push I think he would like to like you. He was asking me about you and I told him you were a most valued praefecto. Let him come to it in his own time. You can't expect to make up nine years in a day. If you keep coming to see him, he will come to know you."

"He frightens me," I said, and scuffed my feet like a child myself. "I don't know how to feel like a mother to him. I just left him here."

"If the gods give us time, the fear will wear off," Urdo said. "I am perhaps not the best person to ask about this." I blushed. I had forgotten for the moment that his mother had left him here, too. "But Rowanna and I have come to a friendship, if not exactly the sort of relationship most men seem to have with their mothers. I think growing up here was an advantage to me, and may well be to Darien. And I was four when she left me here, old enough to know but not really to understand. Darien has never known anything else."

"He said you said it was a good place to grow up," I admitted.

"It was. And he will come to know you. He is your son, after all." I looked up sharply. There was some envy in the king's voice.

"I'm sure you will, the Queen will, you'll get your own son soon," I stammered. Urdo shrugged, and grimaced as if it pulled at his wound.

"That's with the Mother," he said. "And this last few years hasn't been a good time for it. I'd not have been able to give a child the attention they need either. When the War is over there will be time for these things. And for you and Darien to make friends, too."

I bit my lip hard to stop myself crying. Tears of self-pity are the worst sort of tears, hateful to the gods. I swallowed, but I could not stop my voice shaking a little. "He thought I didn't like him."

"Then you'll just have to show him that you do," Urdo said, calmly. "And don't try to rush things. Leaving him Starlight is a really good idea, even if it is going to leave you a horse down. Is Glimmer ready to ride?"

"Next year," I said, getting control of my voice.

"Ah, next year," said Urdo, in a contemplative tone. "Everything depends on what we can do next year. I shall have to send the Isarnagans back, and I ought to send a pennon or two back with them. It will be hard to go on as we have been without them. But we don't want to go on as we have been, of course. I must break the Jarnish kings who oppose my rule, or who support Sweyn's, and to do that I must either fall on their kingdoms one by one or defeat all of them together in the field."

Urdo sighed. "To the distress of careful strategic principles, the alae cannot hold ground and take it only poorly, which means it must be all of them together. So I must give them a reason to do that."

"The kings won't like you getting all the alae together in one place," I said.

"No. They won't like it at all. I'm going to call them all to Caer Tanaga this autumn and talk to them about it, tell them this is our chance to make a real change and stop the War dragging on and on. They're mostly tired of it."

"Even so, they won't like being completely stripped of troops." I was picturing Duke Galba's reaction. "However loyal they are, they care about their homes and their farmers first. Everyone does."

"I won't strip anywhere completely. But they might be down to a pennon instead of an ala. Enough to keep off the raiders. But we can do it, I think. We've never trained with more than three alae together, but I think we could manage seven. Seven alae. Thirteen hundred armigers! Can you imagine? We could break anything they can put against us with that."

"If we can get the Jarns to stand and fight," I said quietly. It was always the problem when we had enough force. Sweyn was no fool and would not come out to fight unless he saw some solid chance of victory.

"If we can, yes. Which means giving them a reason to think they can win." Urdo was smiling now.

"Where?" I asked, but as soon as I had said it I knew. If we had to break all the Jarns there was only one place. "Tevin."

"Tevin. Yes. Exactly." He grinned. "Send Raul in. We'll send out some messages today. Tomorrow I should be well enough to ride, and we'll head back to Caer Tanaga."

I sent Raul in to him and spent an hour talking to Arvlid. She had nothing but good to say of how Darien progressed at his studies. She had matured into a plump woman, though I couldn't think how, on the food in Thansethan. It was hard to imagine her now running ten miles to warn the monks. I soon fell back into my friendship with her, but somehow I could not explain to her about Darien. She knew him too much better than I did. When we left Thansethan he bade me farewell formally, and embraced me formally.

Raul went off that first day to make a harvest truce. We did not have long before the news that we had lost the Isarnagans reached Sweyn. We knew they had spies among Alfwin's troops. Recruits would arrive and swear for the year or the season, and when that time was up go home. A few of them would break their oaths and tell all our doings. Others, meaning no harm, would let slip the general talk of the camps. There would be no way to keep such an important development quiet. We could not stop them going home. As long as they fought for us and not against us while they were with us there was nothing we could do about loose tongues. It would have reduced their numbers too much if we expected all the armsmen to swear their lives to Urdo, as an armiger might. Nor could any king support such a great army. Already Urdo had more sworn followers than any other king since before the Vincans came.

Raul had no trouble making that truce, which would last until the spring thaw. Gerda was pregnant, and Sweyn wanted to be home for the birth. By spring we hoped to be ready again.

Our Isarnagan allies went back to their own land along with Thurrig, his son Larig, and two pennons from Caer Thanbard. We could ill spare them, but we were bound to fulfill our obligation. With Larig went his brother Chanerig, which caused much trouble later. For now it is enough to say that with Elenn's mother died all the advantage we ever had of our Isarnagan alliance.

Within half a month of our return to Caer Tanaga the kings began to come in. Custennin came first with his priest Dewin. Urdo and Elenn sat up late with them talking about the White God. The next morning Dewin's countenance was even more smug than normal. I soon learned the gossip that he had converted the Queen over supper. This news was not a surprise to me. Elenn had long been interested in the White God. She had spent time in Thansethan and she was very friendly with Chanerig ap Thurrig. I had guessed for some time that she would take the pebble. It seemed to suit her. She was a woman who would want the whole world and all the gods to praise in one direction. Dewin could not have been more pleased if he had converted the gods themselves. I had to laugh when I heard it from a dour ap Cathvan. He was among those who had sought an Isarnagan Queen precisely to avoid this situation.

Angas arrived very late that night. The next day Mardol the Crow and Penda of Bregheda rode in together. Urdo took Darien's advice and took them off hunting. Angas and I went with them and found a boar that gave magnificent sport. We were eating it for dinner when Guthrum and Ninian arrived with Rowanna, who immediately started to scold Angas for not bringing Eirann and Teilo with him. He surprised her by listening very quietly until she had finished and then telling her that Eirann was brought to bed of another daughter two days before he left. The whole company drank her health. Custennin then set everyone laughing by asking if the girl were betrothed yet. His son was five years old and he was starting to look for alliances. He looked at the Queen hopefully when he said this, as if to ask about her womb, but she said nothing and only refilled his cup smoothly as if that were all he could want of her.

Then Flavien ap Borthas arrived. Masarn was out of sorts when he told me this news. It seemed he had bet Gredol two night-guard duties that

Flavien would not come. This was rather hard on their pennons, but it would teach them to be more sensible in future. That day I was up on the walls surveying the guard when Haleth called out that she had seen Galba approaching. I walked around to where I would have a clear view of him. It was a month since I had heard from home, and Aurien's new baby had been due any day when Veniva last wrote.

I knew at once when I saw them. Duke Galba was there, and Galba ap Galba in his white praefecto's cloak, and riding between them my brother Morien. Their armsmen and guards came a little behind. I told myself that my father's wounds must have been bothering him too much to make such a long journey. It was the kind of comforting lie we disdained in the alae. I knew. I left the walls without saying anything and went down to the city gates to greet them. When they came closer I could see that all three of them had their hair close-cropped, and then I knew for sure. Morien wore the colors of a decurio. He did not meet my eyes. Duke Galba dismounted first and embraced me.

"I'm so sorry, Sulien," he said, and then all the false hopes faded away as if they had never been, and there was no denying it anymore.

"My father?" I asked. He raised his chin. Morien came forward.

"It was a fever," he said. I remembered now that Veniva had mentioned a fever in the town when she wrote. Some Malmish traders had brought it she had said. "He went among the sick seeking a cure. He found one, but too late for himself."

"It was a noble death," I said. It was almost as noble a death as if he had died for his people on the battlefield. I felt fiercely proud of him even as my heart ached to know I would never see him again. I wished I had had time last winter to go home and talk with him again. I would have to go and see my mother as soon as there was time. I stared at Morien.

"Gwien was my friend, and I honor him," rumbled Duke Galba. He patted my shoulder.

"We have given our second son his name," said young Galba. It was then that I started to weep.

"I have to make my homage to the High King," said Morien. "And you will have to swear as my heir, until I have a child." I frowned. Morien had got married the year before to Kerys ap Uthbad, Enid's little sister. With luck she would have a child soon. I did not much want to be heir to Derwen.

"I don't expect it will be long," I said, wiping my face. "Everyone seems to be having babies."

"Is there news?" young Galba asked.

"Eirann Swan-Neck is delivered of another daughter of Angas," I said. "And my pennon commander ap Sifax has another son. And Gerda has given Sweyn a son at last. This is new news that reached us only yesterday."

"I thought you meant the Queen," said Duke Galba, disappointed. "Almost six years married and no sign of an heir for the kingdom?"

I shook my head. "When we have peace and Urdo has time to be at Caer Tanaga for two months together, no doubt it will be different," I said. "Now come into the city, the High King will want to see you, and we can mourn properly for my father Gwien."

I do not know what Urdo said to the kings. I was not there. Young Galba and I stood on guard outside the Great Hall as the kings went in, magnificent in reds and greens, glinting with gold. Guthrum and Ninian of Cennet wore cloaks with a swan embroidered in gold and trimmed with swans' feathers. They had chosen a swan as their house-badge in compliment to Elenn's gift. Flavien ap Borthas of Tinala wore a jeweled belt. Duke Galba of Magor wore a Vincan drape and carried the little rod that had been the sign of his grandfather's office. Angas of Demedia wore his white praefecto's cloak over dark red velvet. He winked at me as he went in. Rowanna of Segantia had a net of silver over her hair, and her embroidered overdress swept the ground. Her cloak was fur-lined. She barely glanced at us as our spears parted before her. My brother Morien of Derwen smiled at us very awkwardly. He wore fine red-and-green linen and the gold ring from my father's hoard. Cinon of Nene looked at us warily. He looked tired. Custennin of Munew looked indecisive, as always, but today he looked indecisive in heavy green silk with a red half cloak. His pebble hung on a gold chain. Uthbad of Tathal nodded to us, we were his kin by marriage now that his daughter had married Morien. I still missed Enid. Penda of Bregheda marched in proudly, wearing a tall crown. Mardol the Crow of Wenlad followed him, walking slowly. He glanced rapidly at me and at Galba, but his expression did not change. He was wearing dark red embroidered with green and gold and held a rod like Duke Galba's. And that was the whole of the great allied kings of the island. They had all come.

Last of all Urdo and Elenn went in, walking slowly. They were dressed all in white, but their cloaks were purple edged with broad gold bands. These cloaks had been found in a chest in Caer Segant. They had belonged to Emrys and before that to some Vincan emperor. Elenn wore her pearl circlet and all the jewelry she had; she glittered and sparkled with a ring on every finger. Urdo wore only the one plain gold circlet with which he had crowned himself High King under the oak. He looked like a king out of

legend. The look in his eyes was enough to mark him regal. I had seen him
in worn muddy armor looking just as kingly. He made the other lords look
ordinary. I swung the heavy doors closed one-handed and shifted my spear
back upright as I turned back. It might be ceremonial, but it had a sharp
edge. Galba looked at me.

"Do you think they'll agree to it?" he asked quietly in the silence that
followed. The little crowd who had gathered to watch the kings go in had
mostly scattered, or were loitering out of earshot.

"I don't understand how anyone could possibly avoid giving him anything he wants when he looks like that," I said.

Galba laughed. "It's a good thing Glyn didn't hear you say that," he
said, drily. "But I know what you mean. He knows what he wants, and he's
going to get it. Good. It's all very well being down at home keeping off the
raiders and sleeping dry at nights, but I could do with being back where the
excitement is." He sounded a little wistful.

"A straight charge before us, crush the Jarns, and everything simple," I
agreed cheerfully. Then I remembered Aurien and their children. "But it's
not just for fun. I mean it isn't always glory. You were at Caer Lind. Friends
die, we could die—"

"We could die anyway," said Galba, staring out across the courtyard.
"And Urdo's Peace is something worth dying for. Worth living for, too,
most definitely, and well worth getting for my children to grow up without
the fear of the Jarnsmen. But I don't want to see you and the others win it
for them while I'm safe out of the way. Morien can look after the troops
we leave down there."

I looked at the side of his face. His mind was made up. Sorry, Aurien.
"I think if they give Urdo all their support and let him have the alae, he'll
let you fight. I'll speak for your right to do it." There came a roar from
inside. A cheer? Or a cry of horror? I couldn't tell. "If they let him have the
alae." I repeated. "I'm so glad I'm not a king." There came another roar,
this time it was definitely acclamation.

"I think we're going to do it," said Galba, smiling. I couldn't help smiling back.

What can you buy with silver?
The ready goods in the bustling marketplace.
Bread, and seed, far-traveled wine.
Toys, and jewels, and works of craft.
Never a horse.
Neither trust nor love.
And no more land than the gaping grave.
            —Tanagan children's rhyme

We feinted with Sweyn all that year. When I closed my eyes at night I saw the map of the borderland spread out like a great fidchel board, the armies as pieces struggling towards their different ends. We tried to trick him, and he tried to trick us, and it took us almost until the next harvest before we each tricked the other and came to battle.

The grain was tall on the stem and beginning to hang heavy as we came into Tevin. My orders were to go forward to the Jarnish hamlet we knew was there and make our presence known. How to do this was my choice. I could have fired the standing crops and the houses and chopped down the farmers as they fled. There were times when the idea of killing and burning everything between us and the sea appealed to me. This wasn't one of them. I hated acting like the raiders, and no matter what people said it was no revenge. It was not these farmers who hurt and harried us, though our threat to them was a way to make Sweyn fight.

As we rode towards the hamlet the sun beat down on my head. I remembered the story of Elhanen the Conqueror treating his prisoners with honor, even though they were the family of his enemy. The Vincans had so admired him he had won two generations of peace for Sinea. Tricks and lies had little appeal for me. I signaled to Elidir to call up the decurios as the little hamlet came into sight, lying in a loop in the river.

"We're tax gathering," I said. "Any comments?"

There was a silence. Masarn broke it. "Isn't this the place where ap Gavan milked the cow?"

I laughed. "I think you're right. Well if so, I hope there are some more people around than there were that day. Don't attack them unless we're attacked, don't loot until we've tried persuasion. Anyone speak good Jarnish?"

"I've picked up a little," said Gwigon Red-Sword. The others muttered agreement.

"Don't forget I have Haraldsdottar in my pennon," Masarn said.

"Good. Then as soon as the scouts get back we'll ride in and try talking," I said. "Your pennon comes in with mine. Nobody to start fighting without the signal. Gwigon and Gormant, bring your pennons around from the sides to surround the village, in case; Rigol and ap Erbin, stay here and be alert.

Masarn was right. It definitely was the village where Garah had milked the cow. I recognized the way the long straight fields behind the huts sloped down to the river and the way the road narrowed.

Some of them fled when they saw us coming. Others hid in their huts. An ancient man came out and bowed to me. He looked poor and terrified, like most Jarnish farmers. He started muttering rapidly. His accent was very thick and difficult to follow. As far as I could make out the sense of it he was saying they were poor and honest and begging me to spare them. Meanwhile Masarn and Alswith Haraldsdottar had dismounted and were opening the doors of the huts. The rest of the two pennons I had brought in stayed mounted and alert, making the little place look crowded.

A cross-eyed old woman came out of the hut Masarn had just opened and walked over and poked the old man. He jumped, spun round, and relaxed. She must have been his wife.

"Your man says you pay silver?" she said to me. I knew the words for man and pay, and she used the Tanagan word for silver.

"We are the people of the High King Urdo," I said. "We will not hurt you. We want supplies. Root vegetables. Meat. Grain. What you can spare. We will pay silver." I knew very well that silver was almost useless to them so far from any of the king's markets. They could use the coin to make decorations, but they could not eat it or exchange it. Nevertheless, the old man brightened. The old woman looked very suspicious.

"Why you buy?" she asked.

"We need to feed the horses," I said, honestly enough, though we could have managed without whatever we managed to get from them. We had left Caer Rangor two days before with five days' food. We also had a depot fairly near, if we needed it, up on Foreth, which the Jarns avoided, thinking it haunted. We wanted Sweyn to know where we were, to think we were fewer than we were, to tempt him closer. We knew Ayl had come north to join him.

"But why you not take?" she asked. The old man put his hand over her mouth, but she brushed him off and stared at me. Her pale cross-eyed gaze made me uncomfortable.

"We keep the law," I said. I didn't trust my grasp of the language. I called to Masarn, who came up, bringing Alswith. She was wearing armor, like the rest of us, but she had taken her helmet off and her flame-colored hair was streaming free. With that and her pale face, it was immediately clear to them that she was a Jarn. They looked at her suspiciously. The old man took half a step back, hunching his shoulders. "Explain to them that we want there to be a hamlet here next time, too, and don't forget to tell them that everyone who lives in Tir Tanagiri is under Urdo's protection. Tell them about the market right, and the markets. Tell them we pay for what we take, but we will take more than the value of the silver as taxes."

Masarn stood by Beauty's head as still as a statue while Alswith explained. The others still had weapons ready.

"But what when Sweyn hears and murders us all?" the old woman asked. Alswith shrugged.

"Why are you here, a woman of our people?" the old man asked. "Why do you ride bare-faced to war like a burnt-skin?"

Alswith pushed back her thick hair with both hands and took a deep breath. "My father was Harald Cellasson, who the usurper Sweyn killed. He died without sons and lies unavenged."

The old couple put their hands on their hearts and bowed deeply to her. It was something they could understand, even if they had not once been Cella's people, and I think they had. It was the argument that had swayed Alfwin, too, when she first wanted to take oath as armiger.

Then the old man leaned forward, and said, very clearly, "Ohtar Bearsson has passed up river. He has landed near Caer Yavroc." Alswith spun round to me.

"I understand," I said. "When was this?" I asked, slowly.

"Before three nights," the old woman said.

"Three days ago," Alswith translated. The last we had heard, Angas had been keeping Ohtar busy up in Demedia. Our plans involved keeping Ohtar away from Sweyn until the last minute, which should still be three or four more moves away. We also kept Ohtar away from Alfwin. Alfwin said he would fight his wife's father's men, but we did not want to test this more than we had to.

"How many did he have with him?" I asked.

"Fifty ships?" the man said, clearly doubtful. "They go by in the dark,

boy saw the walrus." The white walrus was Bereich's flag, an oddly cheerful beast.

"Fifty?" Elidir repeated from where she waited close behind me. She
sounded incredulous. It did seem rather a lot. I wondered if he meant five.

"Are you sure it was fifty?" I asked, slowly.

"Forty, fifty, maybe sixty?" He seemed sincere. Alswith's eyes met mine,
her lips tightened. That would be more than two thousand warriors, loaded
full. What could he be doing? That must be everything in Bereich that
could float.

"We will have to take this news back," I said. "Elidir, Grugin, get
everyone ready."

"How much food can you spare?" Masarn asked, before the trumpet
had even reached Grugin's lips. The old man had clearly forgotten he was
there, he started.

"You always think of your stomach," I said, as the commands to re-
form and be ready to ride back blew loud and clear.

"Somebody has to if I'm ever going to get back to my wife's cooking,"
said Masarn, patting his belly. The old woman laughed, a high cackle. She
said something rapidly to Alswith. The armigers rapidly re-formed.

"All that is left of last year's grain and three sheep, she says," Alswith
relayed. "And more grain when it is cut, if Sweyn does not burn the place
down for dealing with us."

I tried not to let my astonishment show. This was far away from anywhere we could even try to protect. The old man looked as amazed as I
was; he was just starting to draw breath to splutter.

"Thank you," I said, and bowed to the old woman. "In Urdo's name.
Masarn, you and Haraldsdottar go with her to round it up, take whoever
you need." They went off and I gave five silvers to the old man. This was
generous if we were tax gathering, but no more than fair in fact. They had
been generous. As soon as we had loaded up we rode back as swiftly as we
could to where we had left the others.

When I got back with this news Urdo called an immediate council of
praefectos. We sat in a circle on the floor of his tent. It was terribly hot. I
would have given all three sheep for an hour in the baths.

"I don't believe a word of it," Glyn said. "Fifty ships? Fifty? It must be
what Sweyn wants us to think."

"Fifty ships would be two and a half thousand men, or twice that if he
has made two trips," Raul said, consideringly. "Five thousand would be
close enough to the whole of his fighting force."

It had not occurred to me that he might have made more than one trip. "The farmers didn't want to tell us he was there. They only mentioned it because Haraldsdottar told them who she was," I repeated. Urdo looked thoughtful.

"That could still be a ruse," Glyn insisted. "Sweyn must want us to go north for some reason."

"I don't think they could act that well," I said.

"Jarnsmen usually make very bad liars," said Raul, affirmatively.

"Is it possible he's there?" Marchel asked.

"Barely," Glyn conceded. "Just. If Ohtar put all his men into ships the moment after the last we heard from Angas and rushed down here, he might have got here, three nights ago. But why would he?"

"To try to take us by surprise?" I said.

"Or to try to take Caer Avroc while we're not expecting it?" Luth of the Breastplate suggested.

A horrible thought occurred to me. "They didn't say they saw anyone in them. Maybe he brought them down empty to load up Sweyn's troops and take them back up to swoop down on Angas."

"We could lose the whole north," said ap Meneth, grimly. "If he's here and he has the ships then we have to stop him using them to get away again."

"Yes," said Urdo. "With that many ships under his hand he can move almost as fast as we can, as long as there is water. If we can take or destroy those ships we have gained a great deal, whatever his plans are. Gathering so many together must have been difficult."

"Maybe Sweyn wouldn't mind Ohtar losing those ships?" said Cadraith ap Mardol, thoughtfully. He looked tired. He had come up from the south that morning. "Maybe he wants to tempt us up there to get rid of them, and if we succeed it's not too great a loss to him?"

"Or maybe he wants to get them all together before we're ready," said Luth.

"Then let him," said Urdo. "We are ready now." He reached behind him for a map. In the tent his familiar jumble of maps and writing tablets was stored in a wooden box with a sloping lid. The map of Tevin had been used so many times that the linen was coming apart at the folds. I am sure he knew it by heart, and I could have redrawn it from memory myself. "Marchel, ap Meneth, you know the land best. Take your alae north towards Caer Avroc. Raul, you go with them if you will. Go through the hamlets." He touched his finger to them as Raul acknowledged the request. "Don't harm the farmers, but be seen. The rest of us will follow, four or five miles behind, avoiding the hamlets. We will exchange messengers hourly, or when we need. Use the code words. If Ohtar is there alone, we will join you and fight him. Even with fifty full-laden ships we are many more in force, if not in numbers. If he is there with Sweyn and Ayl we will come up quietly. Attack the ships if you can. Negotiate for a little and then make a stand—two alae is enough to get them to form up. Pick your ground very carefully. Make sure you don't get caught in a pocket between their forces. When they are ready to attack we will take them from the flank. Send your messengers very carefully."

Marchel rolled her eyes. "Tempt them to somewhere where they *have* a flank?"

Urdo took a drink from his waterskin. "Picking ground to fight is something we've all been practicing."

"You believe he's there?" asked Galba. Urdo grinned.

"I don't say I believe everyone who gives grain, but it helps. It almost doesn't matter. Either he is there or Sweyn is trying to split our forces. To make him think we have done so, it is necessary to look as if we're doing it. He will try to catch us. We shall send out scouts wide from the main body in all directions. We don't want Sweyn coming up on us unawares. If we can catch him then we only need an hour to be together again."

"Sweyn could be trying to get us up there while he tries for Caer Rangor again," suggested Luth. I swallowed a sigh. Luth always thought entirely in terms of fortresses and land.

"It doesn't make any difference which wrong place we are in if he tries that," said Urdo. "But I think this news of Ohtar is true, and I do not think Sweyn wants us to know it. Burn the ships. But if we have a choice, try hard to take Ohtar himself alive."

"Why?" asked Cadraith.

"Only a king can surrender a kingdom," said Urdo. "And without Ohtar, Bereich is a real problem. Borthas killed his son, remember, and his grandson has been brought up at Caer Avroc. If he took the crown, it would be the same as giving the country to Tinala. His daughter is married to Alfwin, and their sons are not yet old enough to rule. Alfwin is too much our friend to rule two Jarnish lands at once without the Jarnish lords rebelling. But Ohtar is an honorable man and has no heirs except those grandsons, who will be our friends when they are grown."

Luth frowned. "If we've won, though, we won't have to worry about their politics? Alfwin and Guthrum are our allies, yes, but we can just send the others back where they belong and take back the land?"

Urdo raised an eyebrow, and Raul groaned audibly. "Do you have any idea how many of them there are?" Urdo asked. "We don't have enough people to farm the land we have. Are you going to individually push each Jarnish farmer into the sea? We could kill all the lords and burn the fields and make the farmers swear to us or starve. We may have to, though I still hope to avoid it. Or we may find, if we kill Ohtar or Ayl, that there will be some lord or king we can deal with. But hoping they'll just go away is just stupid." Luth looked at his feet. He was very brave, and his troops would follow him into a dragon's mouth, as the saying was, but he wanted everything to be clear.

"Many of them are our brothers in the faith," Raul added gently, looking at Luth. "Even in Bereich where Ohtar kills what priests he catches, many of the ordinary people have taken the pebble."

"You're both right," said Luth, sighing. "I didn't think it through."

Urdo smiled. "I've been thinking about it for years whenever there's time to think."

"If Ohtar is killed though," said Glyn, "couldn't Alfwin rule in Bereich for his sons and have a regent rule Tevin for him?" Raul looked at him approvingly.

"If need be," said Urdo. "But I would rather keep things as simple as they might be. He may be killed in the chance of war and rearrange the picture, but I can still tell my armigers not to seek him out with their spears."

We made noises of assent. "Anyway, shall we move?" Urdo asked. We all scrambled to our feet.

After two hours the scouts started to report Jarnsmen among the trees. Marchel's reports were much the same. The hamlets were as usual, no sign of armies, but people were moving. Soon it seemed the woods and gullies were full of them, everywhere we could not take a horse. We even felt the occasional arrow. There were never enough of them to charge, and we were very wary of fighting in woods in any case.

We halted where the river widened for the horses to drink. "I don't know about Ohtar, but someone is here," Galba said ruefully.

"It is very hard to estimate what their force is while they're moving like that," Cadraith said. "There seem to be more of them than I'd expect if it's just Ohtar's men. And they're dressed like men of Tevin, not like northerners. When I was up with Angas I thought the Bereichers wore brighter colors." These was not much sign of bright colors among these troops.

"We can outrun them," I said.

"Do we want to?" asked Gwair Aderyn. "We want them in one place."

"And where do we run to?" said Urdo, thoughtfully. "If we ride very hard we can make Caer Avroc, or Caer Rangor not by sunset but tonight. Yet if either of those fortresses is under siege, we might not be able to get in rapidly."

"That would leave us very exposed," Cadraith said, drily.

"We'll have to stop somewhere tonight where we can protect the horses," Urdo said decisively.

"There's that depot up on Foreth," Luth said. "I've been there taking supplies. It's not guarded. The locals leave the place alone because they think it's haunted, and it's been useful to us before. We'd be on a hilltop, and there isn't enough cover for them to creep up and start hamstringing horses."

"There's no water up there," said Gwair.

"The river's near the bottom of the hill," Luth said. "If we water the horses before we go up, we'll be all right. If they cut us off from the river then we can charge through them in the morning."

It seemed like such a sensible idea in the blazing afternoon. Even when we got to Foreth at evening with the mist rising off the river it seemed sensible. The wide hilltop had plenty of room for all the people and horses. To the west was one very steep side, almost too steep to walk up. The other sides sloped more gently and could be ridden. We made our way up the path to the top. There was plenty of food stored there, among the ruins of the old fort, covered over with new wooden boards. We could rest and be ready to go north or south if the scouts found any concentration of Jarnish troops. We set up camp in the remains of the ancient fort, near where the supplies were hidden, away from the table stone which was at the very top of the hill.

The scouts kept reporting that the woods and the gullies and the waterways were full of Jarns. Urdo sent Marchel out with two pennons in addition to the usual scouts. We needed to know where their main body was. Reports came back of more groups of them moving towards us, and then sometime during the night reports stopped coming back. They didn't push the inner ring of sentries set up around the hilltop at all.

When Elidir woke me at dawn to tell me Urdo wanted me they were all around us, clustered at the points where we could charge, most of them directly downslope to the south. The main body was back towards the trees, and a line of pickets was nearer the foot of the hill.

"We can charge now," Luth was saying expansively as I came up. He was wearing his famous blue breastplate and looked splendid. "Right now. As soon as we can be mounted."

"The trees are crawling with them," Galba said, screwing up his eyes. "There are what, maybe five thousand of them right there with Sweyn? That can't be all of them. There are probably that many again in the woods, must be if Sweyn doesn't want us to roll over him."

"There's something else wrong." Urdo seemed to be listening to something. "Anyone been down this slope?" We shook our heads. The nearer part was covered with heather and bracken, far from ideal for riding over. Below it became sheep-grazed turf, sloping gently towards the Jarnsmen. "Sweyn's no fool to stand there and tempt us like that. I don't think the slope is sound."

"If they've trapped it, then they must have done it before we got here," said Luth, his voice catching a little.

"Not your fault," Urdo said, and clapped him on the back. "It isn't as bad as it looks. We can check for holes and trenches and fill them in when they're not looking and surprise them."

"When?" I asked. "Tonight? And charge tomorrow at dawn?"

"Tonight. Yes," said Urdo. "How much water is there?"

Glyn sighed. "I filled all the buckets, but it isn't really enough, certainly not if it gets hot like yesterday."

"It might rain," said Luth. The mist was burning off even as he spoke. "It always rains in Tevin," he added, without much conviction.

"If he knows we have no water, he will wait for Ohtar, if Ohtar is really here somewhere," said Galba.

"Or just until we are too weak to do much damage," Urdo agreed. "Sulien's idea about dawn is a very good one if we could do it."

"They have some archers," said ap Meneth, pointing. "See how many of those men there near the center of the pickets have bows? They never have many, but there are enough there to do damage if we charge here."

"Let's check all the sides and make sure where they are. Also send people down discreetly to check if we're right about the holes."

"Should we try and negotiate?" Cadraith asked.

"I'll send Raul down and see what they say. I wonder where Marchel's got to?" I wondered too. She was in a very bad position—cut off from us, without much in the way of supplies and with no other help within reach.

Urdo went to wake Raul. I sent Elidir to call my decurios and talked to them for a while. I was back at the edge in time to watch Raul pick some little branches from one of the rowan trees that clung between two rocks on the shoulder of the hill and trudge down towards the Jarnsmen.

It was a very long day. My armigers were restless and unhappy. They wanted to fight or move. They were not used to being trapped. None of us were. I couldn't work out what the awful waiting reminded me of; it wasn't Caer Lind, when I had been too tired and strung-out to feel it. Raul went up and down several times. Watching him tramp wearily back up the path, pebble swinging, I remembered. I had felt like this at Thansethan, waiting for Darien to be born. I wished Garah was there to share the thought that the day was pregnant with battle. I didn't know anyone else who would have laughed at it. We gave the horses what water there was. We grew very hot and thirsty ourselves.

In the late afternoon Marchel charged them in their rear. She must have collected every scout between Foreth and Caer Lind; she even had a banner. It looked as if she had a whole ala. She was aiming directly for Sweyn, meaning to kill him and force his sworn men to break the line and chase after her to clear their honor. It would have been a good plan if it had worked. Unfortunately they stood firm and she did not come near him. It was over before we could mount up and come to her aid; she wheeled away to the west as fast as she had come.

"Good," said Urdo, from where we were watching. "Look. She's shifted him." Sweyn was moving his main body around so that they had their backs to the river, although there were still hundreds of them in the trees. "She can't take him in the flank now, but it makes it much better for us. They've nowhere to run to. They'll stay clumped there, too." As the Jarns moved, Sweyn brought some of his pony men around out of the trees and sent them off after Marchel.

"I hope they catch up with her," I said, "it'll probably make her feel a lot better to have something to wipe out."

"No doubt she'll kill what outliers she finds," Urdo said. "But I think Sweyn's sending them out to watch for her coming back, not to bring her to battle. There's nothing like enough of them."

"I've fought them before," Luth said. "They're pretty useless. Our horses could fight them on their own."

"They were the same at Caer Lind," I said, and grinned at him. He was still looking a little downcast. "Useless. Too small to be much trouble. They seem to have learned to ride them a bit better, though."

"Sweyn, or someone, is trying to learn what works for us," Urdo said, turning his head to watch them go.

Just before sunset Urdo called the praefectos together again in his tent.

"Two can play games with mist," he said. "When it is dark and the mist rises tonight we will send the quartermasters and grooms down to cover over the ditches and fill the holes on the south side. They can take the planks from the depot roof. One of your pennons can cover them, Gwair. Also make some half-peeled sticks from the thorn and the hazel trees down on the east side. Put them with the pale sides facing up towards us so that we can see the safe lanes. Then when there is light enough after the dawn we will charge." It would be very dangerous work to do in silence, slitting the throats of their guards, filling holes, marking lanes. Gwair raised his chin. Urdo did not ask for suggestions, and he did not look as if he wanted any. But it had to be said.

My mouth was so dry I squeaked when I began to speak. "What about water? Wouldn't it be better to charge now while we still have strength?"

"This was a holy place once," Urdo said. "They named the Mother here with names of water. I am going to try and call it here again. The land remembers." Galba caught his breath. "Do not raise hopes among the armigers that may be dashed, but be ready to water the horses when we can."

"Water on the top of a hill?" asked Gwair Aderyn. But he did not sound sceptical, he sounded delighted. The praefectos were exchanging pleased looks that we knew a trick Sweyn did not. I frowned.

"I will do what I can. Luth, set up the sentries. Have them watch the main body of the Jarns as well as they can. If they find out what we're doing, we need notice of it. Gwair, organize covering the pits." Just then a sentry burst in, one of Galba's people. "What is it?"

"More Jarnsmen approaching."

"Up the hill?" Urdo leapt to his feet.

"No, my lord. Along the river. In boats. Lots of them. Flying the walrus flag." The sentry was very young. He was trembling.

"Only Ohtar coming. Thank you." Urdo sounded pleased if anything. I could see the fidchel board, our kingpiece trapped on Foreth between their encircling fighters.

"Ohtar?" echoed Galba as the sentry left.

"We knew he had the ships," Urdo said. "It makes no difference, or rather, it makes it better for us. Ohtar is very bold and does not like to wait about. Now I think they will make a stand tomorrow. Go and do what I have told you. Everyone get as much rest as you can. Share out the grain to the horses tonight with the last of the water. Sulien, stay here." The others rose and left us.

I looked at him. He seemed cheerful and confident. I remembered how I had felt at Caer Lind when I was sure we were going to die and wondered if that was how he was feeling now. I just felt tired and dusty and thirsty. But he looked at me and grinned, and I felt my spirits rising.

"Cheer up," he said. "Now water. No matter what cost we have to pay in time to come, what do you know about the old gods and water?"

"I know what Dalitus wrote," I said.

"What?" Urdo leaned forward eagerly.

" 'Never accuse a superior officer of bluffing.' " Urdo stared at me for a moment, then threw back his head and roared with laughter. When he had his breath again he reached out and hugged me. I raised my eyebrows.

"It's good to laugh," he said, stepping back. "But will you help me?"

"Of course, my lord," I said.

—22—

There rise rills in the peat,
waterfalls wear away limestone,
over black-flaking slate slide streams heady as wine
a cool sharp joy to the tongue.
Pools stand under tall trees,
and in the cupped rock, deep lakes.
Reed beds rise from the fen,
green stalks, brown heads, wet-rooted.
Otters splash in cool brown bogs,
dawn dew shimmers on spider silk,
and the rain falls fresh from grey clouds.
The slow rivers sweep the plains
drawing sweet water down to salt sea.
Water flows and returns,
a holy thing is clear water rising up
from Earth's depths, falling from high sky,

a boon to the thirsty, Coventina's gift.

The leaf turns slowly on the still pool.

 —Tanagan charm for purifying water

The sun had set and the moon was rising, silvering the mist that filled the valleys. Around the hill the Jarnish campfires made a sullen glow. We had no fires. In the distance the peaks of the Breghedan hills were dark distinctive shapes against the starry sky. The camp seemed quiet and restrained as we walked through it. Gwair Aderyn was singing softly. I recognized one of ap Erbin's brother's new songs. We walked away from everyone, up onto the highest point of the hill, where the table stone was. Nobody had camped near it. It made people uneasy. I longed for Garah. Garah had a particular love for the Mother, Breda, she called her, Coventina. I thought of how the water had shot up at Caer Lind when I used Garah's charm. I remembered Garah's mother giving me a cup of milk and honey in Coventina's name.

As we walked I seemed to see shapes moving with us, old kings from forgotten times, priestesses carrying curved knives, a small child running through bracken, steely-eyed sentries guarding walls that were long crumbled. If I looked closely at these shapes they vanished, only to reappear again in the corner of my eye when I looked away. As we came up to the stone I saw Osvran standing there, looking hopeful, talking to a shadow of myself whose face was horribly twisted.

Urdo said nothing and did not slow his walking, so I did not know if he had seen anything. He was the king. Perhaps he saw them all the time. When we came to the rock he stopped, and the shadows faded.

"This is the place and I am here," he said, conversationally. I pulled back my sleeves and reached out my arms, palms downward. I sang aloud Garah's hymn to water that had been in my head since we came away from the camp.

There was no sudden change. I did not even notice for a moment that the change had come. Urdo nudged me. The hilltop was no longer the top of the hill. There was another, higher, saddle to the north. A rocky path led up between high banks towards it. It looked as if it had always been there and we had not noticed. Urdo went toward it. I followed him, picking my way as best I could over the stones and the dust. Some of the stone was the stuff of the hill and some was loose shale under my boots. It sloped up steeply, it would be too steep to ride easily but not too steep to lead horses. The moon was shining down on us, lighting our way and giving all the shadows very sharp black edges. Bracken grew on the sheer upward sides of the path. I did not look back. The slope grew steeper, and we came over a lip to find a great leaf-shaped pool stretching before us, filling a bowl in the hills. What hills? I looked up and around and saw that the hills of Bregheda were no longer in the distance but around us; we were among them.

I smelled her before I saw her. The pool was full of dark weed, twisting and twining, and I thought some of it must be rotting. The smell was like overripe plants, like the heart of deep mixed forest, a deeply fecund smell. Even when I saw her I thought for a moment she was a seal lying on the rock. Urdo knew at once. He waded straight out into the water towards her. I followed more carefully. The water was shallow, it did not come above my knees. As we came closer she sat up, and I saw that the weed was her hair. I think all the pool was part of her. Maybe the hills as well. She laughed, and the sound was very merry and very amused, and it echoed around the bowl of hills like thunder.

"So, my husband, now thou seek me," she said to Urdo, speaking in Tanagan. Her eyes were very big and very dark. Her skin was blacker than I have ever seen on a human person. Her breasts looked like the breasts of a woman who has borne children. She was very beautiful and yet wild and savage, and I feared her.

"I have come," said Urdo. His voice sounded joyful and as wild as hers. "I am king of Tir Tanagiri, and I have come by right."

"Yes, beloved, but what brings thee? Dost thou seek a son to follow?" Her voice left no doubt that she was making the offer woman to man, and not just offering a goddess's blessing to his wife's womb. The lake rippled a little, spreading out from her rock, and I saw Urdo sway a little as it passed him. I felt my cheeks heating and was glad of the darkness. She may have seen anyway, for she laughed again.

"That is not why I have come," Urdo said, cleverly sidestepping the possibility of refusal. "I seek water for the horses."

"No small thing thou'rt asking, dearest," she said. Urdo bowed his head.

"I know," he said. "And it is no small thing for me to come and ask. I have never asked before. Until now, I have done it all myself."

"Though thou wed me by the oak tree, all this time thou asked for nothing. When thou'rt dead then I will hold thee, for I know thou truly love me?" Her voice was a little plaintive on this last, but I did not know what she was asking.

"My land, or my people, both, or either. I don't know if there is a difference. I am doing my best, Lady," he said.

"Thou wilt not blame me for thy sister?" Urdo drew in a sharp breath, and shook his head. I had not known Morwen had tricked so many gods.

"Do not speak of it. Her son will never come to my crown." No, I thought, Angas had already proved his faith there. I had forgotten about young Morthu.

"Her great-grandson will, I'm thinking, if the path lies clear before thee."

"That's too far ahead for me tonight, Lady. I know you think far ahead, but the Jarnsmen will have what crown there is if I do not water the horses tonight." She laughed again, and it sounded more like thunder than ever. Her belly rippled, and the pool rocked, splashing around my legs. She seemed to take notice of me for the first time. She smiled, but she looked sad.

"I was with you, by the oak tree," she said to me. "And the child was worth the bearing." I raised my chin. "Ah, stern soldier, dare to love him," she said, very sad now. I could find nothing to say. I didn't know whether I was in time for my love to mean anything to Darien. She looked away, back towards Urdo.

"Ah, thou always knew I'd let thee, small enough a thing to give thee, there's so little we can alter, though we long to, though we love you. Take my water with my blessing. Fetch the horses, let them drink deep, they will never water better, gifts I give beyond thy knowledge, Rhighanna herself will bless me." Now Urdo laughed.

"My great thanks, Lady."

"One more thing that I can give thee, given long into my keeping." She put her hand beneath the water and drew out a sword. The water sparkled as it ran off in the moonlight. It was so silver as to be almost blue. "Crown and stone thou hast already," she said. "Bear this at thy side in battle. Time and past it saw the sunlight. Come and take it, let me kiss thee." The water rippled again.

Urdo turned to me, and there was a strangeness in his voice. "Sulien, go and get the horses. Bring them up thirty or so at a time. Get some people to help bring them up. We'll be all night in any case. I will stay here."

I waded back across the lake and down the path, knowing better than to look back.

I feared to step off the path in case it vanished, leaving Urdo far away. I had no choice when I reached the end of it by the table. It stayed while I woke Glyn and Masarn and Rigol. Glyn quickly got people organizing the horses while Rigol and I led the first group up. It was strange, walking along in the darkness with horses, waiting while they drank and leading them back. I saw no sign of Urdo or the Lady by the lake until we had finished. I did not take every group up, but I was there with the last group, my pennon's horses. When they had finished drinking, Urdo was there, on the shore, the sword strapped to his side. Neither of us said anything. He took Prancer's head and started back down the path.

"It's almost morning, by the stars," I said, when we came back to the stone. It had seemed a long night. We learned later from Marchel and the Jarnsmen that it had been three days for the world beyond that hilltop. "Glyn's given the grain to the horses. And he got me to take buckets down for the people to have water. I hope that's all right. She did say we could take the water with her blessing."

"She did," said Urdo, and I could tell he was smiling. "We will all eat and drink, and when the morning comes we will be ready."

It was all a little dreamlike. It might have been the night without sleep. Almost all the other armigers were well rested. They looked fresh and cheerful. We formed up in alae and pennons to eat what the cooks brought us in the first light, hot oats with some dried fruit, what was left from feeding the horses. It steamed a little in the dawn air and tasted very good.

I had tightened Glimmer's girth before it was really light enough to see, doing it by feel. Urdo was moving among us as we ate and got ready, having a quiet word with almost everyone, raising their spirits and making sure they understood. He needed to know that every praefecto and pennon commander knew their part and was in the right place. He embraced each as he left them, and many of the ordinary armigers, too. I ate standing up, leaning against Glimmer's solid silvery flank. I picked out the pieces of dried apple and gave them to him when I'd finished all the rest. I was just wiping his enthusiastic slobber off my hands when Urdo came up to me, carrying his great banner. It was furled around the pole. It was an heirloom of his house, a huge dark purple banner with no device. Nobody knew how old it was, nor when it had been brought from Vinca. Some said it had been carried by the Emperor Adren when he stormed Dun Idyn four hundred years before. Certainly Emrys had raised it as a sign of his imperial claims. It looked almost black in the dawnlight.

"Will you ride beside me and carry my banner?" Urdo asked. I could hardly speak. I straightened up, stammered some thanks, and took it to feel the weight. The pole was very solid, but the banner itself was as light as our ala banners, for all that it was so much larger. It was made of silk, silk that must travel a year overland through strange lands before it comes to the border of Vincan lands at Caer Custenn at the far edge of Lossia. I fitted the base of it into the cup by my stirrup. It was the first time I had used the banner cup on this saddle except in training. I gave a messenger my shield and spear to take back to the packhorses. I wouldn't be able to use them with this.

Urdo gestured the other praefectos closer. Galba looked enviously at the banner. "Galba, you and ap Meneth will take Sweyn and the right. Luth, you and Cadraith take the left, facing Ohtar. Gwair and my ala will take the center and face Ayl. The difficult part is getting through the bracken. I've told everyone to make it look slower than it is. They will not be expecting us to be as fresh as we are. We still have some benefit from the mist, too. Watch for the marked paths through the obstacles and the instant we are through form up into lines facing forward as fast as we can. All just as we've practiced a thousand times, except for the lanes. Be ready to charge as soon as you see my banner."

"You've got Marchel's three pennons with you, Sulien?" Galba asked.

I shook my head. "They're with Gwair. I have five of my pennons out ahead and my pennon behind the king in case we stop." My pennon had not been very pleased to hear this, they were used to leading the charge.

"We will do our best not to stop," said Urdo. "They won't have faced six alae before, and we know two alae do a lot more than one."

"What about Marchel?" Gwair asked.

"She may see and come out and join us. I'm not counting on it. She's not had many choices down there," said Urdo.

"If Ohtar changes into a bear what do I do?" Luth asked.

"Try to stop your horse bolting," Urdo said, and grinned.

I laughed at Luth's expression. "Unless the whole army of Bereich turn into bears you don't really need to worry," I said. The light was growing. It was almost time, the mist would lift soon. Urdo embraced us all and sent the others off to take their places. The Jarns were moving about, but I couldn't quite make out what they were doing. They seemed to be in a desultory line of battle, though it was tighter on the left, where Ohtar was. I made sure all my decurios knew what we were doing. One would have thought from ap Erbin's face that he was a little boy who had been given a real sword for Midsummer Day. I suppose I should have given him more chances to lead.

I swung up onto Glimmer's back. Urdo and Prancer were beside me. There was music in my head, a song in a language I do not know. It had a strong insistent beat, and it carried me along with it. There are many songs

about that charge at Foreth, but that is not one of them. I believe the Lady
sent it to carry me forward. When I think of that day now I still hear that
music.

The grooms had covered over the pits. They said it was easy. As we
waited I hoped they had done it thoroughly, right down to the bottom of
the hill. Even a few horses down would slow us, probably disastrously. We
had to hit Sweyn fast, before he realized that we were not as weak as he
hoped and caught us standing. Fifteen thousand screaming Jarns was nothing we wanted to fight from a standing start.

Glimmer was ready, more than ready. I patted him, glad of his eager-
ness, but I missed Apple. Apple really loved a fight.

Now the Jarnsmen were forming up into a line of battle, about three
hundred yards from the base of the hill. The three kings were there, each
surrounded by their huscarls, their best men, and farther out their fyrds-
men. They were three distinct hosts. It was said later that there were indeed
fifteen thousand altogether, or even more. At the time it just seemed that
there were a lot of them; the ground was dark with them.

We filtered down through the bracken and through the clear marked
lanes the grooms and Gwair's men had made. Then came the ready signals,
first the raised banners from each pennon, then the trumpet calls from the
alae trumpeters as each was ready. It was a long minute between Luth's first
blast of readiness and Galba's coming sixth and last. It was fully light now,
light enough to see the whole line of armed and armored armigers, six alae,
more than a thousand horse, spread out over more than a mile in a disciplined line across the hillside.

I could hear frantic drum signals from the Jarns below as we got ready.
They must have been surprised when we appeared like that in the light,
through the obstacles, ready. I couldn't see them clearly past the two lines
in front of me, but it looked as if they were tightening up and getting
ready.

Then Urdo drew his sword and raised it high. The upswung blade
caught the light of the sun as it rose out of the clouds and flashed out bril-
liant blue-white. I unfurled the banner. It was bigger than a blanket. I don't
know why the Vincans needed them that size, but it certainly was impres-
sive. Then, as the front line was already moving, Grugin blew the general
charge signal, the great unmistakable trumpet blast, the five notes of "I'm
coming to get you" that means everyone should charge forward at top
speed. The front two ranks were moving off quickly, and it was time for us
to move. I drew my sword as we took the first walking steps before we

began to trot. It looked dark and battered in comparison to Urdo's shining blade.

Then we were moving, fast. The music swelled in my head, weaving in the charge call and the other signals. We were very close together. I could smell the charge, that particular mixture of human sweat and excited horse sweat. It was strange to see each pennon's rally banners and charge banners all going forward together as we moved, the gold and the white streaming back in the dawn wind. The purple banner caught the wind and blew back behind me, the only dark color among all the gold and white. It was like Caer Lind except that this time there were enough of us.

There is no time, and all time, charging behind a line of lowered lances towards a line of trained men who will try their best to stand firm and kill you. Even with the music bearing me up there was time to think, to remember other charges, the hours of practice it takes for people and horses to do this, so close. I remembered Duncan telling me that cavalry must keep moving and never hesitate and Angas yelling at me to relax enough for the horse to do its share. Each pounding step brought us closer and closer, the lances held light as moonbeams pushing points as sure and deadly as doom. Before us stood the Jarnsmen, their faces drawn and ready and waiting, some smiling, some almost bored, many concerned, questioning, very few of them afraid. I remembered Caer Lind, where we had twice broken on their shield wall. They threw their small axes and spears, but we were going too fast for them to hit many of us. Our line curved out slightly to take them as we wanted to. I was sorry that this time I couldn't carry a lance in the front line and be the first to hit them. But I had the banner, and the place of honor. My king was beside me and my friends were around me and my horse was under me. My mouth was open and I was singing, or calling out a battle cry, or screaming. They tell me I sometimes scream in battle, though I do not take notice of it.

A great howl rose from the Jarns on the left. It was the Bereichers all yelling together in the hope of putting Luth off his stride. Then there was no more time to think. We reached the Jarnish shield wall with a shock but no pause. It was strange to see them go over like that, two long lines of men with locked shields just gone under the impact of lances and the weight of the horses. If they hadn't realized as we galloped towards them, then they never had time to realize we weren't thirsty and exhausted before they were down. The line broke, and they were moving back. It was far from the end, for though they fell back they did not flee but regrouped and stood firm for a while with desperate discipline. They were a worthy enemy and no cowards, all king's men. Their shields were almost no protection against the reach of a lance or a cavalry sword, yet they stood firm. "You will feast with your gods tonight!" I heard myself shouting as I struck out with my sword. Most of those who had been charging in front of me were still using their lances. Then a few Jarnsmen started to run away. They fell before me, and I kept moving always, staying near Urdo, using Glimmer's weight against them.

Everything was very clear. We had spread out a little. There was a small clump of Jarnsmen ahead of us, around Ayl. I saw the red eyes of the twisted snakes in the gold ring on Ayl's arm. I had broken bread with him, so I aimed a cut at the man next to him, who went down. Urdo smacked Ayl with the flat of his shining sword as Prancer shouldered into him, then Ayl was sitting in the mud and I kept on. I was laughing.

They were breaking around us like a wave. Glimmer reared up to kick a spearman in the head. For some reason the little details of the horse armor as he moved engraved themselves on my mind, the pattern of holes in the leather that holds the plates. Then Urdo and I were cut off among a thick press of Jarns coming in to protect their king. Alswith brought Masarn's pennon thundering in to save us. I learned later she had snatched up the signifer's banner when he fell. Masarn grinned at me, his teeth showing very white against his skin as he thundered past.

There was no time to thank them then, for the Jarnish horsemen came up behind us. They were brave, for they had lost already, and they must have known it. They did not fight as if they knew it. They kept on very fiercely, though they did not really understand how to fight from horseback. They did better than they had at Caer Lind. They killed several of us, even after I had brought my pennon back together around the king. I saw one of them unhorse Gwair Aderyn. Once he was down and stunned a spearman killed him. I fought with them for some time. I wished I had my shield instead of the banner pole. I doubt the man I thumped with the end of it much appreciated the honor done to him. I needed all my skill at riding to manage without a shield. It felt strange to fight a mounted opponent. It occurred to me even then that if they had greathorses it would be an equal fight, and the part of my head that loves fighting wanted to practice fighting my friends so I could learn the way of it.

Then it was over. They turned to flee, but few of them could reach the trees—the river was behind them. Suddenly Marchel was there, coming out of the edge of the trees beyond the river, cutting off their retreat to the ships. I blinked and wiped sweat out of my eyes. I had no idea where she had come from—I later learned that she had been coming up through the trees and kept her improvised ala still until she could see where she would do most good. Furious battle immediately began to rage around the ships. But not enough Jarns could get away to re-form. They fought on in little knots around wagons and copses, wherever they could rally with their backs to something solid. If they stood in the open we could just roll over them. Those with their backs to something could fight on until we could bring up two pennons and take them from two angles. The only large group of Jarns who were standing firm were Ohtar's men. They had been backed towards the river and did not have anywhere they could possibly retreat without getting their feet wet. But they had drawn themselves up in something like a line. I could see Ohtar himself under his walrus banner, fighting furiously.

Urdo ordered Grugin to blow the signal for the spare horses to be brought up. I was glad to get on Beauty's back and let them lead poor tired Glimmer away. I hopped across, I didn't want to dismount and bring the banner down near the ground. We re-formed, and I looked to where Marchel was fighting. Ap Meneth was coming up to support her. There was no sign of Galba. Luth and Cadraith were still fiercely engaged with Ohtar. I looked at Urdo. There was blood running off his new sword. There were no live Jarnsmen anywhere close.

"Signal Luth and Cadraith to rally," he said to Grugin. "We will form up and charge them again from here: there's room to get up to speed. We should have a five-ala charge." Grugin blew the signal. I sent three pennons out to shield the people changing horses in case Ohtar rushed forward to try to catch them off-balance. The fallen were everywhere, and the smell of blood and butchery hung around them. It seemed impossible that we should have killed five or six thousand men, but that was what they said afterwards. They said that nine hundred and sixty of them fell in that first charge. We lost only fifty, though two of them were praefectos. They had learned to aim at our white cloaks. We lost also a hundred and eighty-two horses, and more than twice that many were wounded. Many armigers were wounded, too, and even more Jarnsmen. Hardly a Jarn left the field that day without some blood spilled to remember the Battle of Foreth Hill.

As Luth and Cadraith were getting ready, a messenger came to us from Galba's ala. There were tears on her face. "Galba ap Galba is dead," she said. "We are going to carry him back to safety. He killed Sweyn."

"We will come over," said Urdo. I followed him, and my pennon followed me. It was not far. The whole ala would have trailed behind us, but I realized in time and signaled to ap Erbin to keep them ready between us and the Jarnsmen.

Galba had killed Sweyn in a way which one often hears mentioned in songs and rarely sees. His lance had gone through Sweyn's teeth and out of the back of his head. It was sticking straight upright in the ground, nailing Sweyn down. Galba himself lay nearby, some of his armigers around him. They were all weeping, Galba had been very well loved by his troops. One of them was holding his mare, Eagle, half sister to my long-lost Banner. A thrown spear had taken him in the chest, straight through the heart. I doubt he had lived minutes after he had killed Sweyn. I hope it was long enough to know what he had done. Absurdly, as they lifted his body onto a shield and began to carry it away, one arm dangling down, I thought of how I had danced with him on his wedding night. The expression on his face was the same, tolerant, slightly impatient, as if there were something he'd much rather be doing. If he could have spoken, he'd have asked me what was so urgent it couldn't wait. Even through that battle music I knew a time would come when I could grieve very much for Galba, and that my grief would be a thin shadow of the grief my sister Aurien would feel, and his father the old Duke, and his young sons.

Urdo drew off his helmet and let loose his hair as a sign of respect. I did the same. My hair was still short from mourning my father, barely reaching my shoulders, a year's growth. I started to put my helmet back on as they carried Galba away. There was no time to mourn yet. I looked over to where Ohtar was still standing out. He had two or three thousand men around him. It didn't look like very many, after this morning.

A messenger arrived from Marchel. She had killed or driven in those trying for the boats and was coming back with ap Meneth to remount and put her ala back together. In front of us the other five ala were re-formed and ready again. Many were drinking from their waterskins and looking brighter and much more refreshed. I did the same myself.

"Shall we wait for Marchel?" I asked as we started to ride back towards my ala, leaving Sweyn's body behind us on the ground.

"No. They can come up behind our line and remount, but I think they can stay in reserve. They must be exhausted," Urdo said.

"Then we use the five who are ready? It's enough. Does Galba or Gwair's ala need anyone to lead? I can spare ap Erbin if need be."

"Not today." Urdo was squinting off towards the Jarnish lines. "Ap Amren has Gwair's ala well in hand, and Emlin ap Trivan has Galba's. I think I will promote ap Erbin soon, though, he's capable and ready for it. And it will please his uncle."

"Will we charge straight away?" I asked.

"Yes—No, look. I think they will surrender," Urdo said. He gestured with his sword, which was shining clean again. Ayl and Ohtar were standing out of their line, talking with a small group of others. Even as Urdo spoke they took off their helmets, gave their weapons to the men with them, and began the long walk across the space towards where our alae were drawn up, empty except for the bodies of their companions. The two kings walked in front, the little cluster of followers, less than a dozen men, straggled a little way behind. Some of them were limping.

We waited for a moment, then Urdo looked over at me and raised an eyebrow. "I ought to call Raul up, but he's way back out of the way with the supply train. Shall we ride forward to meet them?" I grinned, and we rode slowly forward, the lines opening before us, until we came almost up to the kings, out on the trampled bloody grass. When Urdo reined in I stopped beside him, shifted my sword in my hand, and concentrated on the Jarnish kings. I was ready to defend my lord at any moment if they tried treachery. Unlike Urdo's, my sword still showed signs of the hard work it had been put to.

"Truce!" called Ayl, as they came nearer. There was mud and blood on his armor, and he had a great swelling bruise on the side of his head. Ohtar's great bearskin cloak had a sword slash in the shoulder, and when he moved I saw a wound beneath it.

"No," Urdo said, in their language. Ayl went very white. Ohtar looked up at the sky and touched his hand to the bear's head on his cloak. Then Urdo went on. "I seek peace, peace for the land. I do not wish to make a truce with you for a year, and then fight again. I know you are honorable men, and you will keep your word. If you swore not to fight me before next year's harvest, you would not, but the next winter we would see raids from your people and soon again there would be war between us and the shield-splintering din of battle. I do not want you to swear a truce. I want you to swear to the Peace. Peace, between us, and between our peoples. You hold your lands, but within the law, under the Peace, as part of my island. I do not ask this for a year, and not for all time, but for our time, our own lives that we can swear for. But I would have peace between your folk and mine in this time, for a generation, while we live, that we will all live under the law."

"Whose law?" Ayl frowned up into my lord's face, speaking harshly, while the sun glinted on the huge barbaric goldwork of his armrings. When Urdo spoke again it is as if he knew by Ayl's words his battle was won, and his voice was firm and strong. It held hope and a wild fierce joy.

"You will keep your laws and your borders and we will keep ours, and if there is a dispute between your people and ours, or your laws and ours, then it will be judged by kings of both people. And your folk will keep the land peace, and the market peace."

The two kings looked at each other, and the music slowed in my head.

Ohtar cleared his throat. "What of Sweyn?" he asked.

"Sweyn Rognvaldsson lies slain on the field," Urdo said. "Galba ap Galba slew him, and he, too, is dead."

"What of his land?" Ayl asked. "What of his kin?"

"I will give Tevin to the rightful king, Alfwin Cellasson," Urdo said. "And those men of Sweyn's he will forgive will be his men. Those of Sweyn's kin who are grown and yet live and will swear to me and to the Peace I will take into the alae, holding them the equal of my own warriors. The alae will protect everyone from the raiders, and we will have a space to know what the Peace is."

"Aylsfa will have your Peace, if we hold our borders," Ayl said.

"Bereich will have your Peace," Ohtar said. "But you must hold by your word for Sweyn's nephew."

"I have said we will hold no bloodfeud with Sweyn's kin," Urdo said slowly. "Yet before he can be accepted as a brother to my armigers he must answer to me before the law for his involvement in sorcery and his dealings outside the customs of war, him and any man or woman else who does so."

Ayl looked at me. I raised my chin in agreement. I did not hate all the Jarns, only the raiders. Sweyn's kin couldn't be allowed to raise armies and fight against us. Having them in the alae seemed a good solution. Urdo sheathed his sword and jumped down to embrace both men, Ohtar first, then Ayl. The music in my head slowed even more, and the world seemed more solid, less as if I was about to charge again at any moment.

It was then that the Peace began, on the field at Foreth. Afterwards we always counted it so. But then Ohtar turned and brought forward from the group behind the man he was worried about, the man with whom I had just agreed to put away bloodfeud, the man whose name everyone knows I shouted at Caer Lind, Sweyn's nephew, the raider and rapist Ulf Gunnarsson.

2

THE KING'S LAW

Cast out of the homeland, dying nameless,

the renegade, the kinslayer,

ending at last under a stone

cut with strong curses. A hard death

beneath the hooves, on a far hill,

alone and kinless, surrounded by strangers.

—"The Outcast"

Before he had quite come up to us I had thought of nine ways to kill Ulf Gunnarsson. Four of them were not even dishonorable.

Against the line of the river the Jarnish troops were still drawn up waiting, shield to shield. I glanced behind me. Our five alae were mounted and ready, the armigers comfortable on their fresh horses. Ap Erbin sat at the head of my ala, waiting for my signal. A little way ahead of them were Raul, Glyn, and ap Meneth, hovering anxiously with a little clump of messengers. The news that the war was over and that we had made a lasting peace had not yet been announced. They would all have seen Urdo embracing the Jarnish kings, but no trumpet had been blown. If I broke the word Ayl had tricked me into giving, then the battle would start again. I sat still on Beauty's broad back and kept my drawn sword on my shoulder ready to strike immediately if there was any resistance. I felt no desire to dismount and join the others on the ground.

Ulf came forward slowly. There was no honorable way of killing him that would set him down in the mud beneath Beauty's hooves right now. He had not changed much. His straw-pale hair was shrinking back a little at the temples, but otherwise he was just as I remembered him. He was limping a little although he had no visible wounds. I smiled to think that he was still feeling the thrust I had both given and healed ten years before. He wore a single gold arm-ring on his left arm. He looked swiftly at Ohtar and then at Ayl. Then he took a step towards Urdo and began to bend his stiff knee as if he would kneel. Urdo put out a hand to stop him.

"I have said that you must answer to me for your sorcerous dealings," he said. "That must be done first." Now for the first time he glanced up at me. I sat as still as I could and looked at him very evenly, not letting my sword waver. He closed his eyes for a moment, drew breath, and looked back to Urdo.

"Lord King," he said, "I will swear to be true to you, and I shall be true to you, but she sits there with sword drawn. She hates me and means to kill me."

"And have you given her no reason to hate you?" said Urdo, his voice light and cheerful. "I say if you will serve me, you will first answer to me, to me before the law. What has been done in war I will forgive, but what you did and the evil Morwen ap Avren did must be answered for." At Morwen's name Ohtar stepped away from Ulf, leaving him looking very alone. I smiled at him. Ayl happened to be looking at up me. He shuddered and turned to Urdo.

"You said you would forgive what was done in war. Will you be bound in your will by a woman? Or will you make her obey?" Ayl had had the most contact with Urdo of all the Jarn kings, and I think knew him the least well.

"Make her obey? I had rather kill you all." Not one armiger would have doubted that voice, Urdo's certain, cheerful, of-course-this-is-possible king's voice. Certainly Ayl didn't. He went so pale his eyes showed bruised. I thought then that Urdo was just trying to silence Ayl. Years later I found out he really had meant it.

"I don't know what cause I have given you to doubt my word, King Ayl," I said. Ayl shook his head as if to say that he did not do so. I did not give him time to speak. "But if this"—I pointed with the toe of my boot toward Ulf—"will abide by my lord's justice, then certainly I shall." I had absolutely no intention of cleaving Ulf into two parts where he stood unless he made a move against Urdo or the other kings. I might well wish he would so I could, but I did not want to tarnish Urdo's new-minted Peace. Before the law Ulf's life was three times forfeit. He had killed my brother, he had burned my home, and he had given me whole and unwilling into the hand of a god I had not chosen.

"I, too, will accept your justice," Ulf said. "And I will take what doom comes to me," he said, and looked suddenly much more cheerful, as if everything were suddenly much simpler.

Urdo turned and made a hand signal to ap Meneth. He began to ride towards us, bringing his little group with him.

"First, I will announce this Peace," he said. "Then if you choose you may wait with my praefectos while I get this matter out of the way. Because it touches on my kindred and on the gods I would rather deal with this matter alone and in the holy place."

Ayl looked content, but Ohtar frowned hard, glancing at Ulf and then up at me. "You said that when the law concerned a dispute between our people and yours, it would be judged by the lords of both people together," he said. "It seems to me that this is such a case. And if it touches on the gods, as I do not doubt your word, then it seems it is rather the gods of my people than of yours."

Urdo looked almost as if he would laugh. "You are a brave and honorable man, Ohtar Bearsson," he said. "I would far rather have you with me than against me. Will you come up to the holy place and help me judge this matter, then?"

Ohtar smiled. "I will. And this shall be the first test of your Peace."

Ayl caught at an arm of the great dark bearskin Ohtar wore as a cloak and whispered something to him urgently. I caught the word *walkurja*. Ohtar shook him off as ap Meneth and the others came up. The other men who were Sweyn's kin came up, too, and knelt and swore to Urdo. Ulf waited a little apart. He did not fidget. He looked almost relaxed.

"Blow the call that the battle is over," said Urdo to the trumpeter as the last of the Jarnsmen scrambled to his feet. "Let it be blown three times so that everyone may know that Peace is made."

"Peace?" asked Raul, looking only at Urdo. I had expected him to be pleased. He had been working for it as long as Urdo had, after all. But he sounded as if he were suppressing fury, the way he had when Galba and I had overheard him yelling about logistics.

"It is agreed," said Urdo, in his most decisive voice. Ap Meneth beamed. Glyn looked delighted. The trumpeter blew the blast, three times, so that everyone knew that this was a real and lasting peace, not just a brief truce. It rang out very loud in the stillness. Then a great cheer rose up from the alae and was answered by another cheer from the Jarnish lines. I noticed Ohtar grinned to hear it.

Then Luth came up, with the other praefectos close behind him, and the armigers began to dismount.

"We ought to break bread," said Glyn. "But while we have some food we don't exactly have any bread—"

"I will invite you all to a great feast to celebrate the Peace at Caer Tanaga when the harvest is safely in," said Urdo. "We will have much to discuss in any case. For now, Glyn, whatever you have will suffice."

Glyn shamefacedly brought out a circle of cold acorn cake, blackened on the stones of some campfire. It looked most unappetizing. Urdo took it and broke it roughly into three, then handed the other pieces to the Jarnish kings. Then he gestured to me. I was confused for a moment, then realized he wanted me to sheathe my sword.

I hesitated for a moment. It was still sticky with blood from the battle. If I sheathed it like this it would never come out of the scabbard's leather again. I pulled at the corner of my cloak, and stopped. Of course it was my white praefecto's cloak, sewn with golden oaks. Nor did I want to get down to wipe it on the grass. Embarrassed, because they were all looking at me, I pulled out my water bottle and poured the water over the blade. I thought it might take off the worst of it. I'd probably have to get a new scabbard later, but I wouldn't have to cut the blade out. To my amazement as the water trickled down the blade it shone clean, the blood and water ran down together and soaked into the ground. It was the last of the water from the lake. I dried the clean blade on my cloak and hastily sheathed it.

Ohtar looked at his rough triangle of cake and made a face. The stuff was bad enough hot. "Well, defeat is supposed to be bitter," he said, and took a great bite. Urdo gave a surprised chuckle around his chewing. Ayl ate his bread stolidly.

"I have had worse," he said. "Though I will look forward to another of your feasts at Caer Tanaga. Surprising you have anything left here really. I have no idea how you held out that long on the hilltop as it was."

"We had a depot there," explained Glyn.

"With enough food for two thousand horses for three days?" asked Ohtar, sounding incredulous. "Tell me how you did it? Every time someone tried to go up they got lost in the mist and came back hours later claiming they'd only been gone a few minutes. Almost all the men of Tevin and everyone who'd ever been up there was too frightened to do it again, muttering about ghosts. I thought they were afraid of their own fear. But it was exactly the same when I led a party of my best men up. We got lost, we saw strange shapes, we came back after hours to find we'd been gone only minutes. I wondered if you had slipped away, except that the place was surrounded, and whenever the mist did shift a little we saw horses and movement so we knew you were there. Sweyn thought you might be waiting for us to go away. We had water and food, even with ap Thurrig harassing us we could have waited much more than three days."

"Three days?" I asked stupidly, in the little silence that followed.

"Three days," confirmed Marchel, coming up at that moment and sliding to the ground over the lowered head of her horse in her usual manner.

Ulf looked at her with deep admiration and Ohtar touched the muzzle of the bear's head that lolled on his left shoulder. "I have sent to Alfwin and expect him sometime later today. I also sent to Caer Tanaga and to Dun Idyn, though the messengers won't be there yet."

"We will speak of this later," said Urdo. I caught his frown. In my heart I thanked the Owl-Eyed Lady of Wisdom that she had not sent to all the allied kings and to her father and his fleet. There was nobody at the citadel of Caer Tanaga but Elenn, Garah, and enough people who knew which end of a sword was which to repel a direct attack. I did not imagine Angas would have done anything foolish. And sending to Alfwin was a good idea. I would have done the same. Yet I could hardly take it in. If it had been three days, anything could have happened. Yet we had the victory. The victory and the Peace. I looked back from all the cheerful faces to Ulf Gunnarsson, who stood apart dejectedly. Once he was out of the way I could start to think about what came next.

"You didn't know it was three days?" Ayl asked, shaking crumbs from his beard. He was looking at me.

"It seemed like one night," I said. There was another awkward silence before Urdo started giving orders and making arrangements.

I glared at Ulf all the way up the hill. Glyn had given him a horse, a half horse. He knew how to ride it. This was more than Ohtar did. He was clinging to the saddle of his borrowed mount like a three-year-old child who had never been to the stables before. He kept completely still except for the paws of his cloak moving a little in the light breeze. Fortunately the horse Glyn had found him was a very even-tempered bay gelding, one of ap Mardol's spares. He plodded on after Urdo without paying any attention to the fact that nobody was guiding him. I had heard that they did not use horses for anything much in Jarnholme, but I'd never quite realized what that must mean. Urdo's groom, ap Caw, rode close behind him, ready to help if necessary.

The five of us rode in silence up the slope three of us had charged down that morning. It was early afternoon. It is always difficult to judge how much time has passed in battle, and it had taken Urdo a little time writing messages and sending off messengers. Raul had wanted to come up the hill with us. Urdo had spoken to him firmly and quietly, and he had stayed with Ayl and ap Erbin.

When we came up near the top we dismounted. Ap Caw took the horses and tethered them where they could graze. Ohtar looked very glad to be back on his own feet.

"I had no idea the beasts did as much damage to their riders as to the enemy," he groaned, stretching his legs. Urdo smiled.

"There is a knack to it, and it is best to begin early," he said. "But I expect you will be going back to Bereich by water?"

"That's the proper way for a man to travel," he said, wiping sweat from his face with his sleeve.

"That's what Thurrig always says," Urdo said. "In time you two will have to talk about your fleets and what we can do against the raiders. Now we shall go to the holy place."

We left our weapons with our horses. It was a struggle for me to take off my sword belt. My fingers kept slipping on the buckle. I did not want to leave it behind. I hated to be unarmed. Urdo left his new sword with scarcely a backward glance. Ohtar left two big knives as well as his long ax—he had already left his spears with one of his captains at the bottom of the hill. Ulf seemed almost glad to unburden himself of his swords. One was a stabbing blade, and the other was not a Jarnish sword but something almost like a cavalry sword. He had been fighting from ponyback when I saw him at Caer Lind. I wondered if the knee wound made him unfit to fight in the shield wall.

We walked up to the stone table. Even in the heat and the sunshine there was a stillness about it. There was a sense of something waiting. Crickets rasped nearby. High above I could hear a skylark, though it was not visible. There were no clouds either; the sky was the high faded blue that heralds the harvest.

"Let this be heard," said Urdo, in the Tanagan tongue and in the same even tone he had used the night before invoking the goddess. "All gods of earth and sky, and all gods of home and hearth and kindreds of people. All who may have concern in this matter draw near and take note. And may the White God who hears and holds all oaths from all people hold all that we shall say in this place this day to the truth, where all oathtwisting and lies shall be plainly seen as oathbreaking. And I who speaks am Urdo ap Avren ap Emrys, War-leader of the Tanagans, High King of the island of Tir Tanagiri by right of birth, by right of conquest, and by right of election by all principalities." It was the first time I had ever heard him say that. It was the first time it would ever have been true for him to have said it. His voice remained grave and calm. "I will judge as well as I might in equity, before the mighty ones."

"I will swear to the truth," said Ohtar, "I am Ohtar, son of Walbern the

Bear, King of the land of Bereich and War-leader of the people of Bereich. And I, too, will judge as well as I might in equity."

"I will speak truth before the gods," I said, holding out my hands up and then downward, "and my name is Sulien ap Gwien, praefecto of Urdo's Own Ala." Then I remembered, though it felt very temporary to me and I never dreamed I would one day take it up, I added, "And heir to the lordship of Derwen."

Then we were all looking at Ulf. Amazingly, he grinned crookedly at us. "What can I swear that you will believe?" he asked. "You know I have given myself to the Father of Lies, and you know I am assumed to twist all oaths, and what's more you know I did it before." Very slowly and carefully he took a few paces away then drew his little eating knife. I was between him and the kings but I rose onto the balls of my feet, ready to move of he made any attack. But he only nicked the skin of his wrist very lightly and let the blood fall onto the earth. "May my doom find me, may my corpse rot and my name be unspoken if I do not speak truth in this place this day. My name is Ulf Gunnarsson, and I claim no title and am heir to none."

Then he sheathed his knife, again very slowly, and came closer again. Ohtar was looking at him very strangely. "Well," Ohtar said. "Who brings what grievance?"

"As to the charge I am accused of," Ulf said. "Of sorcery I am entirely innocent. It is true, as the lord Urdo has no doubt heard, that I was there when Morwen ap Avren slew King Borthas ap Borthas of Tinala by blackest sorcery. My uncle Sweyn Rognvaldsson sent me to watch. He told me he chose me among his huscarls for this task because I was kin and could be trusted, and I think he chose me over my younger brother because I was not his heir." He smiled at me. "A Jarnish king must be whole and unharmed when he comes to kingship. You struck very true. At least now I know you for a champion, I will not have to endure hearing for the rest of my life that I was lamed by a whore." Blood heated my cheeks. But he had not insulted me.

"It was ap Gwien wounded you?" Ohtar asked, his eyebrows raised.

"Yes," Ulf said, and smiled. "But it was in the normal usage of war, and I do not reproach her for it."

"We were speaking of sorcery," Urdo said drily.

Ulf bowed to him and continued. "I was there when Morwen killed Borthas, as I said. But I had no part in it. Indeed I was sickened by it as I have never been sickened by anything else. It was very black sorcery. She called on no gods, she took his soul to use in her enchantments. She was mad and terrible, she raved and said dreadful things. I told Sweyn I could not watch another such death, and he railed at me and called me coward, and sent me to watch again when she went to kill Osvran ap Usteg."

I bit my lip. Osvran. This hilltop reminded me of him, even on a hot summer afternoon. "He was a brave man, and much he endured. No one should die like that, least of all a warrior who has sent fighting men to the High Feasting Hall. When he was almost dead I called on the Lord of the Slain to come and take him to the end he deserved, and then I slew him. Before Morwen could stop me he died with my sword in his throat. Even though she needed to unravel his soul for power to use for my uncle and our armies I could not bear to let her have it."

His face was twisted at the memory. I believed him.

"That is the only time I have been glad to hear from a man that he killed my friend," said Urdo, quite warmly. I felt a great relief sweep over me. It was seven years since Caer Lind. I had not believed the Hymn of Returning when I sang it for Osvran, but I believed it now—his soul had gone on its way. I could mourn him the way I mourned any friend lost in battle and not as one lost to the world entirely.

"What did the witch-queen do?" Ohtar asked, sounding interested.

"Railed and raved at me at great length. Sweyn was also very angry with me. Then the day after I saw ap Gwien on the field at Caer Lind, screaming my name and covered in blood. I thought she was a walkurja indeed, my doom come straight to find me. Yet I did not die, and the Lady of Angas did, at her hand. And that is the closest I have come to sorcery."

"Very well," said Urdo. "I have been misinformed, for I knew that you were there and thought that you had been her apprentice."

"This is a very bad thing to have said about me," Ulf said. "Even if I am to die I would keep what name I justly have. My brother Arling Gunnarsson, if he lives, can speak for Sweyn's anger with me, and so can my aunt-by-marriage Gerda Odulfsdottar."

"Nobody here has doubted your word," Ohtar said, smiling a little. Ulf shut his mouth, looking foolish.

I suddenly realized that Urdo had thought him guilty of sorcery and bound to die on that account. I drew breath to speak and heard the skylark's clear trill again. I looked up and again the sky seemed quite empty. If the Lord of the Sky was sending a messenger to guide my choice I did not understand how. Everyone was looking at me.

"Ulf Gunnarsson has wronged me before the law," I said.

"Whose law?" Ohtar asked. "He said you wounded him in the usage of war."

"No," said Ulf. He looked deadly serious now and spoke to Urdo. "She was within the usage of war, and I, perhaps, was not. I was seventeen years old and out on my first raid. I was wrong in many ways. I will offer reparation."

"By Tanagan law or by Vincan law," I said hotly, answering Ohtar. "It has never been acceptable—"

Urdo raised a hand. I stopped, and he spoke, very calmly. "Ulf came onto Derwen land in a raiding party, they burned the house and he killed Darien ap Gwien, the heir and Sulien's brother."

"With his own hand?" Ohtar asked.

"Oh yes," I said. "I was there."

Ulf closed his eyes briefly. "I had not known he was your brother," he said, directly to me.

"This is matter for a bloodfeud, true enough, but it is not outside the usage of war," said Ohtar.

"Further," Urdo said, "Catching Sulien alone and unarmed in the woods, he, with a party of others—how many?" he asked, turning to me.

"Six," I said. I hated to think about it and I certainly didn't want to talk about it. It came back to me in detail as he asked, the fight, the defeat, the rape, the smell of leaf mold, and the pattern of the branches above me. I took a deep breath and smelled the sun-warmed clover and feather-headed grass. "Five and Ulf Gunnarsson. Do we really have to talk about that?" Ohtar looked distressed.

Urdo shook his head a little sadly at me, then looked back at Ulf and his voice was a little less even. "With five others you caught Sulien ap Gwien alone and unarmed and raped her. You robbed her thereafter of all joy in the act of love."

Even with my stomach heaving that seemed unfair. I looked at the grass stalks beside my boots. I felt they were all looking at me. "It would have been worse to find out how awful it was after I was married and it was too late," I said, not loudly, without looking up.

"Heider!" breathed Ohtar, sounding not as if he were cursing but calling on the goddess to witness. "She is a king's daughter," he went on, louder. "Our law would have your head for that."

"You mean rape would be acceptable if my father were a farmer?" I asked, startled and horrified. I looked up and met his eyes. He blushed and stammered.

"I will not say these things do not happen, in raids, in war, when there are men together and women of the conquered. I do say this should not have been."

"It doesn't happen in the alae," I said, angry.

Ohtar raised his eyebrows and looked disbelieving. "The women don't like to see it, and even the stupidest got the point after I hanged two of them," Urdo said, flatly. It had never happened in any ala I served in, and I did not tolerate any such abuse under my command.

"Ulf Gunnarsson?" Urdo asked, and his voice now held anger.

"I did it." I took a quick look at him at the sound of the pain in his voice; he was staring ahead over the kings' heads, his hands clasped behind his back. There were tears on his face. He spread his hands. "What do you want me to say? I meant to do it, and I did it, though the two things are very different. I did not know what it meant. In Ragnald's crew we spoke of women as plunder. That was how we saw her. Then after my friends were dead I think some madness was on me, but I did it and knew I was doing it. And, Heider help me, took pleasure in it."

"Being sorry now counts for nothing," Ohtar said. "Can you pay the great fine that must at very least be set on you?"

"I don't know." Ulf shrugged. "I hold no land of my own right. I have been a commander for Sweyn, and Sweyn is dead and his promises rot with him. The land that was my father Gunnar's is under the wave. Some treasure I have, in Caer Lind; if it is still mine, I will willingly give it. But all I know I have is my name and my life."

"Let us finish the tale of your misdeeds before we begin to talk of reparation," Urdo said. "After that you coerced Sulien into healing the wound she inflicted on you, you promised not to kill her, then you left her bound to a tree, meaning her to die of thirst." Urdo kept his tone very even. Ohtar grimaced at Ulf.

"And he dedicated me and gave me whole to a god not of my choosing," I added.

"And have you had no good of that god?" Ulf asked. I caught my breath. I could not possibly answer that. It was true he had come to save me from Morwen, and maybe in battle. Fortunately, I had no need to speak.

Ohtar was looking at Ulf in complete disgust. "You idiot! You—" his face was almost purple, and he lapsed into a flood of rapid Jarnish cursing. I did not recognize most of the words, and the ones I did were all ones I had been told were unfit for polite company. Then Ohtar regained control of himself and caught his breath. With an effort he began again in Tanagan.

"You twisted an oath and you performed a sacrifice you didn't understand, and you did it wrong and you got Gangrader angry with us Jarns. No wonder he was so happy to drink so much of our blood today. What were you using for brains? That's part of the ordeal for kingship, not a way of sacrificing prisoners. Even if you'd been entitled to sacrifice prisoners, which you're not. Only a king may, and you aren't a king and you weren't then and you never will be!"

He spat on the grass and drew breath. "You just don't understand what you were doing at all, do you? When a king sacrifices for victory in battle it must be done in the sight of the gods and the people, for the whole people. Even then it is a wide and difficult thing, to send someone to the gods. Nobody does it on a raid, and nobody does it for no one's benefit but their own. Small wonder your doom has come to find you, you made it for yourself. You took a king's daughter and you gave her good reason to hate you, you put her through an ordeal and you left her alive to come after you. The only wonder is that you have lived this long." He looked at me and spoke more calmly. "I would agree that you did not do as badly as you might of that bargain with Gangrader, Sulien ap Gwien, but that is small thanks to Ulf. He had no right at all to do it. It was not sorcery, it was oafish bungling."

Ulf looked at the ground.

I looked from Ohtar's expression of revulsion to Urdo, who was frowning. He looked back at me. "What would you, Sulien?"

"Can I fight him fairly?" I asked. "I swore to put his arms on my brother's grave. I have hated him for years. But he saved Osvran, so I would give him an even chance. I will give him choice of weapons."

"An even chance? And if you fall?" Urdo raised an eyebrow. "I don't want to lose you. I need you in the Peace as much as in the War." My cheeks burned again, so much that I thought Ohtar might see, and tears came into my eyes. I looked away hastily, though I had little doubt I could kill Ulf in a fair fight. "And you, Ulf? What would you?"

He took a step forward and knelt before Urdo, the sun glinting on his arm-ring. "Lord, I would swear to you, not from the expediency that brought me to you on the field but from my heart. Sweyn is dead, and with him my obligations, I am a free man. In you I see law upheld and a hope of justice given to all of us." Ohtar's eyebrows rose, and he leaned forward staring at Ulf, bewildered. "Or I will go back to Jarnholme if you order it, if I have a place there. Or I will accept a more distant exile if need be. I will go to death when the Chooser of the Slain takes me; he has not called me yet, and I do not hear him calling me today. As for this matter, I freely admit I have wronged her. I would make reparation, as much as I can. It was ten years ago, and I agree with all the harsh words King Ohtar has given me. I was a fool. I will willingly give up my arms to put on ap Gwien's brother's grave. I will do that in any case, whatever happens. I will fight her if you order it, but only if you order it." He looked away.

"Exile is not a choice here. If you live, you will stay in the ala where I can keep an eye on you," Urdo said. I looked between them, confused. I had wanted to kill Ulf for such a long time. Then I thought of a way out.

"Even if I would accept that offer of your arms, I cannot," I said. "The bloodfeud is not mine to end, it is my brother Morien's. He is lord of Derwen."

"Derwen's half a month from here," Ohtar said. "This need to be settled today. You are his heir. You can do it, by your own law, if you would." He was right. "Or you are welcome to kill him fairly, for all of me."

I looked at Urdo. "My lord?"

"It is not the Peace I would best want if one of you must die to make it, but better a fair and open fight now than something else later. I will not stop you fighting if it is what you want. I cannot and will not order you to give up your vengeance. I will say this, whatever happened, what has been spoken on this hill today will not go further than those of us who are here, just that all has been satisfied."

I looked at him for the space of three breaths. He wanted it so much. The Peace was what he had been working for all this time. But my brother Darien, dead and left to rot. The hours sawing my wrist free. The months at Thansethan. "I would fight him," I said. "Choose your weapons." I looked at Ulf.

"I will fight barehanded," he said. I blinked. Yet it was a good choice. He was my height, or close to it. He had the knee injury, but he had some training, and he had a man's strength of arm and body, probably greater than mine. I would have to keep him moving or end it very quickly if he was not to get the advantage. Thurrig always said if it got to wrestling, you'd lost already. Ulf dropped his little dagger on the grass before the kings, and I did the same.

"Let it be, then," said Urdo, sounding saddened. I looked at him apologetically. "And let what is done here on this hilltop be an end of this forever." I raised my chin in acquiescence and so did Ulf. Ohtar looked interested and not at all concerned.

I walked over to Ulf, and he stood there. I swayed a little, and he still

stood there. He did not move at all. I tried to recapture the anger I had felt at him for so long, but it did not come. I could not feel the rage I felt in battle. I only felt a burning bitterness. I feinted a blow towards his head, an easy dodge for him. I put enough force into it to make it worth avoiding, it would strike him hard across the face if it connected. I meant to move in and kick as he moved away. But he did not move away. I felt the blow connect and moved automatically to follow it up and protect my head. But he did not move to attack, he just stood there, rocking slightly with the blow. I stopped and stepped back a little.

"Aren't you going to fight?" I asked, cautiously, ready to strike or leap back and pivot if he did.

"No," he said, and grinned, then spat a bloody broken tooth onto the ground. "The High King did not order me to. I'm just going to stand here. If your honor requires you kill me, go ahead and kill me."

If I had had my sword in my hand I would have run him through that instant. As it was I struck him as hard as I could on the jaw, so that he fell over. But that was the end of that impulse of fury. How can you kill a man who doesn't fight back, who lies on the ground smiling in a hopeful sort of way? I could have kicked him in frustration, but that was not the sort of rage in which I could kill him. I had killed so many men that day, brave men who had done nothing worse to me than stand in my way on the field of battle. Yet now Ulf lay before me and when I reached out for the hate I bore him I just felt confused.

I stood there and stared down at him. High above the skylark called again and was answered by another. I didn't know what I felt or what to do. I wished Osvran or Thurrig could walk up and call me an idiot and tell me what to do next. I wanted to be in a warm dim stall with a horse that needed rubbing down slowly. Six thousand Jarns had died that day already. He lay there, eyes on the sky, smiling. He had given Osvran a clean death. There was a hollow place in my heart where rage had been. I have never understood where it went. I stood there a long moment. It would have been so easy to break his neck. He had wept when he thought of what he did. Would it be shameful to give up my vengeance and let him live? Not as shameful as killing him only to avoid that shame. I looked at Urdo. He was watching, his face very still. He looked like a carved statue of a king set on the hilltop as long ago as the stone he leaned on. I felt as if I had stood here almost forever already, looking down at Ulf. I kicked him in the ribs.

"Oh get up. You're not worth the trouble of killing. Get up and get me

your weapons," I said through gritted teeth. "And we will say this is over and more than over, and you can swear to the High King and then you can be in my ala and then I'll make you wish you *were* dead."

—24—

In the morning battle,

at noon meat

at night rest.

— Isarnagan proverb

It was raining when we brought Galba ap Galba home. It was not the fine light rain that often marks the end of summer; it was a heavy rain that fell day after day from thick grey clouds and stripped the leaves from the trees and made riding misery. The wind blew cold and constant from the west. All the way down through Tevin, through Nene, through Tathal, and on into Magor it rained until the highroads were slick with water and all the tracks away from the highroads were deep with mud. In some places the mud was dark and sticky and came up to Beauty's fetlocks. I thought it no wonder we saw so few people as we traveled.

Urdo had thought to bury Galba with the other dead. There were too many of them to burn. Fifty-two of ours we might have managed, at some cost to the forest, but not six thousand Jarnsmen. So they were given to the earth in the new way, and great mounds were built below the hill at Foreth where they lie still in honor, their weapons beneath their feet. Galba alone of those who fell on the field was carried home and given back to fire and air in the old Tanagan way.

It was Emlin who changed the High King's mind, coming to us almost as soon as we were back down Foreth Hill and before we had dismounted. Ohtar had decided to walk back down. Urdo had just sent Ulf off and had pushed back his hair and drawn breath to say something to me as Emlin came up. Emlin looked nervous but resolute, and his hair was shorn so short that from above I could almost see his neck.

"My lord," he said, to Urdo, and added "Praefecto," to me, perfunctorily but politely, establishing this as a formal and not a friendly conversation. "My lord, they said they are going to bury the Captain, I mean my

praefecto Galba ap Galba. I have put a guard around his body or they would have taken him already."

Urdo swung down to the ground and summoned the groom with a twitch of his head. He did not look as if he wanted formality. "Glyn's people were only following my orders," he said, as ap Caw led the red horse away, "to have everything ready for sunset. What is the matter?"

"My lord, he was heir to his father's land, and three of his grandfathers shared his name and lie on that land, and he loved it so. The old Duke would want him to come home, all those he led know he would have wanted it." I looked around. There were indeed more than a few of Galba's people hanging around watching us anxiously. They had all cut their hair short. I realized as I saw this that they had done this not for close friends or fallen kindred but for Galba, their captain. They had served under him since Caer Lind, but all the same this was something I had never seen. The Vincan troops had done this for their great emperors, for Adren and Aulius and much loved Drusan. Cornelien records that the legions on the northern borders refused orders to cut their hair at the death of Tovran, saying that grief began in the heart and could not be commanded. The order had been withdrawn. I have always thought this sensible, though Cornelien saw it as a dire precedent. All this passed through my mind as I looked from Galba's armigers back to Emlin. He had been to Urdo's strategy feasts, he must know all this as well as I did. He would not have given an order. All the same someone must have suggested it. Few of these armigers would keep Vincan ways at home.

"It is close enough half a month's ride to Magor, without risk to the horses," Urdo said. "And it is summer." There was a bank of low clouds far off to the west behind the hill, presage of the rain that was coming, but as he spoke it was a very hot afternoon. "It would be better to take the ashes to his family."

"Ten days, from here," I said. As I spoke I felt my voice shake, and dismounted to steady myself. The loyalty of the ala had moved me. As I reached the ground I went on, "I think Emlin is right that it is what his father and the land would want. We could make a casket." Emlin looked at me gratefully.

Urdo turned his head sideways and seemed to be listening for a moment. I wondered if he heard messages on the wind from distant Magor. I looked to the southwest and saw only the river and the forest.

Urdo sighed. "I could not do this for all the fallen. But none other here is a king, or a land's heir. Will you take his body home with his ala then, Sulien?" I turned to him.

"If you can spare me, I could," I said, "It is my family duty if not my desire. It will be very hard to give this news to my sister and his young sons."

"The news will be there before you, the red-cloaks are riding already, news of the Peace and those who died to make it will be all over the kingdom as fast as swift horses can carry it. But if you will take Galba's body home you can perhaps give a little comfort. Also—Emlin, do you feel ready to command the ala?"

Emlin shook his head. "No, my lord."

"That is as I also thought," Urdo said, and smiled, "Leading an ala takes different skills from being a tribuno, and you are a very good tribuno." He turned back to me. "Sulien, do you want to live down at Derwen and Magor near your family for a while?" Before I even got my mouth completely open, Urdo put his hand on my arm. "That was a question, not an order."

"No," I said. A great deal of relief seemed to have crept into my voice from somewhere, but my emotions felt out of reach as if they were happening somewhere else and I was hearing reports of them sent by unreliable scouts. I tried hard to speak evenly. "I will take my brother Galba's body home and then come back. To Caer Tanaga?" I asked.

"To Caer Tanaga, yes, to the feast of Peace when the harvest is in. I will take your ala down with me, and Gwair's ala, too." He frowned a little as he mentioned Gwair Aderyn. "I shall miss Gwair. He was the steadiest praefecto I had, and the first to take up my cause. When I was a boy at Thansethan there were very few things I remembered about the time before I came there. It is all a jumble of pictures in my mind. I remember the silks my mother would wear, and how she always smelled so beautiful. I remember running out in the mud and getting filthy and my nurse scolding me, with mud dripping between my fingers. I remember a bee caught against a window somewhere, buzzing and buzzing to get out, to escape, and yet that may have been at Thansethan for they have beehives there and make good honey. I remember riding in front of someone on the saddle of a pony, I remember how the pony's ears looked quite clearly, but I do not know whose horse it was. I remember seeing a goat, too—that was when I first came to Thansethan, the goat's barred yellow eye. Children take notice of animals, I suppose. I remember when I first came there I did not know how to play with other children, and they all knew each other, having been born there or come there very young. That was strange, and lonely. And I remember coming there, riding through the night sitting on the front of Gwair's saddle with my lady mother riding beside us. He used to come and see me once a year as I grew up, to take back news that I was well I suppose. I always looked forward to his visits. He used to bring gifts. I fancied that he must be my father. I do not remember my father at all." He sighed, staring into nothing. Emlin and I looked at one another, wondering if we should stop him, but not quite daring. "Gwair was a good man. He was of no great birth nor was he very skilled in the new ways of fighting, yet nobody ever scorned to serve under him."

"I never knew him well. Did he have children?" I asked, as gently as I could.

Urdo blinked a little and looked at me, his eyes back on the present. "Yes, he has two daughters, one of them is a decurio in Angas's ala and the other is married in Segantia and has half-grown children of her own. Well. Neither will inherit his ala. When you come back I will put ap Erbin in charge of them and send them on to Caer Segant. We can discuss then who you want as your new second."

"Masarn," I said, without hesitation. "He's the right sort of steady."

"We will discuss it next month when you come back to Caer Tanaga," Urdo said. Appointing a tribuno would usually be a praefecto's responsibility. With my ala it was different, as we worked so closely with Urdo I had long since agreed that he would have a say concerning appointments. "You are in charge of Galba's ala while you are there. Then Emlin, you can take care of them for a little. When you come back to Caer Tanaga, Sulien, bring your brother Morien with you. Galba's trained him, and he's been leading a pennon. Let me have a look at him and see if he's up to command. He's the obvious person, if he can cope with it. Do the troops like him, Emlin?"

"He's very quiet," Emlin said, clearly choosing his words carefully, not looking at me. I wondered what he meant.

Urdo looked at him sharply, but just then Raul came up, and close behind him Alfwin, who had a stunned look about him. "You can leave in the morning," Urdo said. "Marchel's ala will be going back to Caer Gloran; you can travel together that far." Emlin went off to tell the news to the other armigers.

Urdo took two long breaths. "Greetings, Alfwin Cellasson, King of Tevin!" he said. "Have you heard that Peace is made?" Alfwin looked as if he had taken a step off the edge of a cliff and found firm but invisible ground beneath him.

"I missed the battle," he said. "We have been hurrying since we got the message from the daughter of Thurrig, and we came too late."

"You have fought for me and beside me these seven years," Urdo said, "And we all know that those on two feet move more slowly than those on four. I am not giving you Tevin wrapped like a bride gift—Sweyn is dead, and I have his older nephew, but the younger one, the heir, is missing, and there may still be some resistance. Still, that is your problem, you are the king here now, rightfully, in your father's place."

"It is not quite that simple, among Jarnsmen," said Alfwin, and his face unfolded from its stiffness, and he grinned. "Yet, I will be king by the time we meet next, I have little doubt."

"If you wish it, if you wish to be received into the church as your wife has, I could crown you here today in the name of the White God," Raul murmured. I could hardly believe his audacity, even if someone had managed to convert Alfwin's wife. That must have taken some doing considering that she had been in Bereich all the time. Ohtar's fierce opposition to the White God was well-known. I wondered for a moment if Alfwin would accept. I knew, as Raul did, that he had spent time with Marchel, who could be very persuasive. Yet even if he had wanted to it would be hardly possible without consulting the land gods of Tevin. Urdo's face went very blank as if he was deliberately keeping all expression away. I thought of the stone on the hilltop. Alfwin looked more stunned than ever.

"This is not the condition on which you give me the land?" he asked Urdo.

"No indeed," Urdo said. "Nor have I made such a condition even to those who have been fighting against us." Urdo looked impassive, but Raul was frowning.

"A great chance is being let slip away," he said.

"We will speak of this later," said Urdo, and his tone was final. "Any choice you make is your own entirely, Alfwin."

"Indeed," said Raul, "I was only asking if it was what you wanted."

Alfwin laughed, with some anger clear behind the laughter. "I am not afraid to face the ordeal, monk," he said. "Lord Tew who gave us this land will not find me wanting." He turned to me then. "Ap Gwien, of your kindness, is my brother's daughter well?"

"She is well, and what's more she did well, very well, in the battle," I said, pleased to have something positive and helpful to say that changed the subject. "I am proud to have Haraldsdottar in my command, she is daring and valiant and skilled, indeed she led back troops today and probably saved my life, and the life of the High King."

Alfwin did not seem to be getting used to surprises. His pale skin flushed red, and he swallowed. I was tired and had quite forgotten that he would be embarrassed to hear a woman of his family praised for skill at fighting.

"The Cellingas have served me well, even in your absence," Urdo said. He was smiling now, but he still looked a little remote.

"Good," murmured Alfwin. "It is not our way, but it is the way of this land, and we are here now." Alfwin was never a fool. He took a long breath, and spoke more firmly. "Good. I am glad we had our part in this victory, even if I came too late. But I will need her for the next few days, with your permission, of course?"

"Of course," I said. "She can come back to the ala when you come down to Caer Tanaga for the Peace feast."

"Ohtar Bearsson will be here soon," Urdo said, before Alfwin replied. "It would be good if you talk to him today. Also we're going to have to arrange quite quickly what we're going to do to help Ayl with the defense of Aylsfa this winter. Aylsfa is not near as strong as it was this morning."

"I thought Luth and his ala would be a good choice," put in Raul.

"Yes, that would work," said Urdo. He looked terribly tired, suddenly. I wondered if we had missed four nights' sleep or only one. "We will have a full council in the morning, with the allied kings. Organize it please, Raul. And we must speak." Raul scratched a note in the wax pad he wore at his waist. It was full of notes already. I left them to it.

I washed, and slept a little, before the sun came near the horizon and it was time for the ceremony. I do not think Urdo can have had time for either. He was moving stiffly and seeing him I thought I could imagine how he would be when he was old.

All those who were neither wounded nor exhausted had been working part of the day on raising the mounds. Glyn, Ayl, and Raul had organized Jarnsmen and armigers working together, and now the mounds made a line along the length of the hill. The mounds would rise higher yet and grow with grass, and the battlefield would become a quiet resting place. For now the dead had been laid within them by their friends and were covered by earth. I did not see them before they were covered. It was the only thing to do in the circumstances, and of course it is the usual thing now. Thirty years ago when I lit the fire for Veniva it was a matter for muttering, and now if my great-nephew heeds my wishes and burns me when my time comes, it will be a great scandal.

One fire had been laid in front of the mounds, a single pyre, too small to burn even one of the dead. We gathered there before sunset, drawn up by ranks, each ala together. None of the Jarnsmen were there, not even Alfwin and his men—they had had their own ceremonies—but every living armiger who had been at the battle was there on the field. Every dead one, too, of course.

Urdo came forward. Exhausted, he somehow looked more kingly than ever. He was still in his armor with his long hair streaming loose on his shoulders.

Urdo lit the fire and poured on sweet herbs and incense as the sun buried itself in the glorious colors of the westerly clouds. I was standing near the front, but afterwards everyone said they had heard every word he said, however far back they were. The gathered troops kept very quiet; there was no noise but breathing and the little sounds of people in armor shifting their weight.

"Who are you who are before me now?" Urdo began, as the fire caught. He did not speak loudly or seem to be raising his voice beyond a conversational tone. He sounded almost as if he were talking to himself. "My armigers, yes, living and dead, but what beyond that? Not Vincans fighting for a distant city, nor yet the desperate defending their doorway, we have come together, and learned, and made a new thing. Maybe never before on the wide earth has there been such a thing."

He took a breath and straightened up and looked out, his eye running over the armigers. "My friends, you came here to fight, and fought, and some of you fell, and some yet breathe, and all of us have won the way through war to Peace."

He turned to face the mound and raised his hands, his palms turned not upwards as if invoking the gods, but outwards, towards them. Then he turned back to us and did it again, and brought them down slowly as he spoke. "I thank you all, for this is to be honored, and all of us who came to this field this day, living and dead alike, shall always be honored for making this Peace."

He drew a breath, then another. It was so silent I could hear birds in the trees. "How much honor shall be done to the dead, and to those who go on from this day, shall be found in our choices from this day forward. Our honor lies in how well this Peace is kept. Those of us who live will mourn those of us who have fallen. We will not forget our comrades who do not go on, and not just those who fell today but all those who fell making this Peace, all these long years of war. This Peace will be their monument. Peace will not be easy. We scarce know what it can be yet, for none of us have known it."

He looked now as if he were looking up over our heads, to something distant we could not see. "It does not mean we shall set down our spears; as we have won this Peace by strength of arm and will, so we will keep it. We will fight no longer for mastery over this our island but to prevent injustice or repel invasion. Those who were this morning our enemies have agreed to the Peace. What remains now is to bring all the will we had for making it to maintaining it, to go on as we have started, and to build the Peace in our actions, breath by breath, all our days."

I had heard him speak like this late at night in his tent, though before it had always been of hopes; it seemed strange to hear it spoken of as something begun. "We have chosen to be as we are, without reservation or withholding or fear. With that strength, we have made this Peace; within it, those who have not, who do not or shall not or will not, take up weapons, who have not had any choice open to them through the years of war but to avoid as they can the paths of armies, shall have this same choice, to be as they would be unto the uttermost borders of their skill, their capacity, and their desire."

He looked down again, and smiled. "None shall be bound by their birth; there shall be one law for all, where a wrong done with a king's power shall receive the same redress as a wrong done unto a king's power, that redress being founded on justice, and no single whim of woman or man."

The fire was burning well now. Urdo poured some more incense onto it, and a great plume of white smoke rose on the wind. "This is the Peace we have won, though we have it still to build and learn. We who are here today have won that Peace for all those who are not here, and for the land. What we have done this day could not have been, without those who died for it, today and on many days. We shall not forget them, in making this Peace we should not have won without them."

Then he named all those who had fallen that day at Foreth. Many around me were weeping, and I found tears on my own cheeks.

Then we sang the Hymn of Returning as the smoke took their spirits onward even though their bodies were bound under the Earth.

His words rang in my ears all down that long wet way to Magor. All I
knew was war, it had been my whole life. Peace was only a word. I had to
learn what it meant.

We rode on through the rain, and every night when we camped we
kept watch, and the pennons took turns keeping the death watch around
poor Galba. I lay down tired and thought of the new walls at Derwen,
thought of feasting and songs, thought of Darien growing up strong and
safe to live—but there my thoughts grew blank. I could not think how we
would live, without war. I tried not to take comfort in the thought that
Urdo would need the alae for a long time yet.

We reached Magor when the tenth day since we left Foreth was drawing to a close. The rain was falling more finely than it had been, and I had
some hope it might stop before the whole island was flooded. Magor
looked well. I saw that someone had been building walls and stables and
barracks since I had last been there, when I first joined Urdo. It was not as
large a place as Derwen had become—it looked like a lord's house with
room for an ala, not like a town. The hall was built Vincan fashion, with a
covered colonnade along the front. I had sent a messenger ahead as we
approached, so when we drew near the household came outside and stood
a moment under that shelter. I drew up the ala neatly outside the hall as
best we could in the miserable weather, our brave banners and bright cloaks
sodden with the weight of the rain.

Duke Galba was there and my lady mother Veniva, holding a baby
about a year old, and beside them a small boy, about three years old, and
behind the whole household of Magor. All of them had cut their hair off
short. We dismounted in unison and I walked forward past the casket
where we were bringing young Galba's body.

Then Veniva took a step forward out into the rain, towards the casket.
As she moved she looked at me for one moment and as her dark eyes met
mine I realized that I was seeing not my mother but my sister Aurien. She
had grown to Veniva's height, and what there was of her hair, which had
been so dark and lustrous, was turned quite white. Her dark overdress was
pinned with the gold-and-pearl brooch from the hoard. She looked old
and deeply grieved. As our eyes met I knew that Urdo was wrong and I had
no comfort to bring here. It might do the old Duke good to know how
well his son died, the boys were too young to understand. Aurien, I knew
then, would understand nothing from me except that in place of her strong
young lord I was bringing a corpse.

There was no time to waste unless we were to wait until the next day. They had set aside a great pile of dry wood for the pyre. It was laid well away from the house under a makeshift roof of boughs. As we walked to it we passed the line of carved stones that marked the places where the dukes of Magor had been burned. Each stone was doubled save the last. That was where Galba's mother lay, and there was space beside her memorial for Duke Galba. He paused beside the damp ground where one day his own grave would be, and walked on.

It is a sad thing to outlive your children.

Even under the shelter I doubt the pyre would have burned in that rain except for all the hair we piled onto it. The armigers had even trimmed their horses' manes and tails and there was so much hair that they said afterwards that Galba was so beloved he needed no wood but returned to ash on hair alone. Emlin and some of the armigers set the casket firmly in place. I set Sweyn's weapons and the spear we had drawn out from Galba's body under the place in the casket where his feet were. As I did so I remembered that in my saddlebag I now had Ulf's swords ready to take to my brother Darien's grave in the woods to fulfill my vow. The ala stood quietly in ranks, bareheaded, their short hair slicked dark in the rain. I could not tell rainwater from tears on their faces.

The older boy, Galbian, his father's heir, took the torch and set it into the wood, then stepped solemnly back. He must have been practicing because he did it very well. The firelight reflected off the wet leather of the armigers armor. Duke Galba spoke, and Emlin spoke. Then we sang, but Aurien was silent until we had finished. Then she let out a great howl, and squeezed the baby tightly so that he howled as well. I took a step to go to them and take the baby, but Duke Galba laid his hand on my arm and shook his head. He understood better than I did. Little Gwien was a good reminder for Aurien then. There are old songs where grieving widows fling themselves onto their husbands' pyres.

As Duke Galba put incense on the pyre there came a great trumpet blast from the hall. I spun round, as did more than half of the ala. It was a messenger's signal, urgent and desperate news. I knew I should have stayed and watched until the pyre burned down. Even though peace had been declared, I could not ignore it. Everyone was at the pyre. I signaled to two of the decurios and walked back through the rain to the hall, trailed by the two pennons. Aurien gave me a look fit to freeze my blood as I left.

The first thing I noticed about the red-cloak was how tired his mare was. She looked about ready to drop with exhaustion. I was horrified that anyone could treat a greathorse like that. Only then did I realize that the man on her back was Senach Red-Eye.

"Sulien ap Gwien with troops, thanks be to the White God and all the hosts of heaven!" he said. He was swaying in his saddle.

"What's happened?" I asked, reaching up to help him down. He slid to the ground and lurched into my arms. He would have fallen if I had stepped back.

"The Isarnagans have landed," he said, his face uncomfortably close to mine.

"What Isarnagans?" I asked. "Black Darag's?"

"They didn't say," said Senach, bitterly. "I didn't stop to ask, but I expect so. We have an alliance with Allel after all."

"Get something for the red-cloak to sit on, someone," I said. "Now, where are they?"

"They landed away on the far western end of Derwen where not many people live and they're coming inland, a great huge army of them, on foot. Thousands of them." One of Galba's armigers brought a great carved wooden chair from inside the hall, and Senach collapsed gratefully into it, his hands working on the eagles carved on the arms. I went down on one knee in the mud beside it so he would not need to waste breath speaking loudly.

"I was taking the news of the Peace to Derwen when we heard a rumor of them, and I went to see. They're not far from Derwen town, I'd say about a day's march then. There's only one pennon inside, under the lord your brother."

"I have Galba's whole ala here," I said, and I was calculating distances as I spoke. I turned to the decurio on my left. Somehow, even though it was a disaster it was a relief to be giving orders and doing something I understood. "Govien, get your fastest messenger to ride to Caer Gloran with this news straightaway. Send the next fastest to Derwen to tell Morien ap Gwien that we are coming. Get another ready to ride to Urdo at Caer Tanaga as soon as I have written a message. Get Emlin here right now. Get the quartermaster. Get anyone else who is well trained in logistics, trained by Dalmer or Glyn. Get Duke Galba, tell him—give him my deepest apologies, but say it is an emergency and we're going to have to ride tonight."

At meat they sat, uneasy peace
forced by their feasting in the king's hall.
Talk fell to fighting, the hard-fought war
between the borders long disputed.

Emer was boasting, keeping count
seized heads slaughtered, the slain of Oriel.
Provoked past endurance, Conal Cernach
replied in kind, corpses of Connat.

Beaten in bragging, Emer sat sneering
"Bold the boasts you gave against me.
If you should meet my mother, Maga,
that would make the counting different."

Conal standing flung a fresh head
rolling the rushes, crashing by her feet;
"So you say, but see, I know her,
met we have, and here is Maga!"
　　—"Lew Rosson's Hall," a Jarnish retelling of an
　　　　Isarnagan story

All of it, the scrambled start, the night ride, the scouts' reports, faded to
nothing as I looked down at Derwen at sunrise, surrounded.

The ala had been riding all night and were bone-tired. I thought it
wise to let them have some rest while I sized up the situation. I left Emlin
setting up camp near a farm about five miles north of the town. It was the
farm I had been visiting the day the Jarnsmen first came to Derwen. We
reached it just before dawn, but the farmers were already about the place,
milking the cows. The woman I had helped to heal was still there with her
daughter and her daughter's husband. She remembered me at once. I asked
about her son who had liked singing, and was sorry to hear he had died of
the same fever that had killed my father the year before. She knew nothing
of the Isarnagans and had not been away from the farm since midsummer.
She was planning to go to Derwen again when the harvest was in, if the
rain had not spoiled it all. It was strange to talk to someone for whom Der-

wen, five miles away, an hour's easy walk, seemed farther away than Caer Tanaga did to me. Her concerns were all with the weather and the crops and beasts, if the world had sharp corners at the edges of her fields it would not have changed her life much. When I told her I had come from Magor in the night she made a gesture of blessing towards the old stone guardian at the farm gate. Then she said that the horses must be very tired and offered us some food. I did not burden her with explaining the distance beyond that we had come in the last ten days and accepted the food gratefully on behalf of the ala.

Then I went forward with the scouts.

We crawled slowly through the heather to the top of a rise that would give a good view of the town. It had stopped raining in the night, though everything was still very wet. I was glad of the protection the riding leathers gave me from the damp, but even so it was uncomfortable. If I did not have a hot bath and then get thoroughly dry soon I felt as if my skin would start to mildew. Crawling uphill I could see the sea before I could see the town and the fields. It stretched up almost into the sky. It was silver-blue and empty all the way to the coast of Munew. There was no sign of any Isarnagan ships. There would not be if they had landed away west near Tapit Point as Senach had said. As a child I had raced Darien up this hill and flung myself down on the dry purple heather to stare up into the summer sky. There had never been reason to come up here since I left home.

I propped myself up on my elbows and looked. The fields and woods stretched out as they always had, the red of berries starting to show in the hedgerows. There was a mist rising from the river. The town looked much the same as when I had last seen it. There were more buildings inside the walls, houses, storehouses, and workshops. The soft pink of the Vincan bricks in the wall of our house contrasted with the golden slabs of dressed sandstone that made up the new town wall, the barracks, and the new stables. There were people moving about inside the town, still too far away to distinguish faces. I prayed to the Lord of Light for Veniva's and Morien's safety. I could do nothing else for them until I could reach them. The wharves stood empty, and the two roads leading down to the water were blocked with wagons turned sideways. The walls were being patrolled, and there were wooden fighting towers set up near the barricaded gates. It was good to know that someone was taking proper precautions.

All the Isarnagans were on the outside still. Senach had not exaggerated. There were thousands of them. There were so many it looked as if they could break the walls by leaning in on them. The ground was dark with people. They had raven banners, black on white.

I started to count the plumes of thin smoke rising in the early-morning light. If each cooking fire meant thirty warriors—then Flerian ap Cado nudged my elbow and indicated something to me on the far side of the town, the direction from which they had most likely come.

"Wagons," she said. I saw them. Fifty or sixty pony wagons were drawn up into a square. Clustered around them were Isarnagan women wearing long shawls, and children of all ages including babes in arms. These were not raiders come in quantity. This was an invasion. They had come to stay.

I had listened to Emlin half the night as we rode, telling me the defenses inside the walls at Derwen. There was no way we could communicate with those inside, other than by lifting the siege. They must be terrified. But they should be safe for a little while unless they did something foolish. I had an ala. One tired ala. A hundred and forty riders, against what looked like the whole mass of Tir Isarnagiri crowded around the town walls. I could make it difficult for them to take the town. I could do a lot of damage to them. But they could take more damage than we could. It might be possible to scare them and scatter them. If I could identify their leader I could probably kill him, though it would be risky. But if they fled where would they go and what would they do? They would scatter into small bands and ravage the countryside. I could not be everywhere at once. The farmers around deserved protection, too. The Isarnagans had brought their families. It would be very hard to make them go back where they had come from.

I put my head down on my arms for an instant, then looked up again. I had seen, but I was no closer to knowing what to do. If they knew how to fight against us they would make a stand in the trees, or just across the river. We could ford it, but it would slow us down. They could do us a great deal of damage from a distance with their deadly little slings that could break a horse's leg. I had no idea what they wanted, or who might be leading them. I wished they were Jarnsmen whose desires and tactics I understood better.

I looked at Flerian. She was the girl who had brought news across the battlefield that Galba was dead. Her grandfather was in the ala, too, Berth ap Panon, Galba's trumpeter. He had been with Galba for years and had served the old Duke before that. Much as I wished for my own ala about me who understood me, I knew these were good people. What was more,

I could never have done that night ride with troops who did not know the land. All the same I would have liked a friend there, someone who would have understood and laughed with me if I said that this was not how I would have chosen to pay a visit to my family home.

Flerian was counting fires, her eyes intent. She saw me watching her and glanced over. "Five thousand, I would say, though they will not all be fighters," she said. "This might not be all of them." She looked over to me as if she was expecting orders that would make the whole thing simple. She was very young, but still she should have known better.

I bit back a groan. She was right, and there was no point in destroying her belief in me. I had been thinking of the problem of scattering them to pillage the countryside, and it was probably already too late. "We'll have to find out what they think they're doing," I said. I glanced at ap Teregid on my left. He was asleep. I poked him. I was too tired myself to be thinking straight. The scouts were out, I would soon learn if they had scattered. I started wriggling backwards until I was far enough down the slope to stand and walk back to where the groom was patiently holding Beauty.

With two alae it might be possible to squeeze them, if we could get them to form up just right. I doubted they would be that stupid. I wondered if I could keep them here until reinforcements arrived. Three would do it, three would squeeze them up against the town wall like a hammer and anvil. They were Isarnagans, not Jarnsmen; they would have no practice at fighting against us and very few long axes. I started counting times to Caer Gloran in my head, but no matter how the messenger and then Marchel hurried she could not be here in less than four days, and more likely five. If Urdo brought my ala from Caer Tanaga as soon as news reached him, or more likely sent them with ap Erbin, they could not be here for ten days at the earliest. He had Gwair's ala there, too. With four alae it would be easy. I would have to find Nodol Boar-Beard, the quartermaster, as soon as I got back and ask how the supplies were holding out. Without access to what was inside Derwen I didn't know how long we could manage. We might well have to send back to Magor.

All these calculations were made more unpleasant because I knew the town could fall before the others arrived, and my family was inside. The walls were strong, but they had been built by human hands and could be torn down the same way. I thought of my mother Veniva, my brother Morien, and my old arms master Duncan, the people I had grown up with. It was true that in my heart my home was in the ala. Yet talking to the farmer in the dawn had reminded me how much responsibility I bore to the people on this land. I had sworn to Morien very lightly, thinking it no more than a formality that he must have a named heir for Derwen until he should have a son. But I had claimed the title before Urdo and Ohtar. It wasn't as if I hadn't cared all through the War when towns and homes were in danger. When Ayl had nearly taken Caer Rangor I had fought on with desperation. Nevertheless, this was different. Somehow these were my people, my responsibility in a way that only my own troops had ever been. I had not understood before.

I rode back beneath dripping trees to the clearing where the ala were resting and finishing up their breakfast. Even though we were ready to move off again as soon as we needed to, there was something of the style and shape of a camp about the ala as I passed through the sentries. People were sleeping by half pennons, the tired horses were cropping the grass, the latrines and cooking area were in the right places. Almost everyone was either asleep, on guard, or tending to the horses. I felt much more comfortable as I moved among the armigers. One of the cooks handed me some smoked mackerel wrapped in a little bread as I passed by. I called out a blessing on him and went on without stopping, munching it.

Emlin leaped to his feet and came towards me as soon as he saw me, swallowing the last bite of cheese he had brought from Magor.

"What good news?" I asked as he reached me.

He grinned. It did him good, it wiped away some of the weariness around his eyes. "Two Isarnagan captives. Not scouts, nobody's seen any of their scouts. I don't think the idiots have scouts. I don't know what to make of the ones we've caught though. They were off in the trees sharing a blanket, about two miles from here, three miles or so from the town. Ap Madog and his half pennon almost rode them down before they saw them. They fought very fiercely resisting capture. The woman got wounded and is being patched up right now. The man has hardly said a word to anyone. He had a sword, so he must have some sort of rank. I've not talked to them yet, just to ap Madog, though I looked them over before sending them to ap Darel. Nobody's reported any sign of anyone else at all yet, away from the main army. I'm so glad you're back. Come and see them, I was just giving ap Darel time to get done before going to them."

"Good," I said. "Well done." Emlin smiled, and I walked along with him towards the center of the makeshift camp where the prisoners were. It would be very useful to have some idea of what the Isarnagans wanted. "Is the woman a fighter?" I asked as we walked.

"She had a long knife as well as a spear, according to ap Madog. So I'd say so. Why would anyone be here who wasn't?"

"Red-Eye was right about the numbers," I said, swallowing the last of my breakfast. "And we saw camp followers and children. I'm very much wondering what that means."

Emlin grimaced. "Whatever are we going to do with them after we've got rid of all the others? Send them back orphaned across the water?"

Ap Darel was just finishing singing a charm and binding up the woman's arm as we reached them. They were clearly Isarnagans, their clothes were woven wool in mottlings of heather colors and their hair, particularly noticeable in a camp where everyone's head was shorn short in mourning, fell in smoothly braided dark loops that would fit easily under a helmet. They were standing in the sunlight almost in the center of the camp. There was a clear space around them. Four armigers were standing guard out of earshot for quiet voices. The one I passed did no more than flick his eyes towards me. They needed sleep. I could still see no way to avoid a fight today. I needed to distract the Isarnagans from the town and let the people inside know we were here. It was also dangerous to risk being caught in the open. But armigers and horses both needed rest.

Emlin and I walked into the cleared space. A spear was lying on the ground where ap Darel had clearly just set it down after using it in the healing. The woman must have been quite badly hurt. The other Isarnagan was standing with an arm around her as anyone might support an injured comrade. I didn't pay much attention to him for the moment. She looked like a fighter, and she looked as if she'd had a bad shock and lost blood. She was quite young, not much over twenty I guessed. She had a scar on her cheek that looked as if it had been made with a long knife from the side a few years ago, before she had finished growing.

"Keep it strapped still for a day or so, then exercise it slowly until it is strong again, and it will be as good as ever," ap Darel said. "You must be careful not to lift anything heavy too soon or you will always have a weakness there."

"If your people don't kill us in the next day or so I shall certainly remember your advice," the woman said, deep amusement clear in her voice.

"We never kill prisoners," I interrupted. They jumped and turned towards me. Ap Darel clicked his tongue in reproach and retucked the last twist of bandage, then turned away to pack up his things.

"That's clear enough," the man said. "Do you always do your best to mend what you yourselves have broken?" He sounded both amused and puzzled. As he turned to face me, stepping away from the woman slightly, I saw that he was a very handsome man. He was tall, too, his eyes were almost level with mine; he overtopped the woman by a handspan or so. He smiled at me with easy confidence, as to an equal. I knew immediately that these were certainly important people, neither scouts nor ordinary Isarnagan fighters. He was as used to giving orders as I was. I wondered even more strongly what they had been doing off in the woods. An officer would surely have somewhere in camp he could withdraw with a friend if they wanted privacy?

"We would prefer not to break things in the first place, but if we must, then yes," I replied, evenly, not smiling. "I am sorry to learn that things are otherwise in Tir Isarnagiri." I had known it already, from the Isarnagans we had fought beside after Caer Lind. They could never be trusted with prisoners. We always used courtesy in these matters, ransoming prisoners or getting the use of their labor. I always remembered Thurrig growling on the subject in training. "Be polite first. There's always time for chopping people up for information later if need be, but putting them back together if it turns out they're important isn't so easy. And the dead may fertilize the soil, but it takes the living to turn it over and plant crops."

"Who are you?" I went on, not giving him a chance to speak. His face darkened in a fierce frown.

"My name has already been given to the doctor, it is too late for secrets," said the woman gently, putting her good hand on his arm. I noticed that she had unusually long fingers and a thick bronze bracelet covered in twisted snake designs. "I am Emer ap Allel," she said. She touched her good hand to her chest and inclined her head towards me, the closest to a bow she could come with her arm bound like that. The man moved a little away from her and folded his arms across his chest. I waited. He said nothing. I continued to wait. At last Emer spoke.

"My companion has a strong prohibition on him from telling any part of his name to anyone when he is with me." She looked at him in a way that made me feel sure she was very fond of him indeed.

"Indeed, it would most surely be my death to give you even so much as my father's name or my land name or the proud use name I have won by my deeds," he said, his tone very light, considering the import of his words. I noted that he had made sure I knew he had a land name and a praise name, even while refusing to tell me what they were. He did not lack pride whoever he might be. "I mean no offense to any of you honorable people," he went on, "and this is as painful to my honor as it is to yours." He bowed to me, to Emlin, and to ap Darel, whose box was by now neater than it probably had been for years, and who was not even pretending not to listen. Emlin's mouth was very slightly open, and I felt quite nonplussed myself. I had heard of curses that worked like that in old stories. I had never met anyone who had that sort of curse on them. There was no way in honor I could demand his name. I wondered if I could get around the prohibition by taking him aside and asking it.

"Go and eat," I said to the doctor. He left with some reluctance, looking back at us as he made his way towards the cooks. I turned back to the Isarnagans, my own stomach rumbling. The fish had just been enough to remind me I was hungry.

"What shall we call your companion then," Emlin asked Emer, getting back some of his composure. This certainly was the oddest prisoner interrogation I'd ever seen or heard of. Somehow it had stopped being something that was going to get me information and take a moment and had become strangely significant.

"Call me anything you see fit," he said.

"Shall I resist the urge to pick something inappropriate, like Fishface, or all too appropriate, like Pretty Boy?" I asked. He bowed, not reacting at all. "Fishface it is, then," I said. His face did not even twitch. Emlin took his hand off his sword again.

Emer smiled at him. I frowned, something about her smile reminded me of Elenn and set me suddenly thinking about her name. She did not look much like Urdo's beautiful Queen but that did not necessarily mean anything. I did not know how common a name Allel was in Tir Isarnagiri, but could this woman be Elenn's sister? If so what did that mean? I really didn't like the man refusing to give at least his father's name. How could he swear not to make war on us if he would not give his name? And what reasons could he have? I almost wished I hadn't said so firmly that we did not kill prisoners. If only Angas were here, or Elenn herself, someone who knew something about Isarnagans.

"I am ap Gwien, and this is ap Trivan," I said, indicating Emlin. Emer again inclined her head and the man bowed. "Now, first, what brings you in arms to Tir Tanagiri?" I was looking at the man, and I saw his eyes flick to Emer. It was very clear he was asking permission to speak. That must make her his superior. This was all very interesting and very strange.

"The king of Anlar has come in arms to win a kingdom for himself across the Windy Sea," he said. This really was terribly bad news, whoever

the king of Anlar might be. I had never heard of Anlar. It was not Black
Darag's kingdom, Oriel, nor yet Allel's Connat. I had no idea if it was some
cloak-sized kingdom, as so many are in Tir Isarnagiri, or a place as large as
Demedia that I did not know about because I had not been paying attention at the right time. I glanced at Emlin, who was looking in fascination at
the woman.

I drew an even breath and spoke as calmly and formally as I could.
"Then the king of Anlar had best turn around and take his ambitions back
to his own island, for this land he disputes is held by Morien ap Gwien,
Lord of Derwen, and through him it is part of the kingdom of the High
King Urdo ap Avren and it will be defended against you."

"Urdo and Sweyn are so bound up with each other neither will turn us
out of this corner," Emer said, "And you children of Gwien have little
more than a hundred and fifty riders here, and perhaps another thirty inside
the walls. We are here in strength."

"Your news is old," I said, "Or you have come too late. Sweyn Rognvaldsson is dead. He fell by the hand of Galba ap Galba on the field of
Foreth close on half a month ago. Urdo has made a great Peace with the
Jarnsmen of Bereich and Aylsfa and our ally Alfwin Cellasson is ruling
Tevin. I may have only one ala to my hand here, but more will come has-
tening at my word. You had best go home, Isarnagans, before our horses
push you into the sea."

"Is this tr—" began Fishface, and stopped as I felt my lips draw back
from my gritted teeth. "I do not doubt your word, Lady," he said, hastily,
"but this is much later news than we have." Emer touched his hand, probably as amazed at his temerity as I was. He stopped and looked down at her,
frowning.

"What will you do with us?" she asked.

"I haven't decided," I said, honestly. "You know we're here, and in
what force, which the rest of your troops don't yet. I will not let you go. It's
also clear to me that you are more than just ordinary scouts, and there may
well be a ransom."

"There will," said Emlin, quietly beside me. "If the lady is not that
daughter of Allel of Connat who married Lew ap Ross, the king of Anlar,
then she must be her sister."

I laughed. I couldn't help it. It was the look on their faces. "My mother
always told me that I should pay attention to gossip because there was a lot
to be learned from it," I said, slapping Emlin on the back. He grimaced at
me, and I realized he had meant to be subtle in giving this information so

they would not guess I had not already known. I choked back another laugh, and Emlin sighed. I could see this was doomed to be another story going about the alae about my stupidity.

"I have only one sister," said ap Allel, stiffly. I coughed a little, not meeting Emlin's eye. I thought I understood why they might be visiting the woods now, if they were married to other people. Even in the alae, though we do not make much fuss about who shares blankets as long as everyone is happy about it, being together without her husband's knowledge would be a shocking thing. Breaking marriage vows is oathbreaking, after all. How could anyone take such a stupid risk for the sake of half an hour, even if they found pleasure in it?

"I take it this is not your royal husband?" I asked. Emer shook her head. The man stared straight ahead. "Do you think your husband would take his army back to Anlar as a ransom for your safety?" I asked, hopefully. Emlin sighed at me. Emer shook her head again, more forcefully.

"I somehow think not," she said, drily. "Though you are free to ask him yourself. I might, of course, try to deceive you as to my value." She smiled. "But by all means let us speak frankly."

"Let's sit down," I said. "If we had your friend's name and your oaths of peace I would send for some food and drink and make you my personal guests."

"It is not possible," he said, helping Emer to sit down on the damp grass. He showed great care for her arm.

"It's not that difficult, is it?" asked Emlin. "Nothing need be said about sharing blankets in the wood. If the lady says she woke very early this morning and wished to walk away from the camp. And if you had been on duty part of the night and so you were also awake . . . Then you decided to accompany her in case the woods were unsafe, as indeed they proved to be?"

It was a good enough story, but very thin. I knew armies by now, even if it were the truth and the Lady of Wisdom herself came down and swore to it, nobody would believe it, though before her husband they would pretend to.

"Thank you for your kindness in invention, but I am no fool, and that is not good enough," said Fishface, giving his words a little sharpness. "To give my name would be my death, as I said, and probably the daughter of Allel's as well. But if you three would eat I would quite understand being excluded." I was hungry, but I shook my head. It was unthinkable. The whole thing would have made more sense to me if it had been her name they refused to give. There were only two possible explanations. He might be her close kinsman, or her husband's, so that their being together broke the law of the Mother. Or there might be a bloodfeud between their kindreds which Emer had forgiven personally but could not persuade her family to forgive. This seemed most likely. It was sad; it reminded me of the old songs about doomed lovers my sister Aurien had once sung endlessly, bent over her sewing.

"Well," Emer said, when we were all sitting, "I believe your news about Sweyn and the Jarnsmen, but we also know things you do not. Our force is not the only Isarnagan one to have landed. I suspect the reinforcements you expect may be distracted by Oriel's and Lagin's armies in western Demedia and in Wenlad." I could only think how much worse it would have been if this alliance of our enemies had come before Foreth. I hoped those armies were not as great as this one. I could not see how they could be unless they had emptied the whole island of Tir Isarnagiri. Emer had a great air of sincerity, and I did not doubt her for an instant. She seemed very regal, even more so than her sister. I was told much later by those who knew her that Emer was very like their mother, Maga, who had ruled a great kingdom and conducted wars and alliances in her own right. She had ruled very well, though of course it all fell apart when she died. This always happened in Tir Isarnagiri.

"Can you negotiate for your husband's army?" I asked. "Are you his war-leader?"

"I am not," she said, and touched her scar and smiled. "Thank you. I have no authority to negotiate, but I can tell you in truth what my husband Lew ap Ross will do. He is an old man and no great warrior. But he has four thousand fighters here, and he will never go home alive without land. The people have come to settle—we gave up land to Oriel and in return they lent us boats and help for this venture." Her eyes rested on the Isarnagan for just an instant as she said "help." He sat looking from her face to mine as we spoke. If he was from Oriel and she was born in Connat, that was almost enough to explain the problem. There had been many wars between those lands.

"Why did you all decide to leave?" Emlin asked.

"Many people wish to leave Tir Isarnagiri since Chanerig ap Thurrig defeated the gods at the last Fire Feast of Bel," said Fishface wryly.

I sat up straight and wondered if I was dreaming. "Chanerig did what?" I liked Thurrig a great deal, but Chanerig I found even more stiff-necked and annoying than Marchel. He was a monk and had sworn vows of abstinence from touching women and from eating meat as well as the usual vows of devotion and poverty. (Almost every woman I knew had said at sometime or another that she found it no hardship to think she could not touch Chanerig.) He almost never talked about anything other than the wonders of the White God. Raul might think that there was no honor other than in serving the White God; Chanerig seemed to think that nothing else was even slightly interesting. He was a single-minded fanatic, and he did not like me. I had never imagined him defeating gods.

"There was a mighty protection set on the island of Tir Isarnagiri that no great evil could ever come as long as we kept up the wards," said Emer. "One of those wards was that twice a year, at the festival of the Lord Bel and on the Day of the Dead all the fires of the island should be put out and then the first fire relit on the Hill of the Ward, and all the other fires be lit only as they saw that fire. It was a wonderful sight every year to stand on a hilltop and see the fires spreading across the land making a chain of lights. When I was a girl in Connat I thought nothing could be more splendid, but it is even more beautiful farther north in Anlar. But just this last year, on the Feast of Bel, Chanerig ap Thurrig lit a fire at Connat before the fire was lit on the Hill of Ward. Many gods and spirits of the land—and many people, too, angry at what he had done, rushed there and fought him all night and at morning he was still alive and his fire was still burning, so most acknowledged defeat and worshiped his god. Almost all of the land spirits did this. It was part of their nature. And some gods worshiped the White God and some sank down into the earth and others left over the waters. As for the people, it seems we must live in a land that is given to the White God or leave."

"What a dreadful thing to do without consent," I said. They looked at each other, and I misinterpreted what they didn't say.

"Thurrig is in Urdo's service and my friend, but I do not approve of that action."

"Nor do I," said Emer.

"So you left?" I said. Emer raised her chin.

"So Chanerig won over the whole island?" asked Emlin. I could not quite believe it either. Arvlid would be pleased. I was amazed and horrified. I was afraid they would find a way to do the same here, and that what they were doing was the same only slower.

"Not all the people are reconciled to it," said Fishface.

"So you thought you would bring your gods and make a new start here?" I said.

"We did," Emer pushed back her hair with her good hand. One ten-
dril had come loose from the coils. "We have come here to the empty lands
to make them our own. We're not going to go back."

"That's fairly told," I said. "So, it seems it must be war, and I am back
to wondering what I am to do with you two."

She drew breath. "Lew will not pay a great ransom for me. In some
ways he might be glad to be rid of me, I have given him no children yet,
and I represent for him an alliance that he has repented of. If you want a
ransom you would get more from my sister. I would say from my father and
my brother, but it would be wrong. Though they value me they have little
enough wealth these days. I am speaking of myself as your captured piece
on the fidchel board." She smiled as she said this last.

"Captured pieces can not change color," I said, "but people may and
sometimes do change sides. You have been honest with me. If you would
rather be sent to your sister than handed back to your husband that is
within my power. Nor would I ask for a ransom from my Queen. I think
you misunderstand the situation in Tir Tanagiri." To say the least. I wished
I was better at putting things delicately. "I am neither tyrant nor bandit. I
am not working for my own personal gain in this situation, although this
land is held by my family. I serve the High King Urdo and the High Kingdom. I am Praefecto of his own ala. I can have you sent to Caer Tanaga. I
will see that it is done as soon as I can spare an escort. What happens there
will be up to Queen Elenn and the High King, but I would think it very
possible they would help you put aside your marriage so you two can be
together—" I thought Elenn might be more ready to forgive an ancient
bloodfeud for her sister's happiness than their father. Also by that time Lew
would most likely be dead, which would make the situation much less
complex for Emer.

"No." Fishface raised a hand and spoke passionately. "You misunderstand. We cannot be together. We are not together now. We have never
been together. We do not wish to be together. If you could forget that you
ever saw us together we would be grateful. Nor do I have any desire to be
sent to Caer Tanaga. Do with me what you would do with any prisoner."

"Very well," I said. "Though I cannot ask Black Darag for a ransom for
a nameless man of Oriel. And a prisoner would usually be sent to
Thansethan to labor, and to take an oath of peace you would have to give
your name." I sighed. He appeared to be an almost insurmountable problem. I almost wished he had been killed rather than captured. Emer was a
problem, too, but once I could get her to Elenn she would be out of my

hands. "You can't spend the rest of your life refusing to tell anyone your name," I added.

He shrugged. "Maybe I had better take a new one and start going by Fishface," he said, unblinkingly. "I admit it is a very vexing problem. Twelve of your horsemen have seen me with my lady, so has the healer, the two of you, the guards, Tia alone knows how many others among the camp here. Maybe I can find a childless rider to adopt me in the sight of the gods and give me his name?"

"If it is death for you two to be together," said Emlin, crisply, "As I have little doubt you are telling the truth, then why did you leave your people and go wandering in the woods together in the first place. Neither of you seems like a fool to risk so much for a moment's pleasure."

I looked inquiring as the two Isarnagans exchanged uneasy glances.

"We had no idea you would be here so suddenly," Emer said. "We thought there were no enemies around. We would have been back in plenty of time." I have never understood that kind of passion.

"And I was to return to Black Darag in the next day or two, as soon as the town fell," Fishface added, "It might have been our last chance to see each other for some time." He smiled at Emlin with easy charm, "I am flattered not to seem like a fool, but I will have to admit it is all illusion."

"It would have been such a long time apart," Emer added.

He looked back at Emer and smiled. She took his hand and looked up at him with an expression that would have made honey seem sour in comparison. I rolled my eyes, thinking that not even incest or bloodfeud was enough of a barrier to that sort of thing.

"And if I don't believe that, what?" Emlin asked. "You weren't running away, you could have got a lot farther before you stopped." I don't know if they would have told us, but it came to me suddenly.

"Did they actually have a blanket?" I asked Emlin. Before he could answer I turned to Emer. "No blanket, eh? Was it the old kingship rite to claim the land?"

"What are you talking about?" Emlin asked.

"When the king is crowned with a circle crown it is a ritual enactment of marriage with the land," I said, thinking how recently Urdo's own marriage with Tir Tanagiri was consummated. "Long ago it was done less symbolically."

She raised her chin defiantly. "Lew is an old fool, but I can rule a land and bring in our gods."

"Did you succeed?" Emlin asked.

"We were interrupted," the man said.

Without thinking I reached out for the land gods that lived in Derwen and felt them respond. I should not have been able to do it. I worried from then until I saw him if my brother Morien might have been killed by the Isarnagans. Only the lord should be able to reach them. Perhaps it was because I had spoken to the Mother. Perhaps it was because I was the heir and reaching in urgency. I found them. Green and growing they were, like the roots of trees and reflections of leaves in deep beds of forest pools. They were quietness and rising sap and rustling leaves and the snow a deer dislodged slipping between trunks was loud as it reached the ground. They were the scents of stone and water running. They did not have human shape or speak in human voices, but I knew them. I knew them as they knew me, as I knew how to run from here to my father's house and never trip and duck under branches without looking, as I could never do in the woods around Caer Tanaga though I should live there all the rest of my life.

They knew me, and I saw myself as I was to them, a moment in a reaching chain of people, feet and flying hair and hoofbeats falling. Apple died at Caer Lind and I never knew what Sweyn's men did with his body. But to the land gods of Derwen he was part of who I was and as they showed me myself I saw him, too. Seated on his back, where I belonged, in the heart of deep forest I reached out to feel disturbances in the land. Emer had not disturbed the balance. She had not had time to reach them. But they were aware of the Isarnagan hordes. I felt them crowded around the town, constricting it, draining the water. Then I was galloping freely on Apple's back away west, to the part of Derwen where hardly anyone lived, the fort of Dun Morr which the Vincans destroyed, the fallen walls open to the sky. Tapit Point was in view in the distance. Apple's nostrils flared, sniffing the sea wind. There were boats far out on the waves. Here, the land said, without words, but I understood, here there is room for these people, who are homeless, who worship our high gods.

I blinked, and reached down to pat Apple's neck, and saw Emlin and Emer and the nameless Isarganan staring at me. I could hear the noises of camp around me. Somebody was cooking porridge with milk. I opened my mouth to speak, and shut it again. I did not know how long it had been. There were sudden tears in my eyes. "You did not succeed," I said, at last, and my voice sounded very strange in my ears.

"No," she said, looking at me. "I know."

"Emer," I said, "can you negotiate with your Isarnagans?"

"Negotiate what?" she asked.

"Would Lew ap Ross, would you, be prepared to hold land under the High King, under the King's Peace? A kingdom under Derwen, off near Tapit Point, where the fort of Dun Morr used to be?"

"Do you have authority to offer that?" Emer asked.

"Only from the land," I said. "That land is empty and will take people. And as far as Urdo is concerned, if there are armies of Oriel and Lagin attacking in the north, then I think making a peace with you, a trustworthy ally, our Queen's sister, in the south to free up the ala to fight in the north would be worth some loss of land. The land you have marched across is mostly empty, our farmers mostly live between here and Magor. That is Derwen land, and I am heir to Derwen. I can offer it, subject to the approval of my brother and my king. If Lew would take it and go there and build a settlement and begin to farm, under Derwen and under the High King, and swear to the King's Peace, all will be well."

I held my breath.

"I think he would accept that," she said, at last, her eyes wide. "A kingdom to be had here without fighting."

"It seems your value on the fidchel board has increased again," said Fishface, neutrally.

"Oh indeed," said Emer, not smiling at all. "If Lew is allied to Urdo."

"Do you hate him so much?" asked Emlin.

"I do my duty," she said, grimly. None of us could think of anything to say.

"I will form the ala up," I said. "We may as well give Lew pause before he does something we will all regret. You can tell him you were doing a holy ritual and the land accepts you on those conditions. You must take them west, and I must speak to Morien and send word to Urdo."

"I hate to be annoying," said Fishface, "but what about me?"

"We drop you off a cliff on the way?" suggested Emlin. "Tell us your name, man, and we can work something out."

We waited a moment, but he stayed silent. Emer looked away.

"The lady Emer ap Allel was alone," I said at last. "She was always alone. We found her alone, and she made an alliance with us alone. You don't exist. You're a figment of anyone's imagination who saw you. You can just sit here until we're gone, and find your own way back to the Isarnagans a lot later and hope nobody notices. I can't guest you or ask your friendship or ask any oath, because you are nameless, so you might just as well never have existed at all."

He stood up, and I scrambled up after him. "Thank you," he said, bleakly, bowed over my hand, and walked away. The nearest guard's spear flashed a warning, and he kept on walking towards it.

"Let him go!" I called, and the guard stepped back. I turned to Emlin. "Get him his weapons back and see he gets out of camp safely," I said. I turned back to Emer. She was watching him out of sight with a very strange expression on her face, as if she was not sure whether to smile or weep. She shook her head a little and looked at me.

"We'd better get on with it," she said.

—26—

"Put no trust in a plan that works too easily."
—Caius Dalitius, "On Military Life"

Emlin was probably the most organized tribuno I ever worked with. In hardly longer than it takes to rub down a horse he had broken camp and got everyone ready. I mounted Beauty and came forward. Some of the armigers were still blinking and rubbing sleep out of their eyes, but they were all mounted and in battle order.

"I'm not expecting to need to fight today," I told them. "But keep alert and be ready, let's give them a show."

We rode over the hill in formation, pennon and ala banners catching the wind, and drew to a creditably sharp halt near the banks of the river. My own ala could hardly have done better.

The mass of the Isarnagans were gathered around the town gate. I gave a hand signal to Berth ap Panon and he gave a great blast on the trumpet. They spun around in a widening wave with a disorganized haste that was almost comical. I sent the heralds forward with branches. The Isarnagans fell back before them and a messenger came out on their side and led them through to their king. Emer came up beside me as we waited for them to return and sat in silence, looking very composed. She was riding a well-mannered dappled half horse that was one of the scouts' spares. When the heralds signaled that I should come forward to meet their leader she rode forward at my side.

As we had agreed, Emlin stayed with the ala. I let him pick out one of the decurios to go forward with me. So three of us went forward, myself, Emer, and Garian ap Gaius. I think Emlin picked him for his lack of curiosity. The heralds had set up their branches at four corners of a square and stood beside them, two of Lew's and two of mine.

We dismounted. Emer slid down with a little difficulty. She managed to land on her feet, but it looked as if it were a close thing. Garian steadied her. I suppose she was used to much smaller horses, because it does not usually take two hands to dismount. Beauty nipped at the dappled mare's hindquarters and she gave him an indignant look over her shoulder. I couldn't help smiling, even as I reminded Beauty of his manners, and so I was smiling as the Isarnagans came hurrying up.

Lew ap Ross was not an impressive-looking man. He was thickset and grey-haired and had grown his moustache longer than his beard in the old-fashioned Isarnagan style. He brought two counselors with him, one a warrior and the other a much older man in a long shawl. Lew's mouth fell open a little when he saw his wife, which allowed Emer to get in the first word, with no time for thought or introductions.

"Good news, my husband," she said. She went towards him and bowed as best she could. "The gods smile on us this day."

"What is this?" asked the older Isarnagan. He sounded a little indignant, as if anything to do with the gods should have come to him first. I suddenly realized with a shock that he must be an oracle-priest of the old tradition. They had been in many of my old nurse's stories. To meet one in broad light of day was like finding a relic out of the barbarous past. The Vincans had outlawed the strange practices and education needed to train them more than four hundred years ago. There had been occasional naturally born oracles since, like Morwen, but nobody deliberately set out to become one in Tir Tanagiri. I looked at him with curiosity and apprehension. There was nothing strange about him except the shawl. He did not have an eagle's beak instead of a nose nor cat's ears. Nor did he not immediately put his hand on anyone's belly and begin prophesying their death conditions. I caught myself before I descended further into childish superstitions. This was a learned man and one of Lew's trusted counselors. I wondered if he really knew the names of all the parts of all the trees.

"Greetings, ap Fial," she said, turning to him. "Will you hear me?"

"We will hear you," said Lew, frowning and gesturing to the others for silence. "How came you here in this company?"

"I woke before the dawn with a strong will moving me to go deep into the woods and commune with the gods of this land. As I am a queen and the daughter of kings, I followed this will and departed, and there deep among the trees I was found by the armigers of this mighty warlord Sulien ap Gwien." She gestured to me, and I bowed blandly. "I was wounded in fighting with them, but they took me to their camp and healed me. There ap Gwien and I spoke long together. There I found that the spirits of the land had spoken to her and moved her. Understanding why we had come out of Tir Isarnagiri, under their guidance she was determined to offer land freely to Lew ap Ross and the people of Anlar. We have come to you to debate if you will take this offer, blessed in the sight of the gods, or if nothing will content you but the blood of those who would be our brothers."

The most amazing thing about this speech was that although it left out several things, there was not a word of a lie in it. Lew ap Ross rubbed his eyes. I looked at him as cheerfully as I could manage. His counselors were clearly stricken speechless. I decided to take advantage of this state of affairs to be specific.

"The land I would offer you lies to the west of here, around the old city of Dun Morr, and it has lain for the most part empty for many years. If you would take it you must hold it in obedience to my brother Morien, who is lord of all Derwen, and the land will still be part of Derwen. But you can rule your people as you would, within the High King's law. You must also swear to keep faith with the High King Urdo."

"You are offering an alliance?" asked Lew, tugging his moustache.

I wished for Raul or someone who was good at explaining complicated political situations. "Sweyn of Tevin was defeated by Urdo at Foreth," I said, "and now all the Jarnish lands acknowledge Urdo as High King. The whole Island of Tir Tanagiri is one kingdom, with many kings under the High King. What I am offering is that your kingdom become part of Derwen, which is part of the High Kingdom. You shall rule your own people as you will under your own laws and traditions, but you will have the Lord of Derwen and the High King over you."

"And what troops must we provide?" asked the warrior, as if he has discovered a hidden catch. I stared at him. That definitely wasn't a question for me to answer. No doubt Urdo would be glad of some Isarnagan levies, but I could not say how many.

"That, and the matter of taxes, will have to be agreed by my brother the High King and by Morien ap Gwien," Emer said, smoothly. "Those are but details, my husband. We should consider the principle. We already have ties of blood with Urdo's people."

"In principle, well, in principle," sputtered Lew, folding his hands behind his back. "What do you say?" he asked his advisors.

The warrior shrugged. In marked contrast to his king he had stood still as we had been speaking, paying close attention to Garian and to me. "I say we fight, we could have it all instead of a part, and we need the stores to get through the winter. Also there is our alliance with Black Darag."

The old priest frowned at Emer and spoke slowly. "I say we take it. It would be spurning your queen and the gods themselves to do otherwise. Rarely do they speak so clearly, even to a queen and the daughter of kings."

"I hear you, ap Ranien. I hear you, ap Fial," said Lew, formally, then hesitated. "Perhaps I should speak to the whole council about this?"

"Speak to them for as long as you like after you have decided, my husband," said Emer. "I think ap Ranien's point about supplies is good. Can we get through the winter without them?"

"If we can fish, yes," said Lew, sounding definite for the first time. "It is seed for next year we will need, if we do not raid."

"Will you give us seed?" Emer asked me.

"I do not know if we can spare it," I said, honestly. "The harvest is not yet gathered, as you know." Emer glanced at me, and I said no more, she at least understood that the ala could prevent them from gaining access to the crops. "Again we must ask my brother Morien, the Lord of Derwen."

"Then let us ask him," said ap Fial, looking right at me for the first time. His eyes were very sharp.

"Are we agreed," Emer asked, putting her hand on Lew's arm.

"If they will give us seed crops for next spring and the empty land, yes," he said.

"Then take your troops back away from the town to your camp where the wagons are," I said, "And I shall go into the town and speak to my brother, and he will speak to you."

"It is fair," said ap Ranien. He made a strange half bow to Lew and went off toward the troops, shouting. Amazingly they obeyed him and headed off in their haphazard milling way towards the trees to the west.

When they had moved what I judged to be out of slingshot, I remounted and rode toward the town gates. I worried for a moment, but they opened at once to my hail.

The last time I had come home to Derwen my mother's steward had mistaken me for a stranger. This time the people shouted my name in the street and cheered. Beauty put his head up and lifted his feet very precisely as he always did for cheering crowds. The people made way for me. Hardly any of the faces were familiar. I recognized Garah's father and the old farmer who had scolded Angas for taking her turnips. Beside her was one of the girls who had been serving in the hall the last time I was home. Now she was wearing armor and holding a spear. She must have joined the ala.

As I came near the house the steward Daldaf ap Wyn came out and stood by the steps down to the forecourt, looking flustered. Close behind him came my mother, Veniva. When had she got old? She moved slowly like an old woman, though she could hardly be more than fifty. She leaned on a cane and her face was lined and she had dark shadows under her eyes. Seeing her I realized that much as I missed my father, however much I wanted to talk to him and hear his thoughts, it must be much worse for her.

I slid down to the ground and handed Beauty's reins to a groom I recognized. "Keep him ready for me," I said. Then I went up the three steps and embraced Veniva formally. She was so thin it felt like embracing a bird; I was afraid her bones would crack. I had mistaken Aurien for Veniva, but I would not do it now I had seen her again. I stepped back a little. "Well met, Mother. Where is Morien?" I asked.

"He was on the wall," Veniva said, "He will be here shortly." Her voice was thinner, and she sounded weary. Though I had spoken in Tanagan, because I had been speaking it with the Isarnagans, she answered me in beautiful precise Vincan, as always. I looked as she spoke and caught sight of my brother galloping up the street towards us. I have never in my life, before or since, been so glad to see Morien. I had been in fear for him since the land had spoken to me. Just beside him rode a young woman. He was wearing fighting armor, and she was wearing riding leathers. After a moment I placed her as the girl Morien had been dancing with when I was there last, Kerys ap Uthbad, poor Enid's sister, whom he had married two years ago. As he swung down, I stepped towards Morien with my heart full of joy that he yet lived and embraced him sincerely. He was still a hand shorter than I was. He stepped aside after he had given me greeting and presented me to his wife.

"Now, what news?" said Morien, impatiently. "Those barbarian bastards have given way without battle. How did you compel them?"

"Have we time for refreshment as we talk?" asked Kerys, smiling hopefully. She was a very pretty girl when she smiled, and I remembered that Enid had been thought pretty, too, before the battle where she lost her arm and got her face scarred.

I shook my head regretfully at her and looked at the others. Morien was waiting for my answer with unconcealed impatience, Veniva just looked tired, and Daldaf was standing by, too close and too eager. He should have gone away, not stayed beside Veniva as if he were one of the family. Maybe we should go inside somewhere private? But there wasn't time. I frowned. It wasn't really any of my business, if they didn't mind it. It didn't really matter. He was my mother's steward, and we were not speaking secrets. "This should not take long." I said. "I have arranged a peace with the Isarnagans. Briefly, they will withdraw westward to farm the empty land around Dun Morr and acknowledge your lordship, and Urdo's."

Morien's eyebrows lowered, and his face darkened. His lower lip protruded. He looked exactly as he had when he had been eight years old and following us around the woods until Darien and I climbed a tree that was too high for him and pelted him with sweet chestnuts. "What right have you to give away my land?" he asked.

"I am not giving it away, but giving you inhabitants for it," I said, a little sharply. "Would you rather they took the town?"

"You have a whole ala out there, you could have pushed them back to the sea if you wanted to," Morien snapped.

"With five thousand of them and me with one tired ala?" I countered, suddenly angry. "I think not. I could have waited and done that with help, but they have landed elsewhere, too, in Wenlad and Demedia."

"And that's more important than Derwen, is it?" asked Morien, stepping forward and pushing his face up into mine. "They've been killing our people and threatening our walls, I don't want to take them in friendship."

I stepped back a little and almost fell down the steps behind me. I was completely unprepared for his reaction, but of course I had not been under siege. Morien stepped forward again. "Why didn't you ask me? Taking it on yourself. You may be special with Urdo, but you are not the head of this family and you do not have charge—"

"I am asking you! I'm asking you now!"

"That's enough," snapped Veniva. Even though her voice was thin it held a commanding edge. Morien swung around to her, his expression the same as when he had complained to her of me when he was twelve and I was sixteen and Darien and I wouldn't let him into the stables because he had pulled Banner's tail. She spoke exactly in the same tone she had used then. "Morien, Sulien could hardly consult you in the middle of a siege. Sulien, Morien's right, the land is not yours to give away."

"I know that," I said, more quietly. I had almost been shouting. Daldaf looked as if he were biting back some strong emotion. "That's why I have come as soon as I can, as soon as they have agreed in principle and moved back from the walls of the town, so that Morien can come and speak to their king."

"They have a king with them?" asked Kerys, wide-eyed.

"He is Lew ap Ross, of Anlar," I said. "His wife is the sister of Urdo's queen. They are substantial people, not raiders. They were brought here in boats belonging to Black Darag of Oriel, who has himself gone north to invade Wenlad or Demedia; they can't leave. We really would have to kill them all, or kill the greater part and enslave the rest, if we would. We can't do that with one ala and local levies." I looked at Morien to make sure he understood. He was frowning and staring at his boots.

"They were shouting Lew's name," Kerys said, biting her lip.

"They will accept peaceful settlement and Morien's lordship?" Veniva asked. Morien made a rude noise under his breath.

"They agreed in principle, my lady mother," I said.

Kerys glanced towards the walls. "So many of them," she said, with a slight shudder. Morien moved to her and put his arm around her; she nestled towards him. "Why have they come?"

"Chanerig ap Thurrig has driven their gods out of the land, and they have come here." I tried to think of something good to say about them and remembered things I had been told. "They are barbarous, true, as we were before the Vincans came, but they worship our high gods and they can learn the ways of civilization." All of this somehow fell into an awkward silence, and I looked around to see why. My eyes came to rest on the white pebble firmly in the center of Daldaf's chest. He looked as if he had swallowed a slug. I wanted to laugh until I glanced at Kerys, who fished under her armor and pulled out a matching pebble.

I caught Morien's eye over her head, he wriggled uncomfortably. "I have talked to the priests, but I have not taken the pebble," he said. "I have responsibilities to the land, and—"

"And I have not permitted it," said Veniva, decisively. "It would be a terrible thing to go against tradition, even if the powers of the land willed it wholly, as they may have done in Munew and Tir Isarnagiri, but they do not here."

"The people—" began Morien, sounding as if he was repeating an old argument.

"Many of the people, yes," said Veniva, very firmly indeed. "Not all of them by any means, even in the town, and very few of them in the countryside." She looked at me and laughed. "You look appalled, Sulien," she said. "They call me the last of the Vincans, and had not thought you would be the last of my children to stand up for tradition beside me. It hurt me very much when Aurien gave way to Father Cinwil's persuasion, and I thought you would have felt the same out there where the King and so many prefer the White God."

"No," I said, quietly, and then more loudly so that others could hear. "The High King compels nobody, and my heart has never changed on such things." I was not accustomed to have my mother look at me approvingly. I felt moved almost to tears.

"We have had this out before," said Kerys gently, but her hand was still on her pebble. "No doubt we will again, but there is an urgent matter to decide, and if we are to talk about our various faiths then I really must insist we go inside and sit down, for we will still be here when night finds us, and maybe still when dawn follows night, as we did when Marchel was here."

"Let us leave matters of the gods then," I said, "and consider the Isarnagans, who are waiting for us."

"As you have left me so little choice I will come and bargain with them," said Morien. "Have you promised them anything else?"

I shook my head. "They were asking for seed crops, but I did not know if you could spare them."

"Can they pay?" asked Daldaf, hopefully.

Veniva laughed. "If they can't pay now, they can pay next year. If we can gather it without being killed in the fields we have no shortage of harvest. Let them pay us back threefold next winter; our farmers will not grudge that at all. And tell them that all their trade must go through Derwen; it will have to in any case, Dun Morr is too far upstream to be a port and there are no good harbors in the west. Add that we will tax all their trade that passes through, just a little. Otherwise I suppose they will pay taxes like anyone else?"

"I suppose," I said. "Morien, do you think it would be a good idea if Mother came out and spoke to them, too?"

Kerys and Daldaf would have come, too, but Veniva persuaded them they should stay and prepare a meal for when the negotiations were complete. She seemed to draw energy from the crisis, or perhaps from having something to do that was different from sitting and waiting.

The three of us walked out of the gates together. The people of Derwen cheered us all. Garian and my heralds looked a little relieved to see me coming back. I sent a message to Emlin that the ala could relax a little as he saw fit and that all was going well. Then I made the introductions and we all sat down on the grass. Lew and Morien scowled at each other. Emer and Veniva smiled graciously.

It wasn't land or taxes that proved difficult. Veniva and Emer between them managed to smooth away the difficulties and get the men agreeing. I think I must have nodded off for a moment while they were discussing details of crops and taxes, because I came awake blinking with Morien yelling at Lew.

"We could if they wanted to move!"

"Don't your farmers do what their lord tells them?" Lew demanded.

I rubbed my eyes and drew breath to answer this before Morien exploded, but he replied quite quietly. "They have a choice, too. If I ordered it, they would move, but where is the need to order these people to leave the land of their ancestors if they do not want to. I don't know how it is in your island, but here we consider farmers to be people." The two men stared at each other, and I almost thought they would start to snort like stallions establishing their positions.

Emer put her hand on Lew's arm as he was drawing breath to retort, and spoke before he could. "Of course they're people," she said, gently. "That isn't disputed. It's just whether they would move."

"If they want to move I'll give them different land, I can do that easily enough," said Morien, a little more calmly. "There is good land to north of here, and up near Nant Gefalion. But if they don't want to move, I don't see why they should be forced."

"Because you offered me empty land, or at least, Sulien ap Gwien did!" burst out Lew, before Emer could stop him again. They all looked at me. Morien looked very angry. I swallowed.

"There really aren't many of them," I said. "Why can't they stay where they are?"

"Why indeed?" asked Emer. "We came through those lands and saw very little sign of settlement at all; there would be no need to throw anyone out to make room for all our people."

"I suppose they could stay," said Lew, grudgingly.

"Whose responsibility would they be?" Morien asked. "They're my people. I can't abandon them."

"They'll still be your people, and so will Lew's people," said Veniva. "The land is yours, too, and you are giving that into his keeping, you will still be the lord even though they govern themselves."

"Within that land I will rule," said Lew, frowning.

"Yes, we have agreed all that," said Emer.

"If they want to come closer to Derwen and have land here, they can do that; if they want to stay they will come under your rule like your people, but you must be fair to them and judge between them equally with your own people," said Morien, sternly. Lew raised his chin in agreement. I noticed Veniva, beside me, give a tiny sigh of relief.

That was the last of the details—after that there was only the oathtaking. It was decided that enough blood had been spilled in the fighting, especially with Emer's wounded arm, that no more was necessary. So we gathered as many of the ala and the Isarnagans and the people of Derwen as could stand around to witness. I witnessed for the High King, with Emlin beside me. Morien called on the gods to hear him, and Lew swore to Morien the same oath Morien had sworn to Urdo, and Morien raised him up and swore to keep him as he deserved. A great cheer went up from everyone, and people who had been fighting that morning were embracing now. I sent the ala to their barracks in the town, and they didn't seem in the least sorry to go. I expect they were all as tired as I was.

—27—

> By the bright wands of the willow
> that grows by Lake Talog
> tell me if she cares for me.
> By the sweet nuts of the hazel
> that grows by the Holy Well
> tell me if she will relent towards me.
> By the tenacious roots of the rowan
> that grows on the slopes of Brin Crag
> tell me if she will come back to me.
> By the spreading branches of the oak
> that grows near Caer Asgor
> tell me what weapon will heal the wound in my heart?
> —Aneirin ap Erbin, "The Woman of Wenlad"

I sent messengers at once to Caer Gloran and to Caer Tanaga. Then I fell asleep in the bath while Kerys was still wringing her hands over my battle scars. I slept for just long enough to feel terrible when I went down into the hall. I got myself a cup of cider and sat in the window seat sipping it and watching. The oil lamps were lit, giving everything a luxurious glow. There were Isarnagans there and people from the ala as well as the town-folk. I was glad it had not been my task to decide who to ask into the hall tonight. Daldaf was moving around with the welcome cup. This time he greeted me as a member of the family. Veniva seemed very occupied with preparations for the feast; she kept going through to the kitchen. Kerys and Morien were dancing together smoothly. Watching them, I thought they were probably well suited to each other. She looked much more natural in a green-and-gold embroidered overdress than she had in armor. She really was very unlike her sister Enid, as unlike as I was to Aurien. Poor Enid had wanted to be a hero and had died in an ambush. If she had lived what would she have become? Kerys smiled and turned and bowed to Morien as the dance came to an end, then she let puffing old Lew lead her out to the next one. She was quite deft at dodging Lew's feet. His moustache waved about as he spoke to her. Morien had got the better of the exchange, for even with her arm bound up Emer was a graceful dancer.

I had come in with no intention of dancing. Indeed if I could have gone straight to bed from the bathhouse without it being a great impolite-ness I would have done so. I enjoyed dancing well enough on winter evenings when we had been penned inside all day, but today I was too tired. Yet when Duncan, my old arms master, came up and asked me to dance, I agreed as quickly as if I had been given an order. He looked older, and what sparse threads of his hair were left were iron grey. I won-dered for the first time how old he was. He still moved like a fighter, and he had a scrape on his cheek that must have come from something hit-ting his helmet hard the day before. He had been my first teacher, and it was his instruction from the time I was five years old that had made me a warrior.

He smiled at me as we went out into the middle of the floor. The music was loud enough that we could talk quietly without much chance of anyone hearing us.

"You haven't changed much," he said. "Oh, you're taller and broader across the shoulders, and a lot more sure of yourself, but I daresay you still lead to the right."

I laughed. "Indeed I do not, for Osvran ap Usteg beat that out of me when we were training with double-weighted swords. Every time I did it he got me with the flat, and he didn't pull his blow either. I had bruises all down my side until I eventually broke the habit. Then when ap Thurrig of the ships taught us Malmish grappling I finally managed to learn not to signal what I was going to do."

"Good," said Duncan, "Useful. And you have done well. I am proud to say my pupil is the Emperor's own Praefecto. I heard that you even carried his standard in the great victory at Foreth Hill. All of you in the alae deserve great praise. I never thought to see the land united and our people winning victories."

"I know," I said. "It was the same for me when I was younger, it seemed as if the world had come to an end and there was only a little space before everything fell in on us."

He raised his chin, giving the dancing only a small part of his attention. "It was so all my life, all we could hope for was to shore up the ruin for a little while, the thought of rebuilding was more than we could imagine. I never thought to see the peace of Vinca come again."

"Urdo's Peace is not the peace of Vinca," I said, raising my voice a little, for we were dancing away from each other. "It is a new thing, he says, so new we must all learn what it is."

Duncan shook his head a little and did not speak until we were close together again. "The young always think they are the first to discover anything," he said. "Those of us who are older know well enough what peace is." He softened a little. "You armigers have done very well to win it, whatever you call it."

"Well, it is not just the alae. There would have been no alae without Urdo, he gave us hope and heart."

"That is a lot for one person to do," Duncan said, swinging me expertly.

"We have all helped, but there would have been nothing without his vision," I insisted.

"I suppose that is what it is to be a real king," Duncan said, "being able to inspire your people to fight for the land." His dark eyes were sad. I remembered what I had learned from Alfwin when he joined us. I wondered if anyone else knew. There were many fleeing from the east in those years, from Tevin and Aylsfa and Cennet. There had been no reason for us to guess that Duncan had once been the Lord of Caer Lind.

"Why did you leave Tevin?" I asked.

Duncan glanced at me sharply. "Why, I was never in Tevin," he said. "Even the name of my country is lost to the Jarns."

"Valentia," I said, recalling Enid bending over an old map in the rain, before Caer Lind.

Duncan smiled. "You haven't lost that amazing memory you had as a child," he said.

"I do think of it as Tevin," I admitted.

"Everything was lost," he said, seriously. "My wife and sons had died in the fighting. There was no doubt we were losing everywhere. Rudwen was all that was left. I left Caer Lind so that she might have a little space to grow up."

He was not looking at me, but over my shoulder, his face was set. "She did grow up," I said, inadequately. She was only twenty-two when she died fighting the raiders who attacked Derwen.

"How did you know I was Lord of Valentia?" Duncan asked. "I had not known Gwien had told anyone."

"He didn't tell me," I said. "Alfwin Cellasson told me how they took Caer Lind, and I thought it too much chance that there should be two men fleeing on piebald greathorses with little girls set before them."

Duncan smiled sadly, looking very old. "Well, then it makes it easier to ask you. I have given good service to your family for nearly twenty-five years now. Do you think your Urdo would give me my land back?"

I choked, missed a step, trod on Duncan's foot, and would have fallen and probably, knocked Flerian over if Duncan hadn't caught my arm and steadied me. As it was, Flerian gave me a puzzled look, and I shrugged an apology. Then I looked back at Duncan. He looked almost as if he were holding his breath. How could he think for an instant that Urdo would do such a thing? He and his people had abandoned the land and broken the ties with it, and the land had accepted Cella and the Jarnsmen instead. In any case he could hardly take up any lordship. He must be past sixty, maybe older, and all his children were dead. His only living nephew was Flavien ap Borthas, who as lord of Tinala could not be his heir. Even if Alfwin hadn't existed and the whole of Tevin had been empty for settlement, he had no people; no king could have thought of giving it to him. I had never thought Duncan a fool to even consider such a thing. There wasn't any kind thing to say, and trying to soften it would probably have made it worse. "No," I said, as soon as I had breath enough. "I don't think there is any chance of that at all. You left the land, and so did all your folk."

"We were forced to flee," said Duncan, stiffly. "But now that it is empty of his enemies the Emperor could give it back, if he chose."

I thought of Alfwin. I thought of the Jarnish hamlet where the farmers had given us corn and told us that Ohtar had come down to fight us. I remembered the ruinous state of Caer Lind when I had been besieged in it.

"It is empty no longer," I said, as calmly as I could. "And the gods of the land accepted the Jarnsmen, with their king Cella, and his son Alfwin after him. Alfwin has been fighting on our side all through the War. They are not enemies but allies."

"He is Emperor, he raised the purple banner, he could—" Duncan began, very stiffly.

I interrupted. "If the Emperor of Vinca had wished to do such a thing, maybe it would have been possible, even though you have no heirs and no people. But Urdo is not Emperor of Vinca, and not a tyrant who can do whatever he pleases." My mind went back to the moment on top of Foreth when Urdo had given his name and titles before the gods. "He is High King of the Island of Tir Tanagiri by right of birth, by right of conquest, and by right of election of all principalities. His Peace is something we are all making."

The dance came to an end, and we bowed to each other very formally, then walked back towards the window where I had been sitting.

"You are right that it isn't Vincan times come again," Duncan said, looking out into the night. "Have you told your mother so?"

"I think she knows," I said, as gently as I could. "She was calling herself the last of the Vincans this afternoon, accepting that. She knows this is a new age."

"I do not think I am the only person who will need reminding," said Duncan, looking very remote. "And if it is a new world indeed that you youngsters are building then you should have told those who thought they were fighting beside you to restore the world of our young days."

I knew well enough that it was nearly sixty years since the last Vincan legion had left Tir Tanagiri and that Duncan's young days had been spent in civil wars as well as fending off the Jarnsmen. I could hardly believe he had really hoped to be given his land back again just like that, when he had abandoned it, and had no heir, and after twenty-five years. I couldn't think of anything at all to say. Fortunately, Lew came up just then. Duncan excused himself to go and help Veniva. Lew was beaming broadly. I suppose he did have a lot to be cheerful about. He was drinking from a smooth red Vincan cup, a particular treasure of my mother's. I hoped he would not break it. I glanced around for Emer, she was part of a group on the other side of the room that included Morien, Daldaf, and her Isarnagan lover.

"Must I go to Caer Tanaga to find my brother Urdo, or will he be coming here soon?" Lew asked, after we had both dispensed with friendly greetings. Calling Urdo his brother seemed a bit much to me, for a wife's sister's husband he had never met.

"You must go to Caer Tanaga for the Feast of Peace," I said, and bowed a little stiffly. "I think my lord Urdo will be sending out invitations by red-cloak as soon as he has the date arranged."

"Then does he ever come out here?" Lew looked curious. I expect he was wondering how much interference he'd have to deal with.

"Sometimes, when it is necessary. He came to help with the defenses after we had been raided by Jarnsmen ten years ago."

"That is a long time now," he said, stroking his long moustache. "Well, I was hoping you would do me the honor of dancing—" I wished I had not danced with Duncan because now it would be impossible for me to say I was too tired to dance. I felt sure he would trample on my feet. I hoped the food would be ready soon. Then Lew surprised me by continuing "—with my nephew." I felt a great relief that I wouldn't have to dodge his feet, whoever his nephew might be, but as he led me across the room my heart sank. He was making for the group containing Emer. He was heading straight for Emer's lover, Fishface himself. When he saw his uncle leading me towards him he closed his eyes for a moment, then he had the nerve to grin. Emer looked a little pale. Morien looked cautiously pleased.

"Sulien ap Gwien, this is my nephew—" Lew began.

"We've met," I said, before Lew could tell me his name. "And I always call him Fishface," We all laughed, though Morien was frowning a little, and Emer's laugh was brittle.

"Where did you—" Lew started, but Fishface took hold of my hand and dragged me off into the dance. I waved an apology at Lew, who said something to Emer, who touched her injured arm. They both stood and watched us benignly. Morien, beside them, was now frowning deeply.

"So where did we meet, Praefecto?" Fishface hissed at me as soon as we were far enough away not to be heard. "I've never been in Tir Tanagiri before, and he knows it."

"Oh, earlier today," I said, quietly. "In the baths perhaps? In the stables? I meet so many people it's easy to forget."

"I don't suppose you've ever been to Oriel?" he asked, swinging me viciously.

I shook my head. "Never been off the island. Better make it the stables, I was there for a while earlier."

"Why couldn't you have just let him introduce me?" By the music he should have swung me again, instead he stepped closer, looking menacing.

"Because I take curses seriously, even if you don't," I said.

"I take that one quite sufficiently seriously to know it'll be my death. I just don't see how you're going to avoid discovering my name for the rest of your life. In fact I'm quite surprised you didn't rush off to discover it as soon as you could. I'm quite sure your eager young captain knew it all the time." Now he swung me, out of time, almost tripping me.

"Ap Trivan? Really?" I said, righting myself. Inability to dance was clearly a family failing. If I hadn't seen Emer dance perfectly well, and Elenn, too, I would have thought it an Isarnagan failing. I wondered whether Emlin did know. We hadn't had time to talk. I had no option but to keep Emer's relationship with her husband's nephew quiet. I would tell Urdo, of course.

"I would imagine so. He seemed quite well up on Isarnagan gossip." I could see Emer's scarred face over his shoulder. Lew, beside her, was smiling and tapping his foot to the drumbeat. Emer was only looking sadly at us. Someone would notice if she kept that up.

"Well, I'm not, and I don't care to be. And unless you want your uncle to wonder even more, then I'd smile if I were you; he's watching us, and you look as if you're going to your own funeral."

He laughed unexpectedly and quite charmingly. "Why, then I shall act the way people are supposed to when they are dancing and compliment your drape and your beautiful amber brooch. Is it Isarnagan work?"

It was the one that had come from the hoard. I shook my head. "It is old in my family," I said.

"I see. What a good thing Urdo has female war-leaders."

"Why?" I asked, cautiously.

"Why, that trick of dashing you off into the dance to get away from the questions would never have worked with a man."

I laughed. "It has been known for men to dance together in the alae, but it is not a usual thing. It would never have worked with ap Thurrig either."

"No indeed, from what I have heard. Indeed my kin and I are lucky it was you we met on this adventure."

We backed and advanced, as we came together again he spoke quietly. "You do realize what my uncle's plotting?" I shook my head. "He suggested to me that it would be a very good thing if I made your brother an offer for you. I suspect he might have suggested the same to your brother, for he was telling me all your faults most apologetically." He laughed again, with a little bitterness. "Oh dear, your face could curdle milk. I am supposed to be a most eligible husband, and most people consider me quite sufficiently handsome."

"They must never have seen a mouth-old salmon," I said.

"Why, how your thoughts do run on fish," he said, very sweetly. "Perhaps we ought to marry at that. No, don't pull your hand away, we're dancing, it will look terrible." He squeezed my fingers so tightly that I would have had to strike him to get free. I had not in any case meant to jerk away. He continued talking very lightly. "I mean it would stop everyone trying to marry both of us off. And as you already know my terrible secret, and I know yours, we needn't have anything to do with each other. You are far better than the last girl Black Darag suggested for me, who was noble and very wealthy but had a laugh like a crow. And even if you don't like my face you must have a terrible time finding dancing partners your own height."

"What terrible secrets of mine has my brother been telling you?" I asked, as calmly as I could, trying to ignore the frivolity.

"Now it's I who should tell you to smile for my uncle," he said, smiling himself as if I had made a joke. "Why only about your relationship with the High King, which is not quite news, even in distant Tir Isarnagiri."

I was surprised how angry it made me. I was quite used to the armigers joking about this supposed relationship, and I had given up doing more than groaning when it was mentioned. I supposed Morien must have picked it up from Glyn's teasing when I was at Derwen a long time ago. But I was horrified to see that it had spread so far. "You listen to much too much gossip," I said, through my teeth. "I do not know why it should please people to tell lies about me, but you are quite mistaken there."

He raised his eyebrows and looked surprised. "I somehow suspected you'd turn me down, alas," he said, and grinned audaciously at me. "Though we'd not be so badly suited as all that. It would cement the alliance nicely, and I've always liked tall women who don't want me. There are so many who do it gets tedious."

There weren't any words rude enough in Tanagan, so I said some in Jarnish, including one or two I wasn't quite sure of the meaning of which Alfwin had used the time Masarn's Whitefoot stepped on his toe. I kept on smiling as best I could as I said them. His own smile never faltered, though behind us Garian was blinking a little.

"Yes, yes," he said at last quietly, as the music came near the end. "If it were a choice between me and a dead leprous female cod you would still indulge your preference for fish, and I can't blame you in the slightest. Indeed I was just being whimsical and reflecting upon irony, and I doubt very much my mother would approve of you either. We will consider the match canceled, though not the alliance between our kindreds. And you may ask your ap Trivan my name, whereupon your opinion of me will sink even lower, if such a thing is possible."

He released my hand, bowed, and left me. I bowed back, automatically, then I blinked after him. I wouldn't want him beside me in battle. For all his quickness one would never be able to count on him being where he was needed. As luck would have it I caught sight of Emlin's cropped head straight away and went over to him.

"Do you know who he is?" I asked, quietly.

"Do you want to dance?" he asked.

"No, I don't, I don't care if I never dance again, and you must be tired, too. Sit down over here with me and tell me quietly what you know about that fish-faced Isarnagan before I put my foot in it." We went and sat in the window. I picked up the cup I had left there earlier. Daldaf, with a flagon in his hand, looked as if he might come up to us. I glared at him, and he retreated.

"He's Conal ap Amagien ap Ross, called Conal the Victor," Emlin said, very quietly.

I raised an eyebrow. "I've never heard of him. He's Lew's nephew then?"

"Yes. His father Amagien the Poet is Lew's brother. Conal's mother is Black Darag's mother's sister."

He sounded like Veniva going on endlessly about dynastic marriages. I could never find it interesting unless I knew the people. "So he fought for Oriel against Connat in their last big war?" I asked. "Come on, Emlin, what are you leaving out here?"

"He fought for Oriel, yes. He's the person who started the war up again. He's Conal the Victor; didn't you hear that he killed Maga of Connat last year?"

I sat quite still, far more shocked than I had thought I would be by whatever his secret was. He had killed her mother, and she—I looked over at Emer, who was talking to Lew and Morien looking quite composed—she was wearing a dark red overdress, wool, not linen, but she did not look too warm. Conal Fishface was dancing with Kerys. I could only see his back, but he was probably saying something outrageous because she was laughing. I looked back at Emer. Now I understood why they couldn't be together. Not some long-ago bloodfeud, her own mother. I wondered suddenly if he had made her some reparation. Even if she had accepted it the rest of her family would not.

"A good thing he was never there at all," I said. "What have we done?"

"I think we have done more for Urdo's Peace than we would if we'd fought," said Emlin, yawning and stretching.

"I shall have to tell Urdo," I said.

"Of course," said Emlin. "Will you go to him now at Caer Tanaga?"

"No," I said. I had decided already what my first step was to be. "I will go to Caer Gloran, where there might be news, and which is on the way north. If there are forces in Wenlad and in Demedia I should be heading that way. If there's no message then I might go east and south to Caer Tanaga to find Urdo and my own ala. It's not much longer to go that way than to go by Magor and the ferry across the Havren."

"Will you take this ala?" he asked.

I looked at him, considering. "No. I don't trust the Isarnagans quite that far. I'll take a couple of pennons—no. I'll take volunteers, a couple of pennons' worth. You ask them, tonight, and before I sleep we must talk over who is going and pick out who will be the decurios and the sequifers. Also tell Nodol Boar-Beard to get supplies sorted out for that many, so we will be ready to leave in the morning."

"At dawn?" asked Emlin, looking weary.

"No, by late morning. We're all tired, and there's no point in pushing people or horses past the best we can do." Emlin raised his chin and looked pleased. What I said was right, but also I wanted to go at sunrise to Darien's grave with Ulf's weapons. "You have to stay here. But I think I must put Morien in charge of the ala. There isn't time for what Urdo wanted: I can't take him back with me."

"You're absolutely right," Emlin said, decisively. "Have you told him?"

"No," I hesitated, fidgeting with the folds of my drape. I had been putting it off. "I wanted to check with you. You didn't seem sure about him."

Emlin looked out of the window at the darkness. "He's your brother."

"Oh speak plainly and never mind that, the important thing is the ala."

He looked back at me, reassured. "Well, Galba trained him well. But he's not fought in war, and he's never really been one of us. He's always been at home and not living in barracks. He's very quiet, and he is the Lord of Derwen, not an armiger the way you and Galba and ap Mardol are. Then again, he's touchy because of that, and if anyone else was in charge of the ala down here he would be a decurio under them, and that would be very uncomfortable for everyone. I certainly wouldn't want to do that, and I don't want to be a praefecto anyway. And unless you stay here there's nobody else."

"I really don't have much choice," I said, and stood up, sighing. "You get on and find out about volunteers for me. I'll ask him." A dance was just finishing, and Veniva raised her hand to signal dinner. "No, wait and do that after you've eaten," I said. "We can discuss the volunteers after breakfast tomorrow."

People began to divide themselves among the alcoves, and the servants brought in plates of food. Daldaf came up and showed me where I should sit, with Veniva, Morien, Kerys, Lew, and Emer. Conal Fishface was not there, fortunately, and I realized that of course he could not eat with Emer. I could not say anything to Morien with the others there. I ate and listened to the others talking and wished I was asleep. Emer and Veniva steered the conversation clear of the shoals, and Lew spoke to Morien much as a steady old sequifer speaks to a young decurio.

As soon as we had finished eating Morien strode out into the center of the room and took the big harp from where the musicians had left it. I had not heard him play since he was a child. Darien and Aurien and I had learned the least amount of music Veniva had considered acceptable and then stopped; none of us had ever come near the big harp. Morien had more of an ear for it. I remembered my mother telling Darien that it was a great thing for a lord to be good enough to give the first tune after a feast, but Darien had laughed and run off with me. Morien, it seemed, was that good.

Then he started to play, and I saw that he was as good as any musicians I had heard at Caer Tanaga. He played an old Tanagan lullaby I remembered my nurse playing, about a girl so beautiful that flowers grew where she walked. I saw Emer smiling to hear it, and wondered if she, too, was thinking about her sister. Then Kerys got up and took the little drum and they sang and played together, ap Erbin's brother's song about the redcloaks. When they had finished, they smiled at each other, for the rhythm is difficult to hold. Emer came forward and murmured to them, and Morien played while she sang an Isarnagan song about a warrior who spent seven days hunting the giant boar and went home to find seven hundred years had passed and all his kin perished.

Afterwards I drummed my feet as loudly as everyone else, and congratulated Morien heartily. Having seen him do something well made it much

easier for me to find words to ask him to command the ala, and we did not
flare up at each other again as I had thought we might. I went to bed and
slept soundly until Daldaf woke me, as I had asked, at first light.

—28—

> On they rushed, that great tide of barbarians, coming ahead as if the
> border and the legion before them meant nothing, crying aloud in their own
> wild tongue as they ran towards the waiting spearpoints. Afterwards I asked
> one of the prisoners what the words meant, and he told me that as near as he
> could put it in Vincan it meant "Death, Death, drink bright blood, whoever
> shall fall shall be counted fortunate!" I asked him why they had not stayed on
> their own side of the border, and he said they wanted to come in to the
> Empire. I asked him if he hadn't known he must inevitably lose against the
> might of the legion, but he just looked at me with his bright eyes and said that
> victory always lay in the hand of Fortune. Yet this was an intelligent man who
> spoke Vincan, a noble among his people. He afterwards served me well and
> rose to the rank of decurion.
>
> —Marcia Antonilla, *The Third Malmish War*

The rain had stopped for the time being. The grass was heavy with
cold wet beads of dew, soaking into my boots as I walked away from
the town. A chill wind was blowing out of the west and I wrapped my
cloak closer. Dusk lingered under the trees. The boles of the birches glimmered pale. The waking birds were calling out to each other and took little notice of me as I walked below them. Once the mattock I had
borrowed chinked against the swords in my bag, and there was silence for a
moment before the birds began chirping again louder than ever. I expected
to have some trouble finding the place, but my feet knew the way. Before
long I was surprised to find myself on a new path through the trees. I wondered who came this way often enough to make a track.

When I came to the place where I had burned my brother I saw a neat
little grave maker. There was a blackened place nearby where someone had
been burning offerings. I bent to look. The stone was local goldenstone
and well shaped, but the letters were not very even. "Darien, son of Gwien,
of Derwen," it read. "I lived dear to my family. I gave up my life when I

was sixteen years old in defense of my home. Here lie my ashes, part of the Earth and all that is holy. I beg you who pass this place to bear in mind my name and think kindly of me."

I bit my lip. In defense of his home, yes, and in defense of me most particularly. I wondered why Veniva, whose letters regularly informed me as to the precise quantities of linen sold that month and how the oil extracted from the flaxseed helped to preserve wood, had never mentioned raising this stone. Reading it I could picture her disputing with Gwien what words would be best to set on it. I felt tears burning in my eyes, but they did not fall. I took out Ulf's swords, wrapped in cloth. I remembered Darien every day, my brother, my best friend. There was always something to make me think of him as he had been. Here I could only remember how he looked when I put him on the pyre, without even his armor, which I had been wearing. His sword still hung at my side. It had seen me through countless battles. I wanted to say something to him, but he was not there. He had gone on.

I raised up my arms to the gods, and called their names. I wished I knew a hymn or a proper form of words to use. Everyone learns the Hymn of Returning, for death is everywhere and nobody knows when it will fall to their turn to send back someone whose name they know. I now regretted that I had never learned any of the other hymns of the Lord of Death. When I was young I had learned what my mother considered essential, and then I had gone on to learn more hymns of healing as I had found people to teach them to me. I had always meant to learn more hymns and praise songs both, but since I had left home there had been so little time for learning things outside my craft. In the alae I often thought myself well taught in such things, for many there had grown up with little chance to learn much about the gods. It was among them, of course, that the priests of the White God made so many of their converts. Now I stood with my arms open in a waiting silence and knew myself ignorant and untaught.

I do not know how long I stood there like that, tears on my face, unable to find words, not knowing what to do next nor how to go on. At last I lowered my arms and drew Ulf's swords out from their wrappings. The rising sun should have shone onto them, but the trees were in the way. "I have brought them as I promised," I said to my absent brother. "Your killer's weapons."

There was a sound from behind me, a rustle and a gasp. I spun round, readying the sword. Veniva was standing there, alone. Her hair was held up by her gold comb. The hem of her overdress was soaked by dew. She was staring at me. "Oh Sulien!" she said. "Why didn't you tell me?"

I lowered the sword slowly and straightened. Even now I couldn't tell her about Ulf and what had happened, either in that clearing or on top of Foreth. We had never talked about it. I might had told Gwien, if he had lived, but even with him my lips might not have obeyed me. "I don't know," I said, at last. "Why didn't you tell me—" I gestured to the stone and the offering place.

She shook her head sorrowfully. "Let us try to do better in future," was all she said. She took the swords from me and looked at them, turning them over in her hands. Then she took a breath and sang a hymn to the Dark Lady, a hymn of grave goods brought late to the pyre and revenge completed. Then together we buried the swords and burned over them the incense and sweet wood Veniva had brought. It was full daylight when we walked back together.

"I shall tell Morien that Darien is avenged," Veniva said when we parted inside the gates. "He should know that, but that will be enough to content him." I embraced her, and she went off into the house with the mattock in her hand, smiling a little. I went to the barracks to find Emlin.

I set off midmorning for Caer Gloran. I took with me two pennons' worth of volunteers. I could have had more if I had wanted to take them. Many of them I had come to know in the ride down, and quite a few of them I remembered from when Galba and I had brought two pennons down to Derwen after Caer Lind. I breakfasted in the barracks with Emlin while we talked over their skills. Then we set off over the hills, the way I had gone so long ago when I first left Derwen. There was a visible track to follow now, very muddy after all the rain. We stopped for the night at the new little settlement by the mines. They called it Nant Gefalion, the blacksmith's stream, because there were so many forges there. There was even a rough wall around it and a wooden watchtower, making it a safe place for an ala to stop for the night. As we rode toward the stables, Marchel's husband, ap Wyn the Smith, came out of one of them and greeted me, asking news of his wife and his brother.

"When I last saw ap Thurrig she was well and in Caer Gloran," I said, leaning down. He was sweating and covered in black dust; even his face had black streaks where he had wiped his hair back. Even though it was twilight, he still had his forge fire burning hot inside. Half a dozen of his helpers were looking on from inside the forge door. "She did very well in the battle at Foreth," I added, in case he had not heard.

"I am proud of her," he said. "I will go back to Caer Gloran to see her soon if she is staying there. And how is my brother?"

"I do not think I know him," I said.

"I thought you had come from Derwen? He is steward there."

It took me longer than it should have. "Daldaf ap Wyn? Of course. You do not look at all alike," I said. That explained why Daldaf seemed to think himself one of the family, if his brother was married to Marchel whose brother had been married to Kerys's sister. It was neither the first time nor the last time I considered how much more complicated kinship ties made the world. "He is very well and took no hurt in the siege."

I declined invitations to drink with ap Wyn when he had finished his forging. I went straight to my tent and slept well that night. When Nant Gefalion was out of sight we were out of Derwen land and into the northern corner of Magor. Although there was nothing to mark the boundary, I could tell when we crossed it. Beauty's hooves seemed to fall differently on the mud.

Our messenger had caught Marchel on her way, and she waited for us where the track joined the road, where I had first joined the ala in battle. The highroad stretched out in both directions. Across it I could see the silver glimmer of the River Havren. It had been raining a little, and now in late afternoon the sun had pushed its way through the clouds, and everything was steaming gently. The horses called greetings and challenges to each other as we came up. Marchel came forward to greet us.

"We may as well camp here tonight and decide what we're doing," she said. "If we go back to Caer Gloran the armigers will make themselves comfortable at home and be hard to start on time, or start out more tired. They've said good-bye; I think it's better not to do it again. And your troops look as if they need the rest."

"We've been doing some hard riding," I agreed, though I would have liked to go the few hours farther to Caer Gloran to have a bath and see Amala. I passed on her husband's greetings and then gave the order to my pennons to camp and rest with the others.

Marchel and I went on to her tent. "Have you heard from Urdo?" I asked as soon as we were inside. She shook her head. We sat down on her blankets.

"It's just too far," she said, picking up a leather cup and pulling it into shape. "That's the worst of it. I wish we knew what he was doing. Even with the highroad going all the way from the gates of Caer Gloran and assuming the messenger changes horses and rides flat out it's a good three days, and another three back of course. I sent as soon as your messenger reached me and again today. I can't expect to hear back from the first message for another two or three days. And even by now it will be completely out-of-date and useless." She sighed.

"I sent when I sent to you, from Magor. He'll have that first message yesterday or today, I think. Then I sent again when they were settled, which message he should have tomorrow or the day after." She poured ale from a full skin into the leather cup and handed it to me. I turned it in my hand as she filled her own cup. "We probably shouldn't wait to hear," I added.

"Of course not." She raised her cup to me, then drained it. I did the same. "Look, are you sure the Isarnagans down there are going to stay peaceful?"

"No," I admitted. "If I really felt sure I'd have brought Galba's ala. As it is I left it with my brother Morien. I don't think they'll break their oaths, and they'll be busy, but I didn't want to leave the town undefended and leave them the temptation."

"Is Morien up to command?" Marchel asked, refilling the cups.

I shrugged, feeling uncomfortable. "He's got Emlin ap Trivan as tribuno, and he's very good." She grunted agreement; she had worked with Emlin before. "He's been a decurio under Galba, and he's the lord down there. Urdo wanted me to bring him to Caer Tanaga so he could see if he was good enough, but there just isn't time really. I've never fought with him and you have—do you think he isn't up to it?"

Marchel drained her cup and passed the aleskin to me. "No, I don't think that. I'd just prefer to have someone more experienced there. He's very young, and he hasn't fought in the war, just against raiders. It's an old argument about who gets promoted, I suppose. But he's had good training and no doubt he'll do. I think you were right to leave them, and it's good you've settled the Isarnagans, too. If only we could deal with the others so easily."

"Have you news of the others?" I refilled my cup, and hers again.

"A messenger from Cadraith ap Mardol and his father, of course. They were at Caer Asgor when they sent it, it reached me as I was setting out. That means it was sent four, no, five days ago now. They were asking for help. The ala had defeated one band. Duke Mardol said he was concerned as to how many others there might be inland in Wenlad. He thought it would take them four days to reach the coast unopposed—they sent me a map of their route. It's no farther from Caer Asgor than from here to Derwen, as the crow flies, but whatever they call him, Mardol can't fly like a

crow, or use crows for messengers either. That would be useful! But Wenlad's all mountains, and there aren't any good roads. There aren't even any
good tracks past Cothan."

"I've never been up there," I said. "You think you should go and
help?" I sipped my ale slowly. I wished there was some way to set the cup
down, or that there was some food to go with it.

"If Derwen's safe, then yes, unless we hear differently from Urdo, and I
really don't think we should wait. The Good Lord alone knows what's
happening in Demedia, but if we go up to Caer Asgor, we're bound to be
nearer to where we're needed."

"Poor Angas," I said. "He hates the Isarnagans, and he's been worrying
this would happen for years. I think you're right, for your ala certainly, but
the sensible thing for me to do would be to get to my ala, whatever Urdo's
doing with it. So maybe I ought to go east towards Caer Tanaga and hope
to meet him on the way?"

"I wish you'd come to Wenlad and help get that sorted out," Marchel
said, turning her cup in her hand so the ale almost slopped over the rim.

"Without my ala I'm just one more lance," I said, "I'd like to get them
and talk to Urdo and then probably bring them up to Wenlad. Do you
know where the other alae are?"

"Mine's here," she began, counting on her fingers. "Galba's is in Derwen, of course. Urdo was going with yours and Gwair's to Caer Tanaga, he
should be there by now unless he's left again already. Cadraith was in Caer
Asgor when he sent to me, and he was heading west. Luth was going from
Foreth to Caer Lind with Alfwin. Angas is somewhere in Demedia. That
leaves ap Meneth who is almost certainly in Caer Rangor still, though he
might have had a message from Wenlad and gone there."

"So might Luth," I said. "I expect Urdo's frantic."

"Not to mention Raul," Marchel said, "This is a most disorganized
invasion." She laughed, and drained her ale again. "Look, I know you want
to see Urdo, but I'm sure he's bringing your ala north, or will be once he
gets the messages."

Anger stirred in me at this. "It is not that I want to see Urdo," I said,
"Or at least, not any more than you do. I want my ala, and I want to know
what's going on and what Urdo wants done first." I drew out a map from
my pouch. "You are going northwest from here, into Wenlad." I traced the
line with my finger. Marchel raised her chin, frowning. "Is that a river or a
road?" I asked.

"River," she said. "Not very clear though. That's the Dee. The road crosses it."

"Urdo keeps saying we need new maps drawn," I agreed absently. "Well, it will take you four or five days to get there, I think, away from good roads. If I go northeast, along the highroad towards Caer Rangor, the way we came down, then if Urdo has set out from Caer Tanaga for the north, I should meet him somewhere along there. Then, if he wants me to come to Wenlad, I can come west along this highroad here and be only a few days behind you, and with my whole ala."

"And if he's not?" Marchel asked. She was looking at the map and not at me.

"Then I'll hear that on the road and go south. I'll at least know where my troops are. As it is I'm not much help to you really, two pennons."

"Better than nothing." Marchel scowled and counted miles with her thumb and days aloud. "So small and well-defined it looks on the map. So big and out of control down here. I'd prefer it if you came with me, but I suppose that will work. Keep sending messengers as often as you can. If all goes well, it won't take too long anyway."

"At least we don't have to worry about what we're going to do with ourselves without any fighting," I said, trying to make a joke of it. Marchel glared at me. I had no idea what I had said wrong.

"We will praise the Lord and none of us will stand for you trying to stir trouble up to stop us!" she said, furiously.

I just stared at her for a moment. "Do you think I invited the Isarnagans in?" I asked.

"You're a heathen, and you want more fighting, and they're all heathens who fled from their homes rather than accept the White God!" she said, looking suspicious.

"I was joking about more fighting!" I said, shaking my head in disbelief. "The ale's gone to your head, Marchel. If anyone's to blame for this invasion it's your brother Chanerig stirring up trouble in Tir Isarnagiri."

"Chanerig brought a whole island under the banner of the White God," she shouted. "His name will be remembered forever among the Fathers of the Church!" She took another swallow of ale, and added, more quietly "Nobody could have expected so many to be willful, or for them to decide to invade us." She looked at me suspiciously. "Though you were very well placed to be there at the right time to settle them without fighting," she added.

I sprang to my feet, spilling my ale on the fleece I had been sitting on. My hand moved of its own accord to my sword hilt. "You are entirely wrong," I said, coldly. "Are you calling me a traitor?"

Marchel rubbed her hand across her eyes and stared up at me. "No," she said. "No, Sulien, I didn't mean that. But you have to decide who you serve, Urdo or your family."

This was nonsense. I was almost too confused to be angry. "What do you mean? You know I serve Urdo—before this I hadn't even been home since the beginning of the war! You're the one who didn't want to be sent to Dun Idyn because you wanted to be near your family; I've always gone where Urdo wanted without complaint. I can't even see what you're accusing me of."

"I'm not accusing you of anything," she said. "Sit down for goodness sake. You misunderstood me. I know you're not a traitor to Urdo, even if you are a godless heathen. But how can you serve Urdo's Peace and your gods?"

I stared down at her, and wondered if she was drunk or if she had gone quite mad like her brother Chanerig. "There has never been a need to make such a choice," I said, slowly and clearly. "Urdo does not force any faith on his followers; not even the conquered were asked to give up their gods. Urdo keeps to the old ways as well as the new. Your god may be splendid in himself, but how can you expect people to serve only one god and ignore all the others? How can you consider forcing them to, if they will not choose to? Where is your loyalty, if it came to it, between Urdo and your god?"

"Urdo is making the Peace where we may praise the White God," Marchel said. "I think we must both be tired and a little drunk, and we are saying things we don't mean. I am sorry if I have insulted you."

"And I you," I said, and bowed, and left her tent. I ate and slept in my own tent, and we parted company the next morning, with formal politeness. I hoped that by the next time I saw her she'd have calmed down.

On the evening of the third day out from the crossroads near Caer Gloran a messenger from Urdo reached me. I was congratulated on solving the problem in Derwen and instructed to go at speed to Thansethan, where my ala was waiting. The messenger was going on to Wenlad so I added a message for Marchel and Cadraith ap Mardol saying that I had received the orders and would be heading for Thansethan. It took another day and a half to reach there. We could have done it more quickly, but not without risk to the horses. As it was I made sure to walk them for a mile or so in the morning before mounting. They were all very tired, and one was lame from a loose stone when we arrived. We came up to Thansethan in a fine rain just as the bell was ringing for noon worship. I led the way to the stable door, afraid we would have to wait until the worship was over before we were let in.

I dismounted and scratched for admittance and found to my surprise the door flung open immediately by the dark and smiling face of Masarn. "Sulien!" he said, and hugged me. Then Elidir pushed past and also hugged me. I had to swing myself back into the saddle to avoid being trampled by what seemed like half my ala all eager to express their delight in seeing me.

"All right!" I said. "I'm very pleased to see all of you, too, but it's only been half a month or so since you saw me!" I tried to count the days in my head but stopped myself, some of them blurred together and there was no need. "Where's ap Erbin?"

They all spoke at once. Eventually Masarn got them quiet. "He's gone with the High King to Caer Lind. He's praefecto of Gwair Aderyn's ala now."

"So who's in charge of you?" I asked.

Masarn grinned. "I was, until I opened the door." he said. "Though I was told to take Raul's advice."

"And has he advised you?"

"Not a word," said Masarn, cheerfully. "It would have been very awkward if he did, him not being an armiger. But he knows better."

"Good. I've brought two more pennons as you can see, volunteers from Galba's ala. They'll be staying with us for a while. Get them settled and their horses seen to. Do you say the High King's gone on?" I couldn't think why he would have gone to Caer Lind, of all places.

"Yes," Masarn said. "He told us to wait here for you. I don't have any orders. But Raul's here, he wants to see you as soon as possible. He knows what's going on."

"Look after my horses then," I said, dismounting. Beauty had his ears back. I patted him and gave the rein to Masarn.

"Shall I come with you?" Elidir asked. As signaler she sometimes accompanied me to make notes and carry papers.

"Not this time," I said. "I'll find out what we're going to do and let you know."

It was very good to be alone for a moment as I walked out through the stables, past my ala's familiar horses, and into the courtyard. It was very peaceful. I wanted to prepare myself to see my son Darien. I hadn't managed to bring him anything, again. My mind somehow refused to stop racing. I wanted to know what was happening.

When I came out into the courtyard, Arvlid was remonstrating with three of my armigers, who were sitting soaking their feet in the pool that fed the water clock. Arvlid was very plump now, and very pink in the face. She could never have run ten miles to warn the monastery; she would have been out of breath after one. I sent the armigers away with their heads between their knees—one of them looked as if she might cry when I asked them if they had just come off the farm. Arvlid was the only real friend I had made in my time at Thansethan, and I was glad to see her. I thanked her for the letters she had sent, and she told me how well Darien was doing at his lessons. "You'll have to get on down to the pasture while you're here," she added. "Darien's been longing to show you his foal."

Then the doors of the sanctuary opened and the people poured out.

Darien came out with the other children. He had grown much taller. I thought he looked thin and wondered if they were feeding him enough. He seemed to be walking on his own in the midst of them. I had a moment before he saw me and his face closed up. We embraced, among the crowd coming out of the sanctuary. "How are you?" I asked. "How is your foal?"

"She's wonderful," he said, his face lighting up again. "She's as beautiful as her mother, and I have called her Keturah."

"That's an unusual name for a horse," I said. The other children giggled.

Darien's back stiffened, and his cheeks flushed red. "It's the name of the star that shone when the White God was born as a man," he explained, in the tone of one explaining that spring grass is green.

"An excellent name," I said, "with her mother being called Starlight." This seemed to redeem my idiocy slightly for Darien. He almost smiled.

"And her father is called Maram, after the White God's apostle who was so stubborn, because he is stubborn you know," a boy a few years older put in, very politely. Darien moved a little towards me, away from the boy who had spoken. Arvlid frowned at the boy, and took a breath as if she meant to speak, but kept her silence.

"Well, a very good name," I repeated, as heartily as I could.

"Shall we go and see her now?" Darien asked, turning to me and Arvlid and pointedly excluding the other children. I wondered if they bullied him.

"I have to speak to Raul first," I said, catching sight of him coming towards me, looking almost pleased to see me. "Will you show her to me later? I'll meet you in the stables."

Darien ran off as Raul came up, and Arvlid gathered up the other children and led them off, except the older boy who had spoken. He was almost a young man—I had boys not much older working as grooms and scouts. He lingered near me, by the pool, looking at me and frowning a little.

"Ap Gwien, thanks be to God," said Raul. "I was afraid you would have gone up to Wenlad."

"I almost did," I said. "What is the plan?"

"Have you heard the news from Demedia?" he asked, in a low voice. Then he looked round and saw the boy still nearby. "No, let's go inside and talk." I followed him into one of the little copyist's rooms in the library where I had spent so much time in the months when I was waiting for Darien to be born.

"Who is that boy?" I asked, curiously.

"That's the youngest son of the old lord of Angas," Raul said, "Our Angas's brother. Which is why I didn't want to speak about it in front of him. He hasn't been told the details. He's been here for the last six months having a bit of education before he comes to Caer Tanaga to the ala." He had grown and changed a lot since he had fought against me to fling himself into the fire that killed his mother at Caer Lind. I would never have known him.

"What's happened?" I asked. "I know some Isarnagans have landed up there."

Raul sighed heavily and pushed back his hood. "When we were fighting the Battle of Foreth and winning the Peace, you may remember Ohtar Bearsson brought all his troops down in boats to fight against us?" I already had a bad feeling. I raised my chin in acknowledgment. "Angas, having an ala and some local levies of foot soldiers, probed into Bereich and found that the defenses were a bluff, it was in fact almost undefended. He rushed all his force to the border, dashed in, and took it while he had the opportunity. He captured Gytha Ohtarsdottar, Alfwin's wife, who has remained with her father all this time. She had been conducting the fight herself after their captain was killed."

"Alfwin will hate that," I blurted.

Raul half smiled. "No doubt. Angas spoke of her in the highest terms in his first letter. She is a great queen." I remembered what he had said of her at Foreth, that she had taken the pebble. Raul went on. "In his next letter, he had heard from Marchel of our troubles and he left his militia but was riding south with his ala to come to our aid. Meanwhile, as Angas was securing Bereich and moving south into Tinala, Demedia, also left stripped of troops, was being invaded by Isarnagans from the west. These are the same Isarnagans who have always raided the coast, the people of Oriel. This time they came in force, largely because of what that idiot Chanerig ap Thurrig did at their fire feast."

"I thought—" I said, and stopped.

Raul put his head on one side and looked at me. "It is possible to serve the White God without being a narrow-minded fanatic, you know," he said, mildly. "I know, as do many at Thansethan, that if people are given the chance to see they will open their eyes. Some people take longer than others." He smiled at me, and there was no doubt that he meant what he said. "But we do not believe in forcing conversions at any time. I wanted to preach to them all after Foreth and see if the spirit would move in them to accept the god of the victorious on the battlefield, as we read happened in Narlahena and in Lossia. But I would never force anyone to come to the White God's table unwilling. When Custennin took the pebble the whole land of Munew sang and rejoiced and praised and worshiped the Lord. All of us who were there heard it. In Tir Isarnagiri it will be regretful praise at best, always looking backwards. Besides which impiety, Chanerig is a fool, and he has wished this invasion on us at a bad time. It would have been even worse if it had come before Foreth, and we have only God to thank, who turns even evil things to his purpose, that it did not."

"That was lucky," I agreed fervently. "So to go back to Demedia, what happened? Angas was away when they arrived?"

"Angas is not such a fool as to leave the country completely unguarded, though he was not expecting anything on that scale. The Isarnagans had a fight on their hands, and a message reached Angas. He immediately sent to us and returned as fast as he could. They are there in great force—both Atha ap Gren and Black Darag are there. Dun Idyn is under siege. There had been an inconclusive battle when last he sent, but it looks as if they are in possession of the western part of Demedia, while Angas has the eastern part and all of Bereich."

My head hurt. "Where is Ohtar in all this? Does he know?"

"We very much hope he is in Caer Lind, so that he will be there when Urdo gets there. He probably knows by now. Urdo will tell him if not. He is hoping to persuade both Alfwin and Ohtar to march or sail north and secure Demedia."

"I see why he went himself," I said. "Will Angas give Bereich back?"

"It is to be hoped that he will, in return for Ohtar's help," Raul said, folding his hands together and staring at them.

"And what am I to do, and my ala?"

"Guard all the south and east," Raul said. I opened my mouth, but he went on. "You can do it from here or from Caer Tanaga, or wherever suits you. There is what's left of Ayl's troops in Aylsfa, you can do something with them if you can get Ayl to agree. Luth is going up to Demedia, but when Marchel and ap Mardol have sorted out the Isarnagans in Wenlad they will be available."

I thought of the vast amounts of territory that were implied in that "south and east," and remembered that the only ala in the west was Galba's ala at Derwen. I would send to move them to Magor, that was near enough if there was trouble with Lew ap Ross or if anyone came up the Havren. That would do, and then my mind turned back to the magnitude of the problem Urdo had dropped on me. The open coastline of Tinala, Tevin, Aylsfa, Cennet, Segantia, and Munew and all the inland country as well. I wondered how much infantry militia the allied kings had and whether they would let me move troops around. I would have to be ready for Jarnish revolts, maybe even Tanagan revolts, certainly for more Isarnagan landings and Jarnish attacks from over the sea, either raiders coming for after-harvest attacks or a real attack with an army from Jarnholme wanting revenge for Foreth. Sweyn's nephew could have got away, Ulf's brother whatever his name was. Raul would know.

"What is the name of Sweyn's younger nephew?" I asked.

Raul laughed. "You have been sitting there chewing your lip without saying a word until it is almost time for the next bell to ring for worship, and that is what you want to know? It is Arling Gunnarsson. He may be dead. He was carried from the field wounded, and nobody has seen him since."

"I hope he is, though who knows who might lead any Jarnsmen who want to fight in that case. Will you talk to the allied kings for me about how many troops they have?"

"I will," said Raul. "Some of that I know already, but we will have to tread very carefully."

I raised my chin absently, agreeing. "After your next worship we must get the maps out and consider troops and logistics. The glory of victory is all very well, but making a show would probably help in some cases." A thought struck me as I stood. "Whatever would you have done if I had gone to Wenlad?"

"I don't know," Raul said, and smiled thinly. "Urdo was absolutely sure you would be coming here; he wouldn't listen to argument. And he was right, for here you are."

I thought that the land had probably told him, but managed not to say as much to Raul, however friendly he was being at present. "Here I am, indeed. Shall I meet you back here after your service?" I asked. "I have to go and see a horse now."

—29—

"If I have no sword, where then shall I seek peace?"
—from a hymn to Sky Father

The month and a half after I left Thansethan I spent mostly in the saddle. There was no fighting except for one skirmish against raiders. Mostly I moved troops around and looked as strong as possible for the kings. There were potential problems almost everywhere that looking weak would exacerbate. I went first to Caer Tanaga and saw Garah and Glyn and Elenn. Garah and Glyn both looked exhausted—all the years of building up supplies to keep the horses fed in the War had left the stores in entirely the wrong place for this new invasion. Dalmer had gone north with Urdo and left it all to them. Elenn was also deeply involved in all the logistic work. I told her about the settlement with Lew and Emer, but not about Emer's relationship with Conal Fishface. It was too shocking, and I did not know how she felt about her sister. I would tell Urdo, and he could decide what to tell her.

I left three pennons there with Masarn. I also left him orders to be ready to respond to any trouble anywhere on his own initiative. I left his own pennon, of course, and the two weary pennons of volunteers who had come with me from Galba's ala. Garah assured me at parting that she would send to me whenever there was any news at all.

We were only one pennon short of a full ala when we crossed the Tamer and rode into Aylsfa. The farmers getting the harvest in stopped in the fields to stare at us as we rode by. In some places they had dug holes in the side of the highroad to get stone for their houses, and it was collapsing down to the level of the fields. I couldn't find it in my heart to reprove the mutters of "barbarians" that ran through the ranks when we saw that.

I ate very good roast boar with Ayl in his strange hall of Fenshal. It has bog and reeds on three sides. This makes it safe from attack but horrible to visit. Both roof and floor are made of rushes, and the walls are wood and mud. It was horribly damp. I reassured him over and over that whatever we could do we would. Those few of his household and fighting men who were alive after Foreth seemed cheered to see us and this proof of Urdo's friendship. They had lost all their confidence with their defeat. I tried hard to be delicate at explaining that he could call on us for help if he needed it. He promised us any supplies we needed if we had to fight in Aylsfa.

Ayl did not fear the Isarnagans, who were not fools to sail all the way around Tir Tanagiri just to attack him when they had no particular grudge. He was worried that Sweyn's first wife, Hulda, who was ruling Jarnholme, or Arling Gunnarsson, if he had survived, would invade across the Narrow Seas at any moment. Hulda, he told me, hated Sweyn for taking a second wife and for sacrificing their daughter to the gods. This would not necessarily stop her deciding to try to avenge him. He was also worried that some of the Tanagan kings would see his weakness and attack. He did not name any of these threats, and I did not like to say that he was fortunate in not sharing borders with the ones most likely to do it.

As far as help went I could say no more than that I would be ready to do what I could. I could not leave as much as a pennon there with him because there was nowhere safe to house the horses and no supplies ready. Greathorses can live on grass alone, but they can't fight on it. Nor do they thrive in wet land, and when they are outside walls they are vulnerable at night. I told him to prepare supplies and have people ready who could ride and knew the ways to the coast in case there was an invasion and the ala needed guiding.

He told me after supper that he was looking for a wife, which I promised to mention to Urdo. I could see this was an excellent opportunity for a closer alliance and that it would be better if he looked for a wife in Tir Tanagiri than if he sent for one from Jarnholme. I wondered if Alswith could cope with him. I couldn't see any Tanagan wanting to live in a damp place like this. But there were proper towns along the coast—I had seen them on the map—Othona and Caer Col. I thought that maybe now there was peace he would live somewhere more sensible. (I was wrong about this. Ayl liked Fenshal and lived there until he died, and his heirs are living there still.) Just before I left he asked after Ulf, who was not with us. Urdo had assigned him to Masarn's pennon, and I had not wanted to change Urdo's direct order without a good reason.

Then I went south, calling briefly at Caer Tanaga to pick up Raul and get Glyn to send one of his sharp young quartermasters to Ayl to help organize the supply situation there. I rode on after only one night, down to Cennet. I ate eels and beans with Guthrum and Ninian and assured them that the Isarnagans would be cleared out of their daughter's kingdom soon. I learned from them that Eirann Swan-Neck and her older children were out rousing the Demedian countryside against the invaders. Guthrum was in no need of troops. Indeed Cennet was probably the strongest and best-armed place on the island as they had lost very little in the War. They'd fought a few skirmishes with Ayl but nothing more. I think Sweyn had thought they would acknowledge him as High King if Urdo were defeated and had not wanted to cause bloodfeuds. I suggested that if they were thinking of attacking Aylsfa, Urdo would be very unhappy to hear it. Ninian replied that the thought had never entered their minds, but she laughed as she said it. They gave us some supplies for the horses, not as much as I would have liked, but certainly a help. It seemed the bean crop had been notably good in Cennet that year. I arranged for most of the sacks to be sent to Caer Tanaga. Beans sustain horses well but with two great disadvantages. The first is the smell, and the second is the interminable jokes everyone makes about the smell. We rode out of Cennet on a dry morning surrounded by a great cloud of both.

We went on westward along the coast to Caer Segant, fighting one little action against some raiders who had put in from Jarnholme in three ships. They were nothing but pirates, and it was a skirmish such as any commander would wish—we either killed or took them all, we took possession of their ships, and without the loss of a single armiger. I gave the prisoners to the monastery at Caer Segant to arrange ransoming or labor and sent the ships on to Caer Thanbard. Then I ate bread and roots with Rowanna. She apologized that I had come on a fast day. She was mourning for Gwair Aderyn in the Jarnish fashion, wearing grey and keeping her head covered. Ninian had kept her head covered, too, but Rowanna somehow seemed to show less of herself than her sister, even though she talked much more.

I was grateful for Raul's presence and skill at making conversation and was sorry when she sent him away after dinner. She had no news for me but after a while I realized she was trying to ask me if I thought Urdo would want to take up the rule of Segantia himself when the Peace was secure. I had no idea, but I told her honestly that I had never heard him mention it. Indeed that was the first time I ever considered that Rowanna ruled Segantia as Avren's widow and Urdo's mother rather than as king in her own right. Urdo never spoke about Segantia any differently from anywhere else. She agreed before we left that if her militia troops were needed I should send for them and they would come under her war-leader. There was one pennon there already, and I left Gormant's pennon with instructions to guard the whole coast between there and Caer Thanbard.

There was some complaining among the armigers who were to be left. They didn't like the south and living among Jarnsmen, they said. This was Gwair's ala's place; they wanted to go back to Caer Tanaga. I comforted them with the thought that I wasn't giving them up, this was temporary, an emergency. I told them that Gwair's ala, now ap Erbin's, would doubtless want to be in Caer Segant as soon as they came back from Demedia.

I went along the coast to Caer Thanbard. I've often wondered why the Vincans never saw fit to build a highroad along the south coast of Tir Tanagiri, linking all the towns there. Instead all the highroads lead inland north or northeast to Caer Tanaga, and there are nothing but tracks, or nothing at all. At least it is difficult to get lost riding next to the cliffs. This was my first visit to Caer Thanbard. I was very impressed with the sea defenses, which Thurrig had built, or restored. I was amazed at the Vincan lighthouse, with mirrors to reflect the lantern and send the beams far out to sea. There was also a very splendid new church inside the town walls. I was invited to the king's hall and ate lamb and plaited honey bread with Custennin and all the great folk of Munew.

Custennin I had met before. He seemed as indecisive as ever, dithering even over what he wanted to eat. His wife Tegwen seemed a bad match for him. She agreed with everything he said and appeared very lacking in spine. I wanted to like his brother Erbin, for his son's sake. Ap Erbin was a good tribuno and my friend. All he had told me of his parents was that his mother had died in battle and his father ruled the wild and rugged end of the peninsula of Munew under Custennin. I was sorry to be very disappointed in Erbin. He began drinking before the food and refilling my cup, too, when I was standing near him. At first I put up with this for ap Erbin's sake, but he soon became drunk on the strong spiced cider. He kept on making lewd propositions even after I had turned him down politely the first time. My mother had warned me about men like that, men who think that being of good family is enough to make any unmarried girl long to share blankets with them and who are vain enough to be offended at a refusal. I have met remarkably few of them. Fortunately armigers are too sensible for problems of that sort.

I spent much of the rest of the evening avoiding Erbin. This meant I spent a lot of my time near Raul, and Custennin's sister Linwen and her husband the bishop Dewin. Even if I had not already known it I would have soon realized that these were the people who really controlled Munew, who made the decisions about what would be done for the land and the people. It was strange to see Custennin, Erbin, and Linwen together, all three children of the last king, Cledwin. It was as if they had all been given the same face, and their personalities had shaped it differently—in Custennin to weakness, in Erbin to self-indulgence, and in Linwen to strength. She was not a pretty woman, but the set of her jaw marked her as someone of consequence. It crossed my mind that if we chose our kings in the Isarnagan fashion, electing the best of the royal kin, she would have been the one anyone would have chosen. I must have been drinking too much, I do not think I had ever thought of such things before except in a purely abstract way. Yet what did it matter? Custennin was weak, but she and Dewin did rule. Except that they did not rule with the consent of the land, and so they were no more than tyrants. Even if Munew was thriving and the crops were good, it wasn't right. "The weakness of monarchy lies in the character of the king" the Lossian philosopher Aristokles wrote almost a thousand years ago. "It lies in the hands of the gods to send us the kings we deserve." Did Munew deserve Custennin? But almost as soon as I had thought it I realized that when it was important the gods did send us the kings we deserved. After all, they had sent us Urdo.

The talk after dinner went very smoothly. There was little danger of a revolt in Munew, and having two pennons at Caer Segant made them feel safer. There was one pennon, originally part of Gwair's ala, in Caer Thanbard. Custennin, or rather Dewin, agreed that they would try to levy some local troops in case of need, but they made no firm promises. I talked about the threat of an Isarnagan landing, but they did not seem concerned. They did agree to providing extra supplies, which I took with me before they changed their minds again. I did not like Munew at all and was glad to be out of it.

From Caer Thanbard I went northeast along the highroad back towards Caer Tanaga, where I planned to exchange three of the pennons I had with me for three of those which had been resting there and then go northward to Tathal and Nene.

Before I got there a red-cloak from Garah found me with the news that Marchel and ap Meneth had won a great victory at Varae in Wenlad. They had trapped the Isarnagan army between the ala and the sea. When they had broken and fled for their boats, Thurrig had sailed into the bay with reinforcements. Between them hardly an Isarnagan had escaped alive. That sort of massacre sounded like Marchel, but not like Thurrig. I rode on, a little surprised. At least there wouldn't be much more threat in Wenlad, though I would need to find a good map to find where Varae was.

When I came to our stables in Caer Tanaga the first person I saw was Ulf Gunnarsson sitting down on the ground fitting an ax head to a shaft. He was surrounded by carpenter's tools and had a wooden block over his stomach where he was drawing a knife down the wood towards him. I suppose without that he would have gutted himself if his hand slipped. A few of the armigers were talking to him as he worked and passing him things. I was surprised how well they seemed to get on with him. I had supposed they would hate him. He did not see me until Starlight's shadow fell on him, and then he nearly did gut himself, wood or not. He jumped up, scattering his tools and knocking over a little pot of linen oil. He bowed.

"That ax head isn't big enough for a long ax," I said. It didn't look much heavier than the sort of ax head people use to cut withies, a one-hand ax, and the shaft he was making was as long as my arm, unless he was planning to cut it down later.

"A long ax is too heavy to use from horseback, Praefecto," he said. "I want a weapon I can use in battle when my spears are gone." I had taken his long sword.

"Carry on then," I said, and went into the stables, oddly unsettled as I always was when I saw him.

Before I had finished rubbing down the horses, Masarn came to find me. He came up to the ropes at the back of Beauty's stall and peered down at me.

"Oh, Masarn!" I said. "Good. Anything happened here? I'm going to leave Second, Third, and Fifth Pennon here with you and take the rest up to Caer Rangor—"

"Sulien," he said, shifting his weight uneasily, "I don't like doing this. I hate being in charge. I don't want to be tribuno." I rocked back on my heels and looked at him.

"What's happened?"

"Nothing! I just really hate being in charge, and I'm no good at it. I could probably cope with the work if you were here, but I hate making all the decisions when you're away. It's too much for me. I can't keep on doing it." He looked wretched.

"But a tribuno has to be able to take charge when necessary—" I said.

"I know. That's why I don't want to be tribuno." He leaned in to the stall, and Beauty shuffled forward, almost treading on my foot.

"Oh Masarn, but I usually stay with the ala, or Urdo is here. This is an emergency!"

"I don't know if you've noticed, but people have been saying 'This is an emergency' in that tone of voice ever since Caer Lind, and that's seven *years*. I'll keep doing it for now, but as soon as things calm down even a little, I don't want to be a tribuno. I don't care about glory, I like regular meals, I hate worrying all the time."

I stood up—my back clicked as I straightened—and I automatically started one of Larig's Malmish stretching exercises. I had been riding too much and not doing anything else for too long. "Do you think you'll be all right working under someone else as tribuno, now?" I asked.

"I should think so. But I'm not sure I even want to be a decurio anymore. Being an ordinary armiger and being told go here and do this is more like it, and even that, well. Well," he hesitated, "I've got a wife and some little children growing bigger, and I like to see them now and then. If the wars are over, I think the ala could get along without me."

"Oh but Masarn, I'd miss you!" I said. "You've been with me since the beginning."

"Yes, I remember you going right over Apple's head, tent-pegging, before you picked up the skill," he said, smiling. "But I'll still be around. My wife lives here in Caer Tanaga. You'll see more of me than you will of ap Erbin or Angas who are still in the alae but off away."

"I suppose so," I said, but I was sad as we walked out of the stables together; it felt as if something good was coming to an end.

We walked up to the citadel, talking about food, about the weather, about the goods laid out on the stalls at either side of the street, and not until we were almost at the top of the hill about the ala. "Gunnarsson's coming on all right," Masarn said. "He's been practicing all the hours of daylight, all weather. His riding isn't up to our standard yet, but he's getting there. He's accurate with a spear, much better than most of our beginners. He's lame, of course, and he knows Jarnish fighting so I haven't bothered him with much footwork yet; wait until he can ride well enough. He wants to be good, that's for sure."

"Do the others like him?" I asked as we came up to the gates.

Masarn looked at me, frowning. "There was some trouble in the very beginning, people teasing him for being beaten in the battle, but I told them to cut it out, and they did. No point in making these things per-

sonal. They're getting used to him now. We've had people who were
hostages for their family's good behavior from the beginning, and it's
never been held against anyone. Also Alswith's been in my pennon for a
long time, even though she's away right now, so they're used to having
Jarns around. I think they can cope with taking people by the each, as
Urdo puts it."

I had mixed feelings about all of this, but before I could sort them out
I heard rapid hoofbeats behind me. I turned to look. A red-cloak was making her way through the crowded street towards the citadel. People were
scattering before her. We went in through the gates, nodding a greeting to
the guards, and waited in the courtyard. She came clattering in a minute
later and blew "Urgent news" on her trumpet. Elenn came out of the great
door before the notes had died away, Raul close behind her.

The red-cloak handed her a thick letter, and another to Raul. Then as
I came forward she handed me another. She held another for a moment
until Garah came running out of the tower door, clutching her clothes
around her. She must have been in the baths when she heard the signal.
Glyn came out of the same door a moment or two later and stood leaning
against the wall. A servant came and handed a steaming drink to the red-
cloak, who dismounted and accepted some food from another servant. I
realized I was putting off reading my letter. I turned it over. It was sealed
with Urdo's running horse. I opened it and read through it rapidly, my eyes
widening as I got through it.

"Sulien," said Elenn, sounding a little unsure, taking notice of me for
the first time. "I see you are here and have the news, too."

"Yes indeed," I said. The courtyard was crowded with people who had
appeared while I had been reading, all listening anxiously. "Splendid news,"
I said.

"Indeed," said Elenn, more firmly. Garah and Glyn were both still
reading her letter, and Garah was pointing out something to Glyn. "We
will be holding the Feast of Peace here at Caer Tanaga in—" She paused
and looked at the letter again. "When the moon is full, that is in half a
month from now."

"Then are the Isarnagans wholly defeated?" asked Masarn, cheerfully
and loudly.

"Not entirely," I said. "But it seems that the mopping-up in Demedia
will take some time, and Urdo has decided not to wait."

My eyes fell again on the letter. '—Without this both Flavien of Tinala
and Penda of Bregheda would adventure north while Bereich and Deme-

dia are beset, which would be disastrous. The war in Demedia is going well enough but will not be over quickly. The alae will remain and continue fighting under ap Erbin and Luth, but Angas, Ohtar, and I will travel south at speed with only an honor guard—'

"Splendid news," said Raul, his eyes still on the letter.

"We must begin preparations for the feast at once," said Elenn to Garah. "The first guests will begin arriving soon."

"Let us go inside and discuss this in comfort," I said. Masarn bowed as if in farewell, but before he'd even taken his hand off his heart I had my hand on his other arm. "Oh no," I whispered. "No slipping away. You're coming right in here with me now. I need you, Masarn. It's an emergency."

"Another emergency?" He raised his eyebrows. "Oh well." Then, to the rhythm we used for tilting at targets, he muttered. "If I wasn't an armiger I wouldn't be here," very quietly, and so we treated the assembled crowd to the spectacle of the Praefecto of Urdo's Own Ala and her Tribuno going in to a council in the high citadel of Caer Tanaga, giggling.

—30—

"Peace in this hall."
"And a welcome to you who keep the peace within it."
—Ritual Guesting Greetings

If this goes on much longer, I am going to strangle Cinon of Nene," Elenn said, storming in and slamming a double-handled welcome cup down towards the table. At the last moment she stopped and set it down gently so there was barely a click as the gold met the board. Even so, I could tell it was empty; she wouldn't have done that if there had been wine in it.

"Not Custennin?" I asked, as she came over to the fireplace where I was trying to help Garah make lists. It was late, after that night's feast.

"Custennin? Definitely not. What's he done wrong? He's happy as long as he can pray with Father Gerthmol every day and dither about the place the rest of the time." Elenn looked surprised as she moved from the shadows into the good light.

"It's the dithering I can't bear," I said, putting down my tablet wax side up and rubbing my hands together. "Never hunt boar with someone who dithers."

Garah was adding a column of figures, her face set with concentration and the tip of her tongue out. She spoke without looking up. "Did you really yell at him?"

"Yes. He was unnecessarily endangering my people's lives, and I told him so. I didn't call him half the things the armigers are saying, but that was only because anger was limiting my imagination." I pinched out my candle. My mother had sent a cask of linen oil with Morien's party with a note to Elenn explaining that it burned well in lamps. Elenn had asked me to read her the note. She had learned her letters but still knew very little Vincan. Everyone was always happy to speak Tanagan with her so she never had the chance to pick it up. Once she understood the note she was delighted and sent the maids down to the storerooms to bring out all the lamps we had to light the banqueting room. The oil did not burn as cleanly as olive oil, so the lamps needed frequent cleaning. It did have the great advantage of not needing to come all the way across the sea from distant Narlahena. Even so, there was only so much of it, and in our own rooms we were still managing with candles for work and firelight for talking.

"Well I'm quite happy with dithering, that just needs coaxing along." Elenn said, settling herself on a low stool. "Custennin's not all that different from my father. Anyway, Linwen and Bishop Dewin are used to managing him. But I'm not sure how I've kept civil with Cinon this far."

"There's only so long we can count on Alfwin's politeness lasting, too," Garah said. She made a mark by the column of figures of food for armigers and horses she'd just been adding, and looked up at Elenn. "Cinon keeps on saying how he's left Nene undefended, which is true I suppose, but he keeps on making out it's Alfwin he's afraid of."

"The man's a fool," Elenn said shortly. "We can't let Alfwin kill him even so; apart from the hospitality issue, his family have been kings since the flood."

"Nobody was a king when the Vincans were here," I said.

Elenn waved that objection away and looked annoyed. "They held the land, they were kings, whatever they were called. Cinon though—it takes a lot to get to the end of my patience, but he's managed it. Constant snide whining is unendurable, and keeping him away from Alfwin is the most I can do."

"Nobody would know," I said. Before I had left the feast I had seen Elenn sitting and talking to him with that friendly attentive manner of hers, as if enthralled by everything he said. I would never have guessed she disliked him.

"Nobody is supposed to know," Elenn said, as shortly as I had ever heard her speak. "That's part of the burden of diplomacy. My mother taught me when I was a girl to keep my own feelings right out of the way of men, smile, and then talk to them the way they like. That way they'll listen to what you want them to hear." She ran her fingers through her hair. "Usually it's nothing like this difficult. Between Lew calling me sister every sentence and dealing with Cinon, I'm worn ragged."

"It's a good thing I'm not a king or a queen," I said.

Elenn and Garah both laughed. At that moment Glyn came in, stamping and shivering. "Sixty-two, and-three," he said to Garah, and she scratched it in. "And by Turth's tusks it's cold in those storerooms!" Then he greeted us and came and sat down on the other side of the fire beside Garah.

"Was that another tactless remark they were laughing at?" Glyn asked me. I just grinned at him; I knew how to get along with him now.

"We were just saying which of the kings we want to strangle," Garah said.

"Flavien of Tinala," Glyn said, without hesitation. "He seems so smooth, but he's going against everything we want. And with Urdo—" he tailed off. We were not using the word *late*. Urdo had set no time for his arrival, but it was now only two days before the full moon. The days since the message arrived had passed in a blur of preparations and preliminary feasting. All the kings were present except Mardol, Angas, Ohtar, and, of course, Urdo himself.

"Flavien is very polite at table," Elenn said. Her voice seemed different somehow.

Glyn shrugged. "Better a man who speaks the unpleasant truth than hides it."

"Cinon spends a lot of time with Flavien," Garah said, frowning.

"Oh, that reminds me," Elenn said. "I've persuaded him to go out for a few hours tomorrow by going hunting with whichever pennon is crossing the river into Aylsfa. You'll need to assign an armiger to be his guard."

"I don't suppose I could send Ulf Gunnarsson?" I suggested. They all laughed.

"I'd like to see his face," Garah said.

"He can't stop seeing every single Jarn as the enemy," Glyn said. "That's stupid, and it won't do, but he's not as bad as Flavien even so."

"Not Ulf, unfortunately," Elenn said. "It's not just the honor, it's someone to make sure he's safe, so it has to be someone who can ride well.

Ulf strikes me as a very courteous fellow and quite suitable, apart from the Jarnish issue, but he's still in training."

"Terrible shame Alswith's not here, then. Fully trained, war hero—" Garah wagged her pen at me, and leaned too far towards me over the fire so the tip was caught by a spark and started to smolder. She sighed and dropped it into the fire, where it burned with a horrible smell of singeing feather.

"Oh well, no shortage of quills at the moment," she said, shrugging and giggled. As well as sending the pennons out boar hunting to distract the kings and to add to the food supplies, we had sent one out fowling on a backwater of the Tamer above Caer Tanaga. They had been very lucky and netted a flock of geese making their way south for winter. Goose and turnip soup thickened with barley is wonderfully warming. Elenn had seen fit to serve it to the kings only once. The rest went to the ala, who were delighted to be able to eat their fill of something good for a change.

"I'll give him someone reliable, even-tempered, and not Jarnish," I said, relenting. "I'll be there myself tomorrow anyway, it's so good to get out and do something in what daylight there is. At least all this hunting is keeping them fed as well as occupied and apart."

"For the feast last year when all the kings came, we were preparing for three months," Garah agreed. She had set her tablets down and was rubbing her fingers free of wax. "And Dalmer said for Angas's wedding they were preparing half a year and had honey sent from Demedia and wine from Narlahena."

"We have some wine, fortunately," Elenn said. "I agree that the hunting is helpful."

"And going over the river and hunting in Aylsfa makes Ayl feel as if he's doing something for us, which cheers him up," Glyn said.

"His brother has been helping me in the hall," Elenn said. I looked at her, frowning, trying to work out what had changed about her. She was sitting up straight, and her voice was more formal. I realized she wasn't prepared to be relaxed in front of Glyn. I could see the uses of diplomacy with the allied kings, but did she need to extend it to everyone male? It seemed unnecessary and a little sad, but I didn't say anything.

"Helping you with the flowers?" Garah asked.

"Where do you get flowers a month before midwinter anyway?" I asked, idly.

"Most of them I dried in the summer and arrange with bare branches and sprays of evergreen," she said. "Sidrok Trumwinsson has been carrying branches for me. He seems to enjoy it."

"He's besotted with you is what it is," Glyn said. "I've seen him making sheep's eyes and sighing. He's enraptured to be in the presence of such beauty. He dreams about you at night."

"Honestly, Glyn, you read that sort of thing into absolutely everything," I said, annoyed.

"Maybe it's because I'm in love," he said lugubriously, pulling a face at me. "I've been meaning to say for a while, Sulien, I don't need to ask your permission, but will you give your blessing to Garah and me getting married?"

I thought at first he was still joking, but when I looked at Garah she was blushing. "Is this what you want, Garah?" I asked, and my voice sounded strange in my ears. She raised her chin and looked at me seriously. I've never understood why anyone gets married if they don't have to produce an heir. But I didn't feel I could tell Garah how awful it was, and perhaps it was easier to endure if you truly wanted children. And they were working together so much, it wasn't surprising they didn't want to say good-bye at night. Garah was looking nervous. "Of course I give you my blessing!" I said, "If you're sure it's what you want."

Elenn was giving me a look I couldn't quite interpret. "Strong children, plentiful crops, good weather," she said, the Isarnagan wedding blessing. Then she got up and hugged Garah and then Glyn. I did the same.

"I shall bake your plait-bread," I said, sitting down again. Garah beamed at me. "If I remember how, and if we have enough honey," I added.

"Shall I ask Bishop Dewin to perform the wedding?" Elenn asked.

"I—" Glyn began, hesitantly, and Garah took over.

"We thought we'd have the Mother's blessing and make vows at dawn in the old way," she said, firmly. Elenn opened her mouth and shut it again. Just then there was a scratch at the door.

"Come in," Garah called, as this was formally one of her rooms. Glyn shrugged as if to say he couldn't think who it could be so late.

A gate guard came in. "I'm looking for the queen," he said, and then seeing Elenn, bowed. "Arrivals, my lady," he said.

"The High King?" she asked, bounding to her feet.

"No, my lady. It's Mardol the Crow, Cadraith ap Mardol and Admiral Thurrig, with some others I don't know. They're waiting."

"Thank you," she said. "I will be down in a moment." The guard went back down the stairs. "Lucky this is here, I suppose," Elenn said, picking up the welcome cup.

"I'll send for the bread," Garah said. "No, I'll go for it, it'll be quicker." Garah ran down the stairs towards the kitchen. Elenn filled the cup from a wineskin that was hanging on the wall. By the time she had finished Garah was back with a plate of salted bread.

"This is all the bread there is until they bake in the morning," she said. "Are their rooms ready? Shall I check them? And ask the servants to bring some food?"

"That would be very good of you, Garah," Elenn said. "Now, will you come down with me, Sulien?" she asked. I stood up, stretched and yawned, straightened my drape and refastened my brooch, then followed her down. As the other kings arrived I had ridden out a few hours from Caer Tanaga to greet them with the whole ala. This served two purposes; it honored them and it made them realize the strength of an ala, and how little they would appreciate being on the wrong side of our spears. Nobody had warned us about Duke Mardol's party. I would have to find out what went wrong with my scouts.

Elenn was still dressed for the banquet. Her overdress was very pale green, embroidered with gold flowers. In the torchlight at the gate it looked white, but the gold shone, as did the gold of the cup. I waited under the arch as she went forward and greeted the armored newcomers individually, offering the plate and cup and then returning their soft words of peace. Then she led them inside to the hall. Thurrig stopped me as we went in.

"Sulien," he growled. "Good to see you. Let's get a drink, eh?"

"Good idea," I said. I found myself grinning at him.

"Did you miss me?" he asked.

"Oh, I don't know how I get by without the sight of your bushy brown beard," I said, though his beard was almost all grey now. "It seems like half an age since I saw you."

"I've been stuck in damned Tir Isarnagiri for half an age," he said. "If I never see the place again, it's too soon."

"What's wrong with it?" I asked. "Apart from you and Chanerig stirring up a hornets' nest?"

"Get me a drink, and I'll tell you," he said.

Servants were bringing out cold roast boar and apples for Mardol and Cadraith and their party. Others were bending down singing charms to light the fires that had been laid for the morning. There was plenty of room. I found space near the end of a table away from the others and liberated a jug of mead and two goblets.

"So, Tir Isarnagiri?" I asked, when we were settled comfortably. Thur-rig had a pig's foot and the jug in front of him.

"They're the most infuriating people in the world. If Elenn wasn't one of them I'd say they were all without exception unbearable, but as it is I shall say that nothing is perfect and so the Isarnagans aren't perfectly dread-ful because they have one mitigating good person. All the rest of them are—well, I won't spoil the clean straw on the floor saying what I think of them. They say a thing fifteen different ways but they never say yes or no, they flatter you in the morning and try to have you poisoned at night, they consult their oracle-priests every hour and refuse to do anything. I got there eager to fight the enemy. After a month I was ready to fight our hosts along with them. After six months I'd have set fire to the whole island and laughed as it went up." He took a deep swallow of mead, and I could see his throat working. He set his goblet down empty.

"Is that why you let Chanerig fight their gods?" I asked.

"Well." He looked uncomfortable and shifted his weight a little on the bench. "Yes. He'd converted the queen's father already, Allel, so it wasn't quite as—it didn't seem as bad as it might. I didn't think it would work the way it did, and Chanerig was so eager to try it, and I was ready to try any-thing that would be likely to make a change." He offered me the jug, and when I had filled my goblet he lifted it to his lips and drank deeply from it. "I can see why you'd be upset, eh? But I've never been much for matters of the gods, not back in Narlahena and not here. I'm not saying I'd have let Chanerig chase out the gods of my people, maybe, but these were stranger gods to me, and anyway I took the pebble years ago to shut Amala up."

"But what did you think would happen?"

"I thought he'd convert a few of their land gods and cause problems here and there. I thought it might help if they weren't all agreeing about consulting their oracle-priests. Also I thought it might maybe stir up trou-ble in Oriel. We'd never once managed to meet on a battlefield in all that time. But what did happen, well, it was amazing. I was standing right behind him with my ax, the whole time, ready to save his life if need be, but I didn't once wet it. He took off his shirt and stood bare-chested with his pebble on. Then he watched the sun go down and lit the fire. This was on the festival of Bel, did I say? All at once they came swarming, gods and spir-its, strange shapes like something out of a dream. They came rushing and howling in from all over the landscape, tall ones like trees and wet ones like streams and bright proud ones shining, men and women, young and old. There were cats with huge eyes and giants and little gnomes, swarms of bees, great bears, everything you ever heard about in a fireside story and didn't want to believe."

It might have been because I was tired or it might have been the drink, but I could almost see them as he described them. I took another mouthful of the summer-tasting mead. "There were so many of them the place was full, all except the circle where Chanerig was standing, with me right behind him. They came forward one at a time and he wrestled them. Some he wrestled with force, beating them to the ground. I taught him to fight myself when he was a boy. Others he fought with words out of his holy books. Others argued endlessly, but always they gave way and another came forward. Most of them he wrestled. The cat he squeezed the life out of. There were people there, too, pressing round, but there were so many land gods they couldn't get anywhere near. Towards dawn the High Gods came striding in, tall and brave, and I thought he was done for. Chanerig clutched his pebble and shouted at them to praise the White God or leave, and they just faded away in the dawnlight. That scared even me. I was tired by then. All night I stood ready with my ax, and sometimes I shifted my weight a little to one foot and then again the other. Then when the sun was up they were all gone, and Chanerig sat on the ground, exhausted. The people rushed up then with weapons, ready to kill him where he sat. Then I took one step forward with my ax, and they looked at him and at me. They'd seen the whole night, too. They just looked, and they saw I was ready to fight them all if need be, and then they turned and slunk away."

I shook my head in wonder and took another drink. "He was still wrong to do it."

"Yes, well," Thurrig rumbled. "I wouldn't have let him try if I'd known what would come of it, all this invading and settling and war in Demedia." He picked up the pig's foot and sucked the sweet meat from between the bones.

"What's this I hear about a massacre?" I asked.

"That was Marchel's idiocy," he said, sounding angry. He banged the pig's foot down again. "Did she never listen to me? Bringing disgrace on my name. I gave her a piece of my mind. I've left her up in Wenlad to see if that will cool her down a bit, she wanted to come here or go back to Caer Gloran, but I wouldn't let her. Isarnagans might be no use for anything— they'll just argue until you're hoarse and never get anything done. But butchering them when they've surrendered, that's wrong, however annoying they are."

"She killed them after they surrendered?" I was horrified. "What did she think she was doing?"

"She had the ala and they were retreating to their ships," Thurrig said, looking grim. "I had finally got out of the island and just happened to be coming along as she was fighting them. We were in our ships, of course, and their ships were still on the beach, so we came up behind them and fired burning arrows into them. They were surrendering on the shore, but before I could get there Marchel and her ala had put them all to the sword."

"But nobody will ever surrender to us again!" I said, appalled. "How could she?"

"She said nobody would know, they were all dead. Cadraith was well behind, his ala had been chasing them, but they hadn't come up, so it was only her and me and our people. But that's no use, the armigers all know, they did it. I know. I'm not telling everyone, but I'm going to tell Urdo and see what he wants to do about it. I hope I can persuade him to be merciful. She lost her temper, I think, that's all there is to it, but it won't do at all."

"Urdo will—" I trailed off. I'd been going to say he'd kill her, and it occurred to me that he very well might. That was against the usage of war. Thurrig shook his head at me.

Elenn came up on the other side of Thurrig and perched on the bench.

"Elenn, my queen, as beautiful as ever," he said, and stood up to bow in the Malmish way, arms at his sides.

She smiled graciously as he sat down again. Then she leaned towards him confidentially and asked quietly "Have you seen Urdo?"

Thurrig shook his head. "Isn't he here? I assumed he was asleep just now. I haven't seen a hair of him, and we've come down just now from Caer Asgor by way of Thansethan. We've not been rushing, but if he's still on the road from Demedia, he's not within a day's ride north of here." He frowned. "What are you going to do if he's late? Postpone the feast?"

"Hold it anyway," Elenn said, looking very determined. I raised my eyebrows. Urdo's letter to her had been very thick, perhaps it had contained specific instructions. "Thank you, Thurrig, Sulien." She got up and walked back to the others, leaving us to shrug at each other.

Thurrig lowered his voice. "How can we hold a feast of Urdo's Peace if he isn't here?"

I shook my head. "I hope Elenn knows what she's doing," I said.

31

The Three Greatest Joys Anyone Can Know
Winning great fame,
making a child
and coming home again.
        —Triads of Tir Tanagiri

More like a month after midwinter than a month before," Beris said, loudly and cheerfully, making my head ring.

I grunted, concentrating on getting my wrist straps tight. The ordinary smell and close air of the stables made my stomach churn. Starlight was saddled and ready and some of the hunting party were already starting to lead their horses out.

"Sulien doesn't want sunshine this morning," ap Cathvan said, laughing. He was leaning on the side of a stall, looking revoltingly healthy. I looked again—when had he got all that grey in his hair?

"You should have drunk milk before you went to bed," Beris said, eyeing me sympathetically.

I sighed. "I was up late, that's all, I'm a bit tired this morning."

"Up late drinking mead with Thurrig?" ap Cathvan asked, though he clearly knew already. "That's what I heard."

"Mead can be terribly deceptive stuff," Beris agreed, shaking her head. "It's the sweetness. You should always drink water before bed, or milk if you can get it. Goat's milk is best, of course, but cow's milk is better than water and water is better than nothing."

I ignored them and pulled on my gloves. That they were right and I had drunk too much the night before didn't make me feel any better. Thurrig had wanted to drink, and the later part of the evening was not clear in my mind. He kept talking about what Marchel had been like as a child and muttering about massacres. He'd never once said what he might do, though, if Urdo executed her. If he'd said he'd take the fleet and sail away to Narlahena, I'd have known he wouldn't really do it, but he'd never exactly said it. Starlight put her head down and whuffled at me. I realized that Beris and ap Cathvan were waiting for me.

"I could get you some goat's milk now?" Beris offered. My stomach heaved at the idea.

"No," I said. "But if you want to be a nursemaid, Cinon is hunting with us today. You can be his guard." Her expression clearly showed that she would have liked to protest the order, but she said nothing. I suppose there would have been more tactful ways to put it, and it wasn't that unpleasant a job. I took a breath and tried to soften it slightly. "Did I accidentally say latrine duty?" I asked. "Looking after Cinon's not punishment, it's an honor; the queen asked me specially to choose someone who was sensible and a first-rate rider." I took up Starlight's reins and led the way out of the stables. The grass crunched with frost underfoot. The sun was rising out of the mists on the river, sending out agonizingly bright spears of light over the woods of Aylsfa on the eastern bank. The pale dawn sky seemed to arch high above instead of hanging a spear's length above the trees the way it usually did.

I could still hear Beris and ap Cathvan talking as they led their horses over the grass behind. "Joined the ala to keep my husband in line," Beris was complaining, for the thousandth time. "Didn't know it would be like this. Nursemaid Cinon! I heard about what happened with Second Pennon. Please tell me Cinon's not an idiot like Custennin?"

"Nothing like as bad," ap Cathvan replied reassuringly. "He knows horses, and hunting. He's not an armiger, but he knows which end of a spear is which. There's nothing wrong with him at all. I'll take you over and introduce you."

There seemed to be too many people clustered down by the ferry. I squinted, but there were still too many. It looked as if the sunshine had brought half the town out of their beds and down to see us off. Elenn was there, wearing a dark green overdress fastened with gold shoulder pins. She was smiling at Cinon and leaning towards him. She almost always came down to bid us farewell and good luck. She was resting one hand on her hound, a great brindled Isarnagan bitch who came up to Elenn's shoulder. She would go hunting with the other dogs, though Elenn rarely rode out herself.

Near the queen stood Linwen, and Custennin, and Rowanna, talking to Father Gerthmol. Even Morien was there, standing with Mardol the Crow. Why were so many kings up so early? There were so many people out that one of the more enterprising shopkeepers who sold hot chestnuts and hot spiced cider in the town had brought out his brazier and was doing a good trade.

I made my way through the crowd, being greeted by friends here and there. Angas's young brother Morthu dodged past me with a shellful of chestnuts, almost bumping into me. He would be joining the ala soon, and I almost spoke to him, but let him go. I caught sight of Masarn buying chestnuts with his wife and children, the youngest standing up precariously, clutching the knee of Masarn's tunic. I made my way towards them, refusing several offers of chestnuts and cider on the way. As I came up the little one sat down unexpectedly with a bump and Masarn lifted him up in his arms, diverting an incipient howl with a practiced joggle.

"What are you doing out of bed when you don't have to be?" I asked. His wife smiled shyly at me and straightened the hat on one of the children. She was a quiet little woman and I never knew what to say to her. I smiled politely back at her.

Masarn laughed. "You look as if you didn't want to get up yourself," he said. "It looked to be a clear morning, that's all, and we thought we'd come down and see you off. It's been raining for a month or more."

"Yes, it's the sort of day the Lord of Light sends now and then to remind us that he's still up there and winter won't last forever," Garah said, startling me by coming up behind Starlight. "I came down for exactly the same reason. Not that I don't have plenty of work to do in the citadel, but I thought a little walk and early light would raise my heart."

"Oh Masarn, have you heard Garah's news?" I asked, remembering it.

"I haven't, but I can guess," he said. "You and Glyn? That's wonderful!" They embraced, making the baby squeal, and then she had to hug the other children, too, so they didn't feel left out. Then, while Masarn was buying her some cider, the little one, up on his father's shoulder, thrust a chestnut into my mouth. In such circumstances I couldn't refuse. It wasn't as hot as it should have been, but it was surprisingly good. I bought a shellful and burned my fingers peeling them. It had been a good season—none of mine were mealy, and all of them were as big as the top of my thumb. They settled my stomach wonderfully. The children fed some of them to Starlight, who ate them one at a time, delicately.

Then Gwigon started loading the ferry. We had said we would start at sunrise, but he had been waiting until everyone was here. It was his pennon and his turn to hunt; I had no intention of interfering with his organization. I just waved to him to let him know I was ready, and he waved me down. I led Starlight down onto the wooden wharf. She balked a little as we neared the side of the boat. She still didn't like it, though I knew she would lie down when she needed to. Cinon and ap Cathvan were ahead of me, waiting for a groom. Beris was with them, looking downcast.

Then I caught what ap Cathvan was saying. "As bold as a spring stallion, Ayl said outright the other day he's going to invite over more cousins
from Jarnholme. And what's to say these new ones will keep the Peace even
if the ones who are here now do? They're not to be trusted. There'll be
more and more of them wanting more and more of our land, mark my
words." Cinon's chin came up in agreement.

I looked around desperately. Ayl wasn't far away, he was standing with
his brother and Lew ap Ross, talking to Elenn. He looked up, he had heard,
and he came a few strides closer. He leaned down towards ap Cathvan. I
was frozen in place. At least it was ap Cathvan he had heard, and not
Cinon, it would be bad if he killed ap Cathvan but not the ruin of the
Peace.

"Don't be concerned about that," he said, calmly and cheerfully.
"The harvest in Aylsfa was good, though I had few enough people left to
gather it, after Foreth. There's no need to worry. You may well be right
about the lamentably large number of Jarnsmen prone to treachery, that's
why we'll stick to cousins and known friends who understand our ways.
Those treacherous types are no good for a country. They can't understand
peace and start up quarrels, but it terribly disturbs a king's drinking time if
he has to be forever putting down rebellions and settling quarrels that
won't stay settled. I know what I'm doing, which is bringing in more
people who can reap and plow and come to the standard when I call
them, that's all."

Ap Cathvan and Cinon both gaped up at him, looking embarrassed. I
wanted to laugh. I had no idea Ayl could act so well, his tone of reassuring
their concern for an allied king was perfect. "I hope—" Cinon began.

That was when the mist lifted and I saw three ships coming up the
river towards us. They had the wind in their sails and they had their oars
out. They were clearly Jarnish dragon-prowed longships. I gave a shout and
looked about for Grugin, my trumpeter. I had seen him earlier. The last of
my hangover blew away as I swung up onto Starlight's back and rode up
onto the bank. Three ships, maybe two hundred fighting men, and I had
my spear. I didn't stop to ask what they were doing here, or who they were,
or how they'd come up all the way up the river between Cennet and
Segantia undetected. I knew the south was stripped of troops. If anyone
wanted to attack Caer Tanaga, there had never been a better time. Could
they have got here undetected? Could Guthrum or Rowanna have
betrayed us? But they were both here, which made it unlikely unless this

was a very deep-laid plot. In any case, three ships wasn't enough. There was an ala in the city, and a pennon right here, we could stop them, unless this was only the advance party. I seemed to be thinking terribly slowly, because I was already signaling Grugin almost before I had realized that the worst problem would be if they didn't land and fight us but went on upstream past us.

Fortunately, they turned their heads towards land almost at once, relieving me of that worry. The pennon formed up as quickly as they could, complicated by needing to lead some of the horses off the ferry again. By the time they were all off, everyone who had been intending to hunt was mounted. Grugin gave Cinon, Ayl, and his brother Sidrok places in the ranks. Ap Cathvan had already found a place. I was pleased to see them showing such courage, even though none of them but ap Cathvan had the first idea how to fight from horseback. I felt sure we could block their way to the gate for long enough.

The moment I gave the first warning, everyone else started milling around. There was a great deal of noise. Kings and rowers and curious bystanders all crushed together. The chestnut seller's brazier somehow got overturned in the confusion. Elenn and her hound were standing very still in the middle of all of it. The other dogs were howling and straining at their leads. Masarn's wife was clutching all three children tightly. As soon as the pennon was ready for battle and I could pay attention to the others, I shouted out to Masarn and Garah to get Elenn back to the walls. I signaled to Garah to take the kings as well if they would go, and to Masarn to send three pennons out to me as quickly as he could. They had hardly moved when the wind, as the ship turned into it, caught the banners on the lead ship, blowing them out so we could all see them.

On the top mast was Urdo's gold running horse. On the other mast flew the Walrus of Bereich, and below it the Thorn of Demedia. It was no attack. Urdo had come at last.

I stayed where I was, at the head of the pennon. Someone, I think it was Masarn's wife, started to laugh with relief. The kings and other people started to straighten themselves up. The dog masters quieted the hounds. Cinon and Ayl dismounted and exchanged a look that almost seemed friendly. Everyone was chattering. Elenn said something to Sidrok, who left the pennon and galloped off towards the city at full speed. Then she moved forward to the edge of the wooden wharf as the first ship glided in. We all watched and waited almost in silence. There were cries on the ship as she came to shore. Someone threw a rope, and Elenn caught it and tied it inexpertly to the mooring post. One of the sailors, a Jarn, leapt up onto the wharf and tied it properly.

Then, while the sailor was fixing a plank for people to climb up more easily, Urdo scrambled up over the side of the wharf and embraced Elenn. He looked well and strong and cheerful. Everyone was smiling in the bright morning sun.

"Welcome home, my lord," she said.

We all cheered. Everyone, from stern old Penda of Bregheda to Masarn's youngest, up on his father's shoulder again, cheered as gladly as Gwigon's pennon around me. I felt sudden tears in my eyes.

Angas and Ohtar came up the plank to shore, and behind them Angas's wife Eirann, with another Jarnish woman, very thin and with her head covered. Sidrok came galloping back with Elenn's welcome cup, almost in time. He had forgotten the wine, and she had to welcome them with the chestnut seller's cider. It didn't matter. She moved among them in the sunlight with the cup, and that was enough.

At the feast that night I sat by Angas.

"They're far from defeated," he said. "We're beating them back though. They've got a lot of ships, and they keep on bringing reinforcements and supplies from Oriel. Ohtar's got a great plan to raid them there in the spring and cut their supply lines."

"You're getting on all right with Ohtar then?" I asked.

"Oh yes," Angas agreed cheerfully, around a mouthful of roast boar. "Once we got the business about Bereich sorted out. That's his daughter we brought down with us, by the way, Alfwin's wife. Did you see her? Tiny little thing: she can hardly lift an eating dagger, but she's a great general in her way and a formidable opponent. I'm glad we're on the same side now anyway."

"How have you sorted out Bereich?" I asked, shaking my head at the proffered ale jug. I couldn't drink the way I used to when I was younger.

"Gave it back unconditionally," Angas said, helping himself to bread. "Handed back as much as I could gather up of the heirlooms and treasures that the ala had collected, too. They were surprisingly good about it. We hadn't done all that much damage—seems they were amazed we hadn't been raping all around us and burning everything in sight. Fortunate it was the ala and not some of my home-raised levies who aren't so polite.

Anyway, ever since, Ohtar's been helping me as much as he can, much better than if I'd asked. Urdo was absolutely right there, as usual." He grinned. "Even before Ohtar got up there I had Jarns on my side. You know Teilo's monastery, founded the year I got married? Well, they work the land with a lot of Jarnish prisoners, the same as at Thansethan. I'd hate to be them, living on Teilo's charity—porridge in the morning, half a boiled turnip at noon, and as much water as you can drink in the evening to remind you of the goodness of the White God. Sermons and readings with every meal. That's what she serves to visitors who can leave when they want to, so it's probably acorn porridge for the poor Jarns." He laughed and drained his cup.

"So anyway, when the Isarnagans were getting closer, Teilo got the prisoners together and said they could have their freedom if they'd fight to defend the monastery. These Isarnagans really hate the White God, of course; they'd been burning every church they found and killing priests. So the prisoners agreed to this, and asked for weapons. She didn't have any, so she told them they could have whatever they could find. So out they rushed towards the oncoming Isarnagan army carrying spades and forks and the tools they used in the fields, and two or three of them charging carrying an eating bench"—Angas patted the one we sat on—"like this, and yelling out, in Jarnish, that they were bringing the mercy of the White God. Eirann actually saw that. She'd been in the hills raising troops and she was bringing them down to save Teilo—she says they were hardly needed. By the time our levies got to the battle most of the Isarnagans had run away very fast back westward and those that were left were very dead indeed, and the Jarnsmen helping themselves to proper weapons."

We laughed together at the thought of it. "What did Eirann do with them?" I asked.

"Recruited them, and they seem to get on all right with our people. Most of them are with Ohtar's forces now."

"So you have a lot of foot soldiers?" I asked.

"Yes." Angas frowned. "Demedia's mostly hills. It makes it hard to use the alae properly. The Isarnagans won't stand to face them either. So far the one big battle we had we got them fighting some of our troops and then brought up my ala from the side. That worked. I nearly spitted Atha ap Gren."

"How did she get away?" I asked.

"One of their little chariots, and people kept getting in the way," he said. "I didn't want to get cut off in the press. They kept stabbing horses and hamstringing them. All that works is to get them to stand, charge, reform, and repeat."

"Getting them to stand is what I kept thinking about in Derwen," I agreed. "I was very lucky there."

Angas looked about and saw Emer and Lew talking to Rowanna a little way away, and shook his head. Eirann was sitting next to her parents not far away. "You were lucky, and I think there'll be fighting in Demedia for a while yet," he said, quietly.

"Maybe I'll come up and help you clear them up," I said, hopefully, mopping up the last of the juices from my meat with the last of my bread.

"I think Urdo means you to stay here," Angas said.

I sighed. "Who's in charge in Demedia now while you're all down here?" I asked.

"Luth and ap Erbin have their alae and their orders from Urdo," he replied. "Tanwen ap Gwair, my tribuno, is leading mine. My sister Penarwen is in charge of political decisions, if any are required urgently, with Teilo to advise her. We're only away for a month, and we had to come."

The next day Urdo wore the plain gold circlet that was the Crown of Tir Tanagiri. He stood on the Stone of the Kingdom in the Citadel of Caer Tanaga and prayed in the sight of all the kings and all the people, and everyone renewed their coronation oaths to him. He announced that he would be writing a law code. Raul prayed, and Father Gerthmol prayed, and Urdo burned incense and made sacrifice of a lamb on the stone beneath the oak, in the old way. People talked in public and in private, in small groups and large ones. The kings came to understand, whether they liked it or not, that this was peace, and a new thing, and if they had disputes with each other they would bring them to Urdo, not take up arms.

That night there was dancing, and feasting, with wine and all the best food brought out. Everyone was dressed very splendidly, with gold and silver everywhere. There was music, and to end the feast Elenn took the welcome cup and went all round the hall to everyone, pledging them to the Peace, and everyone drank, all round the circle. That was Urdo's Feast of Peace at Caer Tanaga, a month before midwinter in the thirteenth year of his reign. So was the island united again, forty-eight years after the last Vincan legion left and thirteen hundred and twenty-three years after the city of Vinca was founded.

32

O all ye works of the Lord,

Bless ye the Lord, rise up and praise him forever.

O ye powers of the heavens,

O ye powers of the Earth,

O ye people of the heavens,

O ye people of the Earth,

O ye Sun and ye Moon,

O ye Stars in your courses,

O ye winds and rains,

O ye dews and frosts,

O ye Winds of the World,

O ye fire and heat

O ye ice and snow

O ye nights and days

O ye mountains and ye hills

O ye waters and ye seas

O ye flocks in the fields

O ye beasts in the woods

O ye birds in the trees

O ye fish in the sea

O ye worms and ye creeping things

O ye Green Things upon the Earth,

Bless ye the Lord, rise up and praise him forever.

—Benedicite, as used at Thansethan, early translation.

I was in the baths with Kerys and Morien the next morning when one of Urdo's messengers brought the message that the High King wanted me immediately. I dried myself and dressed as quickly as I could and ran through the halls. I thought he had orders for me, or wanted to talk about what I'd done in Derwen. He had been surrounded by people since he stepped off the ship, and we had hardly had time to exchange a word. I waved at the clerks in the marble hall and ran up the stairs towards the room Urdo always used at Caer Tanaga.

As I scratched at the door I heard his voice raised, "Unforgivable to assume—come in Sulien!"

I went in. Raul was standing by the window overlooking the court-yard, looking distressed. Urdo was standing by his chair, his hands on the back of it. His table was, as always, piled high with papers and maps and books. He straightened and turned to me. "Hello, Sulien. It's very good to see you. As I told you in the letter, I'm very pleased with what you did with settling Lew at Dun Morr."

I smiled, then I remembered that I had to tell him about Emer and Conal Fishface. But not in front of Raul. "You sent for me?" I asked.

"Yes." Urdo looked tired. He sat down, but said no more. Raul glow-ered. I looked at him, puzzled. I had been working well with Raul since Foreth. He didn't yell at anyone except Urdo.

"Maybe I should have said, why did you send for me?" I ventured.

Urdo laughed. "I want you to stand quietly and witness, and if neces-sary, stop Father Gerthmol killing me." I was unarmored, but I had my sword. I blinked.

"Don't be ridiculous," snapped Raul.

"What are you talking about?" I asked, plaintively.

"I'm going to tell Father Gerthmol that I'm not about to take the peb-ble," Urdo explained.

"I've been arguing for you with Father Gerthmol for the last twelve years!" Raul said. "Anyone could see that the time wasn't right, and the sit-uation was delicate. But now! Now when all the kings are here and have renewed their oaths, when peace has been made, it's the perfect time. It's what you always said."

"This Peace is made without the shield of the White God," Urdo replied. "It will hold better without."

"But you honor the White God, you know you do!" Raul said.

"I do," Urdo said. "But I also honor other gods, and I won't force a decision on anyone." He turned the chair so it was facing Raul and sat down on it.

"Do you mean the Matausian heresy?" Raul asked. "Because that is how Father Gerthmol will hear that statement, however piously you intend it."

"Matau was a fool," Urdo said, impatiently. "I do not say the White God is no different from the other gods. But I will still not take the peb-ble now."

"If this is because of Chanerig—" Raul began.

"What Chanerig did has helped to make up my mind," Urdo inter-rupted.

"But nobody is asking you to do that!" Raul shouted. They were neither of them taking any notice of me at all. This was obviously an argument that had been going on for some time. I leaned back against the wall, then realized my wet hair was touching the plaster and stepped forward a little.

"If I take the pebble, and I am High King, it would be almost as bad," Urdo said. He looked over at Raul very seriously. "Why else do you want me to do it? If I were just one man, then what would it matter? But I honor the gods of the land, and I honor those who find other ways to worship, and I will not see them hurt."

"The powers of the land support you, you can lead them to the light," Raul said. "At Foreth—" He trailed off, awkwardly.

"Yes, at Foreth," Urdo said. "At Foreth the gods of the land gave the greatest proof they support me; Coventina herself gave me water for the horses. I think they have little desire to change. I do not think my desire is strong enough to make them." Raul opened his mouth to protest, but Urdo held up a hand and continued. "Listen to me, Raul. You think that because the land will listen to me then it will do what I want. You saw all Munew come to the light, and you want the whole island to do that. But it is not so simple. The Protectors of Tir Tanagiri hear me, but they will not follow me if I lead them where they do not want to go. It would take my whole heart and my whole will to lead them to worship, and I do not have that will."

"But even so the people need—"

"Raul, I honor you, and I honor Thansethan. There are priests and monasteries I honor less, who believe they should put all the world behind them, or that they should convert the whole world by force, like Chanerig. There are those, like you, who say that the land gods and the people can praise together. There are crops still in Munew. But there are priests who say the people should stop bowing to old stones and offering ale to the first furrow. They say they should take the old names out of the charms and hymns they use every day to start fires and purify water and heal their hurts and do everything in the name of the White God. I would have any change come slowly, in the time of trees and whole human lives. I would have it happen, if it is to happen, because it is better, not in a hurry to be like the king."

Raul frowned and twisted the cord that bound his habit. "Worshiping the White God is better," he said.

"Well, then, so they will choose. I would have everyone free to make their choice. I will not have Ohtar killing your missionaries anymore, but I will not have anyone say that their way is the One True Way for Tir Tanagiri, for see, the High King wears the pebble, and where he leads the whole island must follow. I will not have Alfwin Cellasson or Veniva the wife of Gwien turned from their traditional worship against their will." He smiled at me as he mentioned my mother. "I would not ever have people or the land converting because I did so when their hearts are elsewhere."

"Honor lies in praising the White God," Raul said.

"Does it indeed?" Urdo asked. "Well, you might find honor in one place only, but I have looked more widely and I have found honor among heathens and those who worship the country gods. Sulien there has more honor than Marchel, and I would trust Ohtar further than I would trust Guthrum."

Raul glanced at me, briefly, without expression, and then back to Urdo. "If this is about Marchel—"

"It is not only about Marchel. Though Thurrig tells me she said to him that the people she killed were not only heathen, they were heathen who had fled the chance of conversion and so had no good in them."

Raul shuddered. "She did a terrible thing, and she was terribly wrong," he said. "Not everybody thinks so within the Church, but I think so." He took three swift steps across the room and squatted in front of Urdo, their eyes level. "I would have everyone come to the Lord of their free will. You know that. But examples and encouragement hurt nobody. And with all this talk of choice and will, have a care for your own soul, Urdo."

Urdo raised an eyebrow. "Not even Bishop Dewin will say that taking the pebble openly affects the soul, it is merely an outward symbol of remembrance."

"That's sophistry," Raul retorted. "I was speaking of your soul."

"Bitwini wrote two centuries ago that it is no different if someone takes the pebble with their last words or with their first," Urdo said. "And the apostle Gorai wrote in comfort to the son of Mikal that those who did not come to praise the Lord in their life may find their way there in lifetimes to come."

"All but those who deliberately turn their backs on the Lord," Raul said. They leaned towards each other, staring at each other in silence for a long moment. I was embarrassed to be there.

"Let me worry about my soul," Urdo said. "Praising the White God is not the only way to holiness."

Raul frowned. "The way to God is the way to God," he said.

"There is more to holiness than any one god," I said. Raul looked sadly at me. "You're so sure you're right, it never occurs to you to wonder about the people who really can hear all the wonderful things about your god and still not make that choice. You think everyone will convert in time, with the right argument."

"Yes," Raul said, supremely confident. "Everyone whose soul is not mired in evil. You know, Sulien, you see us as closed and narrow, closing all doors but one and then forcing everyone through that one door. But we are not—we are wide and open, for God embraces all the other gods and whatever you can find in them you can find in him, too. He is the God of gods. The whole ordering of the world fits within him, he made the world, all the worlds, so that everyone and everything has their right place and in time they will come to find their way to that place in his light and his glory. And those who pass through him will find the way to life eternal."

I had heard it all before; he was quoting from their book of memories. "If he made the world and ordered it, why is everything not in that place already?" I asked, as I had asked Arflid long before at Thansethan.

"God made the world and set everything in its place, then he withdrew because he does not want slaves or machines but freely given offerings of praise. In time the world turned to evil and forgot him, except for a few of the faithful in Sinea, so he came into the world as a man to show us the way back."

"Well if he does not want slaves or machines, and if everybody's going to find their own way to him in time, why not let people have that time?" I asked.

Urdo laughed, and Raul threw up his hands. "She's right," Urdo said. Raul turned back to him. "You pressed Alfwin hard after Foreth, and yesterday Father Gerthmol pressed Ayl even harder. He made it sound like the price of marrying Penarwen of Angas." I had no idea what he was talking about. I wondered what Father Gerthmol had done and if it had upset any of Urdo's plans.

"I hear what you are saying about free choice," said Raul, slowly. "But be gentle with Father Gerthmol." He looked up at me. "We can quarrel in front of you, Sulien, it is all in the family. But Father Gerthmol will see your presence as a direct insult. Urdo, he just won't listen to what you have to say if he thinks you're insulting him. He isn't a great holy man, even if he would like to be, but he's a good administrator, he's a good leader for Thansethan. He is getting old, and he is in a hurry to see everyone come to the light. He has supported you all this time in the thought you were his pupil and thought as he did. He won't put insults behind him and suffer; he'll get angry if you throw them in his face."

I caught Urdo's eye and motioned towards the door, only too glad to leave if he wanted me to.

"Stay, Sulien," Urdo said, straightening in the chair and lifting a hand to rub the back of his neck as if it were aching. "Father Gerthmol was not gentle with me yesterday, Raul, or with Ayl, and I must put an end to this. You know as well as I do that Sulien summoned no demon. I have to be firm, and I must do it with all the gods to witness. I would do it before the gods and the people in public if I could, but I do not think he could stomach that. I will force no faith on anyone, nor will I allow any faith to deny any other, and I will have Father Gerthmol understand this in a way he cannot doubt. I will have Sulien here to witness for her gods, and I will have Ohtar to witness for his."

Raul rocked back on his heels as if he had been slapped. "Urdo, no!"

"Yes. He will be here any moment if the messenger I sent has his wits about him."

"He has tortured priests to death! He threatened to kill his own daughter when she took the pebble! This is a bad mistake. I know he is an ally, but he has made so many martyrs in Bereich—" Even as he spoke I could hear sounds in the hall outside, and then there was a scratch at the door.

"Perfect timing," Urdo said. Raul stood and walked back over to the window. "Come in, Ohtar!"

Ohtar came in, and looked at the three of us, clearly puzzled. "Greetings," he said, and bowed in the Jarnish fashion. I closed the door behind him.

"Ohtar, you are going to have to stop killing the priests of the White God that come into Bereich," Urdo said, without preliminary.

Raul took a sharp breath, but said nothing. For some reason Ohtar looked at me. I shrugged. "They want to convert my people," he said.

"Yes," Urdo said. "And those of your people who are unhappy with their old ways and their own gods will convert, if they are allowed to do so. But if your old ways and your old gods are strong, and if the land gods accept your lordship, then most of your people will be happy in their own ways."

"They promise to wash them clean and save them and have them live forever in shining light. It makes everything holy very simple. It is deceptive and attractive. People are afraid, and they hear the priests saying for sure

what will be." Raul turned and looked out of the window. I wanted to say
to him that he couldn't run away from the fight no matter how much he
wanted to. "Also they tell the people that unless they praise the White
God, they will be cast out into darkness for all time. What is the difference
between holding a sword at someone's throat and telling them you will kill
them unless they convert and telling them they must convert or face eternal darkness?"

"I agree," I said. "Many of those among the armigers who convert do
it for that reason. It is one thing to offer someone a chance of praising in
the light and another to threaten them with being cast out into darkness."

"If they are happy with their gods and their ways, they will not change
from them, for threats or promises," Urdo repeated. I thought of Kerys and
of Aurien and wondered what cause they had to be unhappy with the High
Gods. "I am not asking you to convert, or even to listen to the priests yourself," Urdo went on, looking at Ohtar. "I am telling you to stop killing
them wantonly and cruelly. Let them make their way."

"I have been killing them because they are my enemies. They say I am
no king. They breed the horses you ride against us. They take care of your
prisoners."

"Many of the monasteries have supported me, it is true. But we have
peace, we are enemies no longer," Urdo said. "The priests are not under
my control. I cannot control what they say. But if you stop killing them,
they will stop preaching against you."

"They want all the land for themselves, I think," Ohtar said, looking at
Raul's turned back. "They have taken Tir Isarnagiri by force, and they have
taken Munew. They would have all the kingdoms if they could."

"Custennin and Munew chose the White God of their free will," Raul
said loudly, spinning round. "There is no comparison. Chanerig—"

"But who would the land follow, in Munew?" interrupted Ohtar.
"Would it follow Custennin or Bishop Dewin? Who truly rules there?"

There was a silence. "Custennin is king of Munew," Raul said, at last.
"And all kings and all nations shall call his name blessed," he quoted.

"He is king under the White God," Urdo said.

"And what does such kingship mean?" Ohtar asked, quickly.

"It is a new thing in the land," Urdo said. "I think it will come to the
whole land, but in time, when the people and the land are ready. The
White God said that all things have a time and a season, and Kerigano
wrote that we should not presume to think that we know the intention of
God or recognize when that season has come."

"He was talking about all good people choosing to praise," Raul burst in.

"But Sethan himself put a note in his translation saying how many things this thought could be applied to," Urdo said, and smiled at Raul. "Here we see the wonders of reading a text in the vernacular."

Raul's lips twitched into a reluctant smile. "But still," he said. "He says all those who can see will open their eyes in time. He says that everyone will come to their places and praise and the world will be made perfect as it was in the beginning."

"But that time is not ours to force," Urdo said. Then he turned to Ohtar. "Nobody is telling you to convert. I want you to make peace with the monks, and stop killing them on sight."

Ohtar hesitated a long moment, looked at Raul, at Urdo, and at me. Then he shrugged. "All right," he said. "While we have peace I won't kill them, unless they preach against my rule, but I won't encourage the rabble either."

"Good," Urdo said. "For now you can witness, for your High Gods, as Sulien can for hers." Ohtar looked at me shrewdly.

"Shouldn't you ask Emer or Mardol or someone?" I asked. "I'm not a king."

"People will listen to you just as well," Urdo said. "I know your heart. I'd have your mother in if she were here, but she's not. You two stand there and be quiet, witness for me. Raul, come here."

Raul crossed the room in two swift strides to where Urdo sat. "What do you want of me?" he asked, and he sounded as if he felt pain.

"Bring Father Gerthmol, if he will come," he said. "If not, I will go to him."

"He might understand you, but he will never forgive these witnesses," Raul said, very fervently.

"He will want to hear for himself that Ohtar will have peace with the Church," Urdo said.

Raul sighed loudly and went out.

There was an awkward silence, then Urdo laughed. "Making peace among people is hard enough, let alone making it between gods!"

"When we judged on top of Foreth we all swore by our own gods, and they were there to see justice done," Ohtar said. "It does not seem so very difficult to me."

"It does to Raul," Urdo said. He straightened one of the piles of papers. The top one was a map of the northwest coast of Tir Isarnagiri

sketched in black ink. "I never said that I would take the pebble when
peace was made, but it seems that they have all expected it as an accepted
thing. Even Elenn thought I would. It seems people have been promising it
in my name for years."

"You were brought up in the monastery," I said. "They really do think
everyone can be persuaded sooner or later. They're sure of it."

"I do serve the White God in my own way," Urdo said. "But the
whole island is my responsibility. I swore before all the kings to protect the
land and the people."

Then Raul came back with Father Gerthmol. Raul went back to his
post by the window. Urdo stood up, and he and the old priest bowed to
each other. Then he introduced Ohtar, and then me. We all bowed. He settled Father Gerthmol in one of the chairs and sat down again in the other.
I made sure I could jump between them if I needed to. I wasn't really worried about Father Gerthmol killing Urdo, but if he struck him in front of
Ohtar it would make difficulties.

"A misunderstanding has come to my ears," Urdo said. "I have invited
you here to tell you that in the Island of Tir Tanagiri all will be free to worship as they would. No priests will be persecuted or killed for preaching
their faith."

Father Gerthmol looked up at Ohtar, inquiringly, and stared into his
eyes.

"I have agreed to this," Ohtar said, holding his gaze. "As long as they
do not preach against me and say I am no king, then I will not hurt them."

"Praise the Lord!" said Father Gerthmol, looking back to Urdo, who
was sitting still and serious.

"No priest will be harmed, but neither will any one god be raised
above the others." I wondered if the gods were there listening. I felt no sign
of them. "Nor do I plan to take the pebble at this time."

Father Gerthmol rocked back on his chair a little, and looked over at
Raul, who was again looking out of the window. From the courtyard
below the came the cheerful sounds of Fifth and Sixth Pennons starting
their morning weapons training. I wished I was out there with them. "And
why not?" he asked at last. "All this time we have been struggling towards
this Peace in the name of the Lord, and now we have it and still you will
not take the pebble?"

"What would it do if I brought the land under the White God against
its will?" Urdo asked. "What would it do to my oaths as king? What would
it do to my people and to the powers of the land?"

"It would bring them into the light, and make them part of the family of God," Father Gerthmol said. "No longer would the gods be withdrawn, speaking only to kings and lords; everyone would know themselves and their place in the glory and the love of God."

"If so they choose," Urdo said. "But a forced choice is no choice, Father. I would not see those who honestly serve other gods forced from their old ways."

"You surround yourself with enemies of the Church!" Father Gerthmol said, looking from me to Ohtar and back again. "But see," he said, more gently, "people who have not seen the light need not be forced to it by your taking the pebble. After all, who but a king can lead the powers of the land into the light, unless it is done by force as Chanerig did it? You can speak to those powers and bring the spirits of the whole island with you."

"It is not what they want," Urdo said, firmly. "Understand me, even if I had the power, I would force my gods no more than I will force my people."

Father Gerthmol looked furious. "What a chance is being wasted!" he said. "I have indeed misunderstood. From the time you were twelve years old you have been steadfastly refusing to take the pebble, but I believed you were a friend all the same. I thought you would come to serve the Lord, and so would the Peace you were making. It seems I was wrong." He looked again at Raul, and back to Urdo. "While we helped you fight," he said, bitterly, "we were fighting to bring this land into the light, not for you to have power for your own sake. I have misjudged you, son of Avren."

" 'It is a king's duty to his people to make, and keep, and hold peace, within which they may prosper; it is a king's duty to the gods to listen.' Thus I swore and thus you witnessed when I took the crown at Caer Tanaga twelve years ago. The land has as much peace as do men, and the land does not clamor to praise the White God forever. I have no power to demand such praise."

Father Gerthmol stood up in silence and looked at me and at Ohtar. Deliberately, he touched his pebble in a warding gesture. Then he turned and, turning, put up the hood of his robe so that it covered his head. He went to the door. We were all staring at him. When he reached the door he stopped, half turned, and called "Raul!" Raul started. "Come Raul. We must leave now if we are to be in Thansethan tomorrow."

Raul looked from Father Gerthmol to Urdo, took one step towards the

33

"Secrets only remain secret if very few people know them."
—Caius Dalitius, *The Relations of Rulers*

I don't think anything ever distressed Urdo as much as Raul leaving. Ohtar had more sense than I did and didn't waste time running after Raul. He went and got Elenn, and she went in to Urdo. Neither of them came out until it was nearly time for the evening's feast, so it wasn't until then that I told Urdo what Raul had said. He listened to me, and said, "Thank you, Sulien," and went on. He looked terrible. I have had armigers take grief like that after losing a close comrade in battle. We deal with it by pouring strong drink down them and all mourning together. It almost always works. I knew it wouldn't work that time. Raul wasn't dead, he had left of his own will.

It was three years before Raul came back. Urdo got over the shock slowly, but it was a blight on what should have been happiness for him. He worked on his law code, and he started to implement ideas he had had years before. Yet all the time I could feel him reaching out for Raul, as an armiger who has lost an arm will keep reaching for it and remembering. Thansethan would no longer help Urdo, and though that was a heavy blow, it was less of a loss.

Those three years were peaceful ones for me. The war in Demedia rumbled on for two of them. We raided the coast of Oriel, using Ohtar's ships and landing a pennon or so at a time. They would land, kill the few who dared to stand against them, and scatter those who fled, take whatever plunder looked valuable and portable, then burn everything. We did it after the spring planting, and again as soon as the harvest was in. When Ayl heard the details of what we had done he shuddered and said to me if he had known Urdo could be so ruthless he would never have taken up arms against him. I think he wanted to know why we hadn't done this with the Jarnsmen. I don't know if Urdo ever told him.

After two years of this and of defeats in Demedia Atha ap Gren sued for peace and passage back to Tir Isarnagiri. Needing to ask passage, after we had burned their ships, must have been the last humiliation. She swore to Angas she would never set foot in arms in Demedia again. She was ruling all of Oriel by then, some of it in trust for her son. Black Darag was door, stopped, looked again at Urdo and up at the hooded monk. He took another step.

"Raul!" Urdo said, quietly, as if it hurt him to speak.

"I am sworn to obedience," he said, looking straight in front of him. Urdo opened his mouth but said nothing. Raul took another step. Father Gerthmol went out, and Raul followed.

"Thank you for witnessing, you can go now," Urdo said, without looking at us. His voice was thick. Ohtar and I looked at each other. I put a hand on Urdo's shoulder, tentatively. He stood up and walked to the window. "I will speak to you later," he said. Ohtar took my arm and drew me out of the room. I could see Raul at the end of the passage, by the stairs. Shaking Ohtar off, I ran towards him.

"How could you do that to him!" I said. "After all these years. He needs you, Raul, and you know it."

"He needs Thansethan," Raul said, blankly, stopping. Father Gerthmol was halfway down the stairs already.

"He can manage without Thansethan if he must. But he needs you. You're his friend, his clerk, his brother nearly. How can you just walk away?"

"Would you always put your friends before your gods, Sulien ap Gwien?"

I hesitated. "I don't know," I said. "But by all the bright gods, it counts for something that nobody has ever put me in a position where I have to make that choice! It isn't your god you're choosing, it's Father Gerthmol and Thansethan and the Church. That whole quarrel was about letting people find their own way to holiness. But you will do what Father Gerthmol tells you, and not your own heart? You're not like Marchel, you know you're not. And you understand him; you can't walk away like that!"

"I am sworn to obedience. Would you break your armiger's oath?" There were tears on Raul's cheeks. "In any case, if I am with Father Gerthmol, maybe I can make him understand Urdo. If I disobeyed, he would see us both as enemies. Tell Urdo that. I might bring him around." Father Gerthmol was at the bottom of the steps. He called up to Raul. "I must go. Tell Urdo that, and tell him—" He hesitated, took a step downwards. "Tell him he should have listened to me, and I love him." He brushed away tears, smiled grimly, put up his hood, and clattered down the stairs after Father Gerthmol.

dead, we heard, killed by Larig, who was then in turn killed by one of Darag's men.

Thus perished the only one of Thurrig's children to live an honorable life. Chanerig was still in Tir Isarnagiri, founding churches and meddling in politics. He kept sending furious letters whenever our raids happened to kill or capture any of his converts. Marchel and her ala had been disgraced after the massacre of Varae. Urdo said that what she had done was unacceptable for a civilized person, she no longer had his confidence or friendship. She was exiled, never to return, and she could never hold or inherit land in Tir Tanagiri. I think he only gave her her life for Thurrig's sake. Her ala was broken up, the armigers scattered among the other alae, mostly those in Demedia. Her officers were all returned to the ranks. She had given the order, but they had carried it out. There was no longer an ala of Caer Gloran. Urdo made them cut their banners and Marchel's praefecto's cloak into strips and wrap them around sticks and thrust them into a fire like a funeral pyre. They wept as they did it, all but Marchel, whose face stayed set rigid. This shocked all of my armigers. Urdo talked to everyone of signifer rank and above who could get to Caer Tanaga about what an order was and when it should be questioned. I was very glad I took my orders from Urdo himself and had no need to wrestle with such things.

Amala went with Marchel to Narlahena. Ap Wyn and her children went with them. Thurrig looked ten years older after they took ship. He went back to his fleet, and we did not see him often. Amala was not disgusted with Marchel but with Urdo for disgracing her daughter for something she could not see as important. She had never really understood Tir Tanagiri, and I hoped she would be happier in her homeland. Ap Wyn and the boys returned after a year or two, without saying anything to anyone. Veniva mentioned to me in a letter that they had arrived one day on a ship from Narlahena, stayed a few days with Daldaf, and then gone up to Nant Gefalion. He had not cared for Narlahena much and wanted to get on with his work. I mentioned this to Urdo, who said that only Marchel was exiled and the rest of them could come back at any time.

I did not go to Demedia, or to raid Oriel. I stayed in Caer Tanaga with the ala. We trained hard, until we were even better than we had been. There had probably never been an ala as good as we were in those first years of the Peace. We could turn on an arrowhead and we keep spears lined up so straight charging that the points were not a handbreadth before each other. Some of the veterans left to settle down and have babies. To some of these Urdo gave gifts of land and horses and told them to be ready to come back to the banner if they were needed. Others stayed in the alae but went to join other alae stationed nearer to their homes. Some were very restless without fighting and begged to be sent to Demedia. I had some sympathy for them and sent them up to ap Erbin. In return he sent us his tired and lightly wounded armigers. I learned later this gave us a reputation among the Isarnagans for having tireless and invulnerable troops. There were always people in other alae who wanted to come to us, too. After all, they knew we were the best. We also took in recruits. Once they had the basic skills I spread them among the pennons, where they worked hard until they were as good as the veterans. Some of them were better.

Ulf took to his silly ax as if he had been born with it in his hand. Some of the others in his pennon asked if he would make them axes, so we ended up with almost as many axes as longswords in that pennon after a year or so. Urdo spoke to me seriously about Ulf and made me promise not to drive him harder than the others. I did not, nor had I intended to. I drove them all hard, and myself with them. I avoided seeing Ulf alone, but I did not torment him. He became a formidable warrior and a loyal and steady armiger. He had a tendency to have nightmares and wake half the barracks screaming, but he took teasing about this in good part. Alswith asked me quite seriously if I had cursed him, but I told her firmly that any grudge between me and Gunnarsson had been settled at Foreth. Among the others he became quite popular. The Queen liked him, too. When Urdo could not ride with her, she would always take an escort from the ala; and she often chose Ulf. He was nobly born, and his conversation amused her. I could say nothing against it without telling her things I had sworn had been ended. All the same I let her know that I could not eat with Ulf. There were plenty of people in the same situation for bloodfeuds old and new, so it did not cause remark, she just made sure never to invite us into her alcove at the same time. Even Urdo seemed to show him some respect, consulting him now and then about Jarnish issues.

Morthu of Angas was the other notable recruit. He seemed to shape up well enough, though his skills were not outstanding, and I paid little attention to him. I did not like him. He was not an heir to land, yet he acted like one, and somehow the others treated him like one. He seemed to have a great ability to get on with people, though he never bothered to exert this skill on me. I guessed that he blamed me still for his mother's death. It did not cross my mind that he was holding a real grudge against me still, or against Urdo. I thought that he was a very young man who would learn better. Yet even then I would often see him with a group of armigers, talking and laughing, and when I drew near they would fall silent. He spent time out of the ranks, going when he could to see his sister in Aylsfa or to Thansethan where he had friends. He was also a great letter writer, sending great sealed messages whenever the red-cloaks went off. I did not then think anything of this except that he was in love with his own importance.

We had very little real fighting to do. We fought off the occasional raiders, and there were fewer raiders every year now that Ayl was offering land to those Jarnsmen who would settle in Aylsfa and call him lord. We talked about raiding Jarnholme the way we were raiding Oriel, once the Isarnagan war was over, to discourage the raiders. Many of them had learned already that attacking Tir Tanagiri meant death and turned to raiding other less-defended shores. Meanwhile we trained, we practiced formations and drills, we played war games, one half of the ala against the other, and on ceremonial occasions we paraded.

There were a number of ceremonial occasions. Garah married Glyn the summer after the Battle of Foreth. This set off a spate of ala weddings. Urdo gave Glyn and Garah a house just inside the gates of the citadel of Caer Tanaga. I was amazed how many people gave them gifts—all the praefectos sent something and many of the armigers. I was very glad for Garah. I gave them a chest of new linen from Derwen and two plates, newly made by the potter at Caer Tanaga, black and lustrous, as good as anything the king ate from. I also made Garah's plait-bread—it was a little untidy. Veniva had always made it look so easy, folding the bread over and over on top of the fruit while talking about something else. But nobody complained. Garah's parents came down from Derwen for the ceremony. They looked very shy and unsure of themselves, and her mother wept when she saw how splendid Garah looked in her orange dress. "Like a lord," she said. She would have been even more impressed if she had seen Elenn with the needle in her teeth, sewing it with pearls and gold thread every evening for two months before. It was a splendid present, good enough for an heirloom. I remembered Garah's mother giving me a cup of milk when I had come into her kitchen after the attack on Derwen, and I stayed close to them throughout the feasting, guiding them through it.

About a month after that, Ayl married Penarwen of Angas, at Caer Tanaga, with prodigious feasting. Gwilen ap Rhun made Penarwen's plait-bread, and she also made up a fertility charm. She had once been key-keeper of Caer Tanaga, and Urdo's leman, and she had gone up to Demedia when Urdo married to look after one of Angas's fortresses on the western coast. There she had become friendly with Penarwen, and now she came down to Aylsfa with her. Elenn still did not like her, although she always behaved very politely towards her. Their wedding was conducted in the church by Mother Teilo, who had come down from Demedia specially. She let Urdo feel the sharp side of her tongue more than once, but it seemed she was more willing than Thansethan to have dealings with us.

Teilo told Ayl at the wedding feast that now he was married to Penarwen he should adopt a banner in Vincan style. Banners were not a Jarnish custom, but since Guthrum had taken up his silver swan Ayl was the only king on Tir Tanagiri who did not fly one. He had a strange blue standard with a dragon's head on the top which he used as a rallying point in battle. He had the same dragon carved on his ship's prow. Ayl smiled at Teilo and promised to consider it. The next time we saw him he had tied great streamers of light red cloth behind his dragon's head. They certainly caught the wind like banners, but the effect was peculiarly more barbaric than the beast had been alone. The color was one made from a root that only grew in Aylsfa, so it was a good choice in that way. When I congratulated Ayl on his banner he laughed and said that he had done it for his lady wife. I don't think anyone at Caer Tanaga ever got up the courage to ask the very regal Penarwen if she was pleased by it.

It was a summer noted for weddings and for abundant harvests. It seemed the land was pleased with Urdo. That year and the year after were noted for babies, too. Penarwen had a son almost exactly nine months after the wedding, and Garah was nursing her new daughter when the news came in. Masarn's wife had another child, too, a daughter this time, and Masarn was delighted. He liked children. He said he'd even have liked a fifth, if it were possible. I reminded him of the Vincan general Quintus, who was a fifth-born child. He had left the ala by then and was helping his wife with her beekeeping and candlemaking. I missed his steadiness as tribuno, but I still saw him often. Occasionally he would even come to practice, though he would never admit that he missed the ala. He called his new baby Sulien in my honor, and I was delighted. Emer ap Allel also bore a daughter that summer, who in later years became the greatest praefecto of her day and one of my dearest friends. At the time the news meant little to me, though I wished Emer well. I had heard no news of Conal since I left Derwen. I guessed that he was back with Black Darag, in Demedia, killing my friends. We stopped talking about the spate of babies when we saw that it distressed Elenn, whose arms were still empty. In any case there were so many babies born every year in the Peace that we almost got used to it.

I was a little lonely in that time. Urdo was very busy, and Elenn had cooled to me for some reason. Garah and Glyn had the baby, and soon another, which kept them occupied. The ala was not as friendly a place for me as it had been, with Ulf and Morthu there. Though I name them together they were not friends. Indeed Morthu seemed to dislike and distrust Ulf and Ulf plainly despised Morthu. I took comfort in training and in breeding and raising horses, which has been one of my passions ever since. I had friends at hand when I needed them, just not as much companionship as I would have wished in my daily life. But I was not unhappy.

In the third year of the Peace Alswith Haraldsdottar came to me early one morning in tears. She had her flame-colored hair pulled back hard away from her face. She looked so pale she was almost green, except for the shadows under her eyes, which were almost purple. Jarns are an unlovely color even when they are healthy, but Alswith was clearly ill. I had made her signifer after Foreth. She deserved it, and she was unarguably good enough. Then about a year later in a spate of rearrangements I made her decurio of Second Pennon. That had worked well, and I was pleased with her.

"What's wrong?" I asked. I was sitting on the wall around the paddock watching Starlight's new colt, Brighteyes. He looked as if he would be fast. I wanted him to get used to people being present without being threatening, so I was just sitting for the time being, enjoying the sunshine. Alswith swung herself up beside me.

"I feel awful," she said. "It's horrible. I wake up every morning with my stomach heaving and I have to run to the latrines. I can't stand the sight of food. I throw up half the morning. Worst of all, I'm sleepy all the time. I thought I'd poisoned myself with some bad mushrooms, because I had eaten a lot of them, and now I can't stand the sight of them. But it's been a month and it's not wearing off. Then I thought I'd got so I couldn't eat bread anymore, like Talog the cook, you know? So I haven't eaten any bread for five days, and I'm still as bad as ever."

"When did the Moon Maiden last strike you?" I asked, with a sinking heart.

Alswith shook her head. "That's another thing, I didn't bleed at all last month, and now I'm nearly due again. I know you know about magic. Do you know what it is? Can you do a charm for it?"

I stared at her for a moment, trying to remind myself that I had once been just that naive. "Is there any chance you could be pregnant?" I asked, gently.

"No, of course not," she said, laughing. "I'm not married, you know that."

"I do know that," I said, carefully, "But even though it's rare, it does happen occasionally that women who aren't married can still catch a baby. It happened to me. I have a son growing up at Thansethan." A son I couldn't see, though Elenn had visited him and assured me he was well. She had taken a letter and some tack for Keturah and brought me a letter back, all about how Keturah was growing and what ap Cathvan had said and how Arvlid sometimes let him ride out with her when she went to the hamlets with medicines. The letter began and ended with stilted phrases but came alive when he talked about horses. It had been the same when we talked at Thansethan. She had brought a letter from Arvlid too, saying Darien was growing well and strong.

"But really, I've never—" She lowered her voice and used a Jarnish word which I had often heard used thrown around as a curse but never known the meaning of. "—fucked. I don't even let people touch my belly button when we share blankets."

Alfwin was going to be furious with me. I wondered if he would settle for unarmed combat or if he would demand blood. "I don't speak Jarnish very well," I said, gently, "but belly buttons don't have anything to do with making babies. Haven't you ever watched the stallions with the mares? It's the same for people, you know? If you've been doing that then it seems very likely to me that you're pregnant. Who have you been sharing blankets with?"

"Nobody, not for ages, and then it was only ap Erbin because we were so pleased to see each other when he came back from Demedia!" she said, defensively. There were tears in her eyes.

I sighed with relief, I'd half expected her to say she'd been sharing blankets with half the pennon. Ap Erbin was someone it was at least possible she could marry. "How do you feel about ap Erbin?" I asked.

She blushed bright red. "I'm very fond of him," she muttered, looking at her feet.

"And is he very fond of you?" I asked. She said nothing, but blushed harder, so that her face was almost as red as her hair. "Look, Alswith, it isn't normal for women to start having babies until they've had a womb blessing when they get married. If they do, it's usually because the gods really want them to have that child."

"I really didn't know that was"—again she lowered her voice—"fucking. I promised Alfwin and my mother I wouldn't do that. I thought it was something terribly bad, not just sharing blankets like almost everyone does. And I was absolutely sure nobody ever got pregnant unless they were married. Nobody in the ala ever has."

"That's not the problem anymore," I said. "The problem is if you want to keep your baby." I hadn't even touched her, I couldn't say for sure there was a baby. But I knew.

She folded her hands protectively over her stomach. "Yes," she said.

"Right. Then the next thing is to talk to ap Erbin and see if he wants to marry you. The next thing after that is to persuade Alfwin and your mother that it's a wonderful idea, not to mention ap Erbin's parents." His father was that awful lech Erbin, and relations with Custennin had been slightly strained ever since the break with Thansethan. "I think the best thing is if I talk to Urdo, and then if he's agreeable you take your pennon down to Caer Segant and talk to ap Erbin. Then you can go to Tevin and talk to Alfwin."

She was still blushing. "What if ap Erbin doesn't want to?" she asked. "It's an awful thing to ask. People's parents are supposed to arrange marriages."

"People arrange their own sometimes," I said, as reassuringly as I could. "And if the idiot doesn't want to, then you can go to Thansethan and have the baby and leave it there to grow up. That's what I did, and it hasn't stopped me being an armiger." I airily elided the problem of Alfwin.

"Oh thank you, Sulien," Alswith said, fervently. Then she slid down off the wall and was horribly sick in the long grass. Little Brighteyes came charging over to see what was making the awful noises. He didn't have any fear of people at all, just a great deal of curiosity. All his get were the same and still are; they probably will be until the end of time.

I sent Alswith off to drink hot water with mint and went to see Urdo. He was in his room, sitting on the chair by the table working on his laws. Elenn was sitting on a stool beside him, counting something out on a slate. As I came in she must have finished adding a column because, without looking, she reached her hand up and took Urdo's hand and pressed it to her cheek. Neither of them looked up. I felt hot and prickly with embarrassment, and would have turned and gone away, but just then Urdo looked up and saw me. He lifted his hand up quite naturally and greeted me. Elenn stood smoothly and when she had greeted me left, saying she needed to speak to Glyn before she could get on. I was sorry to have interrupted but glad to have Urdo on his own to explain Alswith's problem.

"Oh Lord, what's Alfwin going to say!" was his first comment. When I had explained the whole situation he laughed shortly. "Well, at least ap Erbin is presentable. If I make the two of them a present of some land, I expect everyone can be reconciled to it. There's empty land up near the border of Tevin for that matter, north of Thansethan, and half the people around there are Jarnish. Yes. We can tell Custennin, but we will have to ask Alfwin, that's the important thing. Send her off to Caer Segant, and get her to bring ap Erbin back if he's willing, I want a word with him. Then, I think, you'd better take two or three pennons up to Caer Lind and talk to Alfwin. Don't take Alswith with you; that way he can't get angry with her. Take ap Erbin, though. Three pennons ought to be enough to keep him alive until you've finished explaining." He grinned.

"But I'm no good at that sort of thing!" I protested.

"Alfwin likes you," Urdo said. "You don't have to be diplomatic. Tell him the gods have found him a son-in-law, which is the truth if he can see it."

"But what if he can't see it?"

"He won't be that angry with you, it's not your fault. And ap Erbin can ask him for Alswith. I think among the Jarns it wouldn't happen like that, she'd be disgraced as I understand their customs, so he might be glad to have her safely married. Probably not many noble Jarnsmen would want her after she's been riding round bare-faced in the ala even after her father was avenged."

"I told her if ap Erbin doesn't want to marry her she can go to Thansethan the way I did," I said. "She's not limited to Jarnish options. She's one of us."

"Of course she is," Urdo said, almost absently. "Did you tell her about Darien then?"

"Only that I have a son growing up in Thansethan. That isn't a secret in the ala—they were there, some of them saw him. It isn't a secret anyway. I gave him my name."

"I know," Urdo hesitated, uncharacteristically, and picked up his brown-and-green stylus. "You didn't tell her who his father is?"

"No. I—" My mouth was dry. "I never talk about that."

"Is that why you gave him your name?" He turned the stylus in his fingers as if he had never touched it before.

"Yes. No. Well, yes, and Father Gerthmol was pushing me, and he made me angry." I looked down at the table, pots of colored ink, good parchment, Vincan books, a letter with Ohtar's seal, an untidy stack of accounts.

"He's good at that," Urdo said, wryly, still fiddling with the stylus. "Ulf doesn't know then?"

"I don't think so. I certainly haven't told him."

"You know a lot of people assume he's my son?" Urdo said.

I looked up at him; he was looking at me patiently. I hadn't thought about it, and I felt like a fool. I knew people said we had shared blankets in Caer Gloran, and even that we had secretly been lovers later. I always dismissed it as gossip, the desire of people to talk about other people and giggle. I had never made the connection to Darien. I was still as naive as poor Alswith, with much less excuse. I could feel my cheeks heating, though fortunately it was less visible than for her. "I'm sorry," I said.

"No need," Urdo said, sounding a little shy. "I haven't discouraged people from thinking that. Indeed, in some ways it's useful for me that they do think that. I have no heir. Morwen told me a long time ago, before I even knew who I was, that I would have no heir. She may have been wrong, her oracles were not always right, nor did she mean me well. But I have always acted as if that was the case, because if I do have an heir I can change my plans, but I am not counting on having one."

"Have you told Elenn?" I asked. Morwen's motivations were a tangled net I did not want to touch.

"Yes," he said, and smiled painfully. "She said I should take the pebble and we should make pilgrimages. I have no brother to go to her bed in my place, nor any other close relative, even if she would allow it."

"You could make pilgrimages," I said, awkwardly. I could not imagine her allowing it. It was a very old custom, but it was something that definitely had to be agreed.

"We could. We probably shall. We are presently undecided as to the shrines of what faith we should journey to. But if I have no heir, then sooner or later the kings will ask who will follow me. Some are saying it already. If they believe Darien is my son then it helps them think I may well beget an heir. I am young still, and there is peace." He hesitated, and set the stylus down on the table. "If I asked you to give me an heir, Sulien, would you?"

"I would endure any wounding in your service," I said.

He laughed, one brief note, cut off, a very terrible sound. "I am not laughing at you," he said, immediately. "Only there was so much pain there. My dear, I am not asking that. You have a son, and I do not. If you do not speak to anyone of his parentage it is as good as if he were my own blood, if need be. There may yet be no need."

"I will not tell anyone," I said. Even though this was no more than what I had been doing for years, I heard a raven cry outside, and a great sound of wings sweeping past, as if I had done some momentous thing.

"Thank you," Urdo said.

"But what will you do for an heir?" I asked. "You won't live forever. This Peace would crumble without you."

"Maybe," he said, "though if it is a good enough Peace it would not; the rest of you could hold it. But do you remember what the Vincan emperors did? When the gods sent them no children they chose the best man to be the heir and adopted him as a son. That is what I would do, get to know the young men who are sons or grandsons of kings but not heir to land, men like ap Erbin, or ap Mardol. Then, when I am growing old and the Peace is an established thing, I would call a council of all the kings and offer them my choice for their election. If they choose him, too, then I would adopt him, and he could start doing some of the work of ruling while I am still there to help."

Urdo sounded really enthusiastic about this. "It could work, but it would need to be undisputed," I said.

"Yes," Urdo said. "But the same goes for a child of mine. There's nothing magical about blood."

"The land—" I said, hesitating. "The land does know king's blood."

"That's why any heir would be of king's blood," Urdo said. "The land would have to accept him, too, but I think I could manage that. If the gods spare me."

"It's a bit like what the Isarnagans do?" I ventured.

Urdo grinned. "Yes. For the time being do not talk about this to anyone."

"Are you really thinking of ap Erbin?" I asked.

"No. He was just an example. He's what, five, ten years younger than me? Just somebody like that."

An idea struck me. "Morthu of Angas," I said, slowly. "Is that why he acts like that?"

"No!" Urdo said, sounding shocked. "Acts like what?"

"As if he's much more important than he is. I just thought, he's the right blood, and the right age. I don't like him, though."

"I don't like him either," Urdo said, quietly. He straightened the parchment in front of him. "He reminds me too much of his mother. Angas does not, and Penarwen does not, and the other sister, the one who we saw at the wedding, the one who wants to go to Teilo's monastery, Hivlian, she does not either, although she has some of her mother's oracle talent. But I do not like Morthu; he does not seem trustworthy."

"Good," I said. "I will say nothing about Darien's parentage, not that I would have anyway. And I will stop denying that we shared blankets that night in Caer Gloran on the rare occasions when anyone mentions it in a way in which I am required to do anything but groan."

Urdo laughed. "Thank you," he said. "And I have never denied it, not even when Thurrig congratulated me on my courage."

I laughed with him, and then stopped as I thought of something. "Is that why Elenn doesn't seem to be so friendly now?" I asked.

"Maybe," Urdo said. "I think someone mentioned it to her at Ayl's wedding, or not long after, because she asked me about it. I told her, which is the truth, that I have not lain with mortal woman else since our wedding, and that is all that is her concern." The question of goddesses, which we both knew about, hung in the air. I could still remember her voice, addressing him as husband. Elenn should be able to understand and forgive that strange consummation.

"She really doesn't like ap Rhun," I said.

"I know." Urdo sighed.

"I won't say anything in any case," I said.

"If she has a child, it won't matter anymore, and you can tell anyone anything you like," Urdo said.

"My good wishes for it," I said. "In the meantime, I suppose I'd better get on and help Alswith sort out getting married before she has a baby in about seven months' time."

—34—

Now I will sing of Brichan
whose hall lies empty
the roof fallen, open to the sky.

Brichan, your ears cannot hear me now
you who ceased from care to delight
in feasting and sweet music.

Your sons are slain, your daughters scattered
your kingdom is being forgotten,
your bard is lonely.

Brichan, you were not wise to heed
the words of the Jarnsmen
trusting all of your, allies.

You walked tall and proud
strong-armed, learned,
decorated with weapons.

Death comes to everyone, shabby or glorious.
Men who were generous while they lived
have their eyes pecked by crows.
—Non ap Cunir, "Lament for Brichan, Lord of Bricinia"

There's something about Tevin," ap Erbin said, thumping his mare
hard in the stomach and tightening the girth another handspan. We
were on our way back to Caer Tanaga, two days south of Caer Lind on the
highroad, and it had just started to rain again. The others were breaking
camp and mounting up around us.

I just grinned at him, swinging up onto Glimmer's back. "What's so
awful about Tevin? I thought you told Urdo you were happy to live up
here?"

"In the north means well away from my relatives." He thumped the
horse again on the last word, and she whickered reproachfully as he tightened the girth again. He looked over at me. "Telling them was bad
enough. You've met them, you can picture it; Uncle Custennin whining
about marrying a heathen, Aunt Linwen genuinely shocked, Bishop Devin
talking about trying to convert her, Aunt Tegwen asking if with that pale
skin she wouldn't burn terribly in the sunshine, Great-uncle Cador muttering about sleeping with the enemy and getting my throat cut, and my father
making crude jokes about trying her out for size before the wedding."

"Avoiding that would be worth putting up with the weather in Tevin,"
I agreed. I tightened my wrist straps. "It doesn't always rain anyway.
Remember Foreth?"

"I'll never forget it," he said. "It didn't rain much yesterday either, and
this rain looks as if it might stop after a little while."

I squinted at the clouds. There were rolling hills ahead, and the clouds
were piled up above them like folds of grey blankets. I rolled my eyes.
"Here, maybe, but I think we'll be riding into it all day."

"We ought to be in Thansethan by late afternoon," ap Erbin said. "As we're going to collect the Queen and escort her back, we could suggest it wasn't worth leaving until morning, so they might give us a dry bed for the night."

"All fifty of us?" I asked. "They wouldn't let me in anyway, the last time I saw him, Father Gerthmol was treating me like a demon. No, we'll have to camp again, there if Elenn's not ready to leave and on down the road if she is. Though if we weren't doing this, she'd manage with less of an escort—she has ap Selevan's pennon with her. That ought to be enough."

"Oh well, it was a dry thought while it lasted," said ap Erbin, mounting at last. We formed up and rode off down the highroad.

"Alfwin was less trouble than your own family then?" I asked as we rode.

"Much more polite if a lot more intimidating," ap Erbin said.

"So what did he say when he took you off on your own?"

"I could ask the same," he said, raising his eyebrows. "He asked me a lot of things about the gods, which I answered as well as I could. I told him I'd not try and force any faith on Alswith and the child—children, later. He seemed happy with that in the end, that they should decide for themselves. We talked about land—it seems his older son is heir to Bereich and is up there with his mother while the younger son is being brought up to be heir to Tevin. Alfwin wants me to swear to him the way ap Ross did to your brother, and he will give us responsibility for some land that joins the land Urdo is giving us. I never thought to hold land." He drew a deep breath and looked around at the hills and the gentle rain. "It must be around here somewhere. There's supposed to be an old villa off the road somewhere which we could patch up or use for building materials depending how much it's decayed. We're going to have a big wedding and walk the bounds of the land and do everything properly. What did he ask you?"

"He just asked me about you," I said. It was true. He'd wanted to know all about ap Erbin. He'd seemed concerned that he might be letting his brother down in what was done for Alswith. From the way he had talked it seemed "big wedding" was an understatement. Alfwin wanted his niece to have one of the three most splendid weddings ever seen in the Island of Tir Tanagiri.

"What did you tell him?" ap Erbin asked, sounding worried.

"Urdo told me to tell him the gods had chosen you for a son-in-law," I said. Alfwin had been more impressed by this argument than I had thought he would be.

Ap Erbin looked appalled. "Me?"

"Well, people don't usually get to start babies without being married, the gods must have a hand in it somewhere," I reminded him.

"I suppose so," he said, without much conviction, looking straight ahead between his horse's ears.

"Do you want to get married?" I asked.

"Well, everyone has to marry someone sometime," he replied, "and I do like Alswith and I'd rather marry her than someone I don't know. But it all seems so sudden. Marriage, land, a baby, all at once."

"I suppose it must." The highroad cut through the hills there, and we were almost sheltered from the rain. The sound of the pennons coming along behind us laughing and singing was very loud.

"Did you really tell Alfwin that?" Ap Erbin sounded concerned.

"Yes, but I also told him that you were a very good tribuno when you were with my ala and that you'd been covering yourself with glory in Demedia since, though covering yourself with wounds would have been just as accurate."

He laughed and touched his ear self-consciously. "This was a sling-stone, of all things. An ambush in the mountains. The next one broke my horse's leg, and I was lucky to fall straight over his head and not sideways, or I'd have been crushed. They ran away as soon as we started killing them, cowards that they are. Ap Gwinthew got the one who got me, though, or so he says." He sighed. "I used to hear people all the time saying how much they hate the Jarnsmen and how we ought to push them back into the sea. I never felt like that when we were fighting them, not that I hated them, not even that time at Caer Lind. The Isarnagans, though, they'd never stand to fight, we'd wear ourselves out looking for them. Then if we stopped anywhere without walls they'd sneak into camp at night to stab horses and cut the throats of sleeping armigers. They rape prisoners and farmers and cut their heads off afterwards. I couldn't help hating them."

"I've never fought them," I said. "But Thurrig says the same, and so does Angas."

"I'm glad we got rid of them," he said. "I wonder sometimes if Urdo was too hard on Marchel. When I heard I was shocked, but after I'd been fighting them for a while I could understand what made her do it."

"You wouldn't have killed them after they surrendered," I said, quite sure of it.

"Well, I didn't," he said, and grinned. "Of course I wouldn't. But I understand now how someone might want to. Though as she did it the first minute she saw them, she doesn't have that excuse, of course."

"I'm glad they've gone home," I said. "Did you see the famous Atha ap Gren?"

"Oh yes, several times. She's not really a giant, she's no bigger than you are, and she fights with a spear. I was quite disappointed after all the songs. She's neither so beautiful as to have men kill themselves for love of her nor ugly enough to turn people to stone, though she spikes her hair with lime and it does look horrific. Black Darag was uglier actually, but it might have been the way he was always scowling. He fought with a spear, too, a huge barbed one. Angas nearly killed Atha once, but nobody ever seemed to get near Darag until Larig managed it, and nobody knows how he did it."

"Didn't he tell you?" I asked. We were riding through the hills. A scout came back saying the road was clear and safe with no sign of life, and I sent her on ahead again to scout as far as the river.

When I turned back to ap Erbin he shook his head. "We never saw Larig again. There was a fight at the ships, and then he went off inland chasing Black Darag, and neither of them came back. We heard later that he'd killed Black Darag with his own belly-spear and then Conal the Victor had killed him. It was definitely Conal who gave Larig's head back when we sent them home."

Up in Demedia, killing my friends. I had guessed it. "I might wish to be the far end of a spear from Conal myself," I said.

"He's back across the Windy Sea now anyway, and I hope he stays there," ap Erbin said.

"Killing people is one thing, taking their heads is another," I said, wrinkling my nose.

"Well, we were all at it by the end," ap Erbin said, lowering his voice. "Angas definitely did, and Larig took Darag's by all accounts, and I let my ala do it after a while. It was the only way to make the Isarnagans respect us, and the only way to get them to give our comrades heads back was if we had some to swap."

I was almost glad I hadn't fought in Demedia. Just at that moment another scout came back, signaling trouble. I rode forward to him. "What is it?"

"I'm not sure," he said. "There's a ship burning in the river, and it looks like a Jarnish ship. There's no sign of any people, but there are tracks going towards the woods ahead, and there could be anything."

I had a bad feeling suddenly. Something was wrong. It could be an ambush; lots of people had known we'd be riding this way today. "I'm going to go ahead and see what's happening," I said. I turned to the near-

est decurio. "Elwith, bring five and follow me. Ap Erbin, you take charge of the rest. Ride to the top of the crest where you can see my signals. If I'm not back in an hour, ride back to Caer Lind—or is Caer Rangor nearer across country?" I added. I always forgot the fortress existed if I wasn't there or sitting staring at a map.

"From here I'm not sure. Maybe. Luth is there, though, with his ala," ap Erbin said.

"Ride for there then, but don't go on down this road if I don't come back."

"What are you—what do you think it could be?" ap Erbin asked.

"I don't know, that's what's worrying me," I said.

The five armigers were formed up. I noticed with resignation that one of them was Ulf. I joined them, and the scout led us ahead along the road.

The road came out of the cutting and ran straight downhill towards a loop in the river. Northeast the river curved away in its valley, southwest it went into the trees. Directly ahead, where the river was nearest to the road, lay the burning ship. Most of it was sunk into the mud. The keel and stem were sticking out and smoldering, sending up a smoke. It was pointed upstream as if it had come through Aylsfa from the sea. It could have held about fifty warriors. It was too burned down to be worth trying to salvage.

"Where are these tracks?" I asked.

The scout pointed to them in the wet ground. "It looks as if a group of men in armor left the ship," he said. "These are deep prints. Armor, or carrying something. They went off that way, towards the highroad, angling towards the woods, south. Then they came back and got on the ship again, or someone did, but I'm almost sure it was the same boots."

"How many?" I asked.

"Half a dozen," he said.

"Why would anyone get back on a burning ship?" ap Padarn asked.

"Could they still be on there, dead?" Mael said, making an evil-eye sign.

"Ghosts don't leave footprints," the scout said, stoutly.

"Why didn't they just sail away again?" Elwith said.

"This is very strange behavior for a Jarnish ship anyway," Ulf said, frowning. "This is a stupid place to raid—why come all this way when there aren't many farms and no rich ones. And you couldn't row that thing with only six—where are the rest of them?"

"There are lots of farms an hour or two south along the highroad towards Thansethan," I said. "There are one or two around here, but that's

all. There's all of Aylsfa nearer to the sea, some of it rich and not too well guarded."

"Unless they were raiding from Aylsfa, or from Tevin," the scout said.

"That would be breaking the Peace," Elwith said, much too loudly.

"If we hadn't come along here just now, nobody would have known," Beris said, looking at the ship. "Isn't that Ayl's prow-carving?" She pointed into the flames.

"No," I said, squinting at it. It could have been. "Half of Ohtar's ships have gilded prows, not to mention the raiders we fought off that time near Caer Segant."

"I have a very bad feeling," Ulf said, staring gravely at the ship.

I did too, but I wasn't about to say so. If Ayl had broken the Peace, there would be almost no way to bring Aylsfa back within it. I just couldn't believe he would do that. His kingdom had grown strong again, but he had prospered better in peace than he had in war. He had married Penarwen. He had no reason to do this. Nobody did. "Let's go on."

The tracks led to the highroad and into the woods. We went cautiously for fear of ambush, but none came. It was quiet, except for water dripping through the leaves from high above. Then the scout exclaimed—the tracks left the road to go into the woods to the right. I felt again that this was all wrong.

"There's nothing there," Beris said, "no farm or anything. It's a deer track." Ap Padarn scowled and put his hand on his ax.

"Do we follow?" the scout asked me. "It looks as if they went both ways here, in and out. I don't think they're still there. Shall I go and see? The horses will never get through."

That it was a trap seemed more likely than anything else. All the same, we were armed, and there weren't enough of them for an ambush. I jerked my chin up. "We'll go quietly," I said. "Mael, you stay here with the horses. Yell and go for help if you see anything."

We dismounted with enough jingling of harness and huffing of horses to make a mockery of the thought of "quietly." The scout led the way through the trees. My feeling of foreboding got stronger and stronger as we went on, though it was only for a few minutes. My heart was in my throat as we came into a clearing.

There was only one person there, and she was dead. She was bound to the roots of an oak tree, legs spread apart and blood on her pale plump thighs. Her throat had been cut, and her head lolled backwards. Her clothes were soaked with blood. All of us had stopped still as soon as we saw the dead Jarn. Strangely my foreboding had vanished as soon as I saw her, and I just knew that there was something very wrong. I looked around carefully before going forward. It seemed just like any grove, but there were old faded strips of cloth and twists of bone and carvings hung high in the branches of the trees. There was a blackened ring of stones in the middle where long ago something had been burned to the High Gods. I looked at my companions. Elwith was touching her pebble. Beris was making a Horse Mother sign. Ap Padarn was making a sign of the evil eye. The scout was completely still, as if turned to stone. Ulf was being spectacularly sick into a pile of last year's half-rotted leaves. A pile, not a wind-dropped heap; someone had swept the clearing.

I went forward to the body. Her neck had been cut half-through with something very sharp wielded by someone strong. I lifted her head up carefully and felt an unexpected shock of grief. I had not been surprised it was a Jarnish body, most of the people living around here were Jarnish, or half-Jarnish. But now that I saw her face I recognized her. It was Sister Arvlid, the one person who had befriended me at Thansethan. Her pale eyes were open and staring, and her lips were drawn back as if in pain. I remembered her straining honey and pacing with me, missing her festival, when Darien was being born.

Elwith was beside me. "It's Arvlid of Thansethan," she said, and there were tears in her voice. "She used to ride out to the farms and hamlets with medicines and prayers, praying in Jarnish with the Jarnsmen. Her parents live on one of the farms out here. Those raiders must have caught her on her way and brought her here and killed her. Nothing we can do for her now, but we'll get them!"

I closed her eyes and put her head down gently. Then I pulled her skirts down to cover her legs and give her a little more dignity in death. As I did so I caught sight of something in one of her hands. Reflexively, I straightened the skirts again to cover it. "Why would they bring her here?" I asked. My voice sounded strange in my ears. Ulf was still vomiting loudly, but otherwise the wood was very still.

"Who knows why those raiders do anything," she said, angrily.

"Come here, Ulf," I said. "You know why raiders do things, tell me why they might have done this." His skin was as whiter than milk as he came forward, and his beard was stained and revolting. He couldn't seem to stop retching, though only air and bile was coming out now. The spasms wracked him. "Drink some water and pull yourself together," I said. "If I can stand to look at this, you can. This was a friend of mine, a holy sister from Thansethan."

Silently ap Padarn gave Ulf his waterskin. Ulf poured it over his head, some of it went in his mouth. "They—they—" and he fell to the ground retching the water out again, lying full length in the loam at my feet. I managed to refrain from kicking him, but it was a close thing.

"Elwith, go and tell ap Erbin we're all right, and get him to bring the troops down to the road. Then tell him—just him—to come in here and see this. Don't tell the others what we've found. I want everyone to stay calm. Beris, you go with the scout, quietly, and go around this clearing and see if you find anything at all. If you do, come back and tell me, but I'd be surprised. She's been dead all day, and they got back onto that burning ship."

"Nobody would get onto a burning ship," Elwith protested. "Unless the White God struck it by lightning to set it on fire and punish them for their crimes."

It was a better explanation than anything I had. But they had probably left in another ship, whatever their reason for burning that one had been. "If he was going to strike people by lightning it would have been better if he'd done it in time to save Arvlid, not just avenge her," I said. "I think they've gone, but I'm not sure, so keep watching out."

Elwith went back to the horses, and the others left. Ulf lay in the dirt retching helplessly. "Have you any more water?" I asked ap Padarn. He shook his head. "Go back to Mael and get his waterskin," I said.

As soon as he had gone I bent over Arvlid and drew out the piece of cloth I had glimpsed in her hand. It was a torn scrap of light red cloth the color and width of the streamers Ayl used like a banner. It didn't look as if she had clutched at it; it looked as if it had been pressed into her dead fingers. I put it inside my tunic; then I did kick Ulf, just once and not very hard.

"Get up. I know you didn't do it. I don't think it was Jarnish raiders at all. How would they know to come to this place? This is a trap, and if we don't want to be caught by it we have got to talk!" He groaned. Ap Padarn came back with the water. I poured it over Ulf.

"Never would have thought he had such a weak stomach," ap Padarn said. "Not a pretty sight I'll agree, but you don't see me puking on the ground."

"No," I agreed, crisply. "Go back to Mael, and when the others come remind ap Erbin to come in. Don't spread rumors among the others, and don't tell them what you've seen; we don't want more lost breakfasts."

When he had gone, Ulf sat up. He looked disgusting, splashed with vomit and dirt and with twigs and dirt sticking to his wet hair. He could not meet my eyes, and he looked ashamed to be alive.

"I'm sorry," he said, feebly. "It's just I have nightmares—"

"You didn't do this," I said. He couldn't have done it, but he could have caused it to be done. I had believed what he had said in the sight of the gods on Foreth, but I had to be sure. I put my hand on my sword ready to kill him if I had to.

"Of course not," he said. "No. I could never—"

"Someone wanted me to find it and act in fury," I said, as sure of it as I ever had been of anything. I took my hand off my sword and looked down at Arvlid's body. "If I had ridden into Aylsfa and fired the fields in vengeance for Arvlid, Ayl would have fought, and that would have been the end of Urdo's Peace."

"You're not going to, are you?" Ulf asked, groggily.

"Don't be ridiculous, I've never been further from hot fury in my life." In fact I felt as cold and hard and brittle as ice. "But think. Whoever did this aimed it at me like a knife to the heart. They killed Arvlid to break the Peace, I think. Who was it? If this was meant whoever did this knew, Ulf. They knew something only you and I and six dead men know. Who have you told?"

"Nobody." He shook his head, dazedly, looking up at me. "Nobody, not that they could know to do this. Half the men of Jarnholme know that I was lamed by a woman on a raid in Tir Tanagiri, but I didn't know who you were. I have said nothing to anyone since the judgment."

"Ohtar, Urdo—nobody else at all? I have never told anyone."

"From what we said on Foreth there would not have been enough to know it was an oak tree—an ash would be the tree for the Raven Lord," Ulf said, slowly, stumblingly. He looked up for the first time and saw the bones and bundles hanging in the branches. "What is this place?" A few drops of rain came down through the leaves and fell on his upturned face; he brushed them off irritably.

"An old place of worship for my gods, I think, though nobody has been here for a long time, twenty years maybe. Who else could have known? Think!"

He was silent a while. "Nobody," he said. "A handful of Jarnsmen know where. They are all of them in Jarnholme or dead, I think. Ragnald Torrensson and my brother Arling know where and hate you. But they don't know enough to have done this." He gestured but did not look. "Could they not have meant an atrocity for whoever came?"

"Maybe, but this is beyond coincidence, this was aimed at me, or at you and me, by malice."

"Would you have thought, if I had not been here, that I—" He could not go on. Though there was nothing inside him, the noises he made were disgusting.

"No," I said, though I wasn't sure if I would or not. "You spoke the truth on Foreth, and I believe you."

"I didn't tell anyone," he said, gulping air. I gave him the waterskin, and he took a deep draught. "Nobody could know from me, unless they read my dreams, and such things are only in old stories."

I thought at once of Morwen of Angas, and the thought felt right, though she was dead. Morwen the witch-queen. "Old stories?" I said. "You should never sleep near people you do not trust, especially if you have screaming dreams that wake up half the camp." I rubbed my eyes and reached out to the Lord of Light for clarity. "Is this very like your dreams?" I asked. "It does not seem to me as like as all that."

Ulf staggered to his feet and looked at Arvlid, breathing carefully. "We cut your dress off," he said, just loud enough for me to hear. "But in my dreams they pull my tunic up."

I didn't know what to say. Ap Erbin came through the trees a few minutes later to find us standing silently, not looking at each other.

"What's going on?" ap Erbin asked. "Elwith said—" He came forward and knelt beside Arvlid.

"Gunnarsson, go back to the others," I said. Ulf turned and left without a word, not looking at me.

"Someone is trying to make me angry," I said to ap Erbin.

"It sounds to me as if they've succeeded," ap Erbin said, looking up at me, puzzled. "I've never seen you so furious."

"I don't think this is the sort of angry they want," I said. "What do you think of what you've seen?"

"Sulien?"

"Tell me what you think," I said, speaking through my teeth.

"A dead monk, a longship on fire for no good reason—a Jarnish raid, though a bit inland for one. Maybe some kind of ambush somewhere, which is what you thought when you rode down here. Why are you so very upset?"

I took the cloth out again and showed it to him. "This was in her hand."

He gasped and drew back. "Ayl? But why?"

"If I said we were going to ride into Aylsfa and punish this would you come?" I asked. I raised a hand as soon as he started to speak. "Look a bit closer. What is this place? Why here? Why did they burn the ship? What did they gain by it? How likely is it that she should have torn a banner if she was struggling? A banner of all things, when Ayl only has one? This is a trap, for us and for Ayl. This was done by some enemy of the Peace, and I have to see clearly what to do next."

Ap Erbin frowned and turned the cloth in his hands. "Who could have done it? Why?"

"Someone who hates us and wants dissension. Someone who knew we would be riding down this road today and wanted us to find these things. Who could it be?"

"Arling Gunnarsson? Atha ap Gren?" Ap Erbin's frown deepened as he looked up at the bundles in the trees. "Cinon of Nene? Flavien ap Borthas? Someone who knew the land well."

"The land, of course. That's what to do about it!" I said, interrupting. "Are we in Nene here, or still in Tevin?"

"I think this is actually Segantia, just," ap Erbin said. "We're half a day from Thansethan. Why? What difference does it make?"

"The calm answer to something designed to make us angry is to have a judgment," I said. "This is a murder. I am sure there's something about murder in Urdo's law code, or there will be when it's finished. I want to gather them all here to see justice done to whoever did this. I am angry: I am so angry I want to tear their hearts out. They took Arvlid's life, Arvlid who never did any harm and much good, and they killed her not for anything she was or was not, but just to trick me and break the Peace. I will gather them all here, and I will have the land say who did this."

"Sulien, what are you talking about?" Ap Erbin stood and put his hand on my shoulder. "You're not making sense."

"Somebody who hates us wanted to goad me into breaking the Peace. They thought that this would do it," I said, as calmly as I could. "It might have worked if they had done it better, if I hadn't seen through it. I need to find out who it was to stop them trying again and doing better next time. I need justice done in the open."

"It could have been raiders. She was always riding out from Thansethan, Elwith said."

"This cloth was prepared in advance," I said, but even as I spoke I remembered Darien's letters, saying he rode out with her. If this was an attack aimed at me, where was he? "Stay here," I said. "Camp by the river. Keep a guard on this clearing. Send scouts out as far as you can and bring in anyone you find, both directions on the river. I am going to Thansethan, and then to Caer Tanaga. I will come back with Urdo, I should be back in five or six days, or I will send word."

"I don't understand," ap Erbin said, sounding dazed. "You said they wouldn't let you in at Thansethan? Why are you going? Calm down a moment."

I took a deep deliberate breath, and then another. I reached out to the Lord of Light and felt calm coming closer to me.

"I need to get Urdo and everyone here," I said. "I need to find out if anyone else has been hurt. My son is at Thansethan, and he sometimes rode out with Arvlid."

Ap Erbin stared at me a moment. "Send messengers," he said. "Send scouts all round in groups. You can't do any more than they could. We should set up camp here, by the river. A proper camp with a ditch and rampart. Those raiders or whoever they are have gone somewhere, and not up in smoke."

He was right, and I knew it. I wanted my enemies drawn up in a shield wall before my lowered lance, everything is so easy then. It was the gods' help that gave me the clarity I had, not to go tearing off in my rage and break the Peace myself.

"I'll write the messages. You send out the scouting groups and get the camp started."

"What about—" He gestured to Arvlid's body. "Should we send her back to Thansethan or bury her here?"

"What would be usual in her faith?" I asked. "I only know what they do for people killed in battle. Would it be different for a monk? We're not far from Thansethan: let's just cover her for now and ask them what they want done. And we must keep the armigers away from here: this is a terrible place. Post two guards here, but don't let everyone come and trample about. Let's all get back to the river, and get people out as soon as we can."

—35—

Come little warrior, kick your toes.
Come little shieldman, touch your nose.
Come little warrior, make a fist
Come little shieldman, snatch my wrist.

Come little warrior, duck your head,
Fast, little shieldman, fast or dead.
                    —Jarnish nursery rhyme game

The first report came from the half pennon sent across the river into
Aylsfa. They found signs that a group of people, nine or ten, had left
the water a little way past the bend downstream and headed off inland.
They tracked them for a mile or two cross-country towards a hamlet, but
the tracks vanished into a coppice. They thought from the prints there
might have been a boy with them, someone with smaller feet. The scout
looked wretched and could not meet my eyes when she told me. I sent
another group with some of the best scouts out that way, but nobody could
pick up any trail after they went into the trees.

I paced in the rain all afternoon and everyone kept clear of me except
more scouts bringing inconclusive reports. Everyone was occupied, either
scouting or setting up camp under ap Erbin's direction. After a while, when
most people were eating, Elidir came up and waited for me to notice her.
She had brought some smoked ham and pan bread. I ate it standing up,
choking down each mouthful as if it had been an acorn cake.

A party from Thansethan arrived at the camp just before dusk. It was a
much larger group than I had been expecting. Ap Selevan's whole pennon
was there, with a whole cluster of brown-robed monks riding in the middle. Father Gerthmol was among them, with Raul and nine or ten others.

Ap Selevan came up to me as soon as he had dismounted. "The Queen
insisted we all come, Praefecto," he said. "She said she was safe behind
strong walls in Thansethan, and you might have need of us."

"May the Lady of Wisdom bless her for her good sense!" I said, really
meaning it. Elenn had done me a great favor here, in sending them and in
not coming herself. Another pennon increased my choices greatly—a half
ala made a good-sized fighting force against anything we were reasonably
likely to encounter. Ap Selevan stood there, stolid as ever, dripping from his
riding cape, waiting for instructions. "Set up camp as always: ap Erbin will
tell you where," I said. "Oh, and ask Father Gerthmol if he can spare me a
moment tonight."

Even ap Selevan knew enough about my relationship with Thansethan
to raise his eyebrows at this. "Yes, Praefecto," he said.

"Ask him as politely as you can," I said, and he jerked his chin up and
went off.

I would rather have made a forced march across a marsh in midge mating season carrying my own weight in turnips than talk to Father Gerthmol just then, but I had to know about Darien. I paced a little while longer, waiting for him.

He came up to me with a companion, another brown-robed priest. I remembered him from Thansethan, he was Father Geneth. He had told me the grindingly dull story of his conversion four times, sure that it must move me eventually. They both bowed, and I bowed in return. Father Geneth began by asking about Arvlid. We spoke about her for a little while, making arrangements for a funeral the next sunset. He did not take his hand off his pebble the whole time. Father Gerthmol neither spoke nor looked at me but acted as if he were standing alone in a field. I waited for them to mention Darien. I had asked about his safety in the message I had sent to Thansethan. At last, when it seemed they would leave at any moment, I was forced to ask again.

They looked at each other. Father Gerthmol looked back into the distance beyond my shoulder. Father Geneth met my eyes for a moment, then looked down at the hem of his robe and his sandalled feet below it. "Young Suliensson rode out with Sister Arvlid yesterday as usual," he said.

I don't remember what they said next or how they left me. I paced some more until eventually ap Erbin dragged me off to my tent and made me swallow a cup of some vile Demedian drink he had. From the taste it must have been made of mashed turnips and linen-seed oil, but it burned hot all the way down and he meant well by it. I must have slept that night because I remember waking up in the dawn with a raging thirst.

It rained all the next day. I paced again, almost wearing a rut through the mud of the camp. I kept expecting every report to be that Darien's body had been found. Instead the reports were curiously empty. It seemed there was nobody and nothing moving as far as they could reach. A red-cloak came in from Caer Rangor in the late afternoon saying that Luth and Cinon had gone out hunting, separately, and had not returned, but the message would wait their return. I hadn't been on a hunt that lasted more than a day since Angas went back to Demedia. I cursed them for being off indulging themselves when I needed them. The news of Luth would have been a worse blow if I had been without ap Selevan's pennon. I blessed Elenn again in my heart.

At sunset they buried Arvlid in the grove where she had died. There was a stir when I arrived with the others. There were so many of us there who had been her friends that there was no room in the grove, and we had to stand back among the trees. I think Father Gerthmol would have sent me away, but Raul said something to him and they let me stay. If he was expecting a spectacular conversion, he was disappointed.

It was a calm and quiet service. Father Gerthmol spoke about her—how as a young girl she had warned Thansethan about Goldpate's attack and how she had lived there so long and served the White God. Now, he said, she had been taken to Him and would serve Him in eternal and everlasting worship. Then we sang and everyone piled earth on the mound afterwards, just as if she had fallen in battle. They cut down the grove later, all but the one oak, and built a church and a monastery. Ap Erbin built his house near there, and I hear that now a little town has grown up around it in the river bend, a real town with a school and a marketplace and a stable for the red-cloaks to change horses. Everyone calls the place Thanarvlid. It is not such a bad way to be remembered. I think if she had known that in dying she was making a town and a center for the Jarnsmen who lived in those parts, she would have been glad of it. It is true that she loved the White God and served him all her life, but she also loved her people and tried to do her best for them. That is why she used to ride out among them after all. It wasn't only prayers she took them but medicine and other help. If they were all like Arvlid, I would like the monks much better.

After the service I tried to speak to Raul, but Father Gerthmol would have none of it and almost snatched him away. After that I paced again until ap Erbin asked me if it was helping, and I snapped at him. Then I went and groomed my horses. They didn't need grooming, the groom had taken good care of them. It did calm me enough to sleep.

The next day was the same. I still didn't want to eat or talk to anyone at all. The same thoughts kept going round and round in my head. Every time I saw a party coming back I felt certain the next report would be that Darien's body had been found. Arvlid had been there when he was born; had he been there when she died? Had all that pain and trouble been for nothing, for him to die so young? I had hardly known him. Then I felt angry with myself for being so selfish as to think of my pain and trouble when it was his life that he would have to start all over again after such a short time. Then I would start thinking about revenging myself on whoever had set this up, but being very sure who it was first. This led me into the other maze of trying to puzzle out who had done this and why.

The only new news to reach us that third day was a message from Penarwen that Ayl was away from Fenshal, hunting. No more news came from Cinon and Luth at Caer Rangor, which suggested that they had not returned.

That evening, as I was sitting on a log grooming my horses and thinking in futile circles, I felt Glimmer move sideways uneasily and I realized someone had come up and was standing a little way behind. I drew my hand across my eyes to block the fire's glare and turned around.

It was Ulf, looming over me in the half-light. I was surprised. I had been expecting ap Erbin or Elidir fussing over me again. Most of the others had been avoiding me.

"I'm sorry to disturb you, Praefecto," he said. I stood up; I didn't want him to have any advantage over me.

"What?" I asked, ungraciously.

He took a deep breath. "Whose child is it they are saying is lost?"

"Mine," I said, shortly.

"I knew that," he said. "I have heard 'Suliensson this' and 'Suliensson that' ever since ap Selevan got in. How old is this son of yours?"

I felt a sudden surge of anger. "I don't know what right you think you have to ask me that sort of question?" Glimmer caught my mood and threw up his head and huffed loudly in challenge. The other horses shifted uneasily.

"No right at all," Ulf said, bleakly, as if that were answer enough. It was too dim to make out his features, but I saw him shudder. "But however much Ohtar called me a fool, I think I was right—you are suited to Gangrader and he likes you. I wish he would be content with you and leave me alone."

"Your choice of gods is your own affair, Ulf Gunnarsson," I said. "I don't see why you need to disturb me with it now."

"Because this boy who is lost is your son, you who have never been married, and because you think that the gods are on the side of peace. Gangrader is not like that, he is a god of war-strife and death in battle and vicious jokes."

"It would not be to Gangrader's benefit to have Ayl and his people slaughtered and civil wars come again," I said, quietly. "Even the harvest of the battle crows must grow to ripeness. And despite your dedication and whatever you think, I have always served Urdo and the Peace of the High Kingdom."

"Oh well I know that," said Ulf, and there was a catch that was almost a sob in his voice. "Yours is always the way of honor. But beware of Gangrader's promises, he will twist them. If that certainty that was burning through you in the grove was his certainty, then distrust it."

"If I was in the hand of any god to see clearly the trap laid for me then I do not think it was your Raven Lord," I said, as calmly as I could, wondering if Ulf was drunk. "I will bear what you say in mind, but Gangrader has never made me any promises, and so he cannot twist them."

"Shall I tell you what he promised me?" Ulf asked, leaning closer and whispering. "He promised me a son of my blood would sit on the throne of Tir Tanagiri. My father was king in Jarnholme, and Sweyn was my uncle, it did not seem so unlikely. So I came here with Sweyn, thinking we had been promised victory right up until we lost. And since that I—well, never mind, but Gangrader twists his promises, and I have a son already, don't I? They say you and Urdo are lovers. They say this boy is Urdo's son. I may be an idiot Jarn, but they say he is thirteen years old and I can count. I remember what Urdo said on Foreth. This is exactly the sort of joke Gangrader loves, and why aren't we laughing?"

"Because the boy is very likely dead?" I forced myself to say. The words came out sounding harsh and cold. "Which rather spoils any joke. I will say nothing of his father. It is nothing to do with you, you have no claim on him. He was born at Thansethan nine months after I took service with the High King."

"It would spoil the joke entirely, and so I expect he is alive, preserved by some strange chance. I expect I will die tomorrow," Ulf said, entirely calmly. "That usually happens when Gangrader has arranged for someone to see the point of one of his jokes."

"Ulf," I said, wearily, "if we have a battle tomorrow and we get the chance to charge, I'll happily put you in the front, and if you truly feel like dying you can charge naked and painted blue like the Isarnagans. I don't care. It will make my life easier. But I don't think this is the sort of fight where we'll be so lucky as to have the enemies clearly marked out to be hacked to pieces. If my son is alive, I ask you to say nothing to him or to anyone else of any question of his parentage. We settled our quarrel at Foreth."

"I will not say anything." He trailed off as if he wanted to say something else but could not find the words.

"While you're here," I said, "tell me who might have read your dreams? All the women and half the men in your pennon from what I hear, but who else?"

"Half my pennon if you like to say so, but why would any in the ala wish us harm?" he asked. Put like that it sounded reasonable. "Before I came to the ala?" He paused. "Comrades, who are dead or in Jarnholme with my aunt and my brother, or now in Alfwin's service. Servants. It's hard to think that anyone who chose to share blankets with me would do such a thing."

I could see that it might be. "But any of those people might have a grudge against us now, against you, and have no reason to love Ayl."

"Maybe. And maybe enough to have reason to hate you for killing their friends. Who does hate you?"

"I don't know." It was a horrible question. I couldn't think of anyone who hated me personally. I had killed Jarnsmen enough, but never outside the usage of war. I wouldn't be surprised if they came at me with a knife, but this sort of thing meant real malice. And Darien—I bit my lip. I thought again of Morwen, who had hated me and was dead. "How close to you did Morwen of Angas come?"

He shuddered, I could see it clearly though it had grown too dark to see his face. "She could never have come close to me while I slept," he said. "Anyway she has been dead for years."

"It felt to me like her doing. Like Caer Lind," I said. "I know very well she's dead. I had a part in it. How about her son?"

"Morthu?" Ulf hesitated. "Yes, we shared blankets once or twice, when he first came to the ala. But when he first came from Thansethan Morthu acted like a filly with the spring air in her face; he wasn't always careful about hurting people's feelings. He sought me out, then mocked me afterwards. I don't like him, now that I know him. But why would he hate you?"

"I'm probably being unfair to Morthu," I said, "but I did kill his mother." He was here, he was in ap Selevan's pennon. I had been aware of him watching me pacing several times.

"He's never said anything against you that I've heard," Ulf said, slowly. "Not for his mother's rebellion, nor against the High King. He does speak well of his brother and of Demedia, and he has mentioned that he is a grandson of Avren often enough that nobody's likely to forget it. But what could he want? What could he gain?"

"The grandson of Avren might want the crown of Tir Tanagiri?" I suggested.

"Starting up the War again wouldn't get him that," Ulf said. "Even if he could kill Urdo it would not. He is very young and has less right than his brother. Very few would support such a claim. He would do better to befriend Urdo and be made his heir."

"Then I don't know!" I said, too loudly. The horses shifted uneasily, and I was aware of the camp beyond them, the ditch, the river. I would have liked to mount up and gallop flat out as fast and as far as I could. "I hate waiting!" I said, with sudden impatience. "I wish there was something to do."

36

The Law shall be no one person's tool, to work the will of kings or to thwart it; it shall be the shield of many against one, and the shield of one against many, and the wall between strife of kin. To do these things it must be made so that the law is composed of the best will, the best judgment, and the best wisdom that can be found among many people, and made each time it is made with a clear heart and a choice of what best serves those living and those yet to be born.
— The Law Code of Urdo ap Avren

There were two more days of waiting and pacing and fretting before Urdo came and everything happened at once. I had kept a wide sentry ring out all the time and had news whenever anyone was moving, which was rare enough. There was still no news from Cinon or Ayl or Luth. I had begun to disbelieve the hunting story. It wasn't the weather to linger outside for pleasure. A messenger got in from Alfwin saying that he was on his way. Even though he would not reach me for days I was relieved to know that not every king in the island was lost out hunting. I was very aware how unprepared we were for a civil war. In the afternoon Father Geneth had the nerve to ask me for ap Selevan's pennon back to escort them home to Thansethan. He caught the sharp end of my fraying patience and retreated angrily back to his brothers.

The day Urdo arrived dawned with a thick and persistent mist off the river. The sun could just be made out as a glow in the whiteness. Urdo arrived out of the fogs late in the afternoon, escorted by the scouts who had been out along the road. He had the other half of my ala with him.

"We almost turned back to Thansethan," Gormant told me while Urdo was greeting Father Gerthmol with careful politeness. "We could barely make out the highroad. It's lighter here than it was a way down the road. We're not going to find anything today. What's going on anyway?"

Then Urdo came up to me, and I tried to get my explanations in order. "Where's—" he began, but before he could say any more a huge silvery white dog ran between us. I blinked at it with a strange feeling of recognition. It had come so close I had felt the wind of its passage, but I had no idea where it had come from. It was the biggest dog I had ever seen, bigger even than Elenn's Isarnagan hound. It was almost the size of a small pony. I drew breath to speak, but then the air was full of wild yapping and howling, and people shouting.

There was a tremendous disturbance in the middle of the camp. The ground was shaking. There was a huge shape, black, thrice the breadth of a horse. There was a great rank smell with it that made my stomach turn over. There were white dogs circling it and there were other dogs, too, ordinary hunting dogs. There were people charging in through the tents and lines, mounted, with boar spears. My eyes suddenly made sense of what I was seeing, and I understood that this monster was a boar the size of the boar in the song that Kilok hunted to make the bristles into a comb for his giant father-in-law. Urdo and Gormant and I ran frantically towards the horse lines; nobody on foot has much chance against even an ordinary boar. Other armigers were doing the same thing, and people were yelling and getting in each other's way. I saw Father Gerthmol running away as fast as he could with his robe hitched up around his waist, looking very undignified.

All the horses were very nervous, and many people around me were having trouble getting control. Once I was mounted I could see better, despite the fog. Ap Padarn threw me a spear and I snatched it out of the air. We were behind the boar. The great creature was too tall for me to see over, even mounted, but I could see around him. He had his head lowered and was ignoring the dogs that were running in to nip at him. There was a picket rope tangled around one of his back feet. Even from behind I could see that his tusks were longer than spears and wickedly curved. Several of the hounds had already perished on their points. One of them lay crushed like an old barrel.

To the left of the boar was Ayl, riding a piebald half horse. His brother Sidrok was next to him bearing Ayl's hideous standard, the pink streamers flying back all around it. There was a party of other Jarnsmen from Aylsfa with them: all had their boar spears ready. Ayl looked much as he always did hunting.

In the center, directly ahead of the boar, was Cinon of Nene, on foot. He had only an ordinary spear and a sword. He looked confused and hurt as if someone had just said something that might have been an insult and he wasn't sure how to take it. There were a dozen or so armsmen of his household with him, all men. Right next to him stood my son Darien. His hands were tied together behind him. I was vastly relieved to see him, weaponless and on foot but alive. He had his teeth bared at the boar and seemed poised to spring at it, as if daring it to come on.

To the right of the boar was Luth, on a dappled mare, in his famous blue breastplate, holding a boar spear. He had his pennon with him, similarly armed. He looked as if he couldn't quite believe the size of the boar, but he was signaling to his armigers and clearly selecting his best angle and lowering his spear to go in before the boar decided to move. They looked almost capable of dealing with it.

The boar, strangely, was acting as if it had been cornered in a thicket, despite being in the open in the center of the camp.

This takes time to describe, which it did not take to see. I was already moving in from behind. It seemed to me that if I set my spear straight and moved in from the side with all Glimmer's weight and mine I might just make a heart hit, or at worst turn it from Darien towards me, or towards Luth and his people, who were ready for it. Glimmer wanted to shy away when the breeze brought us a clear scent of it, and I had to urge him on with my knees.

Boars are often fast, though usually the smaller ones are faster than the big ones. Still I was surprised when it charged. It went straight forward towards Cinon and Darien. I could not stop, so I held my spear tightly and rode on, fast. We hit, but the tip of the spear just skittered off the skin. I don't know what happened next. Glimmer tripped, I think, in one of the creature's deep footprints, and threw me off up over his head. I let go of the spear, it would have broken my arm. I pulled my feet from the stirrups and leapt, almost by reflex.

For an instant as I was in the air I saw it clearly. The world was a black boar below me with white dogs circling around it and beyond that people on horses circling and beyond them distant trees. Glimmer had gone on straight after I had left him and was making for the river. It was only then when I saw it whole from above that I knew this was no monstrous beast but a creature of the gods. It was mighty and beautiful and terrible. It had a dignity that was like the dignity of an animal who lives wild and has nothing to do with people, but stronger than that any individual animal can have, even one that had lived to be old. I don't know why I didn't see this when I was down on the ground, but I had not. In that moment in the air I knew other things, too, my own place in the pattern of the world, and Darien's, and Urdo's. It slipped away from me almost as soon as I had seen it; that is not a sight any mortal mind can hold on to and stay sane.

Then I landed on top of the boar. It was not a good landing. It was like hitting the side of a moving mountain or being thumped by an enormous fist. All the breath was knocked out of me, and I felt bruised all over. Even breathing was effortful, and the powerful stink of the boar did not help. It was a moment before I could see, and even then it was hard to raise my head. Darien was there, somehow, beside me, lying completely winded across the harsh thick bristles of the boar's shoulder. I drew another difficult and deliberate breath and then I grabbed him. I heard Urdo shout and saw that he was cantering beside the boar. He looked a long way down. I took hold of Darien and heaved him off, half-sliding and half-throwing him to Urdo.

Then I jumped backwards and was amazed to be caught halfway through the sickening plunge towards the ground. Once again all the breath was driven out of my body. I heard Luth laughing close to me, and after a moment I realized I was lying facedown across his mare's withers. We kept speed with the boar and the three great white dogs that chased it for just an instant, then Luth let his horse fall back and turned her so that we faced back to Urdo and Darien. I noticed to my surprise as they came into sight that Ayl was with them.

Every gasp of breath felt like a victory. Even though the whole fight only seemed to have taken a moment or two we had come so far outside the camp and up onto the hillside that the uproar there seemed quite distant. Luth was still laughing as we drew to a halt. I didn't have breath to move, and I couldn't have sat up from that position, draped in front of him like a sack of turnips. I slid down to the ground, and promptly fell over. My legs wouldn't hold me. I felt ridiculous and terribly undignified, partly because Ayl joined Luth in laughing. Then Urdo dismounted and set Darien down gently on the ground. He was better able to stand than I was; he'd had a gentler landing the second time. From the look of it Urdo had caught him in his arms rather than across his horse.

"Well done!" Luth said to Ayl, slapping him on the back. "We both took it the same moment from different sides. You were right there. If it had been even a little smaller I think we'd have brought it down."

"We would," Ayl said, beaming. "I'd like to hunt with you again, something more our size."

Urdo cut the cord around Darien wrists with his knife. Darien rubbed one and then the other. "Where are you hurt?" Urdo asked me.

"I'm fine," I said, then lost what breath I had to coughing. Luth started laughing again.

"One of these days you'll die from wounds you never noticed you'd taken," Urdo said, looking down at me. He was smiling. But I wasn't wounded, only bruised all over from landing so hard both times. The only blood was where my face was scraped from the boar's bristles.

"What was it?" Darien asked, gazing off into the fog where the boar had vanished. His robe was torn in several places, and his face and arms were scratched, but his voice sounded stronger than mine did.

"A huge boar," Luth said. "I've been tracking it for days and I've got quite lost. I've no idea where we are."

"I've been trying to get hold of you for days," I panted. "What if there'd been an invasion?"

"There hasn't, has there?" Luth asked, looking so startled that I laughed, almost choking with it.

"I've been tracking it for days, too," Ayl said, frowning a little. "I never saw prints that size before. But where were you coming from, Luth, that I didn't see you on the trail? And where are we anyway?"

"I came from Caer Rangor," Luth said, carelessly. It must be wonderful to have a head solid bone all through like that with no room for ideas.

Urdo looked at Darien. "It was not just a huge boar that folk can track from the southeast and the northwest at the same time. It was the Black Boar, Turth," he said. "He's one of the protectors of Tir Tanagiri."

When I heard the name it was as if I'd had confirmed something I knew already. I looked off up the hill after him, but there was already nothing to be seen but the huge prints leading away. Turth was done with us and gone on his own affairs. I wondered why he had come to us out of the mists. To save Darien? To punish Cinon? I took another painful breath.

"A demon?" Darien asked, his voice rising. Ayl looked shocked.

"A spirit, certainly," Urdo said, evenly.

"He didn't hurt me," Darien said, shakily.

"You're as bad as your mother," Urdo said, smiling and shaking his head.

"If I'd known, I should have tried to tell him about the White God and then he—" Darien stopped, and laughed. "Well it's hard to imagine something like that eternally praising," he explained. Ayl and Luth laughed, too. Ayl sat down beside me on the heather the better to have his laugh out.

I did not laugh. Facing that wild dignity to try to make Turth change direction with words would be as futile as doing it with spears. "Father Gerthmol was there, and he didn't try and convert him either," I said. "In fact, he ran away pretty rapidly. So I don't think you need to blame yourself for not trying."

Darien looked at Urdo. "I didn't know there were things like that?"

"All part of the world," Urdo said, gently.

"Chanerig fought things like *that*?" Darien asked. I hated the thought of that even more than when Thurrig had first told me.

"I broke a good boar spear trying it," Luth said.

Ayl gazed thoughtfully down at the tracks the creature had left. "I suppose we just goaded him with our spears?"

"Mine went in a little way, I think," I said.

"He didn't hurt me," Darien repeated. "He didn't hurt—" He looked at me, and floundered for a moment, clearly unsure what to call me. "Er, you, either."

"Neither of you had done anything to anger him," Urdo said. "Unless you count spearing him and flinging yourselves on top of him. Did you *jump* onto Turth's shoulder, Darien?"

Darien squirmed. "I—yes. I went between the tusks. It seemed like there wasn't anywhere else to go right then, the others were all flinging themselves flat but I couldn't see what good it would do."

"It was the best of a bad set of choices," I agreed.

"The tusks slice from beneath," Ayl explained. "If you're flat on the ground the pig has to stop and root you over, or bite you, to get his tusks under you, and they don't want to stop. Didn't help them this time, though—some of them got trodden on. I caught that out of the corner of my eye when I was looking at ap Gwien vaulting onto the top of the thing."

"He gored Cinon through the thigh and trampled about half of his men," Urdo said.

"Whatever had Cinon done to make Turth so angry?" Luth asked, not laughing at all now.

"I suppose it was probably killing Sister Arvlid," Darien said. We all turned to look at him. "Or maybe stealing King Ayl's boat and setting it on fire? They ambushed us as we were going along the road. We thought they were friends to start with. They were going to kill me, too, I think, when they got to the right place, except I was going to run away as soon as I got a chance. They'd untied my legs so I could walk, and I was going to run fast as soon as I had sight of somewhere to run to. Only then it got foggy when we were in the wood and then everyone was there."

Luth opened and shut his mouth a few times, before managing to say "Cinon?" in an astonished squeak.

It took Ayl a little longer to absorb what Darien had said, and say, "My boat? What boat?"

"When was this?" I asked Darien, ignoring them. "How long ago did they ambush you?"

"This morning," said Darien, definitely.

"The gods have been looking after you," I said. My breathing was a lot easier now. "It was five days ago." I looked at Urdo, and he looked back at me for a long moment.

"People get murdered all the time without the gods doing anything at all!" Luth said. "And why did Cinon do all that?"

"Maybe Turth came because he made a sacrifice of a holy sister in a sacred grove in an attempt to break the Peace," I said. But I knew he had come to save Darien; I knew that Darien would be important one day. Urdo glanced at me swiftly.

"Break the Peace?" Luth rubbed his forehead as if it hurt. "Cinon?"

"She was a Jarnish monk from Thansethan," Urdo put in, "and the intention in stealing his royal ship was to make it look as if Ayl had done it."

"Oh!" Luth looked as if that made much more sense. Then he looked at Ayl in a puzzled kind of way.

Ayl just gaped. "My ship? As if I had been raiding and killed a holy sister of Thansethan?" If I hadn't been sure of his innocence before, the complete bewilderment on his face would have settled it.

"It looked very convincing," I said. "If I'd come over the river with troops and attacked you, you'd not have stopped to ask me what I was doing, would you?"

"I suppose not," he said. "Cinon." He shook his head. "Cinon has never trusted me at all, or any Jarns, but he has never made a secret of it. That is more cunning than I had expected to find in him."

"Or I, come to that," said Urdo, frowning.

"Some of it was very stupid," I said. "It does make sense to think it was someone stupid following a plan made by someone cleverer."

"Who, then?" Urdo asked.

"Flavien ap Borthas?" I suggested. "And maybe—" But I looked at Ayl and didn't mention my suspicions about Morthu just then. He was married to Morthu's sister after all. "I thought he would have to have a public trial," I said, instead, because they were all looking at me. "I thought that would be the only way to clear Ayl. I wasn't expecting that boar at all. But if Cinon did it and he is dead, are we going to tell everyone?"

"That Cinon met a king's death in a hunting accident?" Luth asked.

"Or that the gods of the island killed him before me for giving them a sacrifice he had no right to give in a place that was not his," Urdo said. "Those would seem to be the choices. This is the time to decide, now before everyone else gets here."

"What best serves the Peace?" I asked.

"That it was bandits out of Jarnholme who killed Sister Arvlid and the hope that Cinon's son shall learn to be better friends with his neighbors than his father," Urdo said. "Whoever planned this will have learned that this sort of attack on us does not work."

"Or that they will have to plan better next time," I said. I could hear the sound of hoofbeats; it sounded as if a pennon was coming towards us from the camp.

"Or that," Urdo agreed. "All the same there are many in Nene who thought as Cinon did and need time to learn better. Disgracing him after his death would only make them hate us more. But though I was wronged by these actions I was not wronged as much as you, Darien, and you, Ayl. If Cinon lived I would have brought him to justice for his crimes whatever the cost."

"He has been punished by the gods," Ayl said. "That will do for me, though I would have the price of my ship from his heirs."

"That is fair," Urdo said. "And you, Darien?"

"For myself, I would have the Peace," Darien said, sounding very grown-up, but at the same time just like a little boy. "But there is also Sister Arvlid, and so you should ask this question of Thansethan. You said Father Gerthmol is here?"

That was one of the very few times I ever saw Urdo look entirely surprised. "Then it will come out," he said. "Father Gerthmol dislikes me now and does not care for my Peace."

"He can forgive anything except someone deliberately turning their back on God," Darien said, as if he were quoting.

"And does he think that I have?" Urdo asked, angrily. "And do you think so?" Then more gently, "But you are right, he has been wronged."

"No," I said, pulling myself carefully to my feet. I hurt all over, worse than after wrestling with Larig in training. I had to roll onto my side and use both arms to get up. I needed a really hot bath and a rubdown with oil before I stiffened, and I knew I wasn't going to get one. "Arvlid has surely been wronged, and the White God perhaps, and Thansethan maybe a little, but does Father Gerthmol have the right to speak for all of those?" I leaned back against the warm and dappled flank of Luth's mare.

"Only for the last," Urdo said.

Darien raised his chin slowly. "Then who can speak for Arvlid and for the White God?" he asked.

"You were her friend and chosen companion," Urdo said, his eyes on Darien's face. "And what would the White God say?"

"He would say—" Darien hesitated, and when he started again he sounded much more sure of himself, as if he was quoting a lesson he knew he had learned well. "He would say 'Let the dead bury the dead, we should look at what can be done for the living.' He would say 'Blessed be the peacemakers, I shall call them my children.'" There were tears rolling down his face, but they did not reach his voice. "And Sister Arvlid would say what he said to the stones 'Forgive these my blood.' She *did* say it, my lord, she said that to them before they killed her." He was sobbing now, all his self-control gone. I took a step towards him, but it was Urdo he turned to, and Urdo held him for a moment. Then he pulled away, wiped his tattered sleeve across his nose and eyes, and said, in a tear-choked but controlled voice, "So if I can speak for them I would say do what you said you would choose to do."

Then the horses I had heard came out of the tatters of mist. Ap Erbin was in the lead, Raul was behind him on Ulf's Smoky. He did not usually ride a greathorse, nor carry a spear, and he looked a little uneasy in the saddle. Elidir and Grugin were there, leading Glimmer and one of the spare riding horses. The rest were all armigers of my pennon. They drew to a halt when they saw us, and lowered their spears in some confusion. Raul jumped down, dropping his spear carelessly in a way that would have earned him ten days of latrine duty if he'd been under my command. He embraced Urdo, then stepped a little away, and Urdo embraced him. They stood there hugging each other and not saying anything while we all looked on, and then we tried to look at each other instead. Ayl remounted to give himself something to do, and I signaled Grugin to bring up Glimmer and the horse for Darien. I patted Darien's shoulder as we mounted up.

"You did very well," I told him quietly. I wanted to say I was proud of him, but couldn't find a way that sounded right. I patted his shoulder again. Glimmer seemed very pleased to see me and more than a little nervous. I did my best to reassure him that I was there and that it wasn't his fault. Then I directed him over towards ap Erbin. I felt stiff and weary.

"What happened after we left?" I asked him quietly.

"Huge row with Father Gerthmol and the priests," ap Erbin whispered. "Also a kind of fight among the armigers. It was my fault for not doing anything quickly enough, I suppose. But I didn't quite realize what Father Gerthmol was saying. He tried to stop anyone coming after you, saying the beast had taken the evildoers. They were getting in the way of the horses and worrying some of the armigers who follow the White God. Cinon's dead, you know? Father Gerthmol said the White God struck the ship by lightning and sent the boar to avenge Arvlid, and some of the armigers were believing him about you and the High King. Gunnarsson started the fighting though when he knocked that idiot brother of Angas's flat. He was shouting that the beast had taken Ayl and Cinon so Nene and Aylsfa had no kings. Sidrok started looking at that awful standard a different way then, damn him. I was trying to get people ready to come and help you. I couldn't just kill Father Gerthmol, tempted though I was. Lots of ap Selevan's pennon seemed to be agreeing with him, and a handful of Luth's armigers, too. I couldn't leave when things were like that. It could have got sticky and come to real fighting. I kept hoping you were all right and you'd just come back. Where have you been all this time anyway? But then good old Raul—"

Then he stopped, and pointed, astonishment clearly written on his face. I looked, though I wasn't satisfied with this account. Raul was going down on his knees before Urdo. There were tears on his cheeks. "I have no sword," he said, and stopped. Darien had dismounted again and walked up to him with the spear he had dropped. "Thank you," he said gravely, taking it. "My lord, we must go back quickly, but first I would swear to you."

"Not as armiger, old friend?" Urdo said, looking down at him.

"I would serve you in whatever way I can best do so," Raul said. "You know my skills are not in fighting."

"What of your service to the White God?" Urdo asked gravely.

"Whatever I do, I shall be serving the White God according to my own conscience. Father Gerthmol has given me back my vows to Thansethan."

"Threw them in his teeth," muttered ap Erbin to me. "Asked him whose side he was on, and couldn't say a word when Raul said he would answer before the throne of God."

"It was no will of mine or the White God's that I left your service; now that I am free to do so, I return to it, as I should not have left it." Raul went on. Then Raul gave Urdo the spear and took his oath on it, swearing by the White God to strike and go and do as Urdo would command in the words we armigers had all sworn. But instead of giving him back the spear Urdo put it down. He smiled and reached inside his tunic for something and drew it out and handed it to Raul as he raised him. I leaned over to see what it was as Raul got up, and almost laughed because it was so appropriate. Urdo had given him his patterned Lossian stylus.

37

Almighty God, who art a strong tower of defense unto thy servants
against the face of their enemies. We yield thee praise and thanksgiving for
our deliverance from those great and apparent dangers wherewith we were
compassed. We acknowledge it thy goodness that we were not delivered over
as prey unto them; beseeching thee still to continue such thy mercies toward
us, that all the world may know that thou art the Savior and Mighty Deliverer
and join with us in praising thy glory.

— Prayer for Thanksgiving in Victory, as used at Thansethan,
early translation

There is a mosaic in Thansethan of what they say happened next.
"Urdo humbling himself before St. Gerthmol" they call it. My
nephew Gwien saw it when he went on pilgrimage three years before he
died. He told us all about it. He thought it would interest me, being about
Urdo, who he himself barely remembered. The mosaic had just been made
then, with real gold for the crown and silver for swords, young Gwien said,
and the boar lying dead behind made of chips of jet from the beaches east
of Caer Avroc. Ap Lew was impressed at such splendor, but I just snorted.
All I can say is that I was there, and I don't care how fine the colors are, the
boar was never killed and Urdo never bent his knee to Father Gerthmol
nor asked forgiveness, no matter what anyone says.

There was a wind out of the east blowing away the tatters of the mist
before us as we came back to the camp. As we rode downhill I could see the
flat fields of Aylsfa stretching out on the other side of the river. In the trees
there was a dove calling over and over *ro-co-coo, ro-co-coo*. My bones felt as if
they had been hammered on an anvil like iron for a horseshoe. I was hardly
riding, more sitting on Glimmer's back allowing him to follow the other
horses and carry me with him. Urdo and Raul were talking in front of me
and I heard Raul say, "Whatever else, he is an honest man."

Most of the ala were mounted and looking uneasy. Urdo had given
orders and ap Erbin and Luth rode ahead to deal with them and get them
ready to ride. I had suggested we could stay another night at the camp, but
I had forgotten the problem Cinon posed us even in death. I followed
Urdo to the center of the camp. There was a cluster of people there about
the trampled bodies of the slain. As well as the knot of monks there was
Ayl's brother Sidrok and Ayl's other folk, Cinon's surviving men and a

handful of armigers. Ulf was there, looking murderous. Ap Selevan stood next to him, looking dreadfully ill at ease. He had his hand on his sword hilt. Morthu was there, too, standing next to Father Gerthmol. One side of his face was bruised and grazed, making his expression unreadable.

Everyone looked up when we came near, and their expressions were very revealing. Morthu looked furious for an instant, then went immediately back to calm. Ap Selevan took his hand off his sword and smiled. Ulf looked deeply relieved. Sidrok looked confused. The other Jarnsmen looked pleased. The men of Nene looked worried, and so did Father Geneth and most of the monks. Father Gerthmol looked utterly terrified, even more frightened than he had looked running away from the boar.

Urdo drew to a halt, and we pulled up behind him. Glimmer wasn't happy and took a few steps sideways. He didn't want to stop near where Turth had been. He threw up his head and jostled Ayl's horse, and it took me a moment to bring him back under control. Then there was a silence as Urdo looked down at Father Gerthmol, who was clutching his pebble and muttering something under his breath. Then Sidrok's face resolved itself into dignity.

"Ayl! By the Thunderer and the White God, you are safely returned to us beyond our hopes."

"Not all our hopes," muttered ap Selevan, loudly, frowning at Sidrok. Ayl slid down from his horse and he and his brother thumped each other on the back in the Jarnish way of expressing affection. Civilized people would have hugged each other. Then Ayl went down the line of his people, all of them taking their turn to pound and be pounded.

"We are returned, and unharmed," Urdo said, while this was going on.

"And the great fiend you followed?" Morthu asked.

"The boar is gone," Urdo said, in the firm tone he used to indicate that a subject was closed.

Father Gerthmol turned round to face us, seemed to cower for a moment, and looked up at us. Then he clutched at his pebble, drew himself up to his full height, and began to rant.

"Begone, demons and foul fiends come in the form of man and beast, I expel you in the name of the Holy Father, the God Made Man, and the Ever-living Spirit—"

It was so sudden and unexpected that nobody reacted for a moment, except Glimmer, who put his ears back and spooked again. When I'd got him back under control Father Gerthmol was all but foaming at the mouth, trying to cast us all out as demons. The other monks had taken a step back away from him and looked clearly uncertain; one or two of them were looking towards Raul. Father Geneth was trying, much too tentatively, to take Father Gerthmol by the sleeve.

I wanted to laugh, and then suddenly Darien did laugh, high and loud and clear, a sudden peal of irrepressible childish laughter. The next moment I heard Urdo's deep laugh boom out, and then I was laughing, too, and so were many among the crowd, Ulf and ap Selevan and Ayl and some of his people. Father Gerthmol looked furious, and for a moment, terribly embarrassed, then he started shouting again, and waving his arms wildly.

The charm he was saying can have had no power, or maybe the White God was angry with him for calling us demons when we were no such thing. He waved his arms in the face of our laughter, and he was still clutching his pebble. The cord that held it, perhaps worn with so much devotion, snapped, and the white pebble fell. It bounced off one of the bodies and then stuck in the mud in front of Urdo's horse. The event horrified Father Gerthmol much more than the laughter. Anyone would have thought it had been the worst thing to happen for months. He stopped shouting and froze for a moment, staring at the fallen pebble. Then his face suddenly crumpled and he sank towards the ground until he was sitting there, his robe rumpled around him. I thought he might cry, but he did not, he just sat on the ground like a skein of yarn dropped from a distaff.

Father Geneth took a tentative step towards him. At the same moment Urdo swung down from his horse in one easy movement. He picked up Father Gerthmol's pebble, wiped it clean on his cloak, and offered it back.

"No, no!" said Father Gerthmol, cowering away. "He has abandoned me. He has turned his face from me."

"It is possible to make a mistake and learn from it without being damned, Father," Urdo said. "I am no fiend, nor are any of my companions. The beast was a protector of this land, and he has done what he came for and gone on."

Father Gerthmol looked at Urdo, and at Raul, and for the first time ever I saw doubt in his face. "A power of the land?" he asked.

"Yes," Urdo said. "Sometimes they touch mortal places, though never quite in mortal time. You have seen a sight few people have beheld."

Father Gerthmol groped at his chest unconsciously, and finding nothing his fingers clutched at the air. "I should have—few people have such a chance and I threw it away." I looked over at Darien, who had said the same. To my surprise he was not looking at Father Gerthmol but over at Morthu. The two of them were staring at each other with an intensity and

"He was amazingly clever," Darien said, admiringly. "He got out of that one without looking bad to anyone."

"But did he take the pebble?" I asked.

"The pebble is only a symbol," Darien said, grinning. "He has to be king, and with so many people being heathens it's hard for him not to step on someone's toes. Raul's explained it all to me. It might cause panic and riots, and wars, if he took the pebble, and maybe the gods wouldn't go with him and the crops wouldn't grow."

"But—" I couldn't ask again. People were mounted up all around us, and ap Selevan was trying to signal to me that he was ready. I ignored him. "What was that with you and Morthu?"

"Oh." Darien abruptly stopped smiling. "Just letting him know that I know he tried to kill me, and that I'm ready for him now. I thought before that he had some honor, that he'd wait for me to grow up and fight him. I'll kill him then."

Not if I can kill him first, I thought. But there was no way with honor, and he was Angas's brother. Then I realized what I was doing, sending Darien off with him. "Stay in Thansethan from now on," I said.

"He won't try the same thing again," Darien said.

"Don't trust in that. Stay close, and keep people with you." I made a hand signal to ap Selevan to come up. "I've changed my mind," I said to him. "You come with me to Caer Rangor, I may need you. Tell Gormant to come up. His pennon can do the escort duty and take the queen home." Ap Selevan shrugged, frowning a little, and acknowledged the order. Darien looked at me with an expression I could not interpret. Gormant came up, and I told him the change of orders. He looked puzzled but didn't query me.

"Good-bye, then," Darien said. I hugged him, and he stood there. Then as we mounted up and started to move off he called out, "I forgot to tell you. Keturah had a foal. He's beautiful, and I'm calling him Pole Star."

"His great-grandfather had that name," I called. "Did you know?"

He shook his head, and grinned, and rode away with the monks and Gormant's pennon. I took my place in the column of the already moving ala. Luth, Urdo, Raul, and Ayl were at the front, so ap Erbin and I moved to the back, last except for some lame horses and the scouts and pickets, who fell in as we passed them. The whole column was moving north at good speed. We have to camp at nightfall, but we would be in Caer Rangor sometime the next day. There was no question of burning Cinon where he fell, of course—he was a king and had to be taken home.

The mist had lifted and the sun was shining through frequent breaks in the clouds. "Did he take the pebble or not?" ap Erbin asked me quietly as we rode along. He looked as confused as I was.

"I have no idea," I said. From the look of it, nobody else did either.

"He definitely said everyone would be free to worship whatever gods they choose and however they want," ap Erbin said.

"I heard that part loud and clear," I said.

"I think he bluffed them," ap Erbin said, finally. "Father Gerthmol was trying to push him, and it doesn't do to try and push Urdo. He did something they didn't expect, like bringing up the reserves in a flank attack."

"I'm glad I'm not a king," I said.

We camped at sunset. I set a double sentry ring, I was still not sure that there was not more trouble planned. I gave ap Selevan's pennon patrol duty, by numbers, so there would always be someone with Morthu. Then I went to my tent and Elidir heated oil and rubbed me down. It was foul-smelling linen-seed oil, but I didn't care about the smell, only how much better it made my bruises feel. It was a pot my mother had sent with strongmint crushed into it which may have helped the bruises even more but which didn't help the smell.

Urdo came up as I was lying on my back on the grass in front of my tent, waiting for the oil to sink in enough that I could put my clothes on again without having them smell of strongmint and oil for months. "You're lucky you didn't break a rib," he said, looking at my bruises.

"I'll be all right in a day or two," I said. "Maybe I should get the ala to practice belly-flop landings onto horses, except it would be hard to get anything high enough to drop them from."

Urdo smiled. "Luth caught you very neatly," he said.

"Luth's very good with a horse," I said. "I should thank him. Where is he?"

"If you can believe it, he and Ayl have gone off to try and spear some ducks they saw on a pond a little way back."

"I just hope they took guards—and that they don't get lost again," I said. "I'd have thought they'd both have had enough hunting for a month at least."

Urdo grinned.

Talog came over then, walking slowly, a bowl of steaming hot porridge in either hand. "Elidir said you were resting here," she said, handing them to us. Mine smelled of honey, and I could see some fat bacon in it.

"You're both very good to me," I said. "I'd have made it to the cook-fire for my share."

"You deserve a bit of special treatment now and then," Talog said. I was so touched I could feel tears in my eyes. I reached into my pack to find my spoon so nobody would see. "Oh, Urdo, Gunnarsson was looking for you, shall I tell him to come over?"

"If you would," Urdo said. I started on my porridge. It was wonderful. Urdo waited until Talog has gone far enough not to hear him before he asked, "Sulien, did you call Turth?"

I jumped, startled. "No. Certainly not. I wouldn't know how to, and I wanted you to have a trial and call everyone together, as I wrote to you."

"You are heir to land, you could have called him," Urdo said, stirring his porridge. "I did not think you had, but I needed to be sure."

"I wish Kerys would get on and have a baby so I needn't be heir to Derwen," I said. "But I was far from there, and such a thing never crossed my mind."

"Then he came uncalled, after the sacrilege indeed, but I think he came for Darien," Urdo said. We looked at each other for a moment. I stopped chewing. "Luth and Ayl and anyone else who thinks about it will think it natural enough, if they think Darien is my son," Urdo said, very quietly. "It seems the land thinks you have indeed given me an heir as we agreed."

I didn't know what to say, the thought of Darien as High King was so strange. But Turth had come and saved Darien from harm. "He killed Cinon," I said. "But Cinon is not all the threat; he could never have planned that. It may have been Flavien, but I think it might have been Morthu. I don't have real proof, but Morthu hates Darien, Darien is sure of it. And—well, he sends letters all the time, and the way Arflid was killed was based on a dream of Ulf's he could have read."

"A dream of Ulf's?" Urdo asked, raising his eyebrow.

"That's what he said. Ah, you can ask him yourself, here he comes." I had just caught sight of Ulf coming through the next line of tents.

He hesitated when he saw us. Urdo waved him up, and he approached cautiously. He did not look at me at all, until he was close, when he bowed to both of us and said, "Sire, Praefecto." He stood very awkwardly.

"Sit down," Urdo said. He sat down but remained ill at ease. After a moment, Urdo said, "You wanted to see me?"

"It's about when you were gone after the boar," Ulf said. "It's true I started the fighting, but I didn't know what else to do."

"What exactly happened?" Urdo asked. I started to eat again. The bacon put new strength into me.

"The boar appeared," Ulf began. "Everyone was rushing about. I was trying to get mounted. There were more people than there should have been. Then the boar charged, crushing Cinon and some of his men. Suliensson and ap Gwien jumped onto it," He sort of half glanced at me, then fixed his gaze back on Urdo very quickly. "You and Luth and Ayl went galloping off after them. Then there was a moment when everyone stood about with their mouths open. Ap Erbin was trying to organize some people who were mounted into coming after you. Elwith was signaling our pennon together. I tried to get to her, but there were monks getting under our hooves. Then Father Gerthmol came into the center of the camp and started shouting that the beast had taken the evildoers and that nobody should follow them. Ap Erbin started shouting back, and so did some other people. It was all very loud, but whenever any horses tried to move off in an organized way the monks seemed to be in the way, clutching at us, and we couldn't just ride them down. And some of the ala were arguing, too, and even more of them were asking where you were then. And then Morthu of Angas said that we should wait until you came back, if you were going to, and at present it seemed as if Aylsfa and Nene were without kings. He'd just opened his mouth to say something about the High Kingdom. I was really quite close to him, and the only way I could think of to shut him up was to knock him down."

"With your ax?" Urdo asked, very stern.

"No!" Ulf sounded sorry. "With my foot. I kicked him in the back, and then I jumped off Smoky and we had a little go-round. I just hit him. There weren't any weapons involved. But some of his friends came to help him, and some of my friends came to help me, and Father Gerthmol was bleating all the time about God and demons and evil. I punched someone in Luth's pennon as well as Morthu. I don't know who it was, but she'd drawn a dagger."

"Would you know her again?" I asked.

"No, sir," he said, still not looking at me, his face absolutely wooden. I'm sure Urdo also guessed he was lying, but neither of us said anything. "But anyway, about then Raul came forward and just pushed between us, bare-handed, calling out to stop, and we all did stop fighting. He's a brave one, even if he is a priest. Then he had a shouting match with Father Gerthmol, saying you were no evildoer but the true king and that you might need help up there in the hills with that great creature. Then he said he was going, and ap Erbin backed him up. Father Gerthmol said if he did he would throw him out of Thansethan, and Raul said that was fine, he wanted to leave anyway, and Father Gerthmol said he was giving him back his vows. So he looked around for a horse and a spear, and as I was next to him I gave him mine, and Smoky, too. And ap Erbin was giving orders to the whole ala to mount up and take up formation, but I couldn't because I didn't have my horse, so I stayed down." He drew a breath. "Raul and ap Erbin between them had stopped the fighting, but there was still arguing when they were gone. Father Gerthmol said it was clear we'd never see any of them again, and he wanted an escort to take Cinon's body to Thansethan. Cinon's men didn't like that idea; they wanted to take him home to Caer Rangor. Sidrok was asking if he was king of Aylsfa and hinting around taking the pebble if Father Gerthmol would crown him. Not that that would last for two minutes back home with his people. He's not much of a Jarnish king, that one, whatever he thinks. Ap Selevan and I just stood over Cinon, watching each other's backs. And Morthu was saying things, not much, but calling Sidrok brother and doing little things to change the way people were thinking. I wanted to fight him—in fact I was sorry I hadn't used my ax and killed him before."

I found myself raising my chin in agreement. Ulf wasn't looking, but Urdo frowned at me. "There's no proof Morthu is involved," he said.

"He's a snake in any case," Ulf said.

"Being a snake is not proof of evildoing," Urdo said. "Not all snakes have poison in their fangs. And he is the brother of Angas and of Penarwen. Killing him would have serious consequences. Do you have any proof, either of you, that he was involved?" He looked at each of us.

I had to shake my head. I put down my empty bowl and shivered; the evening was becoming cold. I reached over and pulled on my tunic. Ulf said nothing for a long moment. Armigers were moving around the camp, and there was singing a little way off, but nobody came near us.

"That he writes letters isn't proof, and neither is a dream anyone might have read. Nor is Suliensson's word that he hates him. The things he was saying, well, I don't like him either. I will watch out for him, but I must stay within the law I have made, or it is no law."

Now for the first time that evening Ulf's eyes met mine, and for once we were in agreement. "I will change his pennon so that he does not go to Thansethan so much," I said. "I will not kill him without honor, but I will not endanger my son either."

"Do you really think he would attack Suliensson?" Urdo asked.

"Only if he could make it look as if it wasn't his fault," I said. "The way Morthu was looking at him was enough to kill him on the spot. It reminded me of his mother."

"Then don't send him to Thansethan, but don't harm him either," Urdo said.

"But Urdo——" I stopped, I wasn't sure what words could reach him in this mood. "He hates us all, he hates everything we stand for, he is an enemy as sure as Sweyn ever was, or his mother Morwen. I am sure of it from the way he looked at Darien. I am even more sure he had a hand in planning that than Flavien did."

"Well, and if he hates us?" Urdo sighed. "He was brought up to hate me, but then so was Angas, and he is one of my most loyal people. You fought against me, Ulf, and you are loyal to me now. Morthu can come to understand what we are doing, come to realize he was wrong. He is very clever to have planned this, if he did, and he is only eighteen now, and he has only been with us for two years. I don't like him, I admit it, and I've been busy, and I've not been giving him much of my time, even though he's my nephew. You don't like him either, Sulien, so you haven't been giving him much of your time. Little wonder he's had time to plot mischief."

"Mischief?" I said, my voice rising. "Arvlid was raped and killed, and Darien would have been killed——"

"Morthu may have been plotting. He didn't do it. Maybe coming into contact with the reality of it will have taught him something." Urdo shook his head. "It would be wrong of us not to try to teach him better. We can set him good examples and talk to him. We don't even know if he did it. I will not go outside the law on this, or have you go outside the law."

"I wish there could have been a trial within the law for Cinon," Ulf growled. "That way we'd have found out who was helping him."

"That is out of our hands," Urdo said. "But you did well, Ulf. You didn't kill anyone and you stopped Morthu from speaking treason I couldn't have ignored."

"Father Gerthmol spoke treason," I said.

"That was a misunderstanding," Urdo said, firmly, and smiled. "He has admitted he was wrong, and in front of everyone acknowledged that I am king with my own responsibilities." Urdo yawned. "It's late," he said. "Tomorrow I have to deal with young Cinon."

He and Ulf said good night then and went off to their own tents. I went inside mine and lay down, praying that Darien was safe and wishing that Ulf had killed Morthu, whatever it might have done to the King's Law and to the politics of the kingdom.

38

"I have the blood of gods and kings, I have walked among giants beyond
the North Wind, but here I am dying surrounded by fools. When will you
understand it's time to end these squabbles and look forward?"
—Last words of Emrys ap Gwerthus, as recorded by
St. Sethan

The only reason I didn't kill Morthu in the years that followed was
because Urdo trusted in my honor, and I could not violate that trust.
Respect for the law wouldn't have stopped me. I believed Darien, and even
without looking any further at what Morthu might do to the kingdom, I
wanted to protect my son. But the law meant so much to Urdo, and I could
not betray him as Marchel had done. So although Morthu accused me
afterwards of putting him into harm's way when I could, I did not, no more
than for any of my armigers. Neither, which would have been more to my
taste, did I run him through at practice, nor request Ulf to hit him on the
head with his ax. I will not say I did not think of these things, but I did not
do them. Certainly I kept a close watch on Morthu, and certainly that did
not escape him. Also Urdo went out of his way to spend time with him,
and Morthu was attentive to him and to Elenn and seemed to all appear-
ances to be learning our ways as Angas had before him. When next he
acted it was in a way that I did not expect.

There were two good years after Arvlid's death. Apart from Morthu,
the constant worm in the apple, they were very good. Raul was back and
Urdo was much happier. He often had time to talk to me in the evenings
again, playing fidchel or just talking about the alae and the land, or whatever came into our heads; laws, taxes, integrating the Jarnish foot soldiers
into the army, or why it always rains in Tevin. My ala was well trained and
thriving. There was peace at last, real peace, and the land prospered. Foals
were plentiful as people decided to breed their mares now they were not
needed for battle every season. Ap Erbin and Alswith married and had their
baby, and the year after another baby. Garah and Glyn also had another
child that year, and their older children were finally old enough to talk and
play with and understand properly. Babies are all very well, little children
who will say "Tantie Sulien" and beg for rides are better, but talking children who can ask questions about the world and start riding properly are
best of all. I remember putting Garah's oldest and Ayl's oldest both up on

Starlight and leading them around the near pasture at Caer Tanaga. It was a reward for keeping their heels in riding and not making a fuss when they fell off their ponies. They looked very small on Starlight's broad back, and they were almost too excited to keep still. It's strange to think of them being grown-up and married now, and king and queen of Aylsfa.

Both of those years there were very good harvests, and plenty of food for people and animals. My mother wrote to me that they were using the dowager Rowanna's methods of scything grain and hay, and yields were increasing. She also begged me to get the plant from Ayl he used to make his strange pink dye. He gave it to me willingly enough, and I sent it off to Derwen. I visited Magor and Derwen only once, when Veniva sent to tell me that Duke Galba was dying. I was there in time to speak to him. I was sad to see him go; the old man had always been very kind to me. My mother cut her hair for him. He was almost the last of the friends of her youth. Aurien was very cold and formal all the time when I was there. I did not try to push her to a friendship neither of us felt. At Duke Galba's pyre I remembered Galba's, but Emer and Lew were there, decorously beside Idrien and Uthbad, and no messenger came to interrupt with news of an invasion. Aurien ran Magor after that, until little Galbian should be old enough. Morien promised to give her whatever help she needed.

Every few months I rode to Thansethan, escorting Elenn. I visited Darien and spent time with him. I took him leather riding clothes like the ones I had worn at his age, practice spears, and a shield. The best protection I could give him was knowing how to fight. I would have had a sword made for him, but Urdo stopped me, saying it was too soon.

Yes, those were good years. Urdo finished his law code and gathered all the kings together to hear it and agree to it. He gave them all a copy afterwards. Flavien tried to sneer at Ohtar, saying he wouldn't be able to read it, and Ohtar amazed him by quoting back what Urdo had read. He had remembered it from one hearing. The kings were not quite as they had been after Foreth. Cinon was dead, and young Cinon was more polite and cautious. He did not drive Elenn to distraction the way his father had. Young Galbian tried to be as dignified as his grandfather, but he was only eight years old. Mardol the Crow was dead, too, quietly, in bed with a young leman. Cadraith wept when the laws were read and said it would have gladdened his father's heart.

The year after that we all cautiously rejoiced, especially those who were always casting glances at the queen's waistline. It seemed Elenn was pregnant, and by the Harvest Fair it was unmistakable. Everyone was saying there would be an heir for the kingdom by midwinter.

At that time there was a new water mill built at Caer Tanaga. It ground better than the usual sort, for the wheel was mounted vertically and not horizontally in the stream. These wheels are everywhere now, of course, but then it was a new thing and a marvel to us. Nobody then had thought of using the work of the wheel for sawing wood or cutting stone; it did nothing but grind wheat to flour. I did not like it at first because it made such a roar and frightened the horses. After I tried the good bread made from the fine flour I thought it was a wonderful invention. News of it went far and wide, farther and wider than we could have imagined.

The Fair that year was the biggest I had ever seen. There is always something exciting about a fair. Even if there is nothing new, there is always the promise that there might be something wonderful around the next corner.

I have never envied Glyn his job, and then I envied it less than ever. With Elenn pregnant and Garah just brought to bed, all the work of provisioning the ala fell to him. As I passed through the main part of the fair where the farmers were selling their extra produce, I caught sight of him bargaining with a fruit seller. Glyn had grown plumper with time and good cooking. By now he was quite a round man. Little ap Glyn was next to him, jumping from foot to foot and looking bored. The younger one, the boy, was perched on his shoulders pulling his hair; the new baby was left at home with Garah. Ap Glyn Junior was too old to be carried really, but with the coming of the new baby he had slipped back into some of his ways of a year or two before. He missed being the youngest. Both children spotted me before their father did, and I gave them the ala hand signal for silence. I came right up behind Glyn and poked him in the ribs. He jumped, and the child on his shoulders giggled. "Don't buy as many pears as last year," I said. "They were coming out of our ears before spring and half the armigers were giving them to their horses because they were so tired of them."

He laughed. "We got pears in tax from Guthrum and Rowanna last year; I didn't have to buy any. This year Guthrum sent beans and Rowanna sent hay—hay I ask you! I want tax in coin, but Urdo says he won't push it yet."

"Hay, I ask you," the little boy echoed. "Over land, too, the old lady must be cracking at last!"

I crowed with laughter, and Glyn looked terribly embarrassed. "Well," he said. "I don't think we'll have any pears at all this year if I have to pay these prices for them." He shook his head over the baskets at the farmer and put on his most doleful expression. "I don't suppose the thought of all those hungry horses can soften your heart?" The boy on his shoulders pulled Glyn's ear, and the farmer grinned and started to haggle.

"I thought I'd borrow one of your children," I said, before Glyn was too absorbed. Both children immediately started to draw attention to themselves, but stopped when I frowned at them. "Mind, if I do take you I'm expecting really good behavior," I said. "No touching things, and if I'm talking, you be quiet. I want someone to help me with money, and I know you two are better with it than I am."

"You think she'd be joking," Glyn said to the farmer, who was giggling behind her hand at the way the children were raising their chins in agreement. "But no, the Praefecto here lives in barracks and eats in the king's hall and never remembers how many silver pennies there are in a gold victrix, and as for haggling, she has less idea than my month-old babe at home, never mind these two."

I smiled crookedly. Then I went on with both children and Glyn's sincere thanks, wrapped up but not hidden in his teasing. We went quickly through the part of the fair selling food. Next came the artisans. Some were local and had shops in the town all year, but others had come a long way especially for the fair. Here there were fewer people with baskets and more boards set out on the ground. Some even had little tents hung about with their merchandise. There were potters, some selling bowls and jugs and crocks and even beakers, others offering to mend any broken pots. Beris was there having a plate mended with rivets; she smiled at me as we went by. The new pots were very expensive, and I didn't need any, not having a house of my own. The colors and glazes were beautiful. The children were clamoring to get on. We stopped for a moment to watch the tinkers mending broken metal tools. The smiths at Nant Gefalion grumble about tinkers and their work, but few people would buy anything metal if they had to go all the way to a smith to mend it if it cracked. There were craftspeople selling cloth of all kinds, and rolls of yarn. I told the children that you could get a whole set of clothes at the Harvest Fair, cloth and thread and the tinkers would sell you needles to sew it together.

"Would they sell it to you if you came in wearing nothing though?" The little girl giggled.

"The Jarnish ones wouldn't," the little boy said, indicating a nearby tent hung about with distinctive pink cloth from Aylsfa and presided over by two veiled and pigtailed young Jarnswomen. The children roared with laughter at the thought of needing new clothes so badly and not being able to get them. "You could get boots, too, look, leather, and shoemakers to make them up for you if you can't cobble."

"People do that," I said. "I've done it myself, though there are more years where I get the boots I've worn down cobbled together to last me another winter." There was a tannery at Caer Rangor where we bought leather for the ala. The stink of it hung on the air for miles around. I paused and looked at a lovely piece of leather hanging on a tent. It was tanned very pale. I felt it, it was very soft, it would be better for gloves than boots.

"Do you fancy that, Praefecto?" Morthu asked, softly and suddenly. He had come up behind the tent and had a covered basket over his arm.

I was startled. "It's beautiful stuff," I said, honestly. "I don't need any at the moment."

"What a shame," he said, putting out his hand to stroke the leather. I let go of it abruptly and moved away. Although he had said nothing but casual politeness, there was something about him that made my skin crawl. He was a grown man now, with nothing of the boy left about him, and I was suddenly aware of that, as if he wanted me to be. He didn't look like his father or his mother. Indeed he looked a little like Urdo, which wasn't surprising in a nephew. He smiled at me deliberately and continued to stroke the leather. "It's very soft," he said.

I wanted to shudder, or hit him, and deliberately stopped myself. The children were being good and quiet, as I had asked them. I wished they would ask for something or catch sight of something interesting and give me an excuse to leave Morthu. I looked down on him. "Have you been buying leather?" I asked, indicating his woven basket and hoping my voice would stay even.

"No," he said. "Wine. There's a ship in from Narlahena, and they're selling some of their cargo."

"Oh, where?" I asked. He turned and took my arm to show me the direction. I flinched, and I know he felt it for I saw an instant of triumph in his face. I couldn't say anything, what he had done was something any of my comrades could have done without offense. The difference was that he was an enemy and that he did mean offense. I moved away from him and went off with the children, glancing back to make sure he did not follow.

The next place was selling smith's ironwork, daggers and spades and hoes. I had to explain to the children how the handles would be fitted into the implements. They wanted to buy a spade for their grandfather back at Derwen, who only had a wooden one. They haggled for a while, but the smith was not fool enough to sell to a seven-year-old for a promise of coin later. They had to be contented with the thought of coming back and asking their father to pay for one. By the time we went on I was feeling almost calm again.

We passed people selling dyes, then a man selling hot sausages, and the children had to have one each. We went on past people selling spices and trinkets and love potions and cures for all sorts of illnesses. Some of these were real enough healing herbs, but others were not, and in any case I hated to see them sold as wonder cures and not medicine. I wondered if I could ask Urdo if there was anything we could do about that. Then at last we came to the Narlahenans.

They had barrels of wine and a board set out on two big barrels so it was like a table, and they had wine in flasks and flagons spread out an embroidered cloth on top of that. Lots of people were haggling over them as they sampled the wares, including the High King's cook. As well as wine they had some other items, and these were what interested us. The children stuffed their sausages into their mouths and put their greasy hands behind their backs to stop themselves from touching everything in sight. There were glass beads, and glass jars, and glass beakers, all in beautiful reds and blues and some in green. Also there were some books. I looked at them longingly. I doubted if I had enough money to buy one, even if I wanted them. I looked at them quickly. I was disappointed to see they were all copies of the *Memories of the White God* except for one, which was a book of prayers composed in a monastery in Narlahena. I put them back and turned back to the glassware.

The children were pining over some little glass animal beads, very cunningly made and about the size of my thumbnail. I asked how much they were, and was surprised to find they were quite cheap. Ap Glyn insisted on bargaining for me, even though the Narlahenan spoke only Vincan and she spoke only Tanagan and so I was forced to translate all the haggling. The children spoke Tanagan at home and heard Vincan only rarely. The Narlahenan had the same clipped accent as Amala, biting off the ends of words, so I knew he must be a Malm. I bought them a bead each, a little red hare for the boy and a blue horse for the girl. On impulse after the price had been agreed I bought a red squirrel and a blue dog for my nephews in Magor, Aurien's two children. I wasn't planning to go home, but I could send them in my next letter to Veniva. I was sorry Darien was too old for one, and then I saw a blue pig and decided to buy him one anyway. It might make him smile.

The Narlahenan, seeing me buying so many and the gold in my purse, brought out more glassware, some of it very beautiful. I wasn't tempted by any of the glass jewels, but when he brought out a green-glass beaker, almost clear and hardly a finger's width thick, with a gold rim around the edge I hesitated. It occurred to me that when Elenn's baby was born I would need a gift for it, and this was a gift good enough for a future king. The Jarns say it is bad luck to buy a childgift before the child is born. The man was just handing the beaker and the beads to me when someone started to address me in a language I did not know.

I looked up to excuse myself, straightened, and was amazed to have to keep looking up to see a tall woman who looked a great deal like my father. My father had never had a sister, but if he had, this could have been her face—the shape of her cheekbones and her nose and chin were just like Gwien's. Apart from that she looked like the wildest sort of barbarian. Her hair was limed so that it was white and stood straight up in spikes all around her face, and she was wearing sealskin leather clothes. She had wide shoulders, and her bare arms had patterns drawn on them, a snake curled around on one and a stylized horse on the other. The children gasped, and the little boy clung to my leg.

She repeated her question, whatever it was, now grinning broadly. I shook my head. "I don't understand," I said.

She said something else incomprehensible, waving her painted arms, then repeated it very slowly and I realized that now she was speaking very bad Vincan. "You are cousin to me?" she asked.

The glass-seller was waiting for my coin, which I gave him, and I took the things carefully and put them in my pouch. Then he said cheerfully and rapidly, "I'd watch out for her if I were you, lady. She's come from the Ice Mountains, took passage with us from Olisipo. She's got six huge horses and a big ax and she paid for her passage with a pair of carved walrus tusks the size of my legs, and she broke a sailor's arm for trying to get familiar."

"Thank you," I said, and turned away. I turned to the woman, who was waiting patiently. "If I am your cousin, I don't know it," I said, slowly. "Who are you?"

"Rigg, daughter of Farr, daughter of Beven, daughter of Neef," she said, striking herself in the chest. "Neef's other daughter was Larr, Larr came to this island with the horses. Beven was lord and could not come, said come later bring horses. She did not come. Farr did not come. But I have come."

I blinked at her. Laris the giant, I remembered. Rigg wasn't a giant, though she was a handspan or so taller than I was. I wished my father was alive to meet her. "You're the granddaughter of my grandmother's sister, and you've come to join the family?" I wanted to giggle at the sudden thought of my mother's face. The children were tugging at me and asking what I was saying. "She says she's my cousin," I said to them. They gaped at her.

"Not join your family," Rigg said, and smiled. "I not know your family was, not know my mother's mother's sister Larr had family here. She was young fighter when she left, no children yet. I come to keep promise my mother's mother Beren made to Emeris."

"I'm Sulien," I said, belatedly realizing that I hadn't given my name and to cover my astonishment. But then meeting family I'd never heard of was a very strange thing for me. "My father was Gwien, and his mother was Larr."

"She is dead?"

"Yes, she died in the civil wars. My father is dead, too, in a plague."

"Very sad," Rigg said, and bent her head. "Did he have sisters?" she asked.

"No," I said. "No, he was an only child. But I have a brother and a sister. She has descendants."

"Descendants? Word mean son's children? Children of son are better than nothing, but daughters of daughter are true kin."

"Descendants just means children of children, or further," I said. "We count through fathers here, mostly."

"But how is anyone to be sure of a father?" Rigg grinned. "But still you are cousin to me, your face says so. And the children, they are yours?"

"No," I said. "They are the children of my friend, they are mine only for this afternoon. They only speak Tanagan."

She laughed, and made faces at them. They clutched their beads and smiled a little shyly. "And Emeris? He is dead, too, I hear?"

"Yes," I said. It was very strange; she had come out of nowhere and wanted to know about ancient heroes. It gave the whole encounter a dreamlike quality. It was only forty-five years or so since Emrys had died, and indeed Thurrig had known him well, but it seemed to me like a time of legend. "And his son Avren is dead and his son Urdo is High King now."

"I heard that." She smiled. "I did not know Emeris made himself lord here until I came to Narlahenia."

This seemed even stranger. "There is a song about his voyage to the land at the back of the North Wind," I said, carefully. "But not much else is known about it."

"Is called Rhionn, Rigatona in Vincan language," she said. "You not hear about Rigatona, Horse Mother Land, from your father's mother Larr?" she asked.

"She died before I was born," I said. "She died in a battle when Emrys was making himself High King. My father was only a boy. I have her armor."

"Very sad," Rigg said again. "I will keep promise to Urdo. Daughter's daughter of Beren and son's son of Emeris, maybe that is how Horse Mother meant."

"I'm intrigued," I said, and met a blank look. "I'm very curious, interested, in what this promise is. If you can tell me, I'd love to know. In any case I can help you find Urdo." Though in truth I had no idea where he was, probably at the fair somewhere. I could help her find him in the evening, though, which would be much simpler for her than braving his clerks and asking to see him. The children were very restless now. I started to walk on slowly through the crowds, drawing Rigg and the children with me back in the direction of the farmers where I hoped to find Glyn at least.

"Oh, I can tell," she said, as we walked. "It is not secret promise. Emrys won five games but Beren could only prize four."

"You've won five games on the shining strand, won them with your song" I remembered from the ballad. "They say he won a thousand horses with a song. Some people say they rode home over the foam, past the two fiery mountains and on past Tir Isarnagiri until they got here."

"Not riding on waves," Rigg said, and laughed. "He had boat. And not a thousand. No lord could give a thousand horses for her mother's funeral songs. Generous beyond the gods! Fifty-two horses he won, four for each moon. His songs were very good, and all new, and we sing them still. But only forty-eight he took, for there were no horses of summer moon. Never until now were there four such to bring. You want see them?"

"Where are they?" I asked. "You want to go and see some new greathorses from the giant's land?" I asked the children. They did; they both loved horses. We went down towards the quay, past the money changers' tables. I smiled at the bored armigers on duty there. The changers had their scales and piles of gold and silver and copper as always and seemed to be doing fine business. Raul was there, talking to an old man with an amazingly long beard. He didn't even glance up at us as we passed.

Rigg led us down to the water's edge. The river was all but overrun with ships that year. There were Jarnsmen from the continent, local riverboats, Narlahenans, even some big vessels from far away with rowdy crews and big awkward sails. Rowing boats and barges were to and fro to them all

the time unloading cargo, swarming on the usually peaceful river like frogs
in mating season. Rigg's six horses were tethered quietly on the grass in
front of a sealskin tent on a standard patch. Two of them were bays, but the
other four were pale gold, all with white manes and tails and white blazes
on their noses. They were the most beautiful creatures I'd ever seen, the
color of summer wheat fields. A pale-skinned boy was watching them, sitting on a huge bundle of sealskins.

"They're beautiful," I said to Rigg.

She smiled bashfully. "Four horses of summer moon."

I translated this for the children. "They're called summerhorses," and
added to Rigg, "I've never seen horses that color!"

"Emeris did not bring any. Four of all moons, two pairs, but no horses
of summer moon because there were not four to give." The children were
clamoring to have a ride on the summerhorses, and I had to frown at them
to stop them. "We find Urdo now?" Rigg suggested after I'd made friends
with the horses. They were three-year-olds, two pairs as she had said. They
were a magnificent gift, or late prize or whatever. I was sure Urdo would be
delighted.

"Whose are the others?" I asked, indicating the bays.

"Mine," Rigg said. "In truth, I wanted adventure. I am not Beren's
heir. Rigatona seemed small to me. I wanted to see outside. Traders from
Firemountain came, horses were there, I asked to go."

"Beren is still alive then?" It seemed strange to think I had a great-aunt
on some distant island just one step away from legend.

"Oh yes." Rigg looked down at me. "She is old, but nothing happened
to kill her yet. She has four daughters, all live. I have two sisters and a
brother, all older, all taller. Not many wars in Rigatona. The traders said
wars came to Tir Tanagiri. I brought my horses to fight wars."

"You want to fight for Urdo? Join the ala?"

"What is ala? A wing?"

"A wing, an army of fighters on horses," I said, and smiled. "We all
fight together, very many horses. I am Praefecto of Urdo's Ala." It was
good to be able to say something that impressed her for a change.

She said something fast in her own language, and made swooping rushing motions with her arms. "I need words. You mean horses all running
together, with spears? We do not have at home, but I saw in Narlahenia?"

"Yes," I said. "In Narlahenia? An ala? With greathorses?"

"Small horses," Rigg said, dismissively. I thought immediately of
Marchel and wondered what she was doing. The ala was Urdo's idea. "But

all running together, and spears moving together, very beautiful. Yes, I want to join ala," Rigg said, after a moment of chewing her lip.

"You'll have to ask Urdo, and vow to serve him, but I'd be delighted to have you," I said. Just then ap Glyn reached up cautiously and touched the painted horse on Rigg's arm. Rigg laughed, and crouched down, showing her arm and rippling the muscles to make the horse run. Both children thought it was wonderful.

"Did you paint that?" the little boy asked, and I translated.

"Not paint," she said. "Made with needles and dye, like a carving." She jabbed at her arm with her finger to demonstrate. I shuddered, and translated, then the children shuddered, too.

"Come on," I said. "Let's go and find Urdo."

—39—

Then Tiya the Skath dragged Princess Gall up above the city and told her to look, and she looked, and saw that he had caused his men to destroy the aqueduct that brought water for drinking and washing. The ruins lay broken on the hillside.

Gall looked at the ruin, and said "I thought at first you wanted to get revenge for your mother, and then I thought you wanted to take over the rule of the Empire. But now I see that you will not be content until you have destroyed us all, and all that we have built, until our very names are forgotten."

Tiya smiled, and stroked his moustache, and said, "Imprisonment among us is teaching you something. We have stolen your luck. Your towns and farms do not please the Great Rat, and if we took them so that they were our towns and farms that would not please him either, but if it is all laid waste and you wept among the destruction, that would please him greatly."

—"The Fall of Vinca," *The Red Book*

Only a few minutes after we reached the fair Masarn called out to me that Urdo was looking for me. Four more armigers and Senach Red-Eye had given me the same information before I returned the children safely to Glyn, who knew not only that Urdo wanted me but where he was.

"He's showing the ambassadors the waterwheel," he said. "Yes, a beautiful horse—Sulien, you spoil these children."

"I didn't buy a spade for their grandfather," I said, and laughed. "Let me introduce my cousin from Rigatona. Rigg, this is Glyn, the logistical wizard for our ala."

Glyn bowed to Rigg. "I would have known the resemblance anywhere," he said.

"So I would to your children," Rigg said.

I left the children to explain about the marvelous iron spade and went down towards the waterwheel. We walked through the crowd. Somehow everything seemed less exotic with the Rigatonan woman at my side. She exclaimed over ordinary things like turnips and seemed to take no notice of strange spices except to wrinkle her nose a little. We walked along, weaving in and out of people selling hot chestnuts, cider, dripping honeycombs, ribbons, felt blankets, and hunting dogs. I only just managed to prevent Rigg from stopping to buy a great Isarnagan hound like Elenn's.

Urdo and Elenn were standing near the waterwheel talking with Morthu and two foreigners. I wished Morthu would fall in and drown. We made our way towards them. Urdo looked very serious, and Elenn looked gracious and beautiful but slightly tired. Knowing her, that probably meant she was exhausted. Urdo's eyes widened when he saw Rigg. Rigg drew back a little and needed to be reassured about the wheel's clatter. Then she put her chin up and advanced confidently.

When she reached Urdo she bowed. "Urdo, Lord of the Tanagans, I bring greetings and four horses of summer moon from Beren, Lord of Rigatona, in accordance with the prize Emeris won. I am Rigg, daughter's daughter of Beren."

Urdo looked astonished. I don't think he knew any more about Rigatona and Emrys's voyage there than I did.

"Many welcomes to you who come in peace to Tir Tanagiri," Elenn said. I was surprised to hear her speak Vincan. She had learned it late and found it difficult and avoided using it as much as she could. "You must feast with us tonight, and I will welcome you properly."

"Welcome indeed," Urdo said. "Truly today we have been honored by visitors from far countries."

Rigg smiled. "Strangers and family, too," she said. "Now I learn my mother's mother's sister has," she hesitated and used the word carefully "descendants in this land, and this leader of ala is one of them."

"I wish my father were alive to know he had cousins among his mother's kin," I said, into the bewildered silence. For once, not even Morthu could think of anything to say.

Urdo looked more amazed than ever. One of the strangers, a woman with pale skin and dark hair, was smiling. The other, a man who would have looked ordinary enough except for the fact that he was wearing an embroidered drape out of doors in the afternoon, looked bored and turned his attention back to the waterwheel. Morthu smiled as if everything about the situation charmed him.

"Praefecto Ap Gwien, I wanted you to meet Ambassador ap Theophilus, who has come to us from the court of the Emperor Sabbatian at Caer Custenn."

The man turned back to us, now clearly annoyed. He bowed to me, and I bowed back. "We say Sabbatian, the Emperor of the Vincans," he said, correcting Urdo, "not the Emperor at Caer Custenn. There is no other. Even here at the end of the world I know he would want to be given his proper title."

Ap Theophilus's Vincan was so good that it made mine sound like Rigg's in my own ears. I wished Veniva could be here to hear him and know that there were people who could use the language so well and so lightly. As for what he said, it was not as admirable as his command of the language he spoke. While it was true that there was no other, there had been one Emperor in Vinca and one in Caer Custenn for hundreds of years, and if this was no longer the case, it was because the Skath had killed the last emperor in Vinca fifty years ago. His sister's son was still alive and claiming the title while ruling some tiny Malmish kingdom somewhere, the last I had heard. There was no Vincan Empire left, only places which had been Vincan once. If it came to that, Emrys and Avren had claimed to be Emperor of the Vincans, and while Urdo had never said he was, he had flown the great purple imperial banner at Foreth. I am sure ap Theophilus knew this as well as Urdo and I did, but we all just smiled and bowed and said no more. I wondered what the Emperor in distant Caer Custenn wanted with us.

"And this is Ambassador ap Lothar of the Varni," Urdo went on, introducing the woman. We bowed to each other.

"It is such a shame we can't all share a welcome cup now," Morthu said, sounding regretful.

"I should go up to the citadel and get it," Elenn said at once. "Or send—"

"You should rest," Morthu interrupted. "You look tired and pale, you should be sitting down being looked after, not being dragged all around the fair in the heat let alone rushing about finding cups. Don't you agree, sir, she needs to rest in her condition?"

Appealed to thus, ap Lothar could only agree. "Of course you should," she said, in clipped Vincan. "This evening is plenty of time to share a cup."

"But I have some wine here," Morthu said, taking a flask out of his basket. "I bought it from the Narlahenan ship. If only we had a cup."

"My cousin has!" said Rigg, beaming. "She buyed one just now."

I knew she meant nothing but good, but I was annoyed all the same. "I meant to give this to you anyway," I said to Elenn, and took the glass beaker out of my pouch.

"It's beautiful!" Elenn said, and held it up to the light. She thanked me and everyone admired it and Urdo asked how they had managed to pack it to bring on the ship and Rigg explained how she had seen them packing glass in straw. Then Elenn held it and let Morthu fill it with his Narlahenan wine.

It was a peace cup, and we all drank, but I knew right away something wasn't right. I had given Elenn the cup, it wasn't that, it was hers and as fit to welcome strangers with as the gold cup or any cracked wooden one she chose to honour with the ceremony. I put it out of my mind and made conversation with ap Theophilus. His trip from Caer Custenn had taken eight months, if he was to be believed. He had traveled overland through Lossia and Vinca and then taken ship with ap Lothar from the Varnian port of Burdigala. I did not like to ask him why he had come, though I wanted to know. I guessed Urdo had wanted me there because I could speak good Vincan, so I did so, and when ap Theophilus quoted from a poet or philosopher I quoted another as soon as I could. I did not want him to think us barbarians at the end of the world. Urdo looked gratefully at me from time to time.

After a little while, when everyone had seen enough of the waterwheel, Rigg suggested that we go and see her summerhorses, and we started to walk downstream towards the quay. Elenn made a motion to put the glass away as she started off. "There is plenty more wine," Morthu said. "Let us enjoy it while it is plentiful. Soon enough it will be winter and short rations." He filled the glass and drank it, then filled it again and offered it to Elenn. "Will you take another cup of Narlahenan wine?" he asked her. She looked at him over the glass, her face completely composed. We all stopped walking for a moment. I wondered what Elenn was thinking. She never let any of it show. Urdo, however, looked furious. She took the glass and took a sip. She could do nothing else except throw it in his face. Then she smiled graciously and handed the glass not to Urdo as Morthu had plainly expected, but to Rigg. Rigg drained it

thirstily as if it were water and handed it back to Morthu. He refilled it
for ap Lothar and ap Theophilus. Ap Lothar tried to hand it to me, but I
shook my head.

"I'm not thirsty," I said.

"You needn't save it for the cold winter nights, Sulien, I may not be
offering it then," Morthu said, with a comical leer and rise of his eyebrows.
The ambassadors and Rigg laughed, and I wondered how much they
would laugh if I cut his head off right there for making a mockery of a my
lord's hospitality.

Urdo took the cup and held it thoughtfully. The little glass looked very
fragile in his big hand. "Is this the last of it?" he asked. He had seen Morthu
empty the flask out, so he knew that it was. Morthu raised his chin idly,
smiling. Everyone had seen his generous hospitality already, as if he were a
king himself, to offer wine to the king and queen in their own place. Then
Urdo raised the glass, and said, "If this is the last of that brew then I will
offer it to the gods below, that the world might always know honor, and
sweetness, and all things in their proper season." Then he poured out the
wine onto the dry grass, which absorbed it quickly. He wiped the glass on
his cloak and returned it to Elenn, who put it into the pocket of her overdress. As she did so she winced, and then after she had taken a step or two
she winced again.

"Are you all right?" Morthu asked, gently, sounding very concerned. "I
said you should sit down, you need better care taken of you than this. You
look quite worn-out."

Urdo stopped where he was walking with Rigg and ap Lothar and
turned to look at Elenn, but she motioned him on. "I am well," she said,
and walked on. Morthu stepped forward to walk beside me and ap
Theophilus. "You would hardly guess it, but when she is well our queen is
accounted one of the most beautiful women in the land," he said.

"She seems most beautiful to me even now, second only to the Empress
of all the women I have seen," ap Theophilus said graciously. I dropped
back to walk beside Elenn. She did look a little weary, but she had not lost
her looks. If anything her skin had more bloom than ever.

"I am sorry I am too tall to give you my arm to lean on," I said.

She smiled, and it clearly took a little effort. "I am—" she began, and
then stopped. "I think you may have to all the same," she said, in a very
strange voice, and fainted. I only just caught her. Even pregnant and
unconscious she was not very heavy, but heavier than she looked.

"Urdo!" I called, urgently, cutting through the noise of the crowd. He and Rigg came running back, followed by the others. Morthu looked concerned and distressed. Ap Theophilus looked bored, or perhaps that was the natural set of his features. Ap Lothar looked worried. I had both arms full with Elenn and could do nothing. Rigg put one hand on Elenn's belly and the other on her throat.

She said something incomprehensible. When she spoke her own language she spoke about four times as fast as she did in Vincan, and sounded much more intelligent somehow. "Where is—" she said, urgently, in Vincan, and then a word I did not know.

"What?" I asked.

"She means a woman's doctor," ap Theophilus said.

"Somebody who knows about borning babies," Rigg said, even more urgently.

"It isn't time!" Urdo said. I have never seen him so much at a loss.

"Is there a priest of Brioth? Of the Mother?" Rigg asked, looking round at all our blank faces.

"I have had a baby," I said. "Let's take her inside."

"I have helped with babies borning," Rigg said. "My sisters, my cousins, maybe that is enough. Inside, yes, and the rest of you go away." Urdo opened his mouth to say something, but Rigg pushed my shoulder and I started to run towards the citadel. As I saw armigers in the crowd I called out to them to clear a way for me, which they did, making a clear path right to the citadel. Rigg ran beside me. After a moment Urdo caught us up.

"I have had to leave them with Morthu. There was no choice," he said.

"Go back to them," Rigg said. "There is no place for men when borning babies."

"That's nonsense!" Urdo said. "In Tir Tanagiri, men can be there. And I'm the father."

"Fathers are not important," Rigg said. "There is no place for men, especially not father. If it is choose between mother and baby, what do you choose, here where fathers are more important than mothers?"

Urdo looked as if he had been run through the gut with a spear. "Is that the choice?" he asked.

"You have four horses of summer moon," Rigg said. "I brought them across wide ocean for you. You go and ride them, and come back and I will tell you if you have a wife, if you have a child. There is no choice for you to make. Trust the women now; it is a mystery of the Mother and not for men."

"I have met the Mother," Urdo said, furious, panting alongside as we

ran up through the streets of the town. "You can't keep me away, I am the King!"

"And did she promise you a baby?" Rigg frowned. "And what if the queen dies? You can do no good to be there, only harm."

"I wish I knew more about it," Urdo said, sounding lost. Elenn dangled on my arms like a half-empty sack. "Sulien—when Darien was born who was there?"

"Garah and Arvlid," I said. "But Thossa was going to be, except he was busy. My father saw all of us born."

"Pray to the land," Rigg said suddenly. "Pray to the land for her health and the child. Stay under the sky and pray until I send for you."

I think it must have been her complete certainty that swayed Urdo. He stopped where he was and let us run on. After we had gone a little way Rigg said to me, "Maybe it is not against the mystery here, maybe I know her only for a minute, but I know she would not want him to see her. This is better."

By the time we came to Elenn's rooms I was exhausted. I would hardly have noticed her weight on my back, but I had never trained to run with a weight in my arms. Elenn showed no signs of consciousness. Rigg pinched her cheek, and frowned. "Put her down on the bed—is it rushes that can be burned?"

It was, and I did. It was then that I saw the blood on my arms where I had been holding her. It was too much, too soon. I remembered what Urdo had said about having no heirs of his body. I sent a servant for Garah and for warm water for washing. Rigg and I undressed Elenn, and Rigg washed her, singing charms all the time. After a while she opened her eyes and screamed.

Garah was there by then, looking for a clean cloth. She ran to Elenn and held her hand, soothing her. It did not work, nothing worked. Elenn screamed and screamed each time her belly rippled, which it did hard and often. Rigg sang constantly and stroked her belly, and picked her up to walk about. Garah held her hand and crooned charms, I held her up when she needed me, and I turned away everyone who came to the door, whatever they wanted. Urdo did not come. I asked her if she wanted him, and Rigg was right, she did not. She screamed until she was hoarse. I turned away priests all afternoon until Teilo came. I couldn't turn her away, so she came in and prayed over Elenn, which did seem to calm her a little. She stayed afterwards, sitting quietly in the corner so that I almost forgot she was there.

At last, just after nightfall, the baby was born. He was much too small to live. He breathed his three breaths, enough to come into the world and have a name before going on, then he died in my hands. No matter how hard I tried I couldn't get any more breath to stay in him. Poor little thing, all blue and slimy and covered in blood, he wasn't much bigger than one of my hands. They say all babies look alike, but he did remind me terribly of Darien. It was the pale skin, I think, but all the same it wrenched my heart. His fists were clenched and his eyes were black and he looked furious that he'd gone to the trouble of being born only to die again so quickly before getting a chance to learn anything at all. He would have been a good son to Urdo, if he had lived, I am sure of it.

I turned to Elenn to ask for a name for him to take back with him to his next life, and saw that she was beyond giving one. Blood was pouring out between her legs. She was drained almost white. Garah and Rigg were singing hymns frantically and trying to stem the flow.

Then Teilo was there beside me. She had lit one of the lamps, and she peered at the child. "Dead," she said. "Well, the Lord must want it that way, but sometimes it's hard. What name shall we give him, for what time he needs it?"

"Emrys," I said, probably because I had heard the name so much that afternoon, but also because it seemed to suit him in his fury and his desire to see the world he could not live in.

"Don't cry, child," Teilo said to me. "It's a good enough name, even if it is a pagan one.

Everyone calls Teilo harsh, and I have heard her scold Urdo and Ayl as if they were little boys. Raul told me she came to Thansethan and yelled at Father Gerthmol for quarreling with Urdo, telling him he wanted to be thought holy more than he cared to be holy, and Father Gerthmol just stood there and took it. I've heard people say she's been bullying people for the last sixty years. All I can say is that she was never harsh to me, and never reproached me or even tried to convert me, she just stayed there and mourned with me over the baby, and if her hymns were to the White God and mine to the Lightbringer then they felt right together that time.

Then I thought I heard Elenn weeping, and I turned around, and she was sitting up on the bed, crying as if her heart was broken but alive beyond my hopes. I took her the dead child. Teilo and I had washed him and wrapped him in linen, and she knew at once he was dead. She wept more, and Garah and Teilo embraced her. Then she pulled Rigg towards her and kissed her. "I would be dead too, if not for you," she said.

"This is true," Rigg said, "but everyone here helped. And you would be dead with me, if not for your husband. I sent him out to pray to keep him from being in. But he did pray, and he held you here. When your spirit would go out with the blood, he held you in until I could stop it. You should call him in now."

"But what happened?" Elenn asked. "It should have been midwinter. What happened? Did—" And then her voice changed as if she remembered. "That weasel Morthu poisoned the wine!" she said.

"But we all drank!" Rigg said. "Hush now, don't think these things. Sometimes it happens."

"That's right," Teilo said. "Sometimes the Lord sends these things despite everything. You are alive, praise to the Lord, and thanks to the prayers of all here, you can have other children."

"I'll kill him," she said, ignoring everyone.

"I drank the same wine," Rigg insisted. "I would have cramps now if herbs bring on a baby was in wine." She patted her stomach.

Elenn subsided, her eyes burning. She gave poor dead Emrys back to Teilo. Then she turned to me and gripped my arm almost strongly enough to break it. "Kill him for me."

"Elenn—" I hesitated. "Rigg says he couldn't have done it."

"There might be other poisons," she said. She lay back, drained and weak. "I saw his eyes. I know he meant me harm. How can I fight him? Kill him for me, Sulien."

I should have believed her. I should have done it. But Teilo pushed in front of me and knelt by the bed. She took both Elenn's hands and forced her to look at her face. "I will speak to Morthu ap Talorgen, and I will ask him if he has poisoned you, or cursed you to lose the child," she said. "He will not be able to lie to me. If he poisoned you, or cursed you, then we will bring him before the king for justice."

"That is the law," I said, and Garah echoed me.

Rigg shook her head. "I drank more of the wine than you. There was no poison."

"He has a lot to gain by killing me, killing the baby," Elenn said. Her voice broke on the last word, and she wept. Teilo held her and stroked her hair.

"I will speak to him," she said.

"If you accuse him without proof he will laugh at us all," I said.

"He is Angas's and Penarwen's brother, and they won't stand for him being murdered," Garah said.

"He will answer me, or if not he will answer on the holy relics before everyone," Teilo said, inflexible. Elenn just sobbed.

"I want him to answer for it if he's done it," I said. "Just don't burst into the hall and make a fuss."

Teilo snorted and stood, her knees creaking as she straightened. "I know better than that; I have been dealing with kings and kings' houses since before Rowanna married Avren."

"Go to find Urdo," Rigg said to me.

I went towards the door.

"Don't say that to Urdo," Garah said. "Don't upset him more by accusing his nephew of poisoning, unless we need to."

"Thank the Lord you are alive," Teilo said to Elenn. She came out with me. When we were in the hall she made a sign of blessing over the door. "It is a fancy she has taken, I think," she said. "If you're all sure the wine wasn't poisoned, though what he was doing giving wine to the queen I'm sure I don't know."

"Stirring up trouble, I think," I said.

"Very well, but not trying to murder her; he's not such a fool as all that to do it where it would be so obvious. I'll go and ask him as I said." She went off in search of him, her stick tapping along the flags as she went.

I went out into the citadel, amazed to find it was only early evening and most people were eating in the hall. Ap Erbin's brother was singing his song about the woman of Wenlad as I went past. It seemed strange. It felt as if a long time had passed in Elenn's room and it should be a different season. I saw ap Cathvan, and told him the news, and he told me Urdo was out by the stables. I should have guessed and gone there first.

He was standing in the paddock where he had brought the summer-horses, stroking the nose of one of them. He looked up when I came around the corner of the stables, but I didn't need to tell him anything, he had been praying the whole time and the land had told him, or the Mother. There were tears on his cheeks, and when I saw him I started to weep again. It was his child who was dead, and I should have comforted him, but it was the other way around. "He was so—he was so—" I kept saying, and he held me, and said, "Ah, Sulien, hush now, hush," until I did.

Then we went back to Elenn's room. Teilo was there. I looked at her inquiringly, and she shook her head. Urdo kissed Elenn, then he took little Emrys in his hands for a moment and looked at him sadly.

"You were right," he said to Rigg, "I did more good where I was."

Then Garah gave a gasp that was halfway between laughing and crying.

"I'll never understand you men," she said. "Aren't you even going to say how glad you are your wife is alive?"

"She knows how glad I am," he said, smiling at Elenn. She smiled back, weakly. "An heir is not the important thing," he said. "As long as you are well."

I crossed the room to Teilo. "He can't deny he had malicious intentions, but he neither poisoned her nor used sorcery to make her miscarry," she murmured to me. I should never have believed her. I should have demanded an inquiry into his intentions, or just gone and killed him anyway. But I did not.

Elenn was looking up at Urdo. "And will you come to Thansethan with me to pray for a son?" she asked.

"In the spring," Urdo said. "When you are well again. If that is what you want, we will go there in the spring."

—40—

Foam-follower, sea-born,
is it Manan seeking vengeance
riding the wave tops like fields of lilies?
Who will name the wind?

Lifting great feet over the wave wash
wild tossed manes, running the swan road
swords rising red with the sun.
Who came like the wind?

Swords sweeping down in strong arms
reap the defenders to lie like tide wrack
swift steeds speeding scatheless.
Who will blame the wind?
— Amagien ap Ross, "The Sea Raids on Oriel"

The monks of Thansethan, not content with a festival celebrating the end of winter and another celebrating the flowering of the land, have a festival between them to commemorate the date on which their monastery was founded by the great Sethan. It is a great celebration for them, one of the most important in the year. Because it is in the spring they celebrate spring also. They fill their sanctuary with early flowers and give gifts of food, the way civilized people do at the feast of Bel a month later. It was for this festival, which also marked the anniversary of Darien's birth, that we set out for Thansethan.

We went in great state. It was Urdo's first official visit there since he had quarreled with Father Gerthmol. As if that wasn't enough, we were going there to pray for an heir to the kingdom. Elenn and Garah went wild for a month before sorting gifts and food to take. I took half the ala and a new set of armor for Darien. He was about to be sixteen, and old enough to come back to Caer Tanaga and join the ala. Urdo had a sword made ready to give him.

Our foreign visitors were still with us. Rigg had not joined the ala. She spent some time attending to Elenn. She came out to practice whenever I was teaching lancework, but she was not assigned to a pennon or any duties. She created rather a stir at first by inviting all the personable young men of the citadel into her bed in turn, but before midwinter she showed all the signs of having fallen in love with our grumpy Vincan ambassador, ap Theophilus. Even more amazingly, he seemed to return her affection and the sight of them walking the walls hand in hand gazing besottedly at each other became a commonplace of the winter. Soon she was even teaching him to ride, and he was improving her Vincan.

What he wanted with us was hard to make out. I know Urdo tried to have it out of him several times that winter. It seemed he wanted us to acknowledge the sovereignty of Caer Custenn. He dropped hints that Caer Custenn was about to reconquer Vinca, or possibly the whole Vincan Empire. Eventually Urdo told him outright that Tir Tanagiri was an independent kingdom and Caer Custenn lay across a thousand miles of hostile territory. He agreed with this and started talking vaguely about trade, and then even more vaguely about waterwheels and siege engines and ala organization.

Ap Lothar was less of an enigma. She was the sister of Radigis, queen of the Varni, and she came with her sister's authority to negotiate alliances. What she wanted was a straightforward military alliance against Arling Gunnarsson. It seemed that Sweyn had arranged a marriage alliance between Arling and Radigis which Arling had now repudiated in favor of a marriage with a Skath princess. Radigis therefore intended to make war on Arling and wanted our help. Her kingdom, like ours, was made up of the original inhabitants of the land and an influx of Jarnsmen.

"I could send an ala," Urdo mused later, when we were riding out alone. "The question is which, and whether I would get enough out of it. The risks are high, but then keeping Arling occupied on the mainland is worth a great deal."

"Supply would be difficult," I said.

Urdo smiled. "It would. It would either be very expensive or chance losing a whole ala, when I might need them here. That is why I won't do it. But I thought you would be begging me to send you!"

"Maybe I'm getting old," I said. I was thirty-three that year, no longer young and wild, and the thought of going away to fight in strange lands made me appreciate how comfortable I was in Caer Tanaga. We laughed together. Later he told ap Lothar that he would not send an ala to help her invade Jarnholme but would make a defensive alliance against Arling so that if he attacked either one of the kingdoms then the other would send help.

We arrived at Thansethan two days before the festival. While Urdo and Elenn were being formally greeted outside the gates I was amazed to see my mother among the press of people. I slid down from Brighteyes and embraced her. She looked as frail as ever, and the sight of her with her cane and her familiar gold comb brought my home to me as strongly as if I stood there. I only ever twice remember my mother leaving Derwen.

"Mother! What are you doing here?" I asked.

She smiled in her usual grim way. "Your brother and his wife are here for the same purpose as the High King, to pray for an heir. I came with them. Morien thinks I came to make sure he didn't convert while I wasn't watching." She snorted.

"So why did you come really?" I asked.

She rolled her eyes. "To see the grandson you've been hiding away here all these years. I was beginning to wonder if there was something wrong with him, and I'm glad to see there isn't."

I felt my cheeks burning. I wanted to hide in my cloak. I had never exactly told Veniva about Darien, but it was absurd to think that meant she didn't know. "You've seen him then," I said.

"I have. He's about here somewhere, seeing to horses. He's besotted with them, just the same as you and my Darien at that age. He's shown me his four horses already, and told me Urdo's promised him a summerhorse foal as soon as there is one. That's very generous of Urdo, I told him."

"Darien will make a fine armiger," I said. "I'm planning to take him back to Caer Tanaga to the ala after this visit. He's sixteen now. That's old enough."

"Too old to be living surrounded by monks," Veniva said, dryly. "And as for you, don't you think it was time you were getting married? There's no use you pining after Urdo all your life. If he'll go to this much trouble for his Isarnagan queen, he's not going to put her aside no matter how fertile you are. Let me look around for you. I haven't pushed you before because I thought it was as much use as trying to force a donkey, but if you want more children, it's time you were getting on with it."

"Mother!" I was speechless. "I'm not—I don't—it isn't—"

"Oh stop spluttering," Veniva said. "But think about it. That's a good lad you have there, and I'm not any too well supplied with grandchildren, and I'm not getting any younger."

Fortunately, it was my turn to be welcomed to Thansethan then, which saved me from having to think of a reply. I went riding with Darien that afternoon, and that evening there was a feast.

At Thansethan there are no eating alcoves. Everyone eats at one table, or at a series of tables in sight of each other. The prayer they give for before food says that all feuds are set aside at the table. This is all very well usually, where feuds are not a question. It is the way we feast in the ala after a battle, all together. Even then there are sometimes people who have to be excused, and fortunately there are always duties that need to be done.

Ulf was used to the situation and went to eat in the kitchens without prompting or even much teasing from the rest of the ala. The meal that night passed without incident except that Morien and Kerys were seated near Morthu, and they spent a lot of time talking. I was busy dealing with Father Gerthmol's difficult politeness and talking to Veniva and Urdo and Elenn.

The next afternoon, after the morning rituals, I had planned to ride with Darien again. Urdo was closeted with Raul and Father Gerthmol and wouldn't need me. Elenn had gone out riding with Ulf. Before I could find Darien, Morien found me on the way to the stables. He was alone, without Kerys, which surprised me.

"I need to talk to you," he said, very seriously. I raised my eyebrows. "It is a matter concerning the family honor," he added.

My first thought was that he had found out about Darien and was horrified. "What's the matter?" I asked.

"Not here," he said. "We must go out somewhere." When I started to continue towards the stables he frowned. "Can't we walk?" he asked. "We can talk more quietly then." Nobody would have thought he was an armiger, let alone a praefecto, choosing to walk when he could ride.

We went out of the east gate of Thansethan and when my feet found they knew a familiar way to turn I did not stop them. The path lay through the fields and past the spinneys, the trees glowing in new green, towards Goldpate's stone. We walked for a little while in silence. We passed some armigers, exercising their horses, and then a group of prisoners carrying wood from the coppice. After a while we left everyone behind.

"What is it?" I asked, when nobody could possibly overhear us.

"The prince of Angas tells me that the man who killed Darien is in your ala!" Morien was almost shaking with anger now he could let it out. "You told our mother he was dead and his arms were on Darien's grave! And instead here he is eating with us openly!"

"I did not lie to Mother," I said, trying hard to keep calm in the face of his accusation and cursing Morthu in my heart. I kept walking, which helped a little. "Nor did he eat with us, nor ever with me, he eats apart; last night he ate in the kitchen. For the rest, the matter is dealt with, as I told Veniva. He killed Darien, and I put his arms on Darien's grave. He gave them up to me. The matter was settled before the High King after Foreth."

"Settled? How can a matter like that be settled?" His voice rose angrily. "It is bloodfeud, and he must die before it can be settled."

"It is possible to accept a settlement," I said, guilt washing over me.

"Only for *me* to accept one," Morien said, visibly fighting to keep control of his temper. "I am the head of the family, whatever you think. It was not your place to accept any settlement, whatever it was, and I can think of nothing that would have restored honor in that situation except his blood. Bloodfeuds are never settled at once, in the first generation."

"I am your heir," I said, as quietly as I could. I wished we were not out away from everyone, that Urdo was there or Veniva. Urdo was really good at explaining why bloodfeuds going on for generations were a terrible idea. "Until you have another. I could accept a settlement, and I did. Ulf Gunnarsson killed Darien in a raid, when he was seventeen. He gave me his arms in front of witnesses. It was a better thing for the King's Peace that he live than die; he is Sweyn's nephew, and now he serves Urdo."

"I do not care who he serves or for political reasons," Morien said. He was silent a long moment, stamping along the ground. "You do have that right in law, but why did you not tell me?"

"You're difficult to tell things to," I said, honestly. "I should have—I meant to, but when I came home there was the siege, and then you were yelling at me about making peace with Lew. The matter was settled. At the time it didn't seem important that you knew the details."

"You are so arrogant," Morien said, through gritted teeth. Goldpate's stone was in sight now as we came over the crest of the slope which had seen the first charge of all time. "What would happen if you didn't know best, Sulien? Would the world break?"

I looked at him. "I didn't mean to upset you," I said. I put a hand out to the stone and leaned on it. "The matter was settled before the High King. If you are unhappy about it, you should talk to him."

"Oh yes, always your precious Urdo," Morien said. "I will. Because I intend to fight Ulf Gunnarsson. I am a king, too. I know what is right and honorable, not just what is expedient!"

I was furious then. I looked from his sneering face impugning my honor, to the rock they put over Goldpate the kinslayer. If I killed him I would be an outlaw too, and nothing would be achieved. "I think I know enough to defend my honor," I said.

"Your honor? Your honor? It is the family's honor!"

Of course, he didn't know about the rape which made it my honor even ahead of the family honor. I couldn't possibly tell him either, no matter how much he reproached me for not telling him things. "Take it up with Urdo," I repeated. "The matter is settled, his weapons lie on Darien's grave." I was going to have to talk to Urdo about it, but I was sure he could make Morien see sense in a way I couldn't because almost any conversation with Morien made me bristle.

I tried to ignore what Morien was saying, going on and on about my arrogance and the family honor. I stared out over the rolling hills to the south, letting it wash over me. I thought if he got it out of his system now he would calm down and start being reasonable. But he just kept working himself up to higher and higher pitches of anger. "How can you bear have someone around you that killed your brother?" Morien was asking. "Even common decency—"

I realized then that I didn't hate Ulf anymore. All he was to me now was a steady and reliable armiger, more trustworthy than some. He had done well in the riot. He was an honorable man, whatever he had done to me years ago. I shook my head at Morien, whose world was so simple.

"I'll fight him even if you're afraid to," he said. My anger was rising again, and I tried to swallow it. Afraid? I who had led so many charges? How could he say that to me, when he had hardly fought a battle in his life? I struggled to say nothing. Morien would always try to push me as hard as he could so that I lost my temper and he could complain about me to

Veniva. "But don't you even care about Darien?" he asked. "I always thought you two were so close, I can hardly believe you didn't care enough about him to avenge his murder."

He shouldn't have said it. I didn't think, I just hit him, and then when he was on the ground I got down and started to pound him. I probably wouldn't have killed him, he was my little brother. If I'd wanted to kill him, I'd have drawn my sword, and then he'd have been dead. I don't remember that fight at all well. I was angry. I had been angry with him for years. I don't know if he managed to hit me at all. He certainly didn't hurt me.

The next thing that is clear was somebody pulling me off him. I couldn't see who it was, but I recognized his voice. "Are you going to murder me if I let you go?" Conal Fishface asked. He had both his arms very tightly around me, pinning both of mine. I knew three ways to break the hold, but there was no point in letting him know that. Part of me knew I should be grateful to him for stopping me.

"Not just now," I said, and my voice shook. He let me go, and I turned around to face him. He was wearing a cloak fastened together with a beech twig with new leaves on it, but otherwise he looked exactly as I had last seen him. A scar from the fighting in Demedia would have been too much to hope for on that pretty face. "What in Coventina's name are you doing here, Fishface?"

"I am an accredited herald from the court of Oriel, which is to say Atha ap Gren, to Thansethan," he said.

"She must be awfully short of people to send," I said.

"Ah, I am glad to see you restored to your right mind and your usual pursuit of insulting me," he said, and had the nerve to bow. "She is indeed very short of people to send who know how to eat with a spoon and to blow their noses on their sleeve and not with their fingers. We lost a lot of champions in Demedia, as no doubt you know. But I feel I would be just as much within my rights to ask you what you are doing here?"

"I'm—" I took a deep breath. "Urdo's at Thansethan to pray for fertility. Or do you mean right here?" I looked down at Morien in some confusion. He hadn't stirred.

"I already knew Urdo was at Thansethan, I ran into the queen in the woods, which is why I am on this path and not the more frequented one. I wondered why you were engaged in a spot of quiet mayhem in this place." He looked down. "Ah, I recognize your esteemed brother. Don't bother to answer the question, I can entirely understand."

"What if it had been a real enemy?" I asked. "Would you still have pulled me off?"

"I had no idea who you were battering," he said, spreading his hands. "I just saw that they weren't fighting back, and you appeared to be thoroughly absorbed in the pursuit. I thought it might be as well to give you a little time to consider, and if assaulting them further seemed like a good idea then perhaps I could assist."

"He's not dead, is he?" I said, suddenly worried. I stepped away from him. Somehow I didn't want to touch Morien again. Conal bent over and picked him up then set him carefully down on top of the stone.

"His blood beats in his veins, his breath stirs in his lungs," he said. He pulled up one eyelid and then the other. "Neither is he shamming unconsciousness, and he may well be rather ill when he wakes up. If you were to sing some womanly charm over him to make his head and stomach feel better and stop the swelling before it's too obvious, then you may yet be able to pass it off as a friendly family quarrel."

"Do you have a horse?" I asked.

"I do. She is tied up in the trees just there. Shall I fetch her so that she can assist your brother back to Thansethan?"

"Thank you," I said. I didn't much like being in Conal's debt, and Morien's reaction to the thought of Ulf was going to be nothing to Elenn's reaction to him, but I was grateful he had stopped me in time. When he was gone I did sing some charms over Morien, and they may have helped. In any case when Conal came back he was waking up.

Conal gave him some water. "You've had a terrible fall," he said, enthusiastically. "Right onto your face. It's amazing your neck isn't broken. Can you tell me how it happened? Were you perhaps climbing on the rock to show your sister how it could be done and were you unlucky enough to slip off?"

"I must have been," Morien said, frowning at me. "Whatever are you doing so far from home, Conal?"

"I am a herald to Thansethan from Atha ap Gren," he said again, smiling and pointing at the twig on his cloak, which I now saw was intended to resemble a herald's branch.

"Why in Sethan's name is Atha sending to Thansethan?" Morien asked, struggling to sit up. Morien wasn't always a fool; it was a good question.

"In Sethan's name, precisely," Conal said. "She wants some better priests than the ones we are getting, all of whom are friends of Chanerig or, worse, Isarnagan oracle-priests he has converted all full of the spirit of the

White God and eager to make us praise. If we must praise we must, but we think we can do it with a little less rigor."

"Don't say that to Father Gerthmol," I warned him.

He laughed. "I shall say that we want to praise in the tradition of Thansethan, not that we want less rigor."

"There's no less rigor," Morien said. "Father Cinwil, who is Aurien's priest at Magor, comes from Thansethan, and he's very rigorous."

"Well, would less crazy sound better?" asked Conal. "That is Atha's request, and I am here to deliver it for her."

"The queen's here," Morien said, suddenly realizing. "She won't put up with your presence icily the way her sister does."

"I think she will while I have a herald's branch," said Conal, carelessly. "Are you feeling well enough to go back to the monastery, Morien? I have my horse here so you needn't walk."

"It's very fortunate you came along," Morien said, and I echoed him. Conal put Morien on his horse. She was a broken-down old grey mare who looked barely capable of bearing Morien a mile, let alone Conal and his pack all the way from wherever he had left the sea.

"How is my uncle?" Conal asked.

"He is well, and so are all his people. His daughter broke her leg jumping off the stable roof last autumn, but she is as good as ever now."

The three of us went back to Thansethan together, making small talk, and none of us saying what we were thinking.

—41—

In the matter of judicial combats, no one may be forced to fight; they may always choose to set the matter before judgment instead. No one may bring challenge other than in their own person, nor against one whose worth is less than theirs. Challenge may not be made against, nor accepted by, one who has not reached the age of their full growth, nor against anyone who is not whole in body or wits.

If the challenge is answered by a champion, the one on whose behalf that champion fights bears both the price of their proved crime and the price, and the price only, of the blood guilt of their champion to the champion's family. Necessarily capital crimes may be defended against by judicial combats, should the accused party choose to fight, but may not be defended by

champions. No champion shall receive, nor be seen to receive, recompense
above the price of their wounds should they get any.
    —The Law Code of Urdo ap Avren

Nobody could expect Conal to have as much decency as Ulf and to
    eat in the kitchen. Besides, he was a herald, and by ancient tradition
heralds must not be treated badly. Father Gerthmol had just enough sense
not to seat him with us but at one of the other tables. I could see him taking his place among the armigers, his twig now pinned to a fresh tunic. He
looked cheerful and relaxed. Darien was at the same table, still dressed in
brown robes, but I consoled myself that this would not be for long. I sat
between Kerys and Morien, opposite my mother and Raul, to prevent
Morthu from inflaming Morien again. Ap Theophilus sat between Raul
and Elenn. Morthu sat between Rigg and Father Gerthmol, opposite Urdo
and Elenn. Morien looked uneasy at being between me and Rigg. He
wasn't comfortable with our new cousin yet. I saw Elenn search out Conal.
Her eyes narrowed a little as she found him, then she looked away.

It was a fast day at Thansethan. We were given cold smoked fish and
hot pease porridge. There was only water to drink. Elenn did not touch
her food, and when Father Gerthmol inquired she murmured something
and touched her stomach as if she were unwell. Morien spoke to Kerys and
Veniva and said as little as he could to me. He looked a little bruised about
the face but nobody mentioned it. It was an awkward meal. The armigers
and the monks ate merrily, laughing and talking, but we at the king's table
had very little to say. Conal said something that occasioned great gales of
mirth from his companions. Beris laughed so much she choked, and Conal
very solicitously patted her on the back. Ap Padarn said something then
that had the whole table in stitches, even Darien and the monks.

Then Conal raised his voice to say something over the din, and suddenly,
as he did so, the room fell into one of those uneasy silences that occasionally
fall onto even a large hall, so that his voice rang out alone. "So, if you're all
here, where is that jolly Jarnsman your queen takes off to dally in the woods?"

The silence continued for an instant, an appalled hush. Everyone was
looking at Elenn, whose eyes were lowered. Urdo had stopped with his
spoon halfway to his mouth. For a moment I thought it would pass off.
They would act as if they had not heard. People were always making
ridiculous jokes about Elenn and Ulf, though never in her hearing. Gossip
like that rarely got more than a groan in the ala. It was so obviously untrue
and based on so little—Elenn always took an escort when she went riding,

and there were a handful of armigers she preferred, and Ulf was one of them. That was the entire basis for the joke—no doubt Conal had seen them together that afternoon and his putting that interpretation on events was intended purely to amuse his companions. It was just like the joke about me and Urdo or about ap Selevan's love for one of the monks of Thansethan, and deserved as much attention. Even if it had been true it was no crime and would have been nobody's business but theirs and Urdo's.

I had started to breathe again when Morthu spoke up loudly. "Take no notice of the Isarnagan lout! He is speaking nonsense and nobody would give credence to his accusation." Urdo set down his spoon, the chink it made was very loud. He took a deep breath. But Elenn, without looking at him, put her hand on his arm.

"I have been insulted," she said, very gravely. "All of you have witnessed. It is an accusation for which denials would be useless, even though it is entirely baseless. I would therefore challenge Conal to combat, that God may decide who is speaking the truth."

Conal stood up and turned to her. He frowned. "I meant no—"

She cut him off with an abrupt hand gesture. "What good would that do to my honor? You have insulted my honor, and I will have satisfaction." Urdo closed his eyes briefly, but her hand was still on his arm, and he said nothing. I could not see what she was doing. Conal was a big man and a trained fighter, and she was a very small woman who had not handled a weapon for years, if ever.

"If you would insist on fighting then I will accept your challenge," Conal said. He looked puzzled. "I would not see a quarrel—"

She cut him off again, she was clearly determined not to allow him any chance of apology. "Then I will choose a champion to defend my honor," she said, and now she smiled a very small smile, hardly more than a twitch at the corners of her mouth. Morthu was looking very pleased with himself. Urdo looked like a king carved from stone. Father Gerthmol was staring at Elenn as a man might stare at a lapdog who is holding off a wolf. I was startled, too. This was like something from an old song, and an old Isarnagan song at that. Elenn and Conal were both Isarnagan, and I think they were acting in a way that was more natural to them than it was to the rest of us. I thought she would say that Urdo would fight him, and so, I think, did Urdo. Her mother would have. I was not happy at the thought. Conal had killed Larig, who was a very good fighter. But Elenn knew better than that.

"In my husband's ala there are many champions, and I know that if I asked, none of them would deny my claim." There was a sudden roar from

the benches where the armigers sat. They might have felt as if they were in an old song, too, but they would respond to a call from their queen. They surged to their feet shouting and stamping their feet; they all wanted to be her champion. The monks looked stunned. Nearly all of them were clutching their pebbles.

She held up her hand for silence, and the uproar ceased. "I could choose any of these brave armigers, because God and the right are on my side. It is difficult to choose, but so that nobody can ever accuse me of favoring any man among them again I will choose Sulien ap Gwien to defend my honour."

Everyone was looking at me then. Urdo looked completely amazed. I rose and bowed to Elenn, it was all I could do. I looked at Conal. He had a twisted smile on his face. He raised his cup of water and saluted me. I did not want to kill him for making a stupid joke, but I did not see what choice I had. I bowed to him. Near him, Darien was looking at me as if he were proud of me.

"Tomorrow, at dawn," Conal said, bowing back. Then he left the hall. I sat down again and stared at the fish on my plate. It looked like something dead. Now Urdo was looking concerned. I tried to smile at him. Elenn said something quietly reassuring to Father Gerthmol. Everyone was talking again now, loudly. Rigg leaned over Morien to pat me on the back. Veniva shook her head slowly. "This is a bad business," she said. "Dueling has been against the Vincan Laws this last four hundred years."

"Judicial combats are permitted now," I said. "And dueling has happened rather a lot in the last four hundred years, whatever the law said." Kerys laughed. Raul started to explain the law to Veniva. I sat and stared at my food until a monk took it away and the feast was over. As soon as I could decently leave I went in search of Conal.

He wasn't difficult to find. It is hard for a tall Isarnagan with leaves on his tunic to hide in a monastery. He had done his best; a monk directed me to one of the little meditation rooms below the library. I started towards it then made a quick detour to the stables. There was a flask of mead in my saddlebag, and I thought I might need it. I said a brief hello to the horses and promised to take them out soon. Then I went off to find Conal.

He didn't look surprised to see me. He had lit a candle and sat down on the three-legged stool that was all the room contained except for a painting in the plaster of the wall of one of the White God's followers preaching to some animals. I needn't have bothered with the mead; he had some already. "You are an idiot, Fishface," I said, coming in and closing the door.

"I know," he said, lightly. "I go off to the woods with a woman who is forbidden to me. I follow my king to a hopeless war in Tir Tanagiri, and survive when he is killed. I stop you from killing your brother. I make foolish jokes in the presence of the people I am joking about. And worst of all, I get caught red-handed every time."

"If you had no honor, you could leave now and go back to Oriel," I said, bluntly.

He passed me his flask. It was a good silver one, and the mead was good, too, and went down smoothly. "I will have honor if it is all I have," he said, bleakly.

"I don't want to kill you," I said. "Elenn—it isn't her honor, though you shouldn't have said it. She wants me to kill you because you killed her mother."

"It is the only honor she has, and I know it and should not have taken it lightly," Conal said. "For us, we have honor in our deeds, but what does she have, beyond being beautiful and her king's wife and faithful?"

"That may be the way of things in Tir Isarnagiri," I said. "Here, no. She has chosen who she is, and she has the work of being a queen. No one wins a fight where logistics did not get there first. She works as hard and as well as Glyn organizing supply. And she—"

Conal laughed, and reached out for the flask again. "She may well have pride in that, but it is not honor."

"It is," I said, as he drank. "It is a different honor. But honor is not only in fighting well and killing cleanly. The monks here say that everything is honorable that serves the White God; if one sweeps a room or preserves apples in his name and does it well, then that is honorable and holy. I think they are right that there is honor in living as well as one can. They think that life has to serve their God, but I think whoever one serves and however one lives there can be honor in the living of life. She has honor. She is a good queen for Tir Tanagiri." I remembered her walking into the hall with Urdo when he told all the kings we would defeat Sweyn. I remembered her walking out into the archway to greet Mardol and Cadraith, the cup held out. I remembered how she had stood calm and still with her hand on her dog's head when we thought the Jarns were attacking. "But it is not honorable to kill you like that."

"If I die, will you tell Emer?" he asked.

"Tell her what?" I was embarrassed at the thought of delivering a message.

"Tell her that I'm dead, so she doesn't have to hear it in front of Lew and the whole court and take it without flinching. She will do it if she must, but I had rather spare her."

"I'll do it if I can, but think—if you're dead, I'll have killed you; there must be people it would be more fitting to ask."

"I daresay, but few enough who know that she would need telling." He smiled and rolled his eyes. "Well, I am not dead yet. Oh, sit down, do! Has it not crossed your mind that I might kill you?"

I laughed, and sat down. It hadn't, of course. "Perhaps it should have," I said. "You did kill Larig, after all."

"Larig?" he said, as if the name was strange to him. "Larig ap Thurrig? Why do you pick him?"

"Because he taught me Malmish wrestling, and he was a friend and good in battle," I said.

"How do you know I killed him?" he asked, in the same polite tone that he had inquired after his uncle's health earlier.

"Ap Erbin told me," I said. "He was there, and Larig was a friend, and we had some kinship ties."

"Ah, ap Erbin," he said, and then he was quiet for a moment, staring at the candle flame. "You know what happened up there?" he asked, after a moment.

"I know there was hard fighting and head taking and you lost," I said.

He snorted with laughter. "That is it in a nutshell, if you leave out the hills and the rain. Demedia is a dreadful place. The problem was that we were doing just well enough to make it worth carrying on, for much too long. We should have seen we were defeated almost at once and made a truce. Darag was never very good at telling he was beaten, though, not from a boy. We grew up together, you know; he was my foster brother. His mother was my mother's sister, and his father, well, some say his father was the god of the Cunning Hand, the Lord Maker. However it was, his mother and her husband did not get on, and he was fostered early with my mother. His mother and mine were both sisters of the old king, Conar. Conar had no sons, so it was clear that the next king would be me or Darag or Leary, who was his other nephew. All the time from when we were children we would compete, and Darag would never give in. It stood him in good stead then, because after Conar was killed in the war with Conat he married Atha and was chosen to be king." Conal sighed, and handed me the flask. It was almost empty. I finished it. "But in Demedia it did him no good, he couldn't see that we should give in. He wouldn't listen to me telling him."

He sighed again and looked at me. "Did ap Erbin tell you how I found Darag's body?"

"No," I said. "I don't think he can have known."

"Darag and Larig were fighting on their own, up in the hills. From the look of it when I got there afterwards, Darag had thrown his belly-spear at one of Larig's horses and killed it. Then Larig threw the spear back and wounded Darag's horse. That's how I found them actually. The wounded horse ran off, and I followed the blood trail back. Then Darag must have thrown the spear back and killed Larig's other horse under him. He was more accurate with it than Larig, which isn't surprising because it was his spear and he practiced with it. But then Larig drew the spear out of the horse and threw it back again, gut-wounding Darag. He was dead then, of course, losing blood, too weak to stand, except that he wasn't going to give in yet. He dragged himself over to a godstone that was nearby, and he tied himself to it by his belt. I don't know what Larig was doing, maybe he helped him if he was an honorable kind of man. In any case, he was tied to the stone with his belly spilling out, but they must have fought there for a while. When I came up his body was tied to the stone with ravens showing an interest, his sword was on the ground near Larig's right hand, cut clean off. Larig had taken his head, of course."

"Ugh," I said, and opened my flask of mead.

"Ugh," Conal agreed, reaching over for it. "So you see, my killing Larig, which I cannot deny I did, was no great feat of arms, as he was dismounted and lacking a hand. Though, as the sword and the hand were right there I have wondered why he didn't just stick it straight on again?"

"He was a Malm and a follower of the White God," I said. "He'd have thought of that sort of charm as women's spells." I suddenly remembered very clearly Ulf saying to me, "You know spells?"

"I see," Conal said. "I can see that if that sort of thing spreads with the faith in Tir Isarnagiri, there will be rather less sword fighting or rather more one-handed people." He laughed. "I am getting drunk and missing the point," he said. "The point is, of course, that killing a one-handed man, no matter how common they are, is less of a feat than killing a two-handed one, and so you need have no fear on that account."

"I hadn't," I said. "Look, Conal, I don't want to kill you."

"Amazing," he said. "Truly amazing. That's the first time you ever called me by my name. Now I probably will die in the morning. Breaking curses is usually a bad sign."

I ignored that remark. "I have to avenge the insult to the queen's honor, but I don't have to kill you," I said. "In Urdo's law code, there are judicial combats fought to first blood. If you will accept that, and stop, and I say that the queen's honor is avenged and you apologize, at first blood, then that ought to do."

"It won't give her satisfaction," Conal said.

"I will talk to Urdo about it," I said. "If you will accept it."

"If I had so much honor that I strongly desired to die, I'd have seen I died after killing Larig," he said, surprisingly. "My father asked me what I was doing alive after my king was dead, you know. I would have thought he liked me better than that, but then he'd seen the bodies after one of your raids on the coast, and it made him bitter."

"So you'll accept a fight to first blood?" I repeated.

"I will," he said. "But what if that goes against you? First blood can be anyone's. I am counted as good with a sword."

"The gods will be witnessing for Elenn's honor," I said.

"And are you so sure I didn't speak the truth in jest?" he asked, sardonically.

I shuddered at the very thought of Elenn voluntarily letting Ulf touch her. "I think I can safely take that risk," I said, standing up. I let Conal keep the mead flask and went off into the monastery in search of Urdo.

—42—

"Come," she said, and shed no tear
and come they did with Evalwen's spear,
come they did with Evalwen's sword,
the blade still wet that had slain her lord,
come they did with Evalwen's sling
a great big pile of everything.
"Stack them deeper, pile them higher,
the slayer's weapons on the pyre!"
But she would not weep, though her lord be dead,
till they topped the pile with Evalwen's head.
         —"The Bloodfeud of Dun Cidwel," Isarnagan song

Urdo was sitting with Darien near the water clock.

"Here she is!" Darien said, jumping up as he caught sight of me.

The bell had recently rung for a service, and I could hear chanting from inside the sanctuary.

"Were you looking for me?" I asked. I sat down beside Urdo and shivered a little. The night had grown chill. The stars looked very bright and very far away.

"Yes," Urdo said. "Get your cloak from the stables and let us walk a little. It is too chilly to sit still for long."

The stables were warm and comfortable. The sounds of horses moving and eating were pleasant and familiar. There was one circle of mellow golden lanternlight in a corner where someone was singing over a sick horse. I took my cloak from where it was hanging behind Brighteyes's stall, and the three of us went out into the night. For the second time that day I found my feet taking me on the path towards Goldpate's stone.

"Did you find Conal?" Urdo asked.

"Yes. I asked him if he would fight until first blood. It would be wrong to kill him when he was only joking."

"I said that," Darien said.

I looked from him to Urdo. "*You* said that?"

"Yes, Darien said that," Urdo said. "Elenn said that Conal should die for the insult he had given her. Father Gerthmol said she should be merciful, even to an enemy of her house who had given her insult."

"Where was this? And what did you say?" I asked, almost tripping over a tussock.

"It was in Father Gerthmol's room," Urdo said. "I said that first blood seemed to me sufficient, and Morthu said that I was very merciful indeed to so overlook an insult given to my wife before everyone."

"I wish I could fight Morthu," I said.

Urdo laughed, and I thought he sounded angry. "I thought she meant to ask him to fight Conal."

"So did I," Darien said. "I was so glad when she asked Sulien instead. I was afraid Conal would kill Morthu, and I would never have the chance to."

"You are not to fight Morthu without my permission," Urdo said. "You're not ready yet."

"Can I fight him if he attacks me first?" Darien asked. We were under the trees and I could see neither of their faces, no matter how hard I tried.

"Do you really think he will attack you?" Urdo asked.

"Yes, if he thinks he can get away with it he will kill me. He knows I hate him, and besides, I am in his way." Darien said.

"If he attacks you, then of course you can fight back, but don't get yourself killed," Urdo said.

"You need to kill Morthu or send him away," I said, abruptly. "It won't do, he'll keep on and on making trouble like this, until something comes of it."

"He's done nothing that breaks the law," Urdo said. "Teilo questioned him about Elenn, and he neither poisoned her nor made her miscarry by sorcery. I have told her and Teilo has told her, but she won't hear us."

"It's too late to wait until he kills someone, even if you don't count Arvlid," I said. "You must have heard the things he says that make everything worse."

"Yes," Urdo said. We came out into the starlight again, and I could see that he looked sad. "You are right. I can't pass judgment on him, but I can send him away. I can send him up to Angas's ala. That's his home after all. I will do that."

"And when will you give me permission to kill him?" Darien asked.

"Not until you are ready, and he has done something to deserve it, both things." Urdo stopped, and stared out down the slope to Goldpate's stone, a hulking shape in the darkness. "This is where I won my first victory," he said.

He put his hand on Darien's shoulder. "It was not much, compared with what came after, but they all followed me, Talorgen of Angas, and Custennin and Thurrig and all their people. That was the beginning of it all. Then afterward I stood outside the stables and Raul poured cold water over me to clean me after battle. The sunlight broke the drops to rainbows and somehow I knew I would not be going back to the library. All the land seemed to be rejoicing around me. I laughed, and I thought that life need never be less than that."

He paused. "Then that night Father Gerthmol told me before everyone who I was."

"You hadn't known?" Darien asked.

"No, never. I thought Gwair Aderyn was my father because he came to see me."

"The monks didn't treat you differently?" Darien asked again.

"They did, but I didn't know why. When he told me it was as if I'd been a fool not to know before."

"I understand," Darien said. "Life is in the moment when you are living it."

"I have given you a sword today. If you understand that, then I know you will bear it for me in honor," Urdo said. We all stood there a moment longer in silence, then we turned and started to walk back.

"And I can fight Conal to first blood?" I asked, after a while.

"Yes." Urdo sighed. "But don't tell Elenn until afterwards. When it is done proclaim the fight over before everyone, and she will accept that."

"She won't like it," I said.

"No, but she will accept it graciously."

"All right," I said, awkward and ungracious as always.

"Isn't that like lying to her?" Darien asked.

"In a way," Urdo said. "But she—she thinks her honor's been insulted. When she calms down she'll see it's ridiculous and that nobody could take that joke seriously. That's a problem with having power; it's necessary to think before using it, which is one reason why laws are such a valuable tool."

"People do take it seriously though," Darien said. "People are always talking about the Queen liking men."

"People like to talk and joke about these things," I said. "I don't know why, but they do. They seem to want to believe everybody is secretly in love with someone." Indeed it has always surprised me that people find this sort of thing believable. It is as if they want to believe it. Of Elenn they said that she was always talking to men, and she must therefore have been mad to meet them in bed. The truth of it was that she was a beautiful woman who liked to be told she was beautiful, and that was an end to it. Men were like a different animal in her mind. I do not think she really trusted even Urdo to be close to her, let alone all those others they linked her name with. And as for me, well, anyone would have thought I'd have said no to enough people they'd not believe I'd have said yes to others. True, for years I'd not denied that Darien was Urdo's son, and now it was generally believed. Anyone who could count knew that Darien was born years before Urdo's marriage, but enough of these lies stuck that everyone believed that Urdo and I had been lovers outside the law all through the time we had known each other.

"You shouldn't believe everything you hear," Urdo said. "It does sometimes happen that people share blankets without telling anyone, but it is a much rarer thing than gossip will make out."

I realized I never had told Urdo about Conal and Emer. There had never been a good moment, and this still wasn't one. It would be too awkward in front of Darien. "Has Morien spoken to you?" I asked, instead.

Urdo stopped walking. "What? I wondered why you had been fighting. Has he some lover?"

"No!" I said, very definitely. "No, nothing like that at all. It's just that Morthu told him about, well, who killed our brother, and he was unhappy that I had settled the matter without him."

"He hasn't spoken to me, but when he does I will talk to him about it and make him understand," Urdo said, and started walking again. We were almost back at Thansethan.

"Where are we to fight in the morning?" I asked.

"On the west side of the monastery, on the flat field," Urdo said. He did not sound happy. "There will probably be a large audience."

Darien opened the stable gate. "I think everyone will come and watch," he said.

We went inside. "I should get some sleep if I'm to be ready at dawn," I said, and yawned.

Urdo smiled at me. "You take care of yourself. I don't have any doubt of your fighting abilities, but be careful. I don't want to lose you."

As we came out of the stables Beris was going in. "There you are," she said. "Gunnarsson was looking for you, but I told him to go to bed and not bother you tonight."

"I'll make sure to speak to him in the morning," I said, wondering what Ulf could possibly want now.

I slept uneasily, and woke from a dream of battle to Elidir shaking me to say she had my armor and my breakfast both ready.

Darien was right. Everyone was waiting in the grey light. The flat field ran along the side of the west wall of Thansethan. The audience was lined up along the wall. Urdo and Elenn and Father Gerthmol were in the center. As I walked towards them I caught sight of Veniva with Darien and Raul. I waved. Then I saw Kerys with ap Selevan near Elenn, and wondered where Morien was. The whole ala appeared to be there, along with every monk in the place. There were almost four hundred people waiting to see me fight. I wished I had eaten less porridge. It lay in my stomach like a stone.

I bowed to Urdo, and then to Elenn. She was wearing an overdress of pale yellow, stiff with flowers embroidered in silver thread. She had her silver-and-pearl circlet on her head and anyone would have known she was a queen even if they had never seen her before. "I am here as your champion," I said, as I straightened.

"Fight well for me, and in God's sight," she said. Then she took a scarf of the same cloth as her dress and tied it around my arm to show that I was her champion. Then I stepped back and saw Grugin leading out Brighteyes, armored as if for battle.

"Oh no," I said. I turned to the other end of the field, and there was Conal on his old nag. "I'm not going to murder the man," I said, turning to Urdo. "Has he fought on horseback before?"

"What does it matter?" Elenn asked.

"It isn't fair," I said. "And it doesn't look fair." I looked to see if Morthu was smirking in the crowd but couldn't find him. "Somebody must lend him a greathorse." I would have done it myself, but I only had Brighteyes and a riding horse with me.

Father Gerthmol began to say something about his herd, and Urdo had opened his mouth when Darien came running up.

"He can't fight on that!" he burst out. "Please, Mother, lend him Brighteyes, and I will lend you Keturah!"

Veniva came up behind him at a more dignified pace. "The boy's quite right," she called, "It would be a disgrace for him to fight on that."

"I agree," I said. "Darien, go with Grugin and get Keturah ready. I'll take Brighteyes to Conal."

Brighteyes was rested and eager to be ridden. He couldn't understand why I was leading him up the field instead of mounting. Conal looked as if he couldn't understand it either.

"Greetings, Fishface!" I called, when I came near enough. The crowd had suddenly got very quiet, they wanted to hear. I saw Rigg standing by Beris, listening. I wondered briefly where Ulf was. I hadn't caught up with him yet. "I've brought you a proper horse; you can't possibly ride that beast."

"Are you proposing an exchange?" he asked. He was wearing leather armor set with enameled plates.

"My horse will be coming soon," I said. He dismounted and fussed with Brighteyes' saddle for a moment. "You have ridden before?" I asked, very quietly.

"Of course," he said. "I've not trained the way you have, of course."

"We're fighting to first blood," I said. "Urdo has agreed. Get down as soon as you can and I'll follow. The horses know what to do, at least, this one does. His name's Brighteyes. Look after him."

I walked back up the field. Darien was bringing Keturah out. She looked splendid, very like Starlight. The question of her training hadn't occurred to me until I spoke to Conal, but I wished now I had asked for a horse of the ala. I thanked Darien gravely, tightened her girth, and mounted. Then I walked her up to the far end of the field, to make sure there was enough room.

I signaled to Urdo that I was ready. All the fuss with horses had taken a while, and the sun was up already. The rooftops of the monastery were dark against the pink sky, but it was getting lighter every moment. "This is the judicial combat to determine whether Conal the Victor meant insult to Elenn ap Allel, with Sulien ap Gwien fighting for Elenn," he said. "Draw near and witness, all people who have an interest and all gods of earth and sky, and all gods of home and hearth and kindreds of people, and the White God, Father Creator, God Made Man and Ever-living Spirit. Strengthen the arm of the side of right and weaken that of the side of wrong and let justice be done and be seen to be done. You may begin."

I lowered my spear and urged Keturah to a canter and then a gallop and Conal did the same with Brighteyes. I aimed my spear at his spear, and he aimed his at my neck. I felt it give a tiny glancing touch to the armor on my side as I hit it firmly just above his hand. He wavered in his balance, and the shaft of the lance sent him tumbling off Brighteyes' back and onto the ground. I dismounted almost as swiftly and stood waiting for him to stand. I could see people catching the horses and could see Darien reassuring Keturah. I hoped someone was doing the same for poor Brighteyes, who must be very confused. Conal came to his feet and drew his sword. We were right out in the middle of the field, in front of Urdo and Elenn but not very close to them.

We exchanged a few blows. I was glad to see that unlike riding and dancing, Conal did know how to fight. "That is the shortest time anyone has ever lent me a horse," he said.

I laughed. "Well, I thought you said you'd ridden before?"

Then he started to take the fight seriously. His face changed, and he didn't make any more comments. I ducked under a great buffet. The fight was suddenly tremendous fun. I needn't kill him, it was like practicing with a friend only with the lack of hesitation I usually only found in battle. We were both fighting well and easily. We both sprang back to reposition and found ourselves smiling at each other. He was very good. I'm sure he could have killed Larig even if he'd had both hands. I couldn't get near him. He couldn't get near me either. We kept moving and fighting. Neither of us left any opportunity for the other to get in close. I don't think I ever fought anyone better. In battle, of course, there is usually so much else going on that even if one is unhorsed someone will generally interrupt an individual

fight. Single combat is something that is sung about much more often than
it actually happens. I had trained with my friends, and I had fought in all of
Urdo's great battles and innumerable skirmishes, but I never had a fight like
that one with Conal Fishface. He didn't talk at all when he was fighting.
Indeed I think it is the only time I ever saw him when he wasn't talking
and making light of everything. He fought as if it was what he was made
for. Somehow it was a very joyous thing, so that I could not stop smiling as
each new move followed from the one before, and I countered it or
attacked in turn.

We might have fought all day if I hadn't slipped on the mud and gone
forward too fast and got a slash in under his guard and cut the top of his
thigh. As soon as he saw the blood he stopped, and I stopped, raising my
sword.

"First blood!" I cried, loudly. "I have the victory! Elenn is avenged."
The crowd erupted in a great cheer.

"Indeed, I apologize to the Queen of Tir Tanagiri for the insult I gave
her," Conal shouted. He dropped his sword and put his hand to his wound.
"Still sure you could have killed me?" he asked me, quietly. I could have
laughed for his pride, but I did not.

"I have never had a worthier opponent," I said. "But I could have spitted you then if I'd wanted to. Come on, let us go and bow before the
king."

Conal limped forward towards Urdo and Elenn. If Elenn was angry, she
did not show it. She stood unsmiling.

"Again, I apologize for the insult I gave," Conal said.

"Justice is done," Urdo said. Elenn bowed to Conal, and Father Gerthmol, beaming, pinned his herald's twig back on. Elenn took her scarf from
my arm.

"Thank you for fighting for me," she said. I cleaned my sword.

"You fought very well," Veniva said.

"Oh yes, didn't she!" said Darien. I beamed at them both.

It was at that moment that Morthu came running onto the field, looking shocked. Limping a long way behind came Ulf, with ap Theophilus
beside him. Morthu ran up towards Urdo, hesitated, then came on when
Urdo signaled to him to do so. The crowd fell silent again.

"Come quickly!" he said. "Ulf Gunnarsson has been fighting Morien
ap Gwien of Derwen! It was a duel. Please come! He has killed him. He
has knocked his skull in with his ax!"

Morthu looked shocked, but underneath I thought he was pleased.

Kerys began to scream. Veniva slowly and carefully started to pull down her hair. Her face was expressionless. Darien looked shocked. Urdo took a step towards me. I just gaped at Morthu, trying to take in what he had said. He took a step back away from me. Morien must have challenged Ulf. Ulf had tried to find me to get me to stop it. It wasn't surprising that he had killed Morien. Morien had never been any good with arms. He wouldn't have accepted first blood. My little brother's ridiculous pride had got him killed at last. I should have done something to stop him. I thought he'd talk to Urdo, but he was more stupid than I'd thought. Crazily, the idea danced through my head that if anyone in the ala had to kill my brother it was just as well it was Ulf: I couldn't eat with him anyway.

It was only then that I realized what this meant. I wouldn't be with my ala. I was Morien's heir. I would have to leave, leave the ala, leave Urdo and Darien and all my friends. There was nobody else to do it. I would have to go. I couldn't be Urdo's praefecto any longer. I could cheerfully have murdered Morien myself if Ulf hadn't been stupid enough to do it for me. I felt as if the world had gone dark. I walked off with Urdo and Veniva to see the body and hear justice done. Ulf came up to us, his face set in strong lines of desperation. Urdo spoke to him sternly, making sure that the fight had been fair and that Morien had challenged. I heard ap Theophilus confirming that it had all been so. I said nothing, what could I say? I couldn't really blame Ulf for Morien's idiocy. He had tried to find me to stop it. My face was wet with tears, but I stood beside Urdo as calmly as I could and listened to his judgment that Morien should not have challenged over a matter that had been justly settled, the gods strengthened the arm of justice, and Ulf bore no blame in the death. I think Urdo knew I was not weeping for my brother but because I had no desire to leave and take up the duties and responsibilities of the lordship of Derwen.

It was five years before I rode beside my king again.